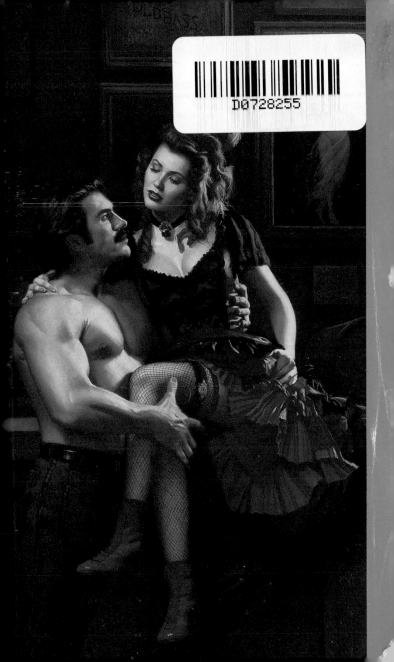

MISCHIEF

"Kindly release me!" Heather snapped. "I'm quite able to stand on my own now."

Black brows arched over laughing turquoise eyes. "In case you hadn't noticed, we seem to be tied together from the knees down," Morgan said.

As the dog gave another tug on the leash, Heather lurched forward once more, bumping hard against Morgan and a rigid object bulging at his hip. As her hand sought to soothe the sharp jab of pain, her fingers brushed something cool and metallic.

Morgan's hand clamped over hers. "It's bad enough your dog has gnawed on my trousers. I don't need you shooting additional holes in them."

Heather's eyes flew wide. "Is . . . is that a gun I felt?" she stammered.

A mocking grin curved his lips. "That, or I'm awfully glad to meet you, honey."

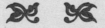

Other Avon Books by
Catherine Hart

DAZZLED
IRRESISTIBLE
SPLENDOR
TEMPEST
TEMPTATION

Avon Books are available at special quantity discounts for bulk purchases for sales promotions, premiums, fund raising or educational use. Special books, or book excerpts, can also be created to fit specific needs.

For details write or telephone the office of the Director of Special Markets, Avon Books, Dept. FP, 1350 Avenue of the Americas, New York, New York 10019, 1-800-238-0658.

CATHERINE HART

Mischief

AVON BOOKS NEW YORK

If you purchased this book without a cover, you should be aware that this book is stolen property. It was reported as "unsold and destroyed" to the publisher, and neither the author nor the publisher has received any payment for this "stripped book."

MISCHIEF is an original publication of Avon Books. This work has never before appeared in book form. This work is a novel. Any similarity to actual persons or events is purely coincidental.

AVON BOOKS
A division of
The Hearst Corporation
1350 Avenue of the Americas
New York, New York 10019

Copyright © 1995 by Diane Tidd
Front cover art by Fredericka Ribes
Inside front cover art by Andy Bacha
Inside cover author photo by Portrait Studios
Published by arrangement with the author
Library of Congress Catalog Card Number: 95-94142
ISBN: 0-380-77731-2

All rights reserved, which includes the right to reproduce this book or portions thereof in any form whatsoever except as provided by the U.S. Copyright Law. For information address Maria Carvainis Agency, Inc., 235 West End Avenue, New York, New York 10023.

First Avon Books Printing: September 1995

AVON TRADEMARK REG. U.S. PAT. OFF. AND IN OTHER COUNTRIES, MARCA REGISTRADA, HECHO EN U.S.A.

Printed in the U.S.A.

RA 10 9 8 7 6 5 4 3 2 1

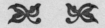

I dedicate this book to the real Heather, my own dear daughter. Your brother Brent was the hero in *Dazzled*. Your brother Sean was my villain in *Irresistible*. Your turn has finally come, and I must say, you make a sassy, delightful heroine. What can I say? You're perfect!

Also, as always, I want to say "thank you" to my warm, wonderful husband, for being so patient, understanding, and loving through all the trials of being married to a slightly crazy authoress. I love you, sweetheart!

❧ 1 ❧

May 1882

"What do you mean, you can't go on to Dodge City with me?" Heather Blair-Burns exclaimed, staring at her traveling companion in dismay. "Etta, you must go with me! You must! The train is about to depart, and we simply don't have time to debate the issue!"

The older woman shook her head in firm denial. "No, Miss Blair-Burns, I don't have to do any such thing, and I'm not going to. I've been offered a position as a Harvey Girl right here at the depot restaurant, and I'm going to take it and stay in St. Louis," she said, nodding toward the dining room at the far end of the train station. "I'm sorry, but you'll just have to travel the rest of the route by yourself. I have my own interests to look after, and I'm not about to let such a grand opportunity pass."

"Travel on by myself?" Heather echoed in disbelief, as if Etta had just suggested she parade stark naked down Main Street. "But it's not at all proper! It just isn't done! Mama would have a fit! Moreover, she most certainly will not appreciate your abandoning me halfway through my journey, and in the middle of the night."

The woman sighed. "You do tend to exaggerate. St.

1

Louis is more than halfway from Boston, and six o'clock in the evening can hardly be considered the middle of the night. You'll be in Dodge City in another fifteen hours or so, asleep most of the way. I'm confident you can make it that far by yourself without mishap."

Heather's lips pursed into a pout as she berated, "Where is your sense of honor and loyalty, Etta? You've been with us for the past twelve years, and you can't tell me you'll earn more working in that restaurant than you do as my maid."

"No," Etta agreed, "but there are other compensations that should more than make up the difference."

"Such as?" Heather demanded.

"It's a known fact that Harvey Girls are well respected and much sought after by men looking for proper wives. Most marry within a year or so. As I'm nearing thirty, and would very much like to find a husband and have a family of my own before it's too late, that is a most encouraging enticement."

"Oh, for heaven's sake!" Heather huffed. "There must be a host of lonely bachelors in Dodge City as well."

Etta wrinkled her nose at that suggestion. "The selection here is undoubtedly superior."

"Then come with me to Dodge and I'll have my father buy you a return ticket on the first train back to St. Louis. Surely you can wait that long to snag a man."

Etta shook her head. "No, I won't risk losing this job to another girl. Positions such as this one don't come along every day, you know. They are few and coveted. I'm lucky to have fallen into this one so easily."

On the verge of losing her temper, not at all an uncommon reaction on those rare occasions when she was thwarted, Heather snapped waspishly, "I cannot believe how silly you are behaving! And stubborn! It isn't like you, Etta, to act so foolishly, as if the world will cease spinning if you don't catch a husband in the next five minutes."

"Easy for you to say," Etta remarked with a sniff. "You're young and pretty, all of eighteen, with so many suitors after your hand, it took you a full six months to decide which you would accept. Now here you stand, all but officially engaged to one of the richest gentlemen in Boston, and you have the temerity to chide me for wanting a man of my own."

She shook a thin finger at Heather, her eyes as bright and angry as Heather's. "You're spoiled rotten, Miss Blair-Burns, as pampered as that snippy little dog of yours." Etta gestured disdainfully toward the fluffy Pomeranian prancing nervously at the end of his leash. "Let me warn you, young lady, one of these days someone is going to come along and prove that the sun doesn't rise for you alone. It almost makes me wish I'd be around to see it."

"Ooooh!" Heather stamped her foot in outrage. "If you hadn't already quit, I'd fire you here and now!"

A few yards away, Morgan Stone stood watching the other passengers board the train. His sharp eyes assessed each person briefly but thoroughly, particularly the men, watching for likely troublemakers. As an employee for Wells Fargo, it was part of his job to head off potential problems before they could develop, to further ensure the safe transfer of valuable shipments of gold, bank monies, and sizable business payrolls. On this specific run, he and his friend and fellow agent Drake Evans were working undercover in an attempt to apprehend the band of robbers who had recently hit three separate trains bound for Dodge City. The gang had successfully stolen several thousand dollars, and the directors of the express company were downright irate—and determined to put a stop to the thefts.

At Morgan's side, Drake commented casually, "Looks like the usual run of folks this evening. With the exception of that little gal with the copper hair.

She's a beauty, isn't she? What do you suppose has her so riled?"

Morgan glanced toward where Drake was looking in time to see the lady in question stomp her dainty foot. He gave a low chuckle. "She looks mad enough to bust her corset, doesn't she? Those two women have been arguing for a good ten minutes now. If they don't stop soon, they'll both miss the train, and more than likely not notice until it's five miles down the track."

"The gentlemanly thing would be to apprise them of that fact, I suppose," Drake suggested with a sly grin. "Course, it could be dangerous to interrupt two cats while they're hissing at each other."

"Afraid you'll get your nose scratched, old buddy?" Morgan taunted, his broad smile revealing an even row of gleaming white teeth beneath his dark mustache. He gave a mock sigh. "Well, I guess I'll just have to take the lead and show you how to handle the situation."

Before Drake could reply, Morgan strode toward the women. He'd just reached them, and was about to alert them to his presence, when the train whistle blew loud and long. The younger woman gave a start of alarm. In quick succession, she tripped over the lump of fur at her feet, spun about in an awkward half pirouette, and promptly fell into Morgan's arms. The puffball gave a sharp yelp, and with excited yaps, began to run in circles, winding his leather leash tightly about the surprised couple's legs, lashing them together.

As she tripped and lost her balance, Heather gave a startled cry. Suddenly her flailing hands caught at something hard and solid, and she grasped hold tightly. Her momentum carried her into a broad wall of cloth, and it was several seconds before it dawned on her that she was clutching a man's arms, with her nose buried in the front of his shirt and his large hands clamped about her waist.

But that was not the worst of it. To her immense mortification, she realized that she was leaning full against him, with her legs wedged between his and her breasts flattened against his ribs. Her heart was pounding an erratic rhythm—or was it his she felt hammering in hard, thunderous beats? And what was that odd tingling that seemed to emanate from his fingers to her waist in hot ripples? She tried to draw a deep breath, only to freeze when the action brushed her breasts more intimately across his rock-hard chest, creating another strange, shocking wave of fluttering heat.

Slowly, her face flaming in embarrassment, Heather raised her head. Her wary brown eyes skimmed upward over a set of broad shoulders, the sturdy tanned column of his neck, and a square, stubbornly set chin. Her gaze lingered momentarily on the sensual curve of a male mouth and the neatly trimmed mustache grazing his upper lip. His nose was straight as a blade, set between high, prominent cheekbones, above which shone a pair of brilliant turquoise eyes, framed by thick dark lashes. At the moment, his eyes were studying her with quizzical humor.

Morgan had caught her purely by reflex, and abruptly found her pressed firmly against the length of him. The feather on her bonnet quivered, tickling his cheek—an insignificant distraction compared to the feel of her breasts crushed against his chest, poking provocatively at him through several layers of clothing. Her slender hips lay cradled in the vee of his slightly spread legs, snug against his manhood, which was fast responding to this unexpected feminine enticement, however unintentional it might be.

He stared down at her upturned face and could not hold back the grin that tugged at his lips, or resist the urge to tease her. "I've heard of women throwing themselves at a man, but roping him in the process is certainly a new trick."

She blinked up at him with huge brown eyes, still obviously bemused. It took a moment for his words to register, but when they finally did, she pushed away from him with such haste that she would have toppled backward if he hadn't still been holding on to her trim waist.

She swatted at him with dainty, gloved fingers. "Remove your hands from my person this instant!" she demanded. "Can't you recognize a lady when you see one?"

"Then you didn't throw yourself into my arms?" he taunted, feigning disappointment.

"I most certainly did not! I tripped and fell against you entirely by accident. Any gentleman with an ounce of sense or common decency would realize that."

"I didn't know they had rules of etiquette for situations such as this," he said with a grin. "However, I'd have assumed that a bit of gratitude might be in order. After all, I did save you from a nasty fall. Twice."

"Thank you!" she snapped peevishly. "And kindly release me. I am quite able to stand on my own now."

Black brows arched over laughing turquoise eyes. "I doubt that. In case you hadn't noticed, we seem to be tied together from the knees down." With an earthward glance, he added on a frown, "And I think the varmint responsible is currently trying to tear off my pant leg."

Following his look, Heather was immediately contrite, embarrassment staining her cheeks. "Oh! I'm sorry. Piddles! Let loose, you naughty dog! Etta! For goodness' sake, lend a hand at untangling us, will you?"

As Etta set about attempting to unbind them, Morgan studied the animal in question with scornful eyes. "You call that thing a dog?" he scoffed in disbelief. "It looks more like a hairy tumbleweed with teeth. I can only hope he doesn't live up to his name and take a notion to relieve himself on my best boots."

"After comparing him to a weed, it would serve you right if he did. Piddles is very sensitive, and quite

intelligent. Moreover, he earned his name by daw-
dling on his daily outings, so I doubt you need fear
for your precious footwear."

Morgan shot the mutt another dubious look. "Now,
why doesn't that ease my mind?" he muttered.

Piddles was snarling and snapping in an effort to
elude capture, holding Etta at bay. As the dog gave
another tug on the leash, Heather lurched forward
once more, bumping hard against Morgan and a rigid
object bulging at his hip. At the sharp jab of pain, her
hand instinctively sought to soothe the ache. In doing
so, her fingers brushed first cloth, then smooth
leather, then something cool and metallic.

Suddenly Morgan's hand clamped over hers, and
he eased her hand from his side, his turquoise gaze
wary. "It's bad enough your dog has gnawed on my
trousers. I don't need you shooting additional holes
in them."

Heather's eyes flew wide. "Is . . . is that a gun I
felt?" she stammered.

A mocking grin curved his lips, tilting his mustache. "That, or I'm awfully glad to meet you, honey."

She blinked up at him, obviously confused.

"Never mind," he told her with a shake of his head.
"I doubt you'd understand if I tried to explain it to
you."

She risked a glance downward and spied the
weapon holstered at his side. "You . . . You *are* wearing a gun!" she gasped.

He gave a curt nod. "There's no cause for alarm.
It's common practice in the West."

Etta had finally succeeded in unbinding the leash,
and Heather hastily stepped away from him. "Why?"
she blurted.

"Mainly for protection."

"Oh, Etta! Did you hear that? Now you simply
must change your mind and come with me, or Mother
will never forgive you!"

Just then the train whistle let loose another long
blast, and again Heather nearly leapt from her shoes

at the sound. Morgan reached out to catch her elbow and steady her.

"You're a jumpy little thing, aren't you?" he noted with a chuckle. "And I believe you are about to miss your train. Nearly everyone else has boarded."

"Oh, dear!" Heather was completely flustered. Her owlish gaze flitted from him to the train, then to Etta. "Etta! Please!" she wailed. "You must come with me this instant! Forget all that nonsense about a new job and suitors. If you haven't caught a husband by now, you probably never shall, so you might as well stay on as my maid."

Etta's eyes narrowed, her mouth forming a tight, thin line in her pinched face. "Heather Blair-Burns, you ungrateful brat! After all the manners your mother and I taught you. Well, mark my words, missy, your arrogance will be your downfall yet, and you won't have me to blame for it." With that, Etta practically tossed Piddles into Heather's arms and marched off in a huff.

Morgan let loose a low whistle. "Whew! You ladies can be vicious when you cut loose."

Heather rounded on him with flashing eyes. "I don't recall soliciting your opinion, sir."

He merely shrugged and grinned. "Maybe not, but you got it, didn't you? And if you're really nice, perhaps I'll even help you carry your baggage to the train, as long as you tote that overgrown rat and keep him off my ankles."

"All aboooard! Last call! All aboooard!"

Heather turned and saw the conductor about to signal to the engineer. "Wait!" she called. "Wait! I'm coming!"

Frantically she tried to gather her belongings, which were heaped about her feet, but there was no way she could manage Piddles, her handbag, her overnight case, and another small traveling bag all at once.

Morgan watched her fumbling attempts for a minute, then gently pushed her aside and collected the rest of her luggage himself. "Morgan Stone, at your service. After you, Miss Burns," he drawled. "You're keeping an entire train full of passengers waiting."

"Blair-Burns," she corrected automatically, hurrying ahead of him.

"How's that?" he asked.

"My surname, Mr. Stone. It's Blair-Burns, of the Boston Blairs."

Droll humor laced his deep voice. "I stand corrected, princess."

No sooner had they entered the passenger car than the train lurched into motion, throwing Heather backward against Morgan, her buttocks slamming against the front of him, and her head bumping into his chin, knocking her bonnet askew. On a grunt, with his hands full, Morgan quickly slung an arm around her middle. It banded just below her breasts, more by accident than design, hugging both her and Piddles, who promptly nipped at Morgan's knuckles.

Heather gave a sharp gasp, and seemed intent on railing at Morgan again. Figuring he might as well fire the first volley, he yanked his hand free, giving Piddles a well-deserved rap on the snout in the process. Then, tipping his head close to Heather's ear, he asked wryly, "Are you always this clumsy, or are you trying especially hard to hold my attention?"

Her elbow rammed into his ribs as she levered herself away from him. "Don't flatter yourself!" she spat, glaring over her shoulder at him. "And if you don't cease being so familiar, I'll be forced to report you to the conductor and have you put off the train. Or turn Piddles loose on you!"

"Fine. Next time you take a tumble, I'll let you fall smack on your fancy little Boston butt."

They made their way to the first-class car, which, because of the higher fare, was less than half-filled with passengers. As Heather was arranging her seat, Drake pushed past Morgan, shooting him a rueful scowl. "You always have all the luck," he grumbled in a confidential tone. "I'm stuck up front with the rest of the ordinary folk, while you ride in style with the aristocrats."

Morgan smirked. "Luck of the draw. Next trip I'll ride point, and you can guard the rear."

"Just mind whose rear you're guarding," Drake offered with a low chuckle, eyeing Heather's rounded backside as she bent to settle Piddles on the seat cushion next to her own.

Drake had sauntered away by the time Heather turned to relieve Morgan of the bags he was still holding. "Thank you for your help," she said stiffly. "You may leave now, if you please, and seek your own accommodations."

"How gracious of you," Morgan replied sardonically. "And they say a good deed never goes unrewarded. Obviously the author of that phrase never met up with the likes of you, Miss Blair-Burns of Boston."

"Oh, for heaven's sake!" she muttered irritably. Snatching up her purse, she fished out four pennies and thrust them into his hand. "There! Now, please be gone!"

He gazed comically at the coins, then at her, and murmured in farcical wonder, "Golly garsh, I'm rich! Wherever *will* I spend it all!"

"I couldn't care less," she announced, flouncing into her chair and staring directly ahead, pointedly dismissing him.

Morgan dribbled the pennies into her lap, one by one. When she failed to respond, he flicked his fingers at her slip-slanted bonnet, cocking it straight again atop her copper curls. She glowered up at him and grabbed at her hat. Having gained her attention once more, he tipped the brim of his Stetson in an insolent salute, backed off two steps, and promptly lowered his long frame into the empty seat facing hers.

❧ 2 ❧

"**W**hat do you think you're doing?" Heather inquired with a scowl. "You can't sit there."

Morgan cocked a brow at her in arrogant reply. "Pardon me, but I was under the impression that my ticket allowed me a seat, the same as you and any other paying passenger."

"Oh, you are going to be a boor about this, aren't you?" She sighed. Casting him another peevish look, she said, "A gentleman would at least remove his hat in the presence of a lady."

He grinned, displaying those shark-white teeth, and doffed his Stetson. A lock of thick black hair tumbled rakishly across his forehead. He brushed it aside with long, tanned fingers, then reached into his vest pocket and drew out a thin cigar.

"You're not going to smoke that vile thing here, are you?" she inquired, wrinkling her nose at him. "They have a smoking car for that purpose, to relieve the rest of us of the stench."

"Don't fret, princess. The conductor will be along any minute now, and after he's collected my ticket, I'll take myself and my stinking cigar off to more appropriate quarters."

"It can't be soon enough," she informed him shortly.

"Does travel disagree with you, or are you always this prickly, Miss Blair-Burns?"

11

Her nose inched upward. "I fail to see how that is any of your concern."

The conductor chose that moment to intervene, requesting their tickets. Morgan produced his promptly, while Heather rummaged through her handbag in what proved to be a futile search.

"Oh, but I know I had it!" she proclaimed weakly. "I'm sure it was here when I boarded. Unless . . ." Her voice trailed off as another possibility began to dawn on her. "Oh, drat! Etta had our tickets. The silly woman neglected to give mine to me. Now what shall I do?"

"If your friend is on the train, I can collect it from her," the conductor assured her.

"But she isn't," Heather wailed. "She decided to stay on in St. Louis."

"Well, ma'am, that does present a problem," the fellow said with a stern look. "By rights, I should stop the train and put you off immediately, unless you can provide some proof that you actually purchased a ticket."

"If I had the ticket, I would have the proof!" Heather retorted miserably. "I bought first-class passage from Boston to Dodge City. There must be some way to verify that without resorting to such drastic measures." Her dark eyes took on a pleading, persuasive glow.

The conductor took pity on her. "I suppose, if you know where your lady friend is staying, we can telegraph back to St. Louis when we hit our first stop. If she can produce the missing ticket, you can continue your journey."

"Oh, thank you!" Heather breathed gratefully, awarding him a winning smile. "I knew you were a reasonable person."

"In the meantime, however," the man continued, "I'll have to ask you to pay the fare from St. Louis to Columbia. That will be twenty-four dollars, please, to be refunded to you when we confirm your story."

Heather gaped up at him in disbelief. "I told you, I've already paid it."

"So you did, miss," the man concurred with a skeptical air.

"Are you insinuating that I am a liar, sir?" she countered huffily, drawing herself more erect in her seat.

"Let's just say I'm leaving room for doubt," he told her. "If you knew how many people, men and women alike, try to grab a free ride by spinning me a tale of woe, you'd know why I have to follow the rules. My job depends on it."

She glared up at him. "Once the owners of the railway discover the manner in which you treat decent, paying customers, you won't have to worry about such things. My family has a lot of influence, sir, and your insolence is going to cost you dearly."

The conductor frowned, then turned a questioning gaze on Morgan, who had been silently observing the dispute. "Are you with this woman?" he asked.

"Nope. Miss Blair-Burns and I just met," Morgan told him with a sympathetic smile. He puffed on his cigar and chuckled. "Sassy little spitfire, isn't she? To hear her, you'd think she owns all of Boston."

The conductor stared hard at Heather. "Listen, lady, I don't care who you are. I have my orders. Now, make it easy on both of us and pay up, will you?"

"I wouldn't pay you even if I did have the money," Heather insisted. "Which I don't. All but ten dollars of my traveling allowance is spent."

The conductor considered that for a moment, then announced with feigned cheer, "Well, aren't you the lucky one! Ten dollars will just buy you a seat with the rest of the third-class passengers. It's a bit crowded, and you'll have to sleep sitting up on an unpadded bench, but if we can fit you in with someone who's had a bath in the last month or so, it won't be so bad."

He reached out to help her from her seat. "Come along, miss. We'll get you settled in the other car."

"That won't be necessary," Morgan broke in. "I'll pay the lady's fare."

Heather's backbone stiffened even more. "A Blair never takes charity, Mr. Stone."

"Then I'd suggest you consult with the Burns side of your ancestry, princess, because I can guarantee you won't care for the accommodations in the third-class section. As the conductor has said, it is crowded and smelly and uncomfortable, not to mention dirty and abounding with people of meager income and questionable character. Somehow I just can't see you fitting into their midst real well."

Though she was sure both men were exaggerating the condition of the third-class section, she didn't want to chance it. "If I allow you to pay for my ticket, you must consider it a loan, to be repaid as soon as I can correct this situation."

Morgan inclined his dark head. "A loan it is, then, if it makes you feel better."

Puzzlement darkened her eyes. "Why are you willing to help a perfect stranger, Mr. Stone?"

His teeth flashed again in that ever-more-familiar grin. "Well, I wouldn't go so far as to say you're perfect, Miss Blair-Burns, but I am enjoying the pleasure of your company."

The conductor let loose a disbelieving snort as he accepted the money Morgan handed him and moved on. "Better you than me, mister," he mumbled, shaking his head.

Heather glared after him. "That man should not be allowed to serve the public. His attitude is altogether too abrasive."

Morgan chuckled. "I'm too forward, the conductor is too abrasive, your maid is full of nonsense. Is there anyone, besides yourself, who *does* meet with your approval?"

"Don't be absurd. There are numerous people I appreciate and admire. You simply aren't one of them," she added candidly.

"If you got to know me better, I might be," he countered.

"I have no wish to know you any better, Mr. Stone. In fact, I don't want to know you as well as I do now."

Any other man of her acquaintance would have taken the hint and changed seats immediately. Morgan merely laughed, his eyes twinkling as he graced her with a roguish wink. "That's a shame, since we're already such 'bosom buddies,' so to speak."

Heather's face flushed so bright that her hair looked pale by comparison. "Mr. Stone!" she gasped.

He rose and gave her bonnet another tap as he stepped into the aisle. "Don't get your tiara on a tilt, princess. And do try to miss me while I'm gone."

She was still trying to formulate a properly scathing retort as he ambled off toward the smoking car.

My goodness! Heather thought, fanning her flaming cheeks with a gloved hand. *What a thoroughly exasperating man!* He was audacious to a fault, an unsettling blend of cocky confidence and wicked charm. Precisely the sort of scoundrel a lady should avoid. Yet, with those fascinating turquoise eyes and rugged good looks, combined with that disarming smile, he was impossible to ignore. Moreover, he seemed fully aware of his appeal and prepared to employ it to its maximum advantage. An intriguing, disturbing, tempting rascal!

Heather shook her head, as if to dislodge that last idea. Still, the thought remained that Morgan Stone's presence had an odd effect on her. Rather like that light-headed, stomach-lurching sensation one experienced when first riding an elevator. A mere smile and she was breathless; a touch, and she was all atingle. Even now she could swear she still felt the fiery imprint of his hands on her waist, his hard chest pressing against her breasts.

With a shaky sigh, she decided that she was becoming far too fanciful of late, prone to all manner of strange notions and sentiments. Perhaps she needed a tonic to soothe her rattled nerves. Yes, that's all it was. Her reaction to Mr. Stone was no more than an extension of her anxious state these days. After all, she'd had more than her share of excitement in the past few weeks, enough to upset even the most stout-natured person.

It had all started when Lyle had proposed marriage last month. Of course, that had come as no great surprise to anyone, least of all Heather, since the two of them had been keeping company for six months. It had simply been a matter of Lyle garnering enough nerve to ask her, and Heather deciding whether or not she would accept.

After some consideration, Heather had agreed, much to everyone's delight. Lyle Asher was quite a catch, after all, and a girl couldn't do much better. He was reasonably attractive, polite, polished, and sprang from one of the oldest, wealthiest, and most prestigious families in Boston. Among other flourishing enterprises, the Ashers owned a publishing company, which Lyle was being primed to manage.

If Lyle was a bit pompous and stuffy, that was understandable. His American ancestry could be traced back to the landing of the *Mayflower*. Then again, so could Heather's—on her mother's side, at least. The Blair lineage was every bit as distinguished in its own right.

It was Heather's father, Angus Burns, an impoverished Scottish immigrant, who had put the only real blemish on the family's illustrious reputation—first by courting and marrying Heather's mother, and then by abandoning her soon after Heather's birth. Fortunately, Nelson and Elise Blair quickly arranged an annulment, which saved their daughter Betsy the public disgrace of a divorce. It was a mark of their social stature that Heather was blessedly spared the label of bastard, since everyone knew Angus and Betsy had been legally wed and Nelson and Elise proudly acknowledged Heather as their granddaughter.

Heather's rightful place among Boston's elite had

been guaranteed ever since then, as had Betsy's. Even Nelson's death and the loss of his warehouses in Boston's disastrous fire of 1872, followed almost immediately by the financial panic of 1873, had not spelled economic ruin or eroded the Blairs' status and popularity. Nelson had left sufficient investments and funds to ensure that his surviving family could maintain their home on Beacon Hill and their comfortable lifestyle.

Or so Heather had thought all these years, while she'd been growing up to become the Belle of Boston. Now, just shy of her eighteenth birthday, with marriage and a secure future ahead of her, she had discovered the shocking truth. Her father, Angus, was not dead, as her grandparents had informed her when Heather had asked about him at the tender age of five. Nor had she and her mother and grandmother been living on Nelson's savings and dividends for the past ten years. Angus had been sending money since Nelson's death, supporting the three Blair women with regular deposits to their bank account. Her father—Angus Cameron Burns—was alive and well, and living in Dodge City, Kansas!

Even now, had it not been for her grandmother's sudden death, which had subsequently delayed formal announcement of Heather and Lyle's engagement, Heather would not have known any of this. Nor, it seemed, would Betsy have been enlightened to the truth. Only after Elise's funeral, during a meeting with the family attorney, Mr. Rice, had either of them discovered that Angus Burns was their benefactor and their sole support, and had been for the last decade.

Upon learning this, Betsy had nearly had a stroke herself. She had taken her father's word that Angus had been killed in a barroom brawl two years after deserting her and their baby daughter. Now to learn, after all this time, that Angus was alive! That he was paying their debts! Virtually keeping the roof over their heads and the food on their table! It was almost too much to comprehend!

"It can't be!" Betsy had argued in stunned confusion. "Angus died years ago, and he certainly didn't have that kind of money. Besides, why would Father and Mother have kept this from me? Why would they let me believe he's been dead all this time if he's not?"

"Perhaps they thought it best, under the circumstances. After all, your marriage to Mr. Burns was annulled," Mr. Rice had suggested.

"But for Mother to accept support, and never say a word to me about it. I simply can't fathom it."

"Nor can I," Heather had put in. "Maybe it's not the same Angus Burns, or if it is, perhaps he left funds when he died that are being regularly transferred to our account."

"No, your father was as poor as a church mouse, I tell you," Betsy said in agitation. "Charming, but penniless."

Again the lawyer disagreed. "To the best of my knowledge, Mr. Burns is alive and healthy. The money is wired regularly at the first of every month from Dodge City, and your Boston bank sends statements to him there."

"Well, there is only one way to settle this matter, Mother. You must write to this fellow and find out who he is, and why he is supplying our income," Heather suggested.

Betsy gaped at her, then suddenly gave a weak, humorless laugh. "God help us if it's all been some awful mix-up and he stops sending money, daughter. We'll be out on the streets!" She paused a moment, and added almost prayerfully, "And God help us if it is our Angus—back from the grave after all these years!"

So had begun a strange, strained correspondence, which had confirmed Angus's identity. His reply was stilted and formal in tone, assuring them that he would continue to support the two of them, asking only that his former wife send word now and then about their daughter's progress. That was when Betsy had first suggested to Heather that she should write to Angus herself.

Heather had been appalled. "Mother, I can't! I wouldn't know what to say. Why, I know our grocer better than I know Mr. Burns."

"Then it is high time you got to know him, don't you think? He is your father, after all."

"Is he?" Heather had countered belligerently. "If so, why haven't we heard from him in nearly eighteen years? Not so much as a Christmas greeting, let alone some indication that he cared. Furthermore, how can you even suggest such a thing, after he deserted us?"

"Perhaps he regrets not being here to see you grow into the beautiful young lady you've become," Betsy proposed kindly, sadness clouding her face. "And he has missed so much. Your entire childhood. Write to him, dear. Tell him about yourself, share your plans to marry. We do owe him that, at least, for supporting us these past years and demanding nothing in return."

"Oh, all right! But I will not invite him to the wedding, Mother. You are far more forgiving than I will ever be."

One blasted letter to the man who had sired her, and somehow everything had gone awry. The next thing Heather knew, her mother was urging her to postpone her engagement party until late summer, and to accept Angus's invitation to visit him in Dodge City. After much debate, Heather had reluctantly agreed, partly out of a growing curiosity about her father, and partly out of concern that Angus might curtail deposits to their bank account if she didn't go.

"Come with me, Mother," Heather had begged. "At least you know what he looks like. It will save me the embarrassment of not recognizing my own father at the train station."

"Angus's invitation did not include me, and I wouldn't go if it did. I suspect this will be awkward for you both, but it would be more so if I went along.

For all I know, your father may have remarried years ago and had six more children with another wife. No, Heather, this is your time to acquaint yourself with your father, and he with you. I have no wish to intrude, or to rake up old wounds and heartaches at this late date."

"Yet you think I ought to meet the man who abandoned me almost the instant I was born! Oh, why couldn't Angus Burns have had the decency to be dead? How dare he interfere in my life now. It's simply not fair!"

Still and all, here she was on a train to Dodge City—her engagement to Lyle temporarily delayed, her well-ordered world turned upside down, her emotions in a state of turmoil, and her nerves so thoroughly jangled that she was even imagining an attraction toward that horrid Morgan Stone. Heaven have mercy! What could possibly happen to further complicate her life?

❧ 3 ❧

Morgan made his rounds, walking through the railroad cars, checking to see that nothing suspicious was going on. After assuring himself that all was well, he settled himself in the smoking car and ordered drinks for himself and Drake, who soon appeared to report that his half of the train seemed to be equally secure.

"Looks like we're in for a fairly quiet night," Drake commented. "Could be our bandits have stolen all they want for now, and are going to give us a break."

"I wouldn't bet on it," Morgan replied. His mustache tilted up at one corner as he joked, "The way things have been going lately, our elusive robbers are probably avid collectors of mismarked coins, and there are several bagsful of those in the mail car, being returned to the mint to be melted down. Besides, I have a feeling, like an itch I can't quite scratch, that tells me we shouldn't let our guard down just yet."

Drake chuckled. "That *itch*, as you call it, is probably due to one feisty red-haired filly who has you dancing attendance on her like a randy stallion."

"Ha!" Morgan scoffed. "She's got her highfalutin tail so far in the air that no self-respecting male would venture anywhere near it!"

Drake's eyebrows rose in mock alarm. "You saying you're not interested? If that's the case, you'd better check your pulse, 'cause I think you're either dead or crazy!"

Morgan grinned. "Oh, she's a tempting bit of fluff, all right, but so full of herself, it's ridiculous. Still, she is amusing, if only because she rises to the bait so eagerly that it's impossible to keep from provoking her. She practically begs to be teased."

Some time later, after collecting his travel bag from the storage area where he had left it earlier, Morgan arrived back in the first-class car to find that during his absence the conductor had converted the seats into sleeping berths. All of his fellow passengers, except his delightful seat-mate, had already retired into their cozy curtained cubicles for the night. At the moment, Morgan's earlier comment about Heather's tail being in the air seemed particularly appropriate. Apparently she was searching for something beneath the low berth, for she was wriggling stomach-down on the floor, her head and shoulders buried beneath the bed and her derriere hiked up in a most inviting manner. With each intriguing wiggle, her night shift twisted more tightly about her, and inched a bit higher along her legs.

With a wide grin, Morgan sauntered silently to his own bunk, which abutted hers, propped one broad shoulder against it, and whispered loudly, "You know, Boston, the problem with playing 'ostrich' is that while you remain oblivious to approaching danger, your posterior provides a very appealing target."

Heather gave a startled jerk and banged her head smartly on the underside of the bunk. Morgan couldn't be sure whether she issued the irate growl, or whether the sound came from her nasty little dog, who promptly poked his snout from between the bed-curtains and bared his sharp teeth at the intruder. Morgan snarled back, his brows rising in tandem with the hem of Heather's gown as she hastily squirmed out into the aisle.

"You . . . you infuriating beast!" she hissed, sitting up and tugging frantically at her twisted gown. Her eyes sparked dark flames at him. "Where did you spring from so unexpectedly?"

He sent her an amused look. "I assure you I arrived in the usual manner. Since they'd anticipated my appearance for many months, my birth came as no real surprise to either of my parents."

"That is not what I meant, and you know it, you sneaky snake!" She wobbled to her knees, clutching at the mattress for support as she tried to rise. Her foot tangled in the material of her long gown, sending her sprawling awkwardly toward him.

He caught her deftly, a deep chuckle rumbling from his throat. "Please tell me your middle name is not Grace," he quipped.

"It's Elise, after my grandmother," she blurted automatically, her senses already swamped by the intense heat radiating from his body to hers. Once again, her breasts were crushed against his hard chest, his fingers almost spanning her small waist. Her flesh felt as if it were being branded through the thin cotton gown.

Before she could recover her wits, one warm hand left her waist, lifting to catch a loose tendril of her hair. As his fingers skimmed lightly along the shell of her ear, she shivered in reaction. His thumb traced her jawline, lifting her chin, urging her stunned gaze to his, then rose to caress the delicate outline of her lips ever so tenderly.

Gleaming turquoise eyes held hers as he murmured, "Have you ever been kissed, Heather Elise Blair-Burns?"

"Y-yes," she stammered, as if under a sorcerer's spell.

"Like this?"

His mouth swooped down to cover hers. His lips stroked hers as gently as a summer breeze, warming them. Testing. Teasing. Tasting with tantalizing sips, until she melted into his embrace with a dainty quiver. Only then did he allow himself to deepen the kiss, drawing her lush lower lip between his teeth, nipping at it, holding it captive for his laving tongue, suckling insistently—and when she gave a shaky sigh, his tongue darted between her parted lips into the sweet depths of her mouth.

As his tongue slid over hers, lightly grazing the roof of her mouth, Heather emitted a muted gasp. In the next instant her jaws clamped shut, trapping his tongue between her sharp front teeth.

"Aaargh!" Morgan's eyes popped wide, meeting her own astonished gaze, even as his fingers tightened on her lower jaw, trying to pry it open. " 'Et go, da' it!" he mumbled frantically.

Before she could decipher his words, let alone think clearly enough to act upon them, Morgan let loose another muffled yell and began to twitch as if in the throes of some strange malady, his left leg kicking out repeatedly. Awestruck, Heather finally released her hold on him, and only then did it dawn on her that Morgan was not having some sort of demented fit. He was merely trying to disengage Piddles's teeth from his knee!

"Damn!" he grumbled. "Between you and your mangy mutt, I'll probably die of rabies!" He smacked the dog on the snout, and Piddles backed off with a yelp, taking a large chunk of Morgan's trouser leg with him.

"How dare you hit my dog!" Heather exclaimed.

"How dare you bite me!" Morgan retorted.

"You had your tongue in my mouth, you . . . you pervert!"

"Hellfire! If you're that blasted shocked, it's a sure bet you've never been properly kissed before. Doesn't Boston breed any real men, or are they all a bunch of timid limp-wrists?"

"That kiss was not at all proper, Mr. Stone."

"Neither is dashing around in your night shift in a public train car, Miss Prim and Proper."

"I was not dashing about! I was attempting to re-trieve my hairbrush from my luggage, not an easy feat once these ridiculous seats have been converted to berths. And I certainly never intended for anyone to see me, most especially you!"

His mustache tilted up on one side. "Are you sure about that?"

"Positive."

"In that case, I'll gladly retrieve your hairbrush for you, as soon as you apologize for nearly gnawing off my tongue, and letting your louse-infested pet rip yet another swatch out of my trousers."

"I hope you hold your breath and turn blue waiting for an apology from me," she told him tartly. "Furthermore, Piddles does not have lice, and I don't want you touching my luggage, me, or anything that belongs to me ever again!"

"Afraid I'll get my grubby hands on your lacy little undergarments, princess?" he taunted.

"When cows start singing opera," she countered stiffly.

"I'll look forward to it with great anticipation," he assured her with a lewd wink.

She was still contemplating an appropriately cutting rejoinder when a man's voice called out quietly from a nearby berth. "Say, folks, all this has been entertaining, but I really don't care who gets into whose britches. I'd just like to get a little shut-eye, if you two would tone it down some."

Heather's chocolate brown eyes grew huge, her face flaming. Without another word, she dived into her berth and yanked the curtain closed behind her.

Morgan's low chuckle followed her. "Nighty-night, Boston," he crooned. "Sweet dreams."

"Only if they're of you with your mustache on fire!" she muttered peevishly.

Morgan awoke just before dawn with the odd feeling that there was an unfamiliar weight on his chest. The weight shifted slightly. Morgan frowned and squinted one eye open. Its twin followed suit. There, snuggled comfortably on his bare chest, was a lump of fur that bore a disturbing resemblance to Miss Blair-Burns's snappish little dog. His scowl deepened.

It was bad enough having to stuff his lanky six-foot frame into a space not much larger than a cigar box, without having to share it with an ill-tempered, overgrown muskrat!

"All right, flea-trap," he grumbled, giving the pup a nudge with his hand. "Enough is enough."

Piddles woke with a snarl, his pearly teeth bared for action as he lunged immediately for the offending hand. Sharp canine claws raked across Morgan's naked torso. "Oww! Dang! Let loose, you fool fuzzball!"

Piddles merely tightened his jaws, not hard enough to break the skin, but enough to issue fair warning that any further agitation would be taken as a declaration of outright war.

"Okay, okay, simmer down," Morgan advised. "I suppose you know that's my gun hand you're sinking your teeth into. You couldn't have grabbed for the other one, could you?"

He paused a moment to review his ridiculous situation. "Hey, Boston!" he called out softly, not wanting to rile the dog any further.

No response.

"Hang it all, wake up, woman!"

There was still no sign of life from beyond the curtain separating her sleeping booth from his.

Carefully stretching one cramped leg, Morgan thrust his foot against the curtain, in the general vicinity of his slumbering neighbor's pillow, or where he supposed it should be. "Hey, Heather! How about lendin' a little help here, dumplin', before I'm forced to strangle your precious pooch."

Something thumped against the top of Heather's head, jarring her from a sound sleep. Before she could open her eyes, it smacked her again. Shaking her head, her vision somewhat unfocused in the dim predawn light, Heather stared in mute speculation at the cloth-covered object that had landed mere inches from her nose. "What in the . . ."

"C'mon, princess," a gruff voice beckoned. "I'm in

dire need of rescue. Get a move on, before this lousy cur of yours chews my fingers off."

The "thing" near her face wiggled, and Heather finally recognized it as a foot. Morgan Stone's stocking-clad foot!

"*Mr.* Stone! Kindly remove your stinking foot from my face!" she snapped, gingerly prodding at it with the tips of her fingers.

"*Miss* Blair-Burns," he mimicked back, "kindly remove your stinking dog from my chest. And while you're at it, maybe you could get him to unclamp his teeth from my hand!"

It took a long, silent minute for his message to fully penetrate her sleep-fogged brain. Then she issued a weary sigh. "Drat!"

"I'll double that, and raise you three damnations. Now, call off this pint-sized carnivore!"

"Piddles! Here, puppy! Come to Mama, baby!" she called out more sweetly than Morgan would have thought possible.

Piddles whined, wagged his tail, and stayed where he was.

"Piddles, don't make Mama angry, now. Be a good doggie and come here." She snapped her fingers in sharp command.

"Try whistling for him. He doesn't seem to be taking you seriously, Miss Sweetness and Light," Morgan suggested mockingly.

"I don't know how to whistle. For your information, that is considered a very unladylike talent."

"Then get your sweet butt over here and collect him," Morgan grumbled. "He's your pet, and I didn't ask for his company. I suppose I've shared my bed with a couple of dogs in the past, but they've all been females and had an invitation."

"Are . . . are you decent?" she questioned hesitantly.

Morgan chuckled. "On occasion."

"Mr. Stone, you know what I meant. Are you dressed?"

"For the most part. Don't worry, darling, there's

nothing important exposed. Not that I could do much about it if there were, you understand, with this hairy cocklebur attached to me."

Begrudgingly Heather crawled out from beneath her covers. On the off chance that any of her fellow passengers were up and about at this ungodly hour, she peered carefully up and down the aisle before hoisting herself from her bunk.

With some trepidation, she parted the curtain of the connecting cubicle and stuck her head and shoulders inside. "All right, Piddles," she said, eyeing the animal sternly. "Enough of this nonsense! Let loose of Mr. Big-Bad-and-Brave before he sets up a howl and wakes everyone else."

"Is that a slur on my manhood?" Morgan demanded. "I'll have you know that I was only considering your tender feelings, or I'd have murdered the rotten monster ten minutes ago."

Heather grabbed the pup, who promptly released his victim. She started to turn away. "My hero!" she jeered.

Only then, with Piddles off of Morgan, did her gaze skitter over the broad male chest before her . . . a bare, hairy chest! Her eyes widened to the size of large walnuts. Her mouth flew open, and she stared in speechless astonishment. Finally, after about ten seconds, she found her tongue again, though her exclamation was not quite what Morgan had expected to hear.

"What have you done to my poor dog? You've ripped his fur out!" she wailed. Her glassy gaze switched from Morgan to Piddles, as she upended the unsuspecting Pomeranian and surveyed his belly. A frown creased her brow. Again her eyes sought Morgan's chest, studying it thoughtfully. Tentatively she reached out and caught a tuft of the dark, swirling fleece, tugging at it.

"Ouch! Take it easy there, Miss Curiosity!" he advised, even as a rumble of laughter erupted from deep in his throat and amusement lit his turquoise eyes.

"That's mine, and I'll thank you to leave it there for the next woman to enjoy."

"Oh, my gosh!" she murmured in disbelief. Never having seen a man's naked chest before, she was totally flustered. "It *is* yours! No wonder it's so much darker than Piddles's fur! Gracious me! I...I... you..."

She was saved from her ticklish predicament by the unexpected advent of another. With an ear-piercing shriek and a horrendous grinding of wheels, the train suddenly gave a mighty lurch. Before Heather could grab for anything to steady herself, both she and Piddles were thrown to the floor, followed immediately by Morgan, who toppled from the bunk and landed half over her. All around them, other passengers found themselves in similar straits, pitched violently from sleeping compartments amid a shower of unsecured belongings. In the blink of an eye, the narrow aisle was strewn with tangled bodies and upended baggage.

Morgan's befuddled mind registered several things at once. The sudden jolt and continuous screech of the wheels told him that, for some reason, the engineer had abruptly applied the brakes. The rapidly slowing train was rocking precariously along the track, the cars weaving and bobbing like ships in a storm. He saw Heather fall, felt himself sliding, momentarily powerless to help himself or her. As she hit the floor, Piddles popped from her arms like a cork from a bottle, a fuzzy yelping blur hurtling through the air. The pup landed safely upon the back of a portly gentleman lying in the aisle several feet away, while Morgan fleetingly marveled that he'd never imagined a dog could fly, let alone so high or so far.

All of this flashed before Morgan's awed eyes a split second before he crashed down atop Heather, his upper body driving the breath from hers, his face planted firmly between her breasts. Then, as he struggled hazily to assess the situation and any resultant damage, a new set of impressions bombarded him. Her flesh beneath the thin cotton nightgown was pliant and warm and fragrant with an alluring womanly scent that filled his nostrils and set his senses reeling. Of course, what else would he smell, with his nose buried in the valley between her breasts and his cheeks pillowed on the supple mounds? He could feel the rapid thud of her heart reverberating against his lips, literally making them vibrate with each beat of her pulse, each quivering breath she took. On impulse, he nestled more fully into her, his lips nuzzling the soft sides of her breasts, his breath moistening the gauzy cloth shielding the plump globes from his touch. Unconsciously his fingers curled over firm flesh, and it occurred to him that his palm rested high on her right thigh—her bare thigh. The raised hem of her gown barely brushed the edge of his hand. So near . . . so close . . . so tempting.

She wriggled, and he gave a muffled groan. Blast it all! This did have to happen when he didn't have time to enjoy it! With much regret, he willed himself to recall that, like it or not, he had a job to do—and no time to wallow in lustful fantasies.

Beneath him, Heather lay gasping, not altogether certain what had caused her current plight or what to do about it. Stunned, she felt Morgan's weight pressing her down, his hard body holding and heating hers, the soft bristles of his mustache tickling her chest through her night shift. Beneath his mouth, his moist breath nearly scalded her scantily clad flesh. His wandering lips seemed to sear their imprint into her skin as they caressed the inner curves of her breasts. His warm, firm fingers clutched at her thigh, further jumbling her senses. Her head was spinning, her body feverish . . . yearning . . . awash with strange and mystifying sensations. Her pulse pounded an erratic beat. Her breasts tingled, her stomach fluttered, her breath caught in her throat. Unaware that she did so, Heather strained toward him, seeking more of this wondrous, forbidden intimacy.

Then, as suddenly as it had begun, it was over. She blinked up at him, still baffled and disoriented, as his body lifted from hers. For just a moment, she thought he looked as shaken as she felt. She must have been mistaken, for in the next instant, he grinned down at her, sent her a devilish wink, and drawled, "Wish I could stay and play, darlin', but duty calls."

Before she could organize her thoughts, Morgan levered himself up, yanked on his boots, grabbed his shirt and gun belt, and began threading his way through the tangle of limbs and luggage toward the rear of the train car. By the time he reached the door, he was fully dressed.

Almost as an afterthought, he turned and called out to her, "If someone comes along with a gun and demands your money and jewels, don't give him any sass, Boston. Just be smart and politely hand over your valuables. I'd hate to see you get hurt."

❧ 4 ❧

Morgan loped through the next railcar, dodging fallen passengers as best he could and cursing the fact that he still had half a dozen compartments to negotiate before he reached the mail car, where money, gold, and various other valuables were locked away in a large safe. Outside, the pearl gray of predawn still shadowed the land, and he could detect no movement through the soot-smeared windows. No masked riders. No sounds or flashes of gunfire. But the train was still grinding slowly to a halt, and the churning in the pit of his stomach, which usually heralded disaster, was growing in intensity.

He'd made it fairly rapidly through two cars, and was between the second and third when the train gave another mighty lurch. Morgan, balanced on the narrow hitch that connected the cars, made a mad grab for anything to curb his fall. He missed . . . and for one dreadful moment anticipated the awful probability that he was about to meet an agonizing death beneath the huge metal train wheels.

Fate was kind, in a rather bizarre manner. As his legs went out from under him, they split in opposite directions, spraddling Morgan astride the crossbar. He landed hard, the air whooshing out of his lungs, which was the only thing that spared him the embarrassment of letting loose a scream that would have been heard from coast to coast. Acute pain lanced through him, and bright stars streaked his vision like clusters of multicolored comets. Amid the numerous distinctive curses that echoed through his brain was also the vague thought that it was a good thing he'd never seriously considered having a family, for there now loomed the disheartening prospect that he might no longer be capable of fathering children of his own.

Doubled over at the waist, clutching the iron bar with one hand and his battered anatomy with the other, Morgan managed to hang on as the train stuttered to a full stop. Through dint of will, he stumbled dizzily to his feet, wobbling on watery knees, and somehow managed to repress the threatening nausea. Miraculously, he was alive, though he might well spend the rest of his days as a eunuch.

Irrationally, his mind still blurred with pain, Morgan immediately pinned the blame on Heather. "It's all her fault! The damned woman is a jinx! A Jonah! Her blasted clumsiness is as contagious as the plague! First I tumble from my bed, and now I'm practically gelded!"

Still grumbling to himself, Morgan hoisted himself aboard again and hobbled hurriedly through the remaining compartments toward the mail car. With any luck at all, there was no holdup in progress. Maybe the unscheduled stop was simply due to some obstruction on the tracks.

This slim hope evaporated at the sight of a small band of riders galloping past the windows on horseback. The improving light outdoors revealed that each wore a hat pulled down over his face, and a bandanna drawn over the lower half to conceal his identity. All were armed.

"Drat! What a hell of a way to start the day!" Morgan mumbled, drawing his own weapon, an act that promptly elicited shrieks of alarm from several female passengers. He ignored them with cool indifference.

He'd reached the end of the last car, just ahead of the mail car, and was debating the best way to proceed, when Drake slipped through the door to join him. He eyed Morgan askance, noting the grease smears on his friend's clothes. "What the devil did you do, crawl under the train while I was clambering over the top of it?"

Morgan glowered. "I slipped, if it's any of your business. Did you happen to get a head count on our greedy friends?"

"Two up front. The one who was guarding the engineer is out cold, with the fireman ready to clobber him again if he so much as twitches. Another is making his way through the cars, collecting booty. I figure we can nab him after we take care of his cohorts, if the conductor doesn't get him first. My guess is four raiding the mail car, two in and two out."

Morgan nodded. "You take the two on the outside. I'll net the pair inside."

Several cars up, Heather was blatantly and irately disregarding Morgan's advice. Faced with an armed, masked bandit, she stubbornly refused to aid him in his quest for loot. "If you want my jewel case, you'll have to dig it out from beneath the berth yourself!" she informed him haughtily. "Evidently you have no notion of how difficult it is to retrieve anything from under there. Perhaps you and your companions should have thought of that before attacking the train while its passengers were still abed. Had you waited an hour or two, everyone would have been up and dressed, and the berths converted to a decent seating arrangement once more."

The beleaguered outlaw glowered with puckered brows and fiercely squinting eyes, the intended evil effect weakened somewhat as he shook his leg, trying to dislodge a growling Piddles. He glanced downward. "Lady, does this pint-sized ankle-biter belong to you?"

"Yes, and he's very protective, so you'd better watch yourself," she warned.

"How'd you like if I turn him into a rug for you?" the robber threatened.

Heather glared at him, her chin jutting out defensively. "That goes to show what an uncouth scoundrel you truly are!" She bent, scooped Piddles into her arms, and faced her tormentor again.

"That's better," he said. "Now, you've got exactly five seconds to hand over your best baubles and money, or I'll plug both of you full of holes. You can start with those pretty silver earrings, and that ruby ring you're wearing."

"It's a garnet, you cretin," she corrected, angrily tugging the ring from her finger. "And the earbobs are platinum."

He shrugged and held out his free hand. "Well, they gotta be worth somethin', even if they ain't real valuable. Your cash next, and be quick about it."

Muttering curses that would have made her mother faint, Heather dug beneath her pillow for her handbag. As she started to open it, the bandit yanked it from her hands and did it himself. Dumping the contents on her bunk, he frowned. "Is this all?" he asked incredulously. "A measly ten bucks and a few loose coins? Jeez, woman, you travel kinda light, don't you?"

"That's the lot," she told him smugly. "Take it or leave it, buster."

"Oh, I'll take it, along with this pretty little watch," he said, scooping the small pile into the bulging canvas sack tied to his belt.

"I hope you rot in hell," she railed, as he tipped his hat and continued down the aisle in search of better plunder.

"I won't mind much, I reckon, as long as the devil don't let mean-mouthed females like you in," he called back.

While Drake engaged his pair of bandits in a hearty exchange of gunfire, Morgan shot through the locked door of the mail car and hurled himself inside, rolling and firing as he went. Right off, he winged one of the men, whose gun flew out of his hand. The other hurriedly backed out of the safe, only to meet the business end of Morgan's Colt as he turned. The postman and the rail guard both lay unconscious amid a clutter of mail.

"Hope you don't mind me inviting myself to the party, fellas," Morgan commented with easy nonchalance. "Now, raise those hands above your heads and keep them there, while I check on my partner."

Morgan edged toward the open window, from which the bandits had been tossing bags of money to their fellow robbers. "Drake? I've got these two covered," he called.

His answer was another spurt of gunfire, echoed by Drake's livid curse. "Shitfire! They're gettin' away! Three of 'em! I'm goin' after 'em! Meet you in Dodge!"

"Hey! Throw me a rope first!" Morgan hollered.

A coil of rope sailed through the window, followed by the sound of receding hoofbeats.

"Okay, fellas, it's time to see how handy you are at hitching knots." Morgan tossed the rope to the uninjured man. "You get the honor of hog-tying your buddy. Do a good job, and I won't be tempted to put a loop around your neck and hang you from the ceiling."

Morgan stood back and watched with a critical eye. The first outlaw was securely bound, and Morgan was looping the rope around the remaining man's hands, when he heard a furtive noise behind him. Before he could turn, something hard connected with the back of his skull. There was a sickening swirl of mist and yellow dots, and then the world went black.

Morgan drifted toward consciousness with foreboding and a whale of a headache. It felt as if his skull had been cracked open. With the caution of a man who dreads the worst, he raised one eyelid, only to be speared by bright sunlight. He groaned, automatically trying to lift one hand to the source of the pain. Only then did he realize that his arm would not move, that he was half lying on it, and that something was binding it to his side. It took him another few seconds to deduce that he was lying on the floor of the mail car, bound hand and foot.

"You ain't goin' anywhere, mister, so you might as well relax," a voice above him advised.

With effort, Morgan opened his eyes and looked up, past a pair of trousered legs and the long barrel of a shotgun leveled at his chest. The mail car guard, his head raggedly bandaged, scowled down at him. Morgan's own pistol was tucked in the fellow's waistband.

"At least we bagged you, and one o' yer pals, even if the rest o' the gang got away," the man informed him curtly.

"Aw, crap!" Morgan grunted in disgust. "They got away?"

The guard looked perplexed. "I know misery loves company, but I'd have guessed you'd be glad they escaped. Sort of honor among thieves and all that, you know?"

"I hate to disappoint you, but I'm not a thief. You've captured the wrong man, and I'd appreciate it if you'd untie me now. I'm fast gaining a lot of sympathy for Christmas turkeys."

The other man gave a sharp laugh that seemed to reverberate through Morgan's throbbing head. "It'll be interestin' to see if you keep that sense o' humor when they fit the noose around yer neck."

"Hang it all!" Morgan grimaced as the guard's chuckle continued. "I suppose you think my unfortunate choice of words is funny, but you won't be laughing long. You, my blundering fellow, have seized an agent of the Wells Fargo Express Company."

With an amused quirk of his bushy eyebrows, the guard commented, "Is that so?"

"It is," Morgan avowed solemnly. "I've been working undercover to apprehend the very criminals who hit the train this morning."

"Yeah, and I'm one of Santa's little helpers," the guard said with a snicker. "Glad to meet ya."

Morgan sighed. "Look, if you'd just go fetch the conductor, he can at least confirm that I'm a paying customer and not part of the band that robbed the train."

The guard shrugged. "He's already been back here and told us that, but it don't prove much. We figure a couple o' you yahoos could've been stationed on the train, to help out from inside, 'specially since we caught you red-handed, with money stickin' out o' yer pockets and a big bag o' gold clutched in yer greedy paw."

Morgan blinked in confusion. "Now, wait just a minute. I didn't even touch that money. I was holding my gun on two of the bandits when someone clobbered me from behind."

"Likely story."

"Who hit me, anyway? You and the postmaster were already out cold."

"Beats me," the guard told him. "Maybe Hal did it. The conductor," he clarified. "You was layin' there with all that loot and he was bendin' over you when I come to. By the time we got you tied up, Shad was startin' to wake up. Lucky for you, nobody was hurt serious, but I suppose they can only hang you once any way you slice it."

"If it means anything, I'm glad no one was mortally wounded, even if I wasn't a part of it. At the moment, I'm not so sure about my own injuries, however. My head is killing me!"

"Yeah, well, we'll do our best to keep you alive till we can get you to Dodge and arrange a decent lynchin' for ya," the guard assured him. "And the sheriff is sure to be plumb tickled to oblige."

* * *

The train was two hours late arriving in Dodge City. It was still half a mile down the track when the engineer blew the whistle in a distinctive series of sounds that signaled ahead to the depot that the train had been robbed. By the time the locomotive chugged sluggishly to a halt at the station, mass pandemonium had already erupted. Townspeople were pouring from nearby stores and homes like packs of rats from a flooded den, all racing toward the train. The stationmaster was pacing worriedly, while the ticket agent hopped from foot to foot like a jackrabbit with blisters.

"Somebody get the sheriff!" the engineer yelled from the cab.

"He's on his way!" yelled back someone in the growing crowd.

"Clear a path, folks," Sheriff Watson ordered, pushing his way through the throng. In his wake trailed one deputy, the mayor, and Dodge's resident judge. Morgan had quite a welcoming committee awaiting him when the guard shoved him down the steps onto the boarding platform and into the presence of the town lawmen. The second prisoner, still half-groggy, stumbled up next to him, where they both stood on display.

"Well, well! What have we here?" Watson crowed in delight. Morgan wondered that the man kept from wringing his hands in absolute glee. No doubt the good sheriff was envisioning an easy reelection.

"Brought ya a couple of fresh-trapped birds for yer jail," the guard said, his chest puffed up like a rooster's. "It'll be up to you to make 'em sing, and we're countin' on ya to get 'em to tell who the other outlaws are and where they plan to stash all the money they stole from the train today."

"Oh, we'll make them talk, all right," the sheriff assured him in a voice loud enough for half the town to hear. "Then we'll hang the pair of them like the buzzards they are."

A cheer went up from the crowd.

"Now, hold on here, George," the judge said. "Mayor Webster's done a fine job of trying to clean up the reputation of our little town, and we don't want to tarnish it by turning into a mob of vigilantes. These men are entitled to a fair trial, and I'm bound to see that they get it. Then we'll measure them for hemp neckties."

Watson nodded, albeit a bit reluctantly. "Quite right, Judge Swanson. How long do you think it'll take to round up a jury and get things rollin'?"

Swanson, looking thoughtful, took a moment to consider his reply. "We could rush things and convene court this afternoon, but you're going to need some time to pry some information from these two first. Besides, I've got me a poker game over at Gus's Gurdy that I'd hate to miss out on. Tell you what. Let's plan for tomorrow morning around ten o'clock. And make sure you give these prisoners a good supper tonight, and a hearty breakfast in the morning. It might be their last, and every condemned man has the right to a decent final meal. Oh, and try not to rough them up too badly. We want them alert and kicking for the festivities tomorrow."

"You sure you don't want me to fluff their pillows tonight and tell 'em bedtime stories, too?" the sheriff asked mockingly. "Or leave the cell door unlocked so they can get to the outhouse without bothering anyone for the keys?"

Rather than take offense, the elderly judge winked and chuckled. "I dare you to speak to me like that during court tomorrow, George. You'll be spendin' time in your own cell for contempt before you know what hit you."

"More'n likely, it'll be your gavel landin' upside of his head, Nels," the mayor chortled, rousing a spate of appreciative laughter from the spectators.

Morgan wasn't laughing. He'd thought once they reached Dodge, there would be someone of reasonable intelligence who might listen to his denial of the charges against him. But matters were looking more bleak by the minute, especially with Judge Swanson practically champing at the bit to pass sentence, while trying to look benevolent for the sake of propriety and a few dozen votes come election time. Fair trial? More of a farce, was a better bet. A travesty of justice.

Morgan glanced around, scanning the crowd, hoping to spot Drake among them. His friend was probably halfway to Texas by now, in hot pursuit of the fleeing robbers. Heaven only knew how successful he'd be in catching any of them, or how soon he'd turn up in Dodge. Meanwhile, unless a miracle occurred, Morgan had approximately twenty-four hours left to live. Chances were good he'd be dead and buried before Drake showed up to vouch for his innocence—or to claim his remains.

Morgan's wandering gaze finally lit on a familiar face. Heather Blair-Burns stood hesitantly on the top step of the train car, holding her beloved mongrel in her arms. She looked a bit lost and bewildered by the goings-on. Evidently she'd never witnessed a lynch mob in the making.

As Morgan watched, a tall, muscular man with a graying head of red hair approached her. Though Morgan couldn't hear their conversation, he saw Heather nod politely. A wide grin split the man's face. Heather's wary expression changed to one of stunned surprise as the fellow promptly enveloped her in his burly arms, swept her off her feet, dog and all, and swung her around in a wide circle. By the time he'd set her down again, Heather's hat had fallen off, her skirt was askew and showing several inches of petticoat, and Piddles was clinging to the man's vest by his teeth.

❧ 5 ❧

When her world finally stopped spinning, Heather was once more looking into the dancing blue eyes of the man who had sired her. He stood nearly a foot taller than she, was sturdily built, and sported a thick mane of hair that still bore traces of the fiery red hue it had been in his youth. His wide smile, which puffed his cheeks beyond the borders of his beard, and those sparkling eyes gave him the overall appearance of a merry giant—with a snarling dog attached to his chest.

Calmly plucking off the animal, he plopped it back into Heather's arms. "Just look at ye!" he exclaimed with delighted wonder. "Why, ye've turned into a beauty, just like yer ma! Nothin' like the wrinkled wee bairn I held in my arms when ye were first born," he added with a wry chuckle.

"Thank you, Mr. Burns," she replied with cool reserve, biting back the questions that clawed at her heart. Had he deserted her and her mother because she'd been such an unattractive baby? Had he taken one look at her as an infant, decided she was too homely to suit him, and run for the hills—or in this case, the prairie? Was his disappearance from their lives all her fault? If she'd been born a boy, a son, would he have stayed?

Angus Burns's face clouded up. "Here now! What's this Mr. Burns business? I'm yer pa, lass. While I know that might take some gettin' used to, ye could at least call me Angus, or Gus if ye prefer, which is how I'm known by most folks hereabouts."

"I suppose Angus would suit. That's how my mother refers to you."

Angus gave a snort of disgust and disbelief. "I'm surprised she dinna wipe my existence from her mind the minute the door slammed behind me."

"I'm sure she would have been delighted to do so," Heather concurred. "My grandparents certainly managed with little trouble."

"No doubt," Angus muttered darkly. In the next instant he brightened. "C'mon, daughter. Let's collect yer bags and I'll show ye where ye'll be stayin' for the next few weeks, help get ye acquainted wi' the town. Dodge is a tad rowdy still, but a lot more civilized than it used to be a few years back. I have a notion ye'll like it well enough, after ye've had time to get to know yer way around and meet a few people."

As she followed his lead, walking along and gaining a quick impression of the rough little cow town, Heather doubted Angus's predictions. At first glance, Dodge City was not impressive, except perhaps for its total lack of beauty. The streets were unpaved, grooved with deep ruts carved through several inches of half-dried mud. The adjacent buildings were similarly worse for wear, the majority drab in color and weather-beaten, a few slanting so precariously that it appeared a mild breeze would send them tumbling.

Here, in the main business district, there was not a single tree or blade of grass in sight. In place of actual paved sidewalks, such as more civilized cities now possessed, this pitiful excuse of a town offered wooden walkways in front of the stores. At intervals, rough planks sufficed as a means to cross intersections, but for the most part folks had to plod in ankle-high mire simply to get from one side of the street to the other.

As they passed various establishments, Heather quickly noted a distinct shortage of women's apparel and millinery shops, tea parlors, pastry shops, curio and jewelry stores, not to mention the complete lack of anything resembling a bank or museum. However, there seemed to be an abundance of restaurants, drugstores, dance halls, billiard halls, and even a couple of art galleries and an opera house. The closest thing to a department store seemed to be the mercantile. There were also a few saloons, which had Heather frowning in distaste and bafflement.

"Mr. . . . uh . . . Angus," she said, "I'm surprised to see that there are taverns which seem to be open and thriving despite the fact that what little research I did in preparation for my trip indicated that intoxicating liquor has been banned in Kansas for two years now."

"We dinna pay much attention to that here in Dodge," Angus informed her with a sly smile. "Mayor Webster don't cotton much to the governor telling him how to run his town."

"What a pity. Personally, I believe in abolishing such establishments myself. I am a proud member of the Boston Temperance Society."

Angus's steps faltered and his smile wavered. "Knowin' yer granny Blair, I should've guessed that." He sighed and resumed walking, more slowly now. "Ah, weel, there's nae hope for it, I reckon."

"No hope for what?"

"Ye'll find out soon enough, little gal." His lingering Scots accent softened the vowel slightly, making the word "gal" come out sounding like "ghel."

Half a block farther along, Angus stopped again and pointed to the opposite side of the street. "We'll cross here," he told her. "That's my place there. Watch yer step now, these boards can be a might slippery."

As they waited for a wagon and two riders on horseback to pass by first, Heather looked with interest at the brick building above which hung a sign proclaiming it to be "Gus's Gallery and Gurdy."

"I know what a gallery is, but what is a gurdy?" she inquired politely.

"Uh, 'tis a short way of sayin' hurdy-gurdy," he admitted hesitantly.

"A hurdy-gurdy?" she echoed. "I don't believe I've heard of that before."

Angus grumbled something she failed to hear, and before she could question him further, Heather needed all her concentration to negotiate the mud-slathered plank beneath her feet. She was still trying to shake clods of mud from her shoes when Angus led her through a set of batwing doors into the shadowed interior of his business.

Even before her eyes had adapted to the dim lighting, Heather's nose was assaulted by a stale yeast odor. As her vision adjusted, she gaped in stupefied astonishment, so completely unprepared for what she saw that she nearly dropped Piddles on his head.

Upon reading the sign over the outer door, Heather had pleasantly presumed that her father owned some sort of art gallery. There were, indeed, paintings on the walls, but as she stared openmouthed at them, she quickly reevaluated her initial, obviously erroneous, assumption. There were fully a dozen pictures, all inordinately large and explicit, depicting various nymphs and sirens in suggestive poses—each woman quite nude and brazenly displaying her charms. As far as actual art was concerned, this blatant exhibit had absolutely nothing in common with it, except perhaps the essential elements of canvas and paint.

To her further dismay, two thirds of one side wall appeared to be mirrored. Reflected in the glass were not only the garish pictures, but a lengthy row of liquor bottles, whiskey glasses, and beer mugs. A long, brass-rimmed mahogany bar extended toward the rear of the hall. Across from the bar, on the opposite side of the room, were numerous round baize-topped tables, at which small gatherings of men were engaged in games of cards. A wide central staircase divided the gambling area from an equally spacious section set up for billiards. At the far end, beyond the stairs, Heather spotted a piano on a small stage. Here a section of the floor space, perhaps reserved for dancing, was ringed with small tables.

"Oh, my goodness gracious! This is a . . . a . . . saloon!" Heather exclaimed loudly.

Angus, who had been standing silently beside her, watching her expressions range from expectation to horror, answered dryly. "Aye, missy, it is. That, and a billiard parlor, and a hurdy-gurdy, which is just a fancy name for a dance hall."

"But . . . but . . ."

Her shrill declaration had more than a few heads turning her way. Belatedly Heather noticed that an audience of men was eyeing her with speculative looks, a few with outright leers.

Angus took note also, and was quick to announce, "I'd like ye all to meet my daughter, Heather. She's from Boston, and raised a lady, so I'll thank ye to keep yer hands to yerselves and remember yer manners, if ye got any. Spread the word that any man stupid enough to make any improper advances toward her will end up nothin' but a pile o' bones and teeth when I'm done wi' him."

"Aw, Gus!" one fellow moaned. "Dangit! That's pure torment! Like letting a fox get a mouthful of feathers, then tellin' him he can't have the bird!"

"This bonny dove is spoken for, fellas. She's set on marryin' some rich city slicker back East, so ye can save yer energy and courtin' for more willin' quail," Angus informed them curtly. "Try any shenanigans, and ye'll not be welcome inside my bar again, if ye're lucky enough to still draw breath."

That rule established, Angus led Heather up the stairs and along the open second-story gallery, which extended the entire width of the building and offered a full view of the activities below. Several doors opened off the corridor, one of which, Angus mentioned, led to his office and private quarters. At each end, an enclosed hall ran the length of the abutting sides of the saloon, providing additional upper-story rooms.

"You certainly have an abundance of space," Heather commented in lieu of anything better to say. She was still struggling to overcome her shock at discovering that her long-lost father was a tavern owner. "You could turn this place into a small hotel if you wished," she suggested, mustering up a shaky smile.

Angus shook his head. "Nae. Wouldna want to put the girls oot on the street. They sorta think o' this as their home, ye ken."

"No, I'm afraid I don't. What girls?"

"Them what work here, o' course."

"Oh, your barmaids live here?"

"Aye." He slanted a sheepish look her way. "Makes it real convenient for the lot o' them to live and work in the same place."

"How many employees do you have, Angus?"

"Just now I'm a wee bit short on help. Down to eight ladies and one bartender, besides myself. I'm hopin' to find another good barman and a couple more girls b'fore the cattle drives get goin' strong. Once those cowpokes hit town in force, business really picks up."

"That certainly sounds interesting," Heather remarked lamely, imagining an army of crude, dirty, thirsty men invading the town. Hopefully she would be on her way back home before it got too bad.

Angus stopped before a door at the rear corner of the hall. "Thought ye might enjoy this set o' corner rooms, since there are more windows," he told her as he ushered her inside. "Not that there's much of a view, but ye'll get more air. It can be wretched hot here when summer sets in. 'Tis quieter back here, too. Less ruckus from the street."

As it was now mid-May, and she intended to stay only a couple of weeks at most, Heather doubted she would suffer much inconvenience, either from noise or heat. Still, she thanked him for his consideration.

Looking around, she found herself standing in a

small sitting room. Through an open pair of doors, she could see into the bedroom beyond. Both rooms appeared neat and clean, though sparsely filled with mismatched furniture. In the parlor there was a lumpy love seat, two overstuffed chairs, a couple of small tables, a pair of dissimilar lamps with faded shades, a thin carpet of nondescript color, and equally dismal curtains.

The bedroom was little better, though the bed was made up with clean linens and quilts, and looked as though it might be comfortable. There was also a small bed stand and lamp, a dressing table with an age-cracked mirror and a wobbly-looking stool, a large scarred wardrobe, and an additional chest of drawers, atop which rested a chipped pitcher and bowl. The wood floor was bare, except for a braided rug next to the bed. Fortunately, there were no risqué portraits on the walls. There was, however, a dressing screen in the corner, painted with Oriental maidens who were bathing.

"I reckon 'tis not quite what yer used to, but the girls helped clean it up, and Arlene sent over one o' the quilts. She made it herself, she did," Angus added with a hint of pride.

"This will do nicely, I'm sure, for the limited time I'll be visiting," she assured him. "Is Arlene one of the women who work here?"

An odd, uncomfortable look crossed Angus's face, making his ruddy cheeks flush even more. "Uh . . . no, lass. Arlene Clancy is the widow woman I've been keepin' company wi' for some time now."

Heather blushed. "I see. Well, that's to be expected, I suppose. Mother warned me that you might have remarried and had more children during the years since you left Boston."

His features taut, he replied stiffly, almost angrily, "Yer ma was the only woman I ever married, or ever intend to marry, daughter. And I haven't any other children, at least none I know of. Once burned, twice shy, as they say."

Heather held up one daintily gloved hand, as if to halt any further speech from him. Her tone was haughty and cold as she said, "Please, sir. There is no need to defend your chosen way of life to me. Frankly, I couldn't care less about your private activities. In fact, I would rather not hear any lame excuses or justifications. Let's just let the matter lie, shall we?"

"That would be best, I suppose, at least for now," he agreed. He nodded toward her bags, which he'd set down near the dresser. "I'll leave ye to unpack yer belongings. Let me know if there's anything else ye need."

He was almost to the hall door when she called out, "There is one thing, if you would. Can you tell me where the . . . the facilities are?"

"Facilities?" he echoed stupidly.

"Yes. The water closet," she elaborated with some embarrassment.

His brow cleared. "Oh, the privy! If ye look out yer back window, ye can't miss it. The little house wi' the half-moon. Just have a care no one else is usin' it b'fore yanking the door open, and flip the latch once ye're inside so no one walks in on ye. We've had that happen more times than I can count."

Heather blinked at him in astonishment, her jaw working ineffectually until finally she croaked out, "Do you mean to say there are no indoor conveniences? No modern accommodations of that type?"

The twinkle in Angus's blue eyes reappeared at last, along with an equally teasing grin. "Afraid not, lass. Ye'll just have to rough it, like the rest o' us poor frontier folk. Course, there is a chamber pot under the bed, if ye'd prefer to use that, but ye'll have to empty it yerself. And there's a tub ye can drag in here and fill wi' buckets o' water for a bath, if ye get tired o' makin' do wi' that puny pitcher and bowl. Ye might even find someone willin' to help ye heat and lug water up to yer room for ye, if anyone has the time or inclination.''

Again he started for the door, chuckling. "Welcome to Dodge, Heather. 'Tis a lang way from Boston, in more than mere miles.''

❧ 6 ❧

Feeling as if she were caught up in an ongoing nightmare, Heather sank into the nearest chair with a heavy sigh. Her sigh escalated into a fit of coughing as a cloud of dust rose from the ancient seat cushion. With watering eyes, she gazed bleakly around her. "Glory! What an absolutely dismal suite," she muttered softly. "Little better than the accommodations aboard that filthy train." Her gaze trailed toward the rear window, and she gave a delicate shudder at the mere thought of using that antiquated outdoor convenience.

Tears of self-pity joined those created by the dusty furnishings. "If that big barkeeping galoot thinks I'm going to use that quaint facility, he has another think coming!" she vowed to herself. "And I will not be reduced to emptying chamber pots like some misbegotten maid, either! Who does he think he is, anyway?"

She slumped farther into the cushion, her face crumpling. "Saints and salvation, I can't believe this! My father running a ... a tavern! Why, if any of my Temperance friends back home ever got wind of this, I'd be drummed out of Boston! And God forbid Lyle should discover the awful truth of my parentage! When Mother learns of it, she'll have the vapors for a solid month!"

As her mind conjured up the image of her dear

mother, and another vision of Angus, she tried to picture the two of them as young lovers. Granted, Angus
Burns must have once been a handsome man, for even
now he was not an unattractive person. His size alone
would have made him stand out from the crowd, and
his eyes were a bright, compelling blue, his broad
smile almost charming. Still, Heather could not imagine her delicate, refined mother falling for someone as
common as Angus appeared to be. No wonder her
grandparents had objected so strongly to the match.
Angus must have fit into Boston society about as well
as a donkey stabled with thoroughbred race horses!

"Thank heaven their marriage *didn't* last!" Heather
exclaimed in relief, as yet another thought occurred
to her. Again her dismayed gaze traversed her dreary
surroundings, comparing them to her exquisitely decorated bedroom suite back home. "Mother would
most likely be tending bar downstairs, had they remained together, and all this tattered luxury would
be ours, day after dreadful day!"

"Just two weeks," she reminded herself with a
grimace. "Fourteen days to abide this awful place,
and I can board the train back to civilization . . . and
proper plumbing!"

A short distance across town, Morgan was no more
pleased with his accommodations than Heather was
with hers. Not that he'd expected much in the way of
amenities, having briefly sojourned in similar jail cells
on occasion, usually on charges of drunkenness or
brawling. Normally he was in and out in fair order,
having spent no more than a night in any one loca-
tion—and never on charges as serious as those he
faced now.

Moreover, he was less than thrilled with the jailers'
none-too-gentle methods of persuasion. At the moment, his jaw ached abominably, his left eye was
swelling shut, and though he didn't think any of his
bones were broken, he suspected he might have a
cracked rib or two beneath the darkening bruises

adorning his torso. It was poor consolation that his alleged outlaw partner, having once more been rendered unconscious, appeared to be in even more pathetic shape. The unfortunate bandit had earned himself worse treatment, primarily because he denied having ever met Morgan before—whereas Morgan readily admitted that his cell-mate was one of the band of robbers who had hit the train.

There was currently a lull between beatings, supposedly to allow the sheriff and his deputy time to question the numerous passengers who were still being detained in Dodge until all valuable information had been gathered from them. A few hapless victims would undoubtedly be convinced to stay and give testimony at the trial tomorrow, whether they wished to do so or not.

Morgan also figured the pause in the interrogation would allow the law officers to recoup their energies, simultaneously giving their prisoners time to reflect on any confessions they might like to tender. Miserable though he was, Morgan was not about to confess to a crime he had not committed. Thus, he could only brace himself for more of the same rough handling he'd already received, and pray he could survive it.

"For what?" he asked himself. "To be hanged after a speedy sham trial? Drake, where the devil are you? Damn! Why is it you're never where you're supposed to be when I really need you?"

"What you mumblin' about in there?" the deputy inquired sourly.

"Just wondering if you intend to charge admission to the trial," Morgan retorted wearily.

"Hey now, that ain't a half-bad idea," the deputy said, brightening. "I'll have to suggest that to the sheriff. Maybe get myself a raise in wages for it."

Morgan grunted in disgust. "Glad to oblige. Just don't expect me to sing and dance and perform card tricks for the crowd. I doubt I'm presently up to such theatrical antics."

* * *

Heather unpacked her luggage, frowning in dismay at the wrinkled state of her clothing and mentally cursing Etta for leaving her to her own devices in this one-horse town. She'd simply have to convince Angus to hire a new maid, since she had no funds with which to do so herself and knew none of the local people. With this thought foremost in mind, she ventured downstairs to find him.

Angus was tending bar, a large white apron tied about his waist, which further impressed upon Heather the unsavory fact that her sire was but a common laborer. She would simply die of shame if any of her friends in Boston ever learned of it!

"If ye're thirsty, I can offer ye a sarsaparilla," he said upon noticing her. "I dinna suppose yer ma allows ye to imbibe anything stronger."

"I'd rather have tea, if you've got it."

"Comin' right up."

"I was wondering if you might help me with another matter. You see, my maid abandoned me in St. Louis. Actually, she found another position and quit my employ. Mother is going to be very distressed when she hears how unreliable Etta proved to be."

Angus nodded and said lightly, "Weel, some folks are hard to please."

"Yes, but all my clothes are wrinkled, and I can't be seen in public in such a deplorable state. Not to mention that I am now without a proper traveling companion."

"More to the truth o' the matter, ye're wi'out a paid slave to tend to yer every whim," Angus surmised, correctly assessing the situation.

Heather's chin rose, her eyes flashing. "I wouldn't have put it quite that way. However, the fact remains that I need a new servant, and was hoping you would see to hiring one for me. I could wire Mother for money, seeing as all my personal funds were stolen during the train robbery, leaving me completely destitute, but she would be terribly upset to learn that I faced such peril alone."

Angus shook his head and laughed wryly. "Askin' yer ma for money would be a mite silly now, dinna ye think, seein' as how I've been supportin' the two o' ye for years? The money would still be comin' out o' the same pocket. Mine."

"I suppose so," Heather conceded diffidently.

He gave her a measuring stare. "Ye know, missy, I'm fast gettin' the notion ye've been mightily spoiled. Could be 'tis time ye learned to fend for yerself."

Her face immediately turned sulky. "Does that mean you are not going to hire help for me?"

He smiled. "Tell ye what. I'll have someone locate an iron for ye, and get one o' the girls to show ye how to use it. Such skills will come in handy once ye're married."

"I very much doubt that, Angus. Lyle Asher comes from a very wealthy family. He'd probably have apoplexy if I even suggested pressing my own frocks. As his wife, I would naturally be above such menial chores."

"Then I'm thinkin' ye'd be better off without the pompous ass. Find yerself a real man, lass. One who knows the value of a good woman."

"Someone like you, who'd run off the first time I wasn't looking?" Heather countered waspishly. "No, thank you, Mr. Burns. I can do very well without that type of husband."

Angus's eyes narrowed into blue slits. "Ye've got a mean mouth on ye, daughter. Furthermore, ye haven't the slightest idea what ye're talkin' about. Get yer mother to tell ye the truth o' the matter b'fore ye go lightin' into me with yer venom. Meanwhile, I'd suggest ye grow up a bit and learn a few useful womanly talents such as cookin' and sewin' and doin' laundry. That way if yer grand plans for marryin' Mr. Rich and Regal dinna pan out, ye can support yerself, and not be a burden on yer parents for the rest o' yer born days."

"That tears it!" Heather declared. "If you think I'm going to stay and listen to you spout ridiculous accusations and nonsense, you are sadly mistaken. I shall be on the first train out of here, and you can trust that you will never see me again!"

Angus smiled blandly. "And just how do ye intend to pay for yer ticket back to Boston, lass? Ye've just told me ye haven't so much as a wooden nickel o' yer oon."

"Oooh!" she shrieked. "You are the most infuriating man I have ever had the misfortune to meet, aside from that awful Morgan Stone, and he turned out to be a train robber! The two of you must have been cut from the same bolt of cloth! Mother was well rid of you, if you ask me."

She marched stiffly back to her room and spent the rest of the afternoon in what her father would have termed "a fine snit."

Morgan was trying to muster up the energy to eat his supper when the deputy announced that he had a visitor. "There's a preacher here wants to pray over your black soul," he said, drowning Morgan's hopes that Drake had arrived at last.

"Just what I need to douse my appetite even more," Morgan grumbled, as the deputy unlocked the cell door and ushered the black-clad minister inside.

The pastor waited until the guard had gone back to his desk before commenting, "Now, is that any way to talk about a well-meanin' man of the cloth?"

Morgan's head jerked up. "Drake?" he whispered, peering up at the face still shadowed by the man's wide hat brim.

"Yep." Drake grinned and waved a hand toward Morgan's untouched dinner plate. "Chicken and dumplings. My favorite. You gonna eat that, or can I have it? I missed my supper."

"My heart bleeds for you," Morgan told him with ripe sarcasm. "I hope you came for more than a meal, something along the lines of a fast jailbreak. The sheriff's got a mean streak, and the judge seems set on a conviction at tomorrow morning's trial, followed by a hasty hanging."

"I sorta got that impression. In fact, the deputy probably wouldn't have let me in to see you if he didn't hope I could wring a deathbed confession out of you. Hellfire, Morgan! You really got yourself in some deep water this time."

"No kidding, genius. Now, what are you going to do to get me out of it? Got any weapons hidden on you? Maybe a spare gun or file in a hollowed-out Bible?"

"Sorry, old buddy." Drake indicated the book in question. "This is the real thing. I borrowed it from my hotel room to enhance the image. Besides, I'm not here to spring you. I'm here to inform you of the latest plan the boss has hatched, which doesn't include blowin' your cover or bustin' you out."

"I hate to be the one to tell you this, but I've already told these yahoos I'm an undercover agent for Wells Fargo. Not that they believed me. If they had, I wouldn't be wearing all these colorful bruises."

"You do look like warmed-over dung," Drake agreed congenially.

"I feel like it, too."

"Well, you'll be glad to know you'll be out of here by tomorrow, though not quite the way you might like."

"Mind expounding on that? It's a little fuzzy to me."

Drake nodded. "As soon as I got an angle on what kind of trouble you were in, I fired a coded telegram to the San Francisco office. The boss wired back, again in the secret code, of course, since we don't want the whole town knowin' our scheme. We're only lettin' the judge and a couple other people in on it."

"What about me? Am I allowed to know, too? Or do you intend to keep me guessing all night?" Morgan grumbled impatiently.

"I'm gettin' to it," Drake replied with a grin. "We've got it all set up. Frank sent a telegram to Swanson, too, requesting that the judge meet privately with me right away. Told him to listen to what I had to report, and that whatever I told him would be the God's truth."

"Good luck," Morgan muttered miserably. "If Swanson has his way, my neck will be several inches longer by midday, and I won't have to worry what to order for supper tomorrow. I'll be dining to harp music."

Drake chuckled. "Knowing you, I would have guessed you'd be roastin' your own meal by pitchfork over hot coals. But that's all wishful thinkin', because I already talked to the judge, and he's agreed to play along with us. For lack of evidence, or witnesses and such, he's gonna put you on temporary probation, like they do with paroled prisoners, though you'll still be under suspicion and surveillance, supposedly on the off chance you might give the law a lead on your fellow outlaws and the stolen money."

"Run that past me again," Morgan demanded warily.

"Swanson's not gonna find you guilty and sentence you to swing, but he's not gonna let you off altogether, either. Instead, he'll remand you into the custody of one of the town council members, someone he can trust to keep our little secret. You'll stay in Dodge for a while, under the watchful eye of the whole town, I imagine, and work for this merchant. That way you'll have an inside track on everything that goes on here and maybe get some information on the real robbers."

Morgan frowned, contemplating the scheme. "Seems to me this plan is shot full of holes." He gestured toward his snoring cell-mate. "What about him?"

Drake shrugged. "He's bound to hang any way you cut it. I'm going to testify against him in court, as are the engineer and fireman from the train."

"At least I won't have to worry about him breaking out and spilling the beans to the rest of the gang. And what will you be doing while I'm selling bonnets and whatnot?"

"I'll be trying to track the gang from the outside, and staying in close touch with you to see what you might learn. Just remember, after the trial you've got to quit claiming you're an agent. In fact, it might be better if you say you made the whole thing up. Tell 'em you're really a traveling shoe salesman or something, and just wanted to look more important."

Morgan winced. "Thanks a heap, Drake. You do know that this whole idea is stupid, and I'm getting the short end of the stick."

"Hey, luck of the draw. It's not my butt sitting in a jail cell right now."

"Why do I get the impression it's still going to be my butt that'll be flapping in the breeze come tomorrow?" Morgan replied with a grimace. "How can you be sure we can trust this judge and his friend?"

"Guess we'll find out in court, won't we?" Drake said calmly. "If worst comes to worst, I'll save your hide, even if I have to do it at the last minute, when they're stickin' your handsome head through the noose."

"Gosh, Drake, that's a real comforting thought." Morgan groaned, rolling his eyes heavenward. "What did I ever do to deserve a friend like you?"

Drake grinned. "Must have been something real bad, I reckon."

Hunger finally drove Heather out of her room once more. She'd missed breakfast, and sulked through the noon hour, and now her stomach felt, and sounded, as if it were forming an intimate relationship with her backbone. Besides, if she didn't take Piddles for an outing soon, he was sure to have an accident in her room, and Heather would bet her last dollar, if she still had one, that her father would make her clean it up herself.

With much reluctance, Heather put the dog on his leash and started for the stairs. Here, on the gallery outside her room, the noise from downstairs was much louder. Raucous laughter drifted upward amid the combined din of loud conversation, the clatter of billiard balls cracking together, the sharp tinkle of glasses and bottles, and the thunderous tones of an out-of-tune piano being played with more enthusiasm than skill.

From her vantage point on the gallery, Heather stared in amazement at the scene below her, as much fascinated as appalled. She'd never been inside a barroom until this morning, and it had been fairly quiet then. Now every available inch of space seemed to be filled with people of every size, shape, and description. Most of the men appeared to be cowboys—at least Heather surmised they were, having never actually seen a cowboy firsthand. For the most part, they were dressed in denim trousers, with leather vests over their shirts. Many still wore sweat-stained hats, while others displayed slicked-down hair with pale, untanned rims where their necks now met their hairline, a conspicuous sign that they'd come directly from the barbershop. Their feet were clad in worn boots, some with spurs still attached.

A smaller number of customers bore more resemblance to gentlemen, and were dressed in white shirts, dark trousers, ties, and cloth vests of varying hues and fabrics. A few had even donned suit coats. One fellow—Heather thought she recognized him as the judge who had been at the train station that morning—sported a top hat. Unfortunately, he'd left it on, which clearly indicated a lack of civilized manners.

A majority of the men, gentlemen or otherwise, had gun belts strapped about their waists, most with empty holsters, thank goodness. Angus had earlier told Heather that guns were not allowed inside the city limits, by order of the sheriff. All weapons were to be deposited in a barrel at the edge of town, to be collected again on the way out. Local residents had their own firearms, however, and not everyone coming into Dodge adhered to the rule. Consequently, it was not unusual to hear gunshots, or to witness a number of shoot-outs in the course of a routine week. The undertaker undoubtedly did a booming business.

It was the women in attendance who most strongly caught Heather's interest, and she couldn't help gawking at them in stunned disbelief. Of the half dozen girls wandering amongst the crowd of men, not one of them was attired in a manner remotely suitable for a lady. Their faces were made up with more paint than it would take to cover the average house, and Heather was sure she'd never witnessed such an outlandish array of feathers—in their hair, dangling from their wrists, draped in long ropes across their bare shoulders. Why, to look at them, it would seem that every bird in the territory had been plucked!

And those gaudy gowns! Merciful heavens! If the lot of them stripped nude and bared their bottoms, there could not have been more cleavage on parade than was now being so blithely exhibited! To make matters worse, the skirts were extremely short, showing an inordinate amount of ruffled petticoats above black net stockings and high-heeled shoes. Why, there were even a number of garters prominently displayed. All this aside from an abundance of garish jewelry—dangling earrings, hair spangles, bracelets, and neck bands.

Heather was still gaping at them in mute fascination when a door down the hall opened and yet another woman stepped into view. This one was adorned in nothing more than what looked like several flounced petticoats atop a lace-trimmed camisole. Her entire costume was bright scarlet, including the large plume that danced a good three feet above her head.

Upon spotting Heather, the brunette marched toward her, offering in greeting a hand tipped with long red-tinted nails. "Howdy, there!" she said with a broad smile. "You must be Gus's little gal. Heather, isn't it? I'm Jasmine."

"Uh . . . hello," Heather stammered, gingerly accepting the proffered hand. Still feeling overwhelmed, she added hastily, "I was just going down to walk Piddles and try to get some supper."

Jasmine's gaze dropped to the Pomeranian. "Oh, what a darlin' doggie!" she cooed, bending to scoop the ball of fur into her arms.

Heather held her breath, not so worried that Piddles would nip at Jasmine, since he generally liked women much more than men, but in concern that Jasmine's bountiful endowments would pop free of their meager confines.

Still cradling the dog, who didn't object at all, Jasmine threw a friendly arm around Heather's shoulders. Instinctively Heather cringed, but Jasmine either didn't notice or pretended not to. "Tell you what, sugar. Let's go get you acquainted with the other girls, then I'll walk you down the street to Vern's restaurant, where we can both get a bite to eat. I'm real partial to their butterscotch pie."

Heather pulled back and reached out to reclaim her dog. "Thank you, but I couldn't take up so much of your time," she replied primly.

"Oh, Gus won't mind none," Jasmine assured her. "And it won't hurt my customers to wait awhile. It might even make 'em appreciate me a bit more when they finally do get my attention," she added with a sly wink.

"Customers?" Heather repeated. "Oh, you mean your dance partners."

Jasmine laughed heartily. "Yeah, I suppose you could call them that, though most of them prefer to do their dancin' on their backs in bed."

Heather stared at the other woman in dumbfounded wonder. "Oh, good and glorious gravy! Angus isn't just running a saloon, is he? He's running a . . . a . . . brothel!"

❧ 7 ❧

Heather awoke the next morning with a headache, a sense of doom, and lingering reverberations from all the shocks she'd received the day before. From morning till night, there had seemed no end to them. She was not looking forward to another day of startling revelations, most especially another verbal debate with her father.

She'd cornered him some time after her enlightening conversation with Jasmine, bluntly accusing him of operating a house of ill repute. He'd leveled another of those piercing stares at her, and calmly explained that there was a difference between participating in such a venture and simply acting as a benevolent landlord.

"I dinna collect any money from what the girls earn. I just rent them their rooms. What they do in them is their oon business."

"In other words, you turn a blind eye to their illicit behavior—in effect condoning it by your silence," Heather stated with disgust. "I find that thoroughly unconscionable."

Angus had chuckled. "If I kenned what that meant, I might agree wi' ye."

"Reprehensible. Despicable. Disgraceful. Take your pick."

"In that case, I'll pass. But tell me somethin', puss. What gives ye the right to stand in judgment of either me or the girls? They've got to have some means o' earnin' a livin', ye know. Not everyone on this earth was born wi' a silver spoon in his or her mouth, like some I could mention."

Heather glared at him. "I realize I've had more advantages than some people, but I still think it's wrong for any woman to do what they do. Why, there must be dozens of other decent jobs they could get to support themselves until they find husbands."

Angus shrugged. "Maybe." A speculative gleam lit his blue eyes. "It strikes me a wee bit odd that after bein' raised all sheltered and pampered, ye'd even have heard o' such a thing as a cathouse, let alone know what goes on in one. How do ye ken they're not just playin' checkers up there, all innocent like?"

"Really, Angus!" she retorted. "I may be privileged, but that doesn't mean I'm stupid. Nor am I deaf or totally uneducated. We do have such establishments in Boston, after all. And while I might not be personally familiar with the activities conducted in one of those places, other people do talk. Rumors fly aplenty, and an attentive person can learn a lot simply by listening. You don't have to leap off a tall building to know the fall will probably kill you," she informed him haughtily.

"Ye do have a point there," he conceded. "Though I think ye should learn to be a mite more tolerant o' folks less fortunate than yerself, missy. I realize that's na a trait common to yer mother's side o' the family, but 'twould be a definite improvement to yer character."

Now, the morning after that disagreeable confrontation, Heather was not joyously anticipating the coming day. For one thing, Morgan Stone's trial was being held this morning, and after learning that she'd become briefly acquainted with the man, both the sheriff and Judge Swanson had requested her presence as a witness at court. Angus had agreed to make certain she attended.

Heather was dreading it. She had never seen a trial before, let alone testified at one. Moreover, she was supremely reluctant to participate in a matter of such extreme importance, the outcome of which could mean a man's execution. Not just any man, either. A man she knew, though slightly. A man who had held her in his arms and kissed her. A man to whom she was strangely attracted, despite her better judgment. A handsome rascal she'd had occasion to alternately despise and desire during their short but tempestuous encounters.

She was still debating with herself, and becoming more nervous by the minute, as she and Angus took their seats in the crowded courtroom. Her anxiety increased when, minutes later, the sheriff entered with Morgan and another prisoner, and led them down the center aisle to the front of the room. As Morgan came even with her, he halted momentarily, long enough to bestow upon Heather a crooked smile that resembled a smirk. Of course, she might have been mistaken in her interpretation of that gesture, since Morgan's lower lip was cracked and swollen to twice its normal size.

Heather was appalled at the change in Morgan's appearance in the mere twenty-four hours since she'd last seen him. Not only was his lip cracked, but he now sported a black eye and numerous bruises on his once handsome face. She could only wonder if he was equally battered beneath his wrinkled, dirt-smeared clothes. The thought that he'd been hurt sickened her, while it was odd that she felt less pity for the other prisoner, who was in similarly sad shape.

She had little chance to contemplate this curious reaction, as the bailiff signaled everyone to rise and announced loudly, "Court is now in session, the Honorable Judge Swanson presiding."

Nels Swanson, attired in the long black robes of his office, sat down and rapped the bench with his gavel. "Be seated, and let's get this sideshow started. Since we're lacking an abundance of attorneys in this town,

I'll hear all the evidence and make a determination myself. No need for all the usual folderol of a jury and such. The sheriff will act as the prosecutor, and I'll do double duty as the defense to call up witnesses. That settled, present your case, Sheriff Watson."

Watson stood. "Your Honor, we've got two men here accused of robbin' the train, and several reliable witnesses to that fact."

"Any confessions yet?" the judge inquired.

"No, sir, but not for lack of tryin'."

"I think we can all see that, Sheriff," the judge intoned dryly. "Call your first witness."

The engineer testified first, followed by his fireman and a passenger by the name of Drake Evans, all solemnly swearing that Charles "Blackie" Black had appeared on horseback and forced the engineer at gunpoint to stop the train. Mr. Evans had then arrived and subdued the outlaw by cracking him on the head with the butt of his pistol. The fireman then took over, guarding the unconscious bandit. All three positively identified the man.

When asked if he had anything to say in his own defense, Black declined to comment, other than to claim he was innocent and being set up.

The questioning then turned to Morgan's participation in the holdup. Jack Dooley, the mail car guard, was asked to tell his version of the robbery. He recalled how both he and the postmaster had been set upon by two armed bandits wearing masks. The outlaws had disarmed Mr. Dooley and forced the postmaster to open the safe before rendering both railroad employees senseless.

"How long did you remain unconscious, Mr. Dooley?" the judge asked when the man had finished recounting his tale.

"I don't rightly know," the fellow admitted. "I come to myself in time to see Hal, the conductor, bendin' over Mr. Stone's body. I helped tie him up."

Swanson nodded. "Is Mr. Stone one of the two fellows who first entered the mail car and held you and the postmaster at gunpoint?"

Dooley frowned. "I can't say for sure. They were wearin' bandannas over their faces."

"Do you recall whether Mr. Stone was wearing a similar bandanna after you regained consciousness and aided in restraining him?"

Dooley searched his memory for a moment. "Now that you mention it, I don't remember seein' one on him, but he might have stuck it in his pocket."

Again the judge took the role of defender. "Who captured Mr. Stone and knocked him out?"

"I figured it must have been Hal."

The postmaster had little more to add. He could not readily identify Morgan as one of the initial assailants, either. Nor could the conductor, when questioned.

"He was layin' in a heap on the mail car floor just like Jack and Zeke. 'Cept he had this big bag of money clutched in his hand and wads of it stickin' out of his pockets. So I right off figured he was one of the robbers, maybe an inside man since he rode the train from St. Louis."

"Did he have a bandanna?"

"Not that I seen. But he did have a gun in his other hand."

"Was his conduct prior to the holdup suspicious in any way?"

"Only when he paid that woman's fare, when she couldn't find her ticket," Hal said, pointing to Heather. "She was bein' a real pain, a regular witch, but he seemed to fancy her for some reason. If that ain't peculiar, I don't know what is."

Laughter broke out in the courtroom, and Heather could have died of embarrassment as all eyes turned her way.

The judge pounded his gavel and shouted for quiet before resuming. "Am I correct in concluding that no one knows how Mr. Stone came to be lying unconscious in the mail car? No one has come forward to profess to the deed?"

Nobody spoke up. "Sheriff Watson?"

"No, sir. And before you ask, I didn't find a bandanna on him, either," he added sourly.

"Mr. Stone?"

"I wasn't wearing a bandanna, and didn't see who hit me, Your Honor, but whoever it was packed quite a wallop. I suppose it could have been another of the robbers."

"And what were you doing prior to being whacked?"

"I had already suspected a robbery might be in the offing, and had gone to the mail car to lend a hand in preventing it. I was holding two of the outlaws at gunpoint, while I had them tie one another up, when someone attacked me from behind."

"The sheriff tells me you claim to be an agent for Wells Fargo, which sounds a bit far-fetched to me. Do you still maintain that is your occupation?"

Morgan slid a hasty glance toward Drake, who gave a slight negative shake of his head. "No, sir," Morgan admitted, feigning a sheepish look to cover his rising frustration, and nearly choking on his next words. "I'm afraid I let the excitement of the moment go to my head. I'm actually just a traveling shoe salesman." Another trickle of laughter arose from the crowd.

"How did all that money come to be on your person when the conductor and Mr. Dooley found you?"

"I guess someone put it there. I sure as he—heck didn't."

"Watch your language, mister," Judge Swanson admonished sternly. "There are ladies present."

Just when Heather was beginning to hope her testimony would not be required, the judge called upon her. She recounted how she and Morgan had first met at the station in St. Louis, how he had paid her fare and made a nuisance of himself by being a persistent pest.

"It never dawned on me that he might be an outlaw, though I was disturbed when I learned he was wearing a gun. Then, on the morning of the robbery, Mr. Stone seemed to be aware of what was happening before anyone else had any inkling of the problem."

"Exactly what gave you the impression that he knew the train was being held up?" Swanson asked.

"He . . . uh . . ." Heather slid a look at Morgan, who was staring stonily at her. On a deep breath, she finished in a rush. "He grabbed his gun and went running from the train car. Just before he disappeared, he advised me that if anyone came along demanding my valuables, I would be wise to hand them over quietly and not make a fuss. It seemed quite odd, especially when I considered it afterward, that he would immediately assume the train was being robbed."

The judge nodded and smiled at her. "Did anything else about him seem questionable or objectionable?"

"My, yes! For someone of such short acquaintance, he was entirely too forward and familiar!"

"In what way?" Swanson inquired.

Again Heather sneaked a quick peek at Morgan. He was definitely wearing a smirk now. She turned wide, innocent eyes on the judge. "I . . . I'd rather not answer that, if you don't mind."

"I'd prefer that you do, Miss Burns."

"Blair-Burns," she and Morgan both corrected automatically.

Judge Swanson's gaze swung from her to Morgan. Morgan shrugged an apology. "Sorry, sir. She insists her name is Blair-Burns, not just Burns. Seems really sensitive about it."

"Please go on, Miss Blair-Burns," the judge suggested. "In what way was Mr. Stone too familiar?"

Heather scowled. With flushed cheeks, she answered curtly, "He took every opportunity to . . . to *handle* my person, with the lame excuse of trying to help me."

When she looked back at the judge, he seemed to be trying to hold back a smile. "I see. Mr. Stone, do you have something to say in response to that?"

"Yes, sir," Morgan replied with alacrity. "Miss Blair-Burns has to be the most clumsy woman I have ever met—or perhaps the most forward. I can't decide which. Throughout our brief acquaintance, she was constantly tripping over her own feet and landing in my arms. Now, I ask you, what was I to do but catch her? Though if I had it to do again, I'd be tempted to let her fall on her . . . face."

"He . . . he kissed me, Your Honor!" Heather blurted out before she thought to stop herself.

"And the little shrew nearly bit my tongue off, too!" Morgan countered.

"He hit my dog!"

"The danged mutt was trying to chew my ankle off! Then he used me for a sleeping mat and bit me when I tried to shove him off me!"

By now the entire courtroom was in an uproar. Nearly everyone, including the sheriff and judge, was laughing heartily. In an effort to restore order, Swanson banged his gavel several times, chuckling all the while. Finally he managed to croak, "Order in the court! Blast it, I said, settle down, or I'll hold you in contempt and fine you all!"

Swallowing one last chortle, he turned to Heather. "Is there anything else you would care to add, miss?"

"Just that my dog, Piddles, is not fond of Mr. Stone, and animals can be excellent judges of character, " she stated primly.

Angus waved his hand in the air, seeking the judge's attention.

Swanson sighed. "What is it, Gus?"

"Weel, Nels, I just thought I'd add my two cents here and admit that Piddles doesna cotton much to me either, and b'sides me bein' Heather's pa, ye all know what a likable sort I am."

Another round of laughter ensued before Swanson said with a grin, "Thank you, Gus. The court will take your modest opinion into consideration."

A couple of other witnesses were called, passengers who had been in the same car with Morgan and Heather and who also recalled his parting words to her. Then Judge Swanson took a few minutes to review the testimony before announcing his verdict.

"I find the defendant Charles Black guilty of armed robbery, his assistance having allowed his fellow outlaws to steal several hundred dollars from the train. I sentence him to death by hanging, to be commenced immediately following this trial."

This met with murmurs of approval from the crowd.

"As for Morgan Stone, I cannot in good conscience hang a man on so little evidence, especially since Mr. Black denies ever having known Mr. Stone before they were both placed under arrest."

Morgan drew an audible sigh of relief in the now silent courtroom. Most of the spectators seemed incredulous at this unexpected pronouncement.

Continuing quickly, the judge said, "However, neither can I release him entirely. Therefore, pending further developments and investigation of the matter, I am remanding Mr. Stone into the custody of Angus Burns for a length of time which I will determine later, or until other arrests can be made and the stolen money recovered."

Amid some grumbling from those in attendance, he went on to add, "Mr. Stone, you are to work for Mr. Burns in whatever capacity he dictates. You are not to venture outside the boundaries of Dodge City unless given liberty by me to do so. You are not to carry firearms until and unless I say you may. You will be on probation, so to speak, still suspect and under observation, so I would advise you to abide strictly to these mandates and make no attempt to flee. Should you try, you will either be jailed again, or shot. Do you understand these rules as I have set them out for you?"

"Yes, Your Honor."

"Any questions?"

"Just one. Does this mean I have to take orders from Miss Blair-Burns, too?"

"Only if her father says so," Swanson replied with a chuckle, rapping his gavel amid a mingling of snickers and muttered protests from the courtroom. "Court adjourned!"

❧ 8 ❧

All during the short walk back to Gus's Gallery and Gurdy, Heather fumed and ranted. "You deliberately set out to make a fool of me back there!" she railed at Morgan, who was none too pleased with the situation himself.

"Oh, really?" he countered. "And what were you up to, besides trying to get me hanged? You didn't exactly paint a glowing portrait of me, either."

"I'll never be able to face anyone again!" she wailed. "It's bad enough my father runs a combination saloon and brothel, but you humiliated me in front of an entire town."

"You'll live," he assured her gruffly. "And I'd damn sure rather endure a little embarrassment than a lot of being dead!"

" 'Tis so nice to see the two o' ye patchin' up yer differences," Gus put in on an amused chuckle.

The two combatants glared at him in tandem. Then Morgan brightened noticeably.

"So you own a saloon, do you, Mr. Burns?"

"Aye, and 'tis Angus," the man corrected. "Or better yet, call me Gus."

Morgan nodded. "Maybe this won't be so bad after all. I was afraid you might operate a clothing store. I could just see myself selling ribbons and lace and ladies' bonnets!" At the mere thought of it, Morgan gave an exaggerated shudder.

"Even that would be a step up for you, wouldn't it?" Heather scoffed. "Imagine a lowly shoe salesman claiming to be a Wells Fargo agent!"

"There is nothing dishonorable about selling shoes. Moreover, who died and made you queen?" Morgan sniped back. "Go back to being a mere princess. It suits you better, at least until you grow up and fit into your crown."

"Now, children, pull in yer fangs and save the bloodshed for later. We've company comin' to greet us," Gus informed them.

Arlene Clancy caught up with them at the entrance to Gus's saloon. Heather's first clue to the slim, smartly dressed brunette's identity was the affectionate kiss Angus gave the lady, though in deference to his daughter's presence, he limited it to a quick buss on the older woman's cheek.

"H'lo, hinny," he said. "I dinna see ye at the trial."

Arlene responded with a smile that warmed her smoky gray eyes. "I was there, darling, though I arrived late and had to sit in the back. I would have met you sooner, but I got caught up in the bustle afterward, and was halfway to the hanging before I managed to break loose from the crowd."

Her gaze turned solemn as it swung toward Morgan. "You are a most fortunate young man. Of course, I suppose you realize it's not over for you yet. There are any number of disgruntled citizens who disagree with Nels Swanson's pronouncement today. They'll be anxiously waiting to see you stub your toe and end up getting what they consider your just deserts."

Morgan nodded in acknowledgment of her statement. "I hope you won't mind if I don't live up to their expectations."

"Not at all," the lady replied sincerely. "It would be a shame to see such a handsome fellow meet such a disastrous end."

Arlene then focused her attention on Heather, who was inwardly debating whether to dislike her father's "friend" at first sight, which was what her daughterly instincts were prompting her to do on her mother's behalf, or to give the woman the benefit of the doubt. Arlene really did seem a decent sort, though for some reason beyond her understanding, it irritated Heather that the other woman had commented on Morgan's good looks. It stunned Heather that she should immediately react in such a proprietorial manner toward Morgan, a response bordering too closely on jealousy for comfort.

"So this is your little Heather," Arlene crooned. "My, she is a pretty thing, isn't she? Aren't you going to introduce us, Gus?"

"Oh, aye. O' course," Gus agreed. "Arlene, this is my daughter, and since ye were at the trial, ye know Mr. Stone as weel. Morgan, Heather, this is my good friend Arlene Clancy."

"I already gathered as much, Angus, but thank you," Heather told him, gracing Arlene with cool regard. "Widow Clancy, I suppose I'll be seeing you again during my visit, but for now you must excuse me. It's been a very trying morning."

"A pleasure to meet you, Mrs. Clancy," Morgan added with a polite tip of his hat. "If you'll pardon me as well, I'll go along inside, so Heather can introduce me to my new co-workers."

At this time of the day, only Bob, the bartender, was working. The girls and the piano player weren't even out of bed yet.

"You'll meet the girls later, and I'll wager you'll be thoroughly delighted," Heather ventured derisively. "After meeting them myself, I was pleasantly surprised to make Bob's acquaintance, and to learn that he had a nice, normal name, instead of some quaint appellation such as Whiskers, or Grizzly, or Tobacco Jack."

Morgan wrinkled his brow in puzzlement. "Why do you say that?"

Bob laughed and explained. "Well, the gals do have unique names, I'll grant you. Let's see," he said, counting them off on his fingers. "Right now we have Jasmine, Lacy, Pearl, Ginger, Crystal, Joy, Velvet, and

Brandy. We used to have a Star, a Bunny, and a Lark. Made for quite a stable of critters."

On this note, Heather left the men to converse and made her way to her room, feeling thoroughly out of sorts. This visit with her father was proving to be more than she'd bargained for. Now she had Morgan to contend with, on top of everything else, and her father's lady friend as well. She shook her head in frustration. *What is the proper etiquette in such awkward circumstances? I wonder. My deportment lessons certainly didn't cover this!*

"I do think your daughter could have been more polite, Angus," Arlene complained with a pout that was still somehow fetching despite her thirty-five years and the few gray strands sprinkled lightly among the darker hair at her temples.

"Maybe in time, when she gets to know ye better," Angus said. "Truth be told, she ain't too keen on me yet, either. B'sides which, she's a mite spoiled. Her mother's fault, nae doubt, and I can see her grandmother's fine hand at work as weel. Both o' Betsy's parents were as haughty as the day was long, and 'twould seem they passed that on to Heather."

"Well, if your wife was anything like her parents and Heather, I can see why the two of you weren't married for long," Arlene commiserated. "The woman didn't deserve a man as fine as you."

Angus smiled sadly. "Betsy wasna filled with conceit, like the rest o' them. She was a sweet, lovely lady. Gracious and warm as sunshine." He heaved a deep sigh. "At least, I thought she was, though it turned out I could nae have been more wrong. There was a ton o' deceit lurkin' in her heart."

"For your sake, I hope her daughter didn't inherit that particular trait," Arlene told him. She placed a sympathetic hand on his arm. "Take care, Angus. I'd hate to see her hurt you the way her mother did."

"Things bein' what they are, do ye still want me to come to Sunday dinner at your house?"

"Of course, and bring Heather along. As you said, perhaps once she gets to know me, she'll see me as less of a threat. After all, it's not as if you and I are married."

Angus's brows rose. "What are ye blatherin' about, woman? Why would Heather see ye as a threat?"

Arlene shot him a slightly superior smile and shook her head at him. "Men! You'll never understand the workings of a woman's mind, will you? Angus, Heather most likely views me as the enemy, not only because she feels I've taken her mother's place in your life, but probably because she's afraid of losing her inheritance or financial support if you and I should wed."

"That's daft!" Angus scoffed.

Arlene shrugged. "Daft or not, I'll wager those are her feelings right now. It would behoove both of us to reassure her on those points."

"Ye can be sure I'll set the lass straight," Angus told Arlene, a scowl drawing his bushy brows together. "If that's what's got her tail in a twist, she couldn't be more mistaken. I'm too auld to be wantin' to start another family at this stage, and too smart to get myself stuck in the matrimonial trap agin."

"You know that, and so do I," Arlene agreed calmly. "But convincing Heather may be another matter."

Angus gave a weary shake of his head. "Lord, 'tis gettin' so a man can't have a life o' his own wi'out somebody tryin' to mess it up for him! Even his oon daughter!"

Arlene nodded in empathy. "I told you before you sent for her that children can be a trial. Next time I offer a bit of friendly advice, perhaps you'll be more inclined to consider it."

Morgan and Gus sat facing each other in the privacy of Gus's office. As far as anyone else knew, Gus was instructing his newest employee on his duties. In reality, a meeting was being conducted between the two men, one in which each was carefully studying the other.

"Did your friend Judge Swanson warn you that no one is to know that I really am a Wells Fargo agent? Or that I'll be continuing my investigation of the train thefts in my guise as your employee?" Morgan asked, initiating the conversation.

"Aye, and ye needn't fret. I dinna intend to tell a soul."

"Even your daughter must not know. Or your lady friend, Mrs. Clancy. No matter how much they might wonder, or how prettily they ask," Morgan insisted.

Angus chuckled. "I ken yer worry, lad. Most women canna keep a secret, howe'er hard they might try. Sooner or later the information simply bursts from them, like a watch spring too tightly wound. 'Tis a rare woman who can hold her tongue from spillin' a confidence."

"True, and I don't think it would be wise to chance trusting either of your ladies."

"Speakin' o' which," Angus commented, "I've noticed how you and Heather seem to strike sparks off one another, and it has me wonderin' what's really goin' on b'tween the two o' ye."

One dark brow arched upward over a turquoise eye. "Are you asking my intentions toward your daughter, Mr. Burns?" Morgan inquired dryly.

"Ye could say so. I've that right, ye know, as her pa, and it did come out in court that ye've shared more than a passin' acquaintance in a mighty short time."

"You're referring to the now infamous kiss, I suppose," Morgan guessed.

"Aye. 'Twould seem to point to some interest on yer part."

"Naturally," Morgan allowed. "Heather is a beautiful woman. Spiteful as hell, with the nature of a born-and-bred shrew, but attractive nonetheless."

Gus nodded. "And ye're a red-blooded man, full o'

yerself, and randy as a goat. Not too ugly to boot. The sort who could turn a young lassie's head, despite herself." Angus winked conspiratorially. "Don't bother tryin' to deny it. It takes one to spot one, and I used to be quite a rake in my younger days."

Morgan's grin was slightly patronizing. "Seems to me you still are, Gus. I couldn't help see the greeting you gave the Widow Clancy. And you a married man! Now, I ask you, aren't you acting a little hypocritically here, admonishing me when your own slate isn't exactly clean?"

Gus's smile melted away, replaced by a thunderous expression. "I'm na married, Stone. If I were, I wouldna be sparkin' Arlene."

Morgan frowned, perplexed. "I beg your pardon? I thought Heather's mother still lived in Boston. Are you saying that you and she weren't married? That Heather—"

Gus cut in quickly, his words sharp and bitter. "Nae that 'tis any o' yer business, but I won't have ye speakin' ill o' my daughter. Heather's ma and I were weel and truly wed when the bairn was spawned. 'Twas only afterward that we had a partin' o' the ways. The Blairs made sure 'twas handled all legal like, wi' no disgrace to either the babe or Betsy. 'Twas an annulment they called it, supposedly less shameful than a divorce, though I had no say in any o' it. 'Twas done wi'out my knowledge or sanction, though I suppose 'twas all for the best in the end. And 'tis all water b'neath the bridge now, done lang sine and best forgotten, except for Heather, o' course. I canna e'er regret fatherin' her, no matter how spoiled she might be after bein' raised by the Blairs."

At the conclusion of Gus's revealing speech, Morgan spoke into the painful silence. "I'm truly sorry, Gus. You're right. None of this was any of my business. But after hearing you tell it, it sounds to me like you got the raw end of the deal."

Gus's blue eyes took on a meaningful gleam. "That ain't nothin' to the trouble ye'll be borrowin' if ye dally wi' my Heather. Bed her, laddie, and ye'll wed her. I promise ye that."

"Oh? Are we discussing the possibility of a shotgun wedding, Gus?" Morgan drawled.

"If the need arises, though I dinna think Heather would be overly pleased either, should that come to pass. She's plannin' t' marry some rich fella back in Boston, a friend o' her ma's family."

"I'm relieved to hear it," Morgan said, though the thought of Heather fancying another man did rankle, surprisingly. "I'll admit up front that I've never considered myself the marrying type. With my job, and all the travel and danger it entails, I don't imagine I'd make a very good husband—or father, for that matter. Moreover, I'm fond of my freedom. Being footloose and fancy-free suits me just fine."

"Then ye'd best keep yer britches buttoned up round my daughter, hadn't ye?" Gus suggested baldly. "Ye can play fast and loose wi' the other gals if ye want, but nae wi' her."

Morgan grinned. "I'll try to control myself. However, you'd better instruct your darling daughter to do likewise. For a lady intent on marrying somebody else, she's making a regular habit of throwin' herself at me, and a man can't be held responsible for what is not his fault."

Gus's smile was as sly as his reply. "Aye, he can. And he will, if ye don't heed my advice. So keep yer mind on yer bartendin' and yer sleuthin'."

"Speaking of tending bar, you are going to pay me an adequate wage for my work, aren't you? After all, I will be doing you a service, and I'll need room and board and such."

"Yer wages include a room here. 'Tis the one at the end of the far hall. I'll show ye in a bit. I'll also pay ye enough to keep ye in food and other essentials, providin' ye're thrifty and tend weel to yer duties, which include a bit o' cleanin' and moppin' and stockin' the bar, and dealin' wi' rowdy customers b'fore they get too riled up and start wreckin' the place."

Morgan grimaced. "How do you expect me to do that when, according to Judge Swanson, I'm not allowed to handle a gun?"

Gus considered that problem. "What about a dirk? Are ye handy wi' one of those?"

"A dirk?" Morgan repeated. "You mean a knife?"

"Aye."

Morgan shrugged. "I can wield one, yes, but with no special proficiency. The Wild West Show certainly wouldn't hire me," he added truthfully. Then, with a speculative glitter in his eyes, he inquired, "You wouldn't happen to have a bullwhip around, would you? I'm a fair hand with one of those, if I do say so myself. My father was a bullwhacker at one time, when he was first getting his trading company started, and I used to ride on the transport wagons with him. He taught me everything there is to know about slingin' leather."

Gus's eyes widened appreciably. "Weel now, as I recall, Nels dinna say nothin' agin' bullwhips. I reckon if a body can keep a team o' oxen in line wi' one, ye can keep a pack o' drunken cowpokes under control in like manner. We'll go buy one this very afternoon, we will, and ye can select the one that suits ye best. Then ye can collect the rest o' yer gear they've been holdin' in the back room o' the train station, and be ready to go to work this evenin'."

"Already?" Morgan groaned. "Have you no pity, Gus? Hell, I feel like I've been pulled backward through a knothole, one leg at a time! That sheriff packs a mean punch!"

Gus laughed. "The way I see it, if ye're weary enough, ye will na have much strength left to go chasin' after Heather. B'sides, I need to put ye to work b'fore yer bruises fade. Ye look downright fierce just now, ye do."

Morgan answered with a crooked smile. "Flattery will get you nowhere, Gus, but a stiff belt of whiskey might do wonders."

❧ 9 ❧

As she stood at the gallery railing, gazing out over the sea of humanity spread out below her, Heather was not in a merry mood. The saloon was once again filled to bursting with all manner of ill-bred men, not the least of which was the brash new bartender sporting the black eye and split lip.

Not that his battered appearance did much to lessen his natural male appeal. Upon meeting him, each of "Gus's Girls" had been thoroughly taken with Morgan, and made no bones about it. They had swarmed around him like bees to clover, gushing and fawning and all but knocking each other down in their efforts to gain his attention. Sixteen painted eyes, simultaneously winking and blinking so briskly that their soot-darkened lashes resembled a horde of fuzzy spiders with the fidgets. It was enough to make a body sick!

And what had Morgan done? Why, he'd lapped up all that feminine adoration like a hog at a trough. The fickle fiend! Even now, he was wearing a delighted grin, laughing and joking and having a high time, as happy as a wolf at a sheep convention. It was thoroughly disgusting, and for two cents, Heather would gladly have volunteered to wipe that foolish smile off his face, and his scraggly mustache with it! Heavens to Hannah! Judge Swanson must have bats in his bel-

fry, to sentence a common criminal to such . . . pleasure!

Still grousing to herself, Heather made her way to
the lower level, where she elbowed her way toward
the bar. En route, she hastily and haughtily dismissed
half a dozen would-be suitors. Finally, after feeling
she'd swum through a sea of octopuses, Heather
emerged at the bar, rumpled and annoyed.

Morgan approached her with a scowl. "Does your
father know you're down here mingling with the riffraff?" he asked.

As she yanked her bodice back into alignment,
Heather forced a false smile. "I passed him about
thirty tentacles back," she intoned dryly.

Despite himself, Morgan laughed.

Heather did not share his amusement. "I might add
that I am not a child to be confined to my room. Furthermore, I do not appreciate learning that the two of
you have been discussing me behind my back. If you
have something to say to me, Mr. Stone, have the
courtesy to say it to my face."

"Sure thing, Boston," he agreed amicably. "Now,
are you just here to flay me with your tongue, or did
you want something to drink?"

She perused the printed list behind the bar. "I'll try
a Baptist lemonade."

Morgan gave a strangled cough. "Uh . . . how about
a regular lemonade? The other's kind of . . . strong.
We wouldn't want to curl your toenails."

"Whatever," she said with a casual wave of her
hand.

He was back with her beverage almost before she
had time to blink twice. "Here you go, princess. Now,
why don't you toddle on up to your room with this?"

"Are you trying to get rid of me, Morgan?" she
inquired suspiciously.

He grinned. "You know, you're not as dumb as you
look."

"Dumb!" she echoed, squinting her dark eyes at
him threateningly. "If you want dumb, mister, there

are a bevy of silly females just itching to show their stupidity where you're concerned!"

"Jealous?" he taunted.

"Of a bunch of floozies? Hardly!"

He slanted her a considering look. "Maybe you should be. Seems to me you could learn a few things from these girls."

"Oh?" Heather cocked an arrogant brow at him. "I suppose you think I'd look better with my face painted up like a clown."

"A dab of color here and there might not be amiss," he informed her bluntly, his eyes twinkling with pure mischief. "You are sort of pale. And the way you've got your hair pulled back isn't altogether flattering, either. You ought to ask Velvet to show you how to pin it up with all those fluffy curls dangling loose."

"I'll have you know that if Etta hadn't quit on me, my hair would look much better than Velvet's ever could!" she retorted. "I'm simply not accustomed to having to style it myself."

"Doesn't look like you're used to pressing your own clothes, either," he intoned with ill-disguised mirth. "Or is it the newest fashion to go around with burn marks decorating your dress?"

"Even scorched, my gown is preferable to the gaudy attire displayed in this place," Heather shot back. "Besides, it might prove advantageous to appear a bit shabby, just so I won't have to fend off so many unwanted advances."

"I imagine that depends on who you ask. Now, I rather fancy that purple outfit Crystal has on," Morgan commented, pointing to the woman who was currently seated atop the piano with her ruffled skirts hiked above her knees.

Heather grimaced. "Indeed!" she mocked. "With those bright yellow petticoats and that matching plume in her head, she looks like a molting parrot that's lost the majority of its feathers in the most strategic spots! I can see you have excellent taste, Mr. Stone."

He flashed her a roguish smile. "I still say you'd look mighty fetching in a dress like that, instead of strutting around with your blouse buttoned up to your eyebrows and your skirts trailing three feet behind you. A man likes to catch a glimpse of skin now and then, or a flash of lace."

"Then you should be downright ecstatic, sir, with all the flesh being flaunted here tonight," she grumbled. "But I should warn you, I've heard that prolonged ogling can cause a person's eyeballs to bulge permanently. Keep gawking long enough, and yours might fall right out onto the floor."

"I'll take my chances, princess," he said with a chuckle.

"I do wish you would cease calling me that," she snapped. "It's highly irritating, and not at all humorous."

He lifted a broad shoulder in cavalier dismissal of her admonishment. "You have to agree it's better than *hinny*, which is what your father called Mrs. Clancy."

"I can't say I like Angus greeting someone other than my mother as 'honey,' but why should you object?" Heather asked.

Morgan laughed, and decided to let her in on the jest. "Not 'honey.' Hinny. Which is actually another term for a mule. And I don't object at all, if she doesn't."

Heather nearly choked on a sudden giggle. "Oh, my stars! I wonder if Angus has any idea what he's been labeling her with that thick Scottish burr of his."

"Probably not," Morgan allowed merrily. "But let's not tell him just yet, all right? It would take the fun out of hearing it now and again."

Heather nodded with alacrity. "I agree. It will be our private joke."

"I thought you'd appreciate it," he admitted, "since I got the notion you aren't too fond of the lady."

"I can't help it," Heather admitted. "It just doesn't seem right that my father should be involved with anyone else but my mother, no matter how attractive or nice Mrs. Clancy might prove to be."

Bright and early Sunday morning, Heather wearily roused herself from bed and set about getting dressed for church. Though not eager to thrust herself amid a throng of strangers, especially after being kept awake long into the night by the noise of drunken merry-makers, she was determined to adhere to the long-standing habit she and her mother had kept for years. At least in church she should encounter people of more orthodox inclinations than those who frequented the saloon—a few solid, dignified citizens with whom she would, she hoped, have more in common.

So thinking, she selected a long-sleeved dress of pale pink brocade patterned with delicate rosebuds and trimmed at bodice, sleeves, and hem with dainty ruffles of lace in a brighter hue of pink. A sprinkling of tiny satin bows enhanced the skirt, which was drawn back into a small bustle, upon which rested a larger bow. With gloves, parasol, shoes, and pert bonnet to match, she presented a fetching figure, though she rued the fact that the wrinkles had not fully hung out of the fabric, which she had dared not attempt to iron lest she scorch this gown as she had her other one.

Until she strolled into the church and down the main aisle, it never occurred to Heather that she might be overdressed. Only then did she become aware, much to her embarrassment, that the standards of fashion in Dodge were somewhat outdated, compared to those of Boston. Of the thirty or so women in attendance, most of them wore dresses that were much more plain than Heather's. Only a couple of the younger women sported pastel colors, and there was a noticeable lack of adornment. At a quick glance, Heather judged that she was the sole bearer of both parasol and bonnet, and that the only jewelry immediately evident on the other ladies was wedding bands, modest brooches, and a pendant watch or two. Thus, even the tiny amethyst studs winking in her ears, and the small matching pendant at her throat, seemed excessive.

Feeling suddenly awkward, as if she stood out like a flamingo among a gathering of wrens, Heather hastened to find a seat, wishing to become as inconspicuous as possible. It was just her luck that the pastor had chosen to preach on vanity this morning. All through the sermon Heather felt as if she were on display, as if every eye, at some time during the oration, turned on her in silent censure. By the time the service ended, she was eager to make her escape, having gained little peace of mind or sense of fellowship for her efforts.

She was not to flee so easily, however. As she slowly made her way down the crowded aisle toward the door, she overheard several comments, many of which she was sure she was meant to hear.

"Imagine wearing such pretentious attire to church! My word, what is this world coming to?"

"Now, Ada, perhaps they're more lenient back East now," another woman offered.

"But earrings! Goodness!"

A third lady spoke up. "Could be the rich wear what they want these days, no matter where they go. A case of 'If you've got it, flaunt it,' though I do think it's terribly inconsiderate and pompous to display one's wealth in such a blatant manner before less fortunate folks."

"Rich?" someone else contributed. "Gus Burns's daughter? Is the man charging that much for drinks these days?"

"Not just for beverages, dearie," another voice contributed sotto voce. "We all know more goes on in that hell hall than slaking one's thirst. And who's to say she's really his daughter? Maybe she's actually his . . . mistress!"

"Oh, surely not! You heard what was said in court

the other day. Even Judge Swanson seems convinced she's Gus's daughter."

"Hmph! I'd say she made quite a spectacle of herself then, too! Seems to be making a habit of it, doesn't she?"

By this time, Heather's spine was as stiff and straight as a ramrod, her cheeks aflame with righteous anger. She was also next in line at the door to shake the pastor's hand, and as she did so, her words, crisp and distinct, carried to one and all.

"Pleased to make your acquaintance, sir. I'm Miss Blair-Burns, from Boston. My father has an establishment on Front Street, as you most likely know."

"Nice to meet you, miss. Will you be visiting our little city for long?"

"That remains to be seen. It really doesn't strike me as a very friendly place. In fact, if you're open to suggestions, I'd like to propose that you preach soon on the sins of gossip and conjecture. I'm sure many of your congregation could benefit from such a lesson."

The minister's face flushed brightly, his eyes not quite meeting hers as he nodded. "I'll consider your recommendation, and please feel welcome to attend again. Our doors are always open to those in need of the Lord's guidance."

"In that case, perhaps you could tell me if there is a Temperance Society in Dodge," she responded.

At this, several muted gasps were heard, and a number of bystanders gaped in undisguised curiosity. One lady, braver than the rest, stepped forward. "There most certainly is, though why you would want to know is beyond me!"

Heather stood her ground and returned the woman's hard stare. "Where are the meetings held, and when?"

Another lady piped up. "Tuesday evenings, seven o'clock, right here."

Heather graced them all with a frosty smile. "Thank you. If I'm still in town, I'll see you then."

* * *

As if her morning hadn't gone badly enough, Heather had to endure Sunday dinner at Arlene Clancy's house. To her credit, the older woman did make an effort to be friendly, if only for Gus's benefit, and had obviously worked hard to prepare an appetizing meal. After eating in restaurants since leaving Boston, Heather should have found it a treat to sit down to home-cooked food. If the atmosphere hadn't been so strained, Heather might have actually enjoyed it.

As she toyed with the food on her plate, she surreptitiously studied her father's "companion." Prejudice aside, she had to admit that Arlene was an attractive woman. She had a slim, willowy figure; a clear, creamy complexion; thick black hair; and hazy mist gray eyes. Heather judged her to be in her mid to late thirties. She sported a few fine wrinkles around her eyes and the corners of her mouth, but she also had straight teeth, high cheekbones, and long, dark lashes.

"Are you enjoying your stay in Dodge so far, Heather?" Arlene asked.

"Not really," Heather replied flatly. "Though I must say it is a lively place, in a rather unique way."

Arlene gave a soft laugh. "Dodge does have its own brand of charm, though it takes some time to get accustomed to it. You must get Gus to take you to the opera house while you're here. Perhaps we could all go together. They do put on some excellent performances."

"We'll see," Heather said noncommittally.

"And you simply must take her out to the ranch, Gus," Arlene added.

Heather's gaze swung toward her father. "The ranch?"

"Aye," he said with a hint of pride. "I have a few acres a couple o' miles outside town. Nothin' big or fancy, mind, but real bonny. Lots o' water and good grazin' for cattle and horses, though I haven't much o' a herd built up yet. And the house is auld and in sad need o' repair. Hardly fit to live in the way it stands now."

"Now, Angus, don't be so modest," Arlene insisted before Heather could reply. After giving Gus an adoring look, Arlene returned her gaze to Heather. "He's right about the house, I'm afraid. When he finishes with some of the major repairs, I've offered to help him decorate the interior. But as far as the land goes, it's about the best you'll find around these parts, and I'd hardly call five hundred acres a pittance, or an equal number of cattle a mere start. He also has a small herd of fine quarter horses, which are always in high demand with ranchers and their hands. Anywhere in cattle country a good quarter horse is practically worth its weight in gold."

"Is that true?" Heather inquired.

"They dinna sell for quite that amount," Angus answered self-consciously, "but they do bring a fair price. If ye're truly int'rested, we'll ride out one day and ye can look the place o'er for yerself."

Heather nodded. "Yes, if it's no bother, I'd like to see it."

"Do you ride at all, dear?" Arlene questioned politely.

"Occasionally. Not expertly, but enough to get me by."

Angus glowed. "Glad to hear it, daughter. 'Twill save us the bother o' havin' to rent a buggy from the livery. Be faster, too. If ye take after yer auld pa a'tall, we'll make a proper horsewoman out o' ye in no time."

"We'll do it soon, then," Arlene said with a smile, deftly including herself in the excursion. "I'll prepare a picnic lunch, and we'll make a day of it. Doesn't that sound like fun?"

Heather swallowed a groan. Oh, yes! With Arlene along, it sounded like a barrel of laughs! Positively the last thing Heather wanted was to abide this woman's presence throughout her entire visit to Dodge. But it appeared her father's ladylove had other plans, which included pushing herself into Heather's life whether she was wanted there or not.

Dredging up a weak smile, Heather replied lamely, "I can scarcely wait."

By early Monday afternoon, Heather was thoroughly out of sorts. Her hair needed to be washed and coiffed, and she yearned for a decent bath in a tub full of fragrant, steaming water. She might just as well have wished for the moon, for there was no way she could heat and lug enough water upstairs to satisfy her needs.

"Why the sour face?" Morgan inquired from his place behind the bar. "Didn't I put enough sugar in your lemonade?"

She raised her head far enough to cast him a dour look. "I want a bath," she complained glumly. "A real bath. I want to sink up to my neck in it, and soak until I turn into a prune. And I want clean, manageable hair again."

He surprised her by replying casually, "Not an unreasonable desire. Admirable, actually, since I've observed that a number of our recent customers could also benefit from contact with soap and water. I'd be willing to wager the cattle they drove into Dodge smell better than some of them do."

"I've noticed," she grumbled. "But would you also be willing to help me get the water and the tub to my room, before I smell similarly offensive?"

"I might," he said, eyeing her askance. "It would depend."

"On what?" she questioned warily.

He grinned. "On whether you'd let me stay and scrub your back for you."

She glowered at him. "I might have known you'd suggest something of that sort, you lecherous boor."

"We could still strike a bargain," he offered. "I'll help you light the stove, if you keep the fire going. You draw the water and heat it, and I'll fill the tub. But only if I get to use it after you're done . . . and only if you agree not to scent our common bath with flowery perfume."

"Truly?" she asked, brightening considerably.

He nodded. "See what compromise and a little honest labor can accomplish? By the way, which room would you prefer to use? Mine or yours?" he added roguishly.

"Pardon me?" she commented with a baffled frown.

"I'm only filling that tub once, darlin', and once it's full, I won't be dragging it from place to place," he explained. "Which means you will either be bathing in my room, or I'll be doing so in yours. Together or separately, whichever suits you best."

"But . . . that's not at all . . ."

"Proper," he finished for her. "I know, but that's the best offer you're going to get from me. Take it or leave it, princess."

"I accept," she decided recklessly. "But we will most certainly not be bathing together, and you'll have to wait until I'm completely finished and have left my quarters."

"Fine, as long as you take your nasty dog with you when you go. I don't want him nipping at my bare a—ankles," he advised her with a mischievous wink.

She shook her head at him, and at herself. "I can't believe I've just agreed to such an outrageous proposal," she marveled.

"Proposition," he corrected with a sly smile. "I never propose this early in the day, and never to a lady who refuses to share my bath or my bed."

❧ 10 ❧

An hour and a half later, Heather still hadn't appeared from her rooms, and Morgan's patience ran out. Bearing a towel and fresh clothes for himself, he thumped his fist on Heather's door. "Hey! Aren't you done yet? I'd like to get cleaned up before the evening rush starts."

From inside, he heard a muted oath, followed by a crash. Over Piddles's excited barking, Heather screeched, "Oh, no! Oh! Help! Help!"

Morgan thrust against the door, breaking the thin lock, and raced through the sitting room into the bedroom. There he found Heather frantically beating a wet towel at the spreading fire from a broken oil lamp. Shoving her aside, he grabbed a coverlet from the bed and threw it over the burgeoning blaze. Cursing and stomping, he soon smothered the flames. Quickly and efficiently, he gathered the blanket and the still-smoldering mound of charred debris beneath it into a smoking mound and promptly tossed the lot out the open bedroom window into the alley below.

Morgan and Heather heaved a mutual sigh of relief. Then, as reaction set in, each began shouting at the other.

"You've just thrown out my best shoes and several of my prettiest shifts and gowns!" she wailed.

"What wasn't reduced to cinders was soaked with oil," he countered. "And what the blasted hell were

they doing scattered all over the floor to begin
with? Good grief, woman! A pack rat must keep
his burrow cleaner than this! Don't you ever hang
any of your clothes up, or fold them and put them
away?"

He gestured to the clutter strewn across the bed,
the bureau, the floor. The disorder was not confined
to the bedroom, but spilled into the sitting area as
well. Nearly every article of furniture in the two
rooms was littered with items of clothing and acces-
sories. All this amid an odd assortment of dinnerware
with food and drink still crusted on them.

"I do not place soiled garments in with my clean
ones," she informed him huffily.

"Obviously you don't gather them up in a neat pile
or bother to launder them, either," he retorted in disgust. "Nor do you dispose of your dirty dishes and
the remains of your meals. How can you stand to live
like this?"

"You needn't act as if this is all my fault, or my
normal state of habitation," she sniffed, poking her
nose in the air. "You are fully aware that Etta deserted
me without warning, and Angus is stubbornly refusing to replace her."

"It's little wonder your maid quit, if she had to follow after you and pick up everything you tossed
about. In less than a week you've managed to make
a shambles of what I imagine were two perfectly clean
rooms before you took up residence in them."

"It's not that bad," she argued.

"It was an accident waiting to happen, lacking only
the clumsy nit who knocked the lamp over and almost caught the entire room on fire!"

She had the grace to look chagrined.

"And would you mind telling why you needed a
lamp in the first place, when it's still broad daylight?"
he inquired.

"I was trying to curl my hair, and I needed the
lamp to heat the curling iron." She waved a hand toward her tumbled mass of copper tresses, a part of

which was frayed and crimped into strange forma-
tions.

For the first time since entering the room, Morgan
took a good look at her. Her satin dressing gown was
splotched with water, and clinging to her body in several interesting locations. During her exertions, it had
slipped aside, baring a good portion of one creamy
shoulder. Her hair hung in a gleaming cascade of
penny-bright waves—all except a few locks above her
forehead, which were standing askew and several
inches shorter than the rest.

He leaned in for a closer view. "Oh, for crying out
loud! You've singed your hair off, haven't you?"

Immediately her eyes misted with tears. "Does . . .
does it look that awful?" she asked in a tremulous
voice. "I tried . . . honestly I did . . . but Etta always arranged my hair, and I just can't seem to do it right."

"It doesn't look as nice as it did," he admitted hesitantly, "but I'm sure once the scorched ends are
trimmed off, it'll be better."

"No it won't!" she sobbed. "I'll just make a mess
of that, too, like I do everything else I attempt!"

"Don't cry, Boston," he all but begged her. "If
there's anything a grown man can't stand, it's a
weepy female." He led her through the maze of
clothes at her feet, to the stool in front of her dressing
table. "Sit," he commanded curtly. "Now, where are
your shears?"

"There's a small pair in my sewing kit," she said,
sniffling. "In the brocade traveling bag in the ar-
moire."

He found it buried beneath another mound of shoes
and skirts. Producing the scissors, he offered, "Do you
want me to get one of the girls to help you, or do you
want to try it yourself?"

Her teeth caught at her lower lip, her huge brown
eyes meeting his in the mirror. "Can't you do it?" she
inquired softly. "I don't dare, and I don't want anyone else seeing what a ruin I've made of it already."

"I can try, but you may not be pleased with the result."

"You couldn't possibly make it any worse than I would," she assured him.

"All right, but don't rant at me afterward."

"I won't," she promised.

With some trepidation, he began snipping at the singed edges. By the time he'd cut away all the burnt ends and evened them out, Heather sported a sassy fringe of hair across her forehead, which really was quite becoming.

"Oh, I do like it!" she caroled, assessing herself in the glass with delight. "Bless you, Morgan! How can I ever thank you?"

"Just clean up this pigsty, and don't touch that curling iron again until someone shows you how to use it properly. Otherwise, you'll likely set fire to the whole saloon, and we won't find your body for a week in all this clutter."

"But I—"

"No excuses," he ordered. "You're sound of mind and limb, and there's no reason why you can't manage a chore as simple as picking up after yourself. Who knows? You might surprise us both and even learn to launder a few of your own clothes."

She twisted around to look up at him, her expression skeptical. "Don't hold your breath, Morgan."

Which was precisely what he was doing at the moment. As she'd turned toward him, her gown had again slipped off her right shoulder and was now exposing the ripe rise of her bosom. Through the sheer veil of her red-gold hair, the smooth swell of her breast taunted him. A scant edging of satin shielded her areola from his avid gaze. A mere fraction of an inch more, and he would know the exact color of it. Was it pink? Or peach? Or tan, perhaps?

"Morgan?" she questioned, noting his fascination. Her eyes followed the direction of his, and she drew in a sharp breath. "Oh, mercy!" Her hands fluttered upward, moving to draw the lapels of her dressing gown together again.

His hands covered hers, preventing the action. "No," he murmured. "Let me see you."

Still holding her hands captive in his, he nudged the robe aside, baring her nipple. His knuckle stroked once over the crest, making it pucker. "A delicate pink rosebud, on the brink of full-blown beauty," he whispered in an awed tone. "Pure perfection."

He knelt and placed a single warm, moist kiss on the trembling peak.

Heather's heart thudded to a stop, then started racing. She went hot all over, then cold, and hot again, in the span of an instant. Shivers chased through her, but otherwise she couldn't seem to move—or to think of anything but the feel of his mouth on her breast, the soft brush of his mustache against her tingling flesh.

With a reluctant sigh, Morgan drew back and draped the garment together over her chest, anchoring her shaking fingers tightly about the cloth. "You'll never know how much you tempt me at this moment, princess. Sitting there all fresh and sweet, with eyes as big and wondrous as a fawn's. Just as you'll never know how it pains me not to take you, here and now ... which I probably would if your hall door wasn't standing wide open with a broken lock. But there will come another time and place, when we're assured of privacy, and I promise you I won't be so gallant then."

While she was still stunned speechless, his lips claimed hers, fast and hard. Then he was on his feet and gone before she recovered enough to stutter, "Y-you arrogant r-rake! You sneaky chameleon! I won't trust you within spitting distance, ever again! No matter how nice or trustworthy you pretend to be!"

Giving lie to her rash declaration, her breast gave a yearning throb. She could almost feel the heat of his mouth still searing her skin. The taste of him lingered on her lips like nectar.

"Oh, Morgan!" she moaned. "Who would have thought a paltry shoe salesman would be such a handsome, beguiling rascal! It's not fair! It's just not fair, or right, for you to make me want you this way!"

A short while later, without the courtesy of knocking first, or waiting for an invitation, Velvet and Lacy strolled through Heather's sagging door. "Heather," Velvet called out. "Morgan said to tell you he'd be up for his turn in the bath in five minutes, and unless you want to see his bare behind, you'd best hurry on out o' here."

"Drat that man! You'd think he owned this place, the way he tries to boss me around!" Heather groused, more to herself than to her visitors.

"If you're complainin', sugar, he can order me around any ole day o' the week," Lacy said with an exaggerated sigh. "He's just about the best thing since pockets."

Velvet laughed and nodded in agreement. Glancing at the untidy room, she commented wryly, "This ain't no way to run a bathhouse, honey. Why, a fella could make off with your corset, and you wouldn't miss it for a month o' Sundays. How do you ever find anything?"

"With difficulty, obviously," Heather responded archly. "And contrary to vicious gossip, I am not running a bathing establishment. I'm merely allowing that . . . snake in the grass to use my bathwater, since he was gracious enough to fill the tub for me. A bargain I much regret making."

"Wish he'd offered me the same deal," Lacy declared wistfully. "I'd have been glad to climb right in there with him and wash behind his cute little ears, and anywhere else he needed cleaned."

Velvet bent to pluck a scorched dress off the floor. "Lordy, girl! What happened here? You been tryin' to iron again?"

Heather shot her a glare. "If you must know, I was trying to heat the curling iron and accidently knocked the lamp over. Our resident hero dashed to the rescue, but he also broke the lock on my door."

"Oh, yeah," Lacy remembered. "He told us to tell you not to worry about that. He intends to fix it right after his bath."

Velvet was still pondering the singed dress. "If you need to borrow anything, I'd be glad to lend you one of my gowns, Heather. I'm sure the other girls would do the same."

"I really don't think our taste in clothes runs along the same lines," Heather pointed out.

Velvet's eyebrows rose noticeably, her friendly smile disappearing. Her frosty tone matched Heather's as she replied, "Forget I mentioned it. Sure wouldn't want you to come down with an itch you couldn't scratch!"

"Now, Velvet, don't be so touchy," Lacy placated. "I'm sure Heather didn't mean anything bad by her remark. Thing is, I wouldn't much want to wear her clothes, either. I ain't used to bein' buttoned up to my ears, and runnin' around with my skirts draggin' the floor and not a hint of rouge on my face. Everybody's different, and it's all in what you're comfortable with, I reckon. Ain't that right, Heather?"

"I assume so," Heather allowed.

"Speakin' o' such," Lacy continued, "Morgan said somethin' about you needin' help fixin' your hair up. I'm no skilled hairdresser, but if you want to come on down to my room, I'll see if I can arrange it to suit you."

Heather mustered up a stiff smile. "Another time, perhaps. For now, I think I'll just twist it into a knot and take Piddles for a walk."

Lacy shrugged. "If you change your mind, you know where to find me. And if you get lonesome and need another woman to talk to sometime, just give a holler, sugar. As long as it isn't durin' workin' hours. Three in a bed is okay for some folks, but it ain't my cup o' tea."

During her entire stroll, Heather attempted to decipher Lacy's parting statement, mentally trying to envision what three people could possibly do together in the same bed. It proved an impossible riddle, especially since she wasn't sure what *two* people—a man and a woman—did in bed together, besides sleep. She had a hazy notion, knowing it had to do with private areas of their bodies, and often resulted in the creation of babies, but precisely what that experience entailed was beyond the realm of her imagination. She supposed she would simply have to wait until she was married to be enlightened to the actual facts of the matter. Then Lyle would undoubtedly show her.

That thought brought an abrupt frown to her face, stopping her short in her tracks. Why, she wondered curiously, was the concept of sharing a marriage bed with Lyle suddenly slightly distasteful to her—while the idea of exploring such intimacy with Morgan was so very intriguing?

❧ 11 ❧

Heather's initial reception at the Temperance meeting on Tuesday evening was nearly as cool as the one she'd received at church on Sunday morning. Twelve women glared stonily at her, and then proceeded to ignore her, talking around her as if she weren't there. Of course, part of their agitation may have been due to the fact that Heather, out of sheer stubbornness, had worn an even more becoming frock than she had at Sunday services. This evening she was attired in a mint-colored satin dress, with forest green fringe, and a saucy little bonnet perched atop her head at a jaunty angle. She'd even dared to bring Piddles along, with a matching bow tied about his neck.

"Ladies, we must do more to inhibit the sale of alcohol," Mrs. Toddy, the society's president, announced. "The cattle drives are just beginning for the season, and the situation is bound to get worse as the summer progresses. Soon we'll be overrun with inebriated drovers. There must be something we can do to alleviate the problem."

"Trudy, we've done everything but stampede their cattle," Sue Barton pointed out. "We can't keep those men from invading our town. If we dared to try, we'd be the ones run out on a rail. Most of our husbands owe their livelihoods to these hungry, trail-weary throngs of cowpokes who spend their pay on baths and new clothes and haircuts and such. Without this

102

summer influx, merchants would lose a good deal of their yearly income."

"Unfortunately, you're right. But short of setting fire to every saloon in town, how do we keep these men, and our own for that matter, sober and orderly?"

"Let's review what we've tried thus far," suggested Margaret Hinkle, their bespectacled secretary. Rifling through her copious notes, she recited, "We've passed out literature in front of the taverns . . ."

"Which might have had more effect if a majority of these cowboys could read," Nellie Sherman put in wryly.

Margaret continued undeterred. "We've conducted group protests, singling out various establishments each time."

"And gotten doused with everything from stale beer to the contents of chamber pots for our pains," Anita White contributed with a grimace. "Last time it took me two days to rid my hair and clothes of the odor and filth."

Peering through her thick lenses, Margaret nodded dejectedly and read on. "We've tacked signs to posts from one end of town to the other. We've marched in the street with banners, singing hymns."

"I, for one, have had quite enough rotten food tossed at me," Sharon Tibble told the rest of the group. "My best blouse has now been reduced to a mop rag."

"Have you offered these men alternative recreation as an incentive to better behavior?" Heather asked calmly.

A dozen heads swung in her direction, twelve jaws slightly ajar. "What in daylight are you talking about?"

"What sort of recreation?"

"Indeed! Are you suggesting we entertain these men with methods similar to those the harlots in your father's dance hall employ?"

Heather smiled. "Not at all, but I do think you are swatting at insects with shovels, when we all know

you can catch more flies with honey than with vine-
gar. The idea, ladies, is to gently, tactfully, persuade
these pathetic wretches to partake in more respectable
means of diversion."

"How?"

"Yes," a second woman said. "To quote another old
adage, 'You can lead a horse to water, but you can't
make him drink.' After weeks on the trail, these
thirsty, lonesome cowpokes have only two things in
mind. To get roaring drunk and fall into bed with the
first available woman."

"Then it's up to you to convince them that what
they really want is to slake their thirst with less intoxicating beverages and to gain the companionship
of a respectable lady."

Anita's brow wrinkled in thought. "You know,
girls, maybe she has the right idea. Maybe we've been
going about this all wrong. Instead of whining and
bullying and generally making nuisances of ourselves,
perhaps we should try a different tactic. What if we
arranged a few picnics and church socials and invited
everyone, including the drovers, to attend? We could
serve lemonade and iced tea and baked goods and
fresh-cranked ice cream. It's a rare man who would
pass up an opportunity to wrap his tongue around a
spoonful of that!"

"Or maybe a barn dance at the livery stables,"
Sharon contributed. "With punch and apple cider and
fried doughnuts."

"How about a songfest? Or a talent contest, with
singing and music and such? And prizes for the best
performers?"

"We could have a street bazaar, with goods for sale
and maybe even a kissing booth," Margaret put in
wistfully.

"And a dunking booth for any of the men who get
. . . overheated, shall we say, at the kissing booth."

A speculative look entered Trudy's eyes. "We could
probably raise a lot of money for charity that way,

and for ourselves, and give the saloons a measure of competition in the bargain."

She turned to Heather and extended a welcoming hand and an apology. "I regret that we were so hasty in our condemnation of you, Miss Blair-Burns. You have introduced an excellent concept this evening and renewed our waning enthusiasm. I hope you will favor us with your continued attendance, for as long as you are in Dodge."

"Hear! Hear!" the others agreed.

A sunny, genuine smile curved Heather's mouth. "Thank you. I'm glad to have been of some help. However, I can't claim full credit, as our Boston Temperance Society, of which I am a proud member, has been employing such diversionary methods for some time now."

"Still, we appreciate your sharing them with us. It's given us a whole new perspective on the situation."

"I'm delighted. However, I'd be even more thrilled if I could envision some way to influence my own father to my way of thinking. It's very disconcerting, not to mention embarrassing, to belong to the Temperance movement when a member of one's family runs a saloon."

The meeting of the Temperance Society broke up early that evening, each woman excited and eager to begin the new assignment of devising and planning innovative entertainment that would lure the cowboys from the saloons and into sobriety. They would all meet again next week to compare notes.

Heather emerged from the church, vaguely surprised to find that night had fallen while she'd been inside. As she gazed about at the darkened streets with their eerie shadows, she was glad that she'd brought Piddles along with her, and that Morgan had promised to meet her here. She wouldn't have wanted to walk back to the saloon by herself. Not that she had any fear of getting lost, since Dodge was not that large. But once the cowpokes got a few drinks under their belts, they could get awfully unruly, and a wise person, particularly a lady, didn't traverse the streets alone after sundown.

"Will you get home all right?" Anita White inquired as they descended the short flight of steps to the church grounds.

"I suppose so," Heather replied. "Angus is sending Mr. Stone to accompany me back. I'm sure he'll be here soon." Her eyes searched the surrounding darkness, failing to find any sign of him. "At any rate, Piddles is a wonderful deterrent to any stranger who might wish to approach me. He detests men."

"Margaret and I will walk partway with you, if you like," Anita offered. "We both live on Chestnut Street, only a couple of blocks from your father's Gallery. We always prefer to go in groups of two or three if we have to be out after sunset. Usually no one bothers us, but we feel safer in one another's company."

Heather accepted gladly, wondering peevishly why Morgan hadn't appeared to escort her as he was supposed to do. He certainly wasn't proving very reliable, at least as far as she was concerned.

As Anita had predicted, the three women met with no trouble in the quieter residential area just north of Front Street. Both ladies invited Heather to tea in their homes the following week. Then they waved her on her way, admonishing her to take care as she approached the business district.

After parting from her new friends, Heather hurried along, not nearly as brave now that she and Piddles were on their own. While she'd never been particularly fond of the darkness, neither had she been especially afraid of it. Until now. Suddenly it seemed as if something sinister lurked behind every bush and building. A dog barked, probably smelling Piddles, and Heather nearly leapt from her shoes, the hair on the nape of her neck prickling and standing on end. Piddles gave a low growl.

Heather was scurrying past an alleyway behind the corner drugstore, which also doubled as the post office, somewhat cheered that she had only half a block to traverse now, when two men suddenly charged out of the dark toward her. Her first scream was one of startlement, her second of sheer panic, as her assailants grabbed her and dragged her into the murky shadows of the alley. In the throes of terror, she kicked and screeched and wriggled like a madwoman, vaguely aware that Piddles was barking and snarling in his own attempt to defend her. A large, hard hand clamped over her mouth, muffling her cries for help. Seconds later, she was thrown to the ground, one attacker raising her arms over her head while the other pressed his heavy body over hers.

"Hold her arms good and tight, Willie. She scratches like a she-cat!" the man atop her hissed. "And keep her quiet, or we won't get any fun out o' her b'fore we have to kill her!"

Her eyes wild, her cries smothered, Heather thrashed beneath him, trying in vain to buck him off of her. Above the frantic beat of her heart, she heard the fellow stifle a grunt of pain as her shoe connected with his shin. His partner in crime gave a muted yell, followed immediately by a pained yelp from Piddles. Ruthless fingers pawed crudely at her breasts, pausing only to claw at the delicate fabric at her throat and viciously rip it apart, baring her breasts to his view and his brutal touch.

Cringing, whimpering, tears of fright and anguish blurring her vision, Heather uttered a silent, urgent prayer. *Oh, Lord! Help me! Please don't let them commit this horrible atrocity upon me! Strike them ... or me ... dead first! Please!*

Morgan was striding angrily back toward the saloon, muttering to himself and cursing Heather for not being at the church when he'd arrived to escort her home. Drat that infernal woman anyhow! Couldn't she ever do as she was told? It wasn't as if he relished this task of playing nursemaid to the little witch. He had better things to do with his time, after all, than to keep track of her. Now, since he hadn't passed her on the way, he'd taken a different route back, methodically searching for her street by street, though the blasted twit was probably safe in her room at this very moment.

He was just turning the corner at Second and Chestnut when a woman's shrill scream rent the night. The eerie sound skated up his spine like slivers of ice. Another echoed it, then more, accompanied by the frenzied barking of a small dog.

Morgan was sprinting in the direction of the clamor before his brain even registered the fact. He had no doubt that it was Heather who had shrieked, though now she'd ceased her cries for help. He heard a loud yelp, and knew it must be Piddles trying to defend his mistress and perhaps earning a swift kick for his efforts.

Halfway down the block, Morgan spied a fuzzy lump in the street. Piddles. With a furious wriggle, the animal bounded to its tiny feet and charged into the alley, dazed but not defeated.

Morgan darted after him. Rounding the rear corner of the building, he spotted several forms, dimly visible in the darkness. One was hunched over another. A third appeared to be stooping a couple of feet away. As Morgan closed in on them, the shapes came clearer. One man was holding Heather's arms. The other was hunkered over her, tearing at her clothes, both so involved in their foul play and deafened by Piddles's barking that they failed to hear Morgan's approach.

Just as Morgan was about to grab the fellow atop Heather, Piddles raced between the man's legs. Snarling and snapping, the tiny dog sank his sharp teeth into the man's groin. Morgan grinned wickedly as the man let loose a high-pitched howl.

"Good boy, Piddles. You handle that one, and I'll take care of this one." With that, Morgan launched himself at the second assailant.

Caught off guard, the man was not prepared for Morgan's attack, but brawny fellow that he was, he rallied swiftly. After a brief scuffle on the ground, he managed to squirm out of Morgan's hold. Both men bounded to their feet.

It was only by chance, in the gloom, that Morgan happened to see the glint of a long, lethal blade, as his opponent suddenly produced a knife. Mentally damning the fates, and Judge Swanson, for rendering him unarmed, Morgan warily faced his enemy. The two adversaries circled slowly, their eyes straining, ever watchful of the other's next move. At the very instant the other man struck forward with the knife, Morgan kicked out to intercept the blow with his foot. The hard toe of his boot smashed into his attacker's wrist, sending the knife sailing harmlessly into the dark alley. With a pained screech, the fellow grabbed at his injured arm and made a quick dash for the street, his partner stumbling fast behind him, Piddles still clinging to the seat of his pants.

With no other sounds to mute them, small broken whimpers now claimed Morgan's full attention. He turned to find Heather huddled in a quivering ball, her arms clasped tightly about her head. The sight of her like this, so shattered and shaken, sent pain and rage lancing through him. His heart ached for her. His brain screamed out in primal fury that anyone had dared to harm her. The urge to protect and shelter this woman—his woman—nearly overwhelmed him, surprisingly intense, sending him to his knees beside her. Anger still warred with compassion, his emotions in tremendous tumult, as he reached out and gathered her into his arms.

Her immediate reaction was to cringe away from him, her hands flailing weakly in an effort to push him away. Her pitiful moans, like those of a frightened kitten, tore into his heart, as if to pierce his very soul.

"Heather, honey, it's all right. It's me. Morgan. I've got you, darling. You're safe now. Safe."

His crooning message must have penetrated her shock on some level, for she ceased struggling and gave herself over to his comforting embrace. Salty tears wet his shirt as she clung to him, quaking violently and weeping as if she might never stop. He drew her closer, cuddling her tighter to him, his own hands trembling as he gently stroked her hair and let her cry out her fear.

Piddles crept quietly up beside them, whining inquisitively, obviously worried for his mistress. He tried to poke his cold nose between them, but finding little space, finally settled for laying his head on Heather's leg in an attitude of anxious anticipation. For once, he showed no inclination to attack Morgan.

At last, when Heather's sobs dwindled to soggy hiccups, Morgan asked softly, "Are you badly hurt? Can you tell me?"

"N-n-no!" she wailed.

He didn't know how to interpret her answer. He asked again. "Are you in great pain? Where does it hurt, sweetheart?"

"I-I'm m-mostly scared, I think," she stuttered between chattering teeth.

Morgan wasn't so sure, but he knew they couldn't just sit here and wait for those ruffians to return, or others like them. Still, he hesitated to lift her, lest her injuries prove to be more severe than either of them realized.

"I'm going to carry you to the saloon. Then we'll send for the doctor. I'll try not to cause you any more pain than necessary, but we can't stay here. We need to get you inside. I suspect you're suffering from shock, if nothing worse."

"I-I can walk. I th-think."

"Honey, your legs are shaking so badly, you wouldn't manage three steps on your own," he informed her, his voice gruff with lingering fear. "Now, just hang on to my neck, and try not to be any more of a nuisance than normal."

He rose easily, her slight weight an insignificant burden compared with the riot of unfamiliar sensations still bombarding him. Never before had he experienced such powerful and mixed feelings toward a woman. At the moment, he felt almost as stunned as she was. Uncomfortable with his inner turmoil, he mentally retreated behind the more secure facade of sarcasm and displeasure. He was much more accustomed to dealing with anger and irritation than with these softer, warmer tuggings in the region of his heart.

"I hope to hell you're not badly hurt," he told her, cradling her to his chest as he set a fast pace toward Gus's Gurdy. "I wouldn't want anything to prevent me from enjoying myself when I paddle your backside! Why in tarnation did you set off on your own, instead of waiting at the church like you were supposed to? Damnation, woman, you don't have an ounce of sense! When God passed out brains, you must have been standing behind the door and missed out entirely!"

❧ 12 ❧

Sensitive to Heather's torn clothing, and any humiliation she might endure because of it, not to mention the ruckus that would ensue if he took her through the front entrance looking the way she did now, Morgan carried her up the back stairs to her room. Fortunately they met no one along the way. He was still ranting and raving as he laid her gently on the bed. Piddles immediately hopped up to lie beside her, eyeing Morgan warily but otherwise making no move to interfere.

Heather hadn't uttered a word as he'd carried her home, and that alone made Morgan more nervous than he might otherwise have been. He lit the lamp and got his first good look at her, and was stunned at the listlessness in her normally bright eyes. "All right. I'm going downstairs to get your father, and send someone for the doctor. I don't want you to move a muscle until I get back." Not that he supposed she would. She looked completely drained of energy. "I mean it, now. Do you understand me, Heather?" he prodded when she failed to reply to his command. Normally she would have lit into him like a termagant on a rampage.

Clasping her ripped bodice to her chest with one hand, she reached out to him with the other, clutching his hand in desperation. Fresh tears dribbled down her cheeks. "Don't leave me," she begged in a pathetic voice. "Please, Morgan! Don't leave me!"

Her voice rose in panic, and fearing she might become hysterical, Morgan perched lightly on the edge of the bed. Tenderly stroking her mussed hair from her forehead, he murmured, "I'm right here, princess. You're safe in your own bed now. Nothing and no one is going to hurt you. I promise."

After a moment she calmed a bit, and he tried again. "Honey, I've got to go for your father and the doctor. And probably the sheriff. I'll be right back, so fast you won't even know I'm gone."

"No! Oh, God, Morgan! No one must see me like this!"

"Okay. Okay. Just simmer down. You're upsetting Piddles, and we don't want him wetting the bed, you know," he cajoled.

She managed a weak laugh. "I'm not hurt, at least not the way you mean," she assured him, sobering almost instantly. The haunted look came back into her chocolate brown eyes. "I . . . I haven't thanked you for saving me from . . . from . . . " she choked out, swallowing back another round of sobs.

His face hardened as images of Heather being held down and assaulted by those two brutes flashed in his head. "Are you telling me the absolute truth? Because if you're not," he warned, "I'm going to tear this town apart hunting for those sons of bitches, and they'll wish they were dead before I'm finished with them. In fact, I just might do it regardless. I'm feeling a bit savage myself at the moment." His fingers brushed lightly over the bruises even now staining her cheeks and throat, where cruel hands had left their mark.

"They didn't finish what they started," she insisted tearfully. "Thanks to your timely arrival. I got roughed up some, and was scared out of my wits, but that's all. I swear it."

Once again she clutched his hand, drawing it to her quivering breast. "Oh, Morgan!" she wailed anew. "I was so frightened! So dreadfully frightened! I never want to be that afraid of anything again! I don't think I could bear it! I . . . I thought I was going to die!"

That possibility had crossed Morgan's mind as well. Would those men have raped her and left her there like some wounded animal? Or would they have killed her afterward? The thought of that wicked knife stabbing into her body made him almost ill.

"They intended to kill me, you know," she said between sobs. "I heard one of them say they were going to, after . . . after . . ."

"Hush, now," he told her, drawing her close and holding her trembling body against his own. "It's over. It's all over."

Gradually she calmed, relaxing against him, absorbing the warmth of him into her chilled bones. "I'm so tired," she murmured. "So awfully tired." Still she clutched his hand as if it were a lifeline she dared not turn loose.

"Go to sleep, princess," he urged softly.

"Stay," she whispered drowsily. "Hold me. I don't want to be alone, and you make me feel so safe."

"I've got you, sweetheart. Don't worry about anything. Just let yourself go. I'll be here to guard you."

Within minutes, she was asleep, though an occasional shudder still shook her—and him. Gently, taking care not to wake her, Morgan eased off the bed and drew a light coverlet over her. Then he tiptoed out the door and shut it softly behind him.

With a heavy sigh, he started downstairs, dreading telling Gus all that had transpired. Still, it had to be done. Even if Heather didn't require medical attention, the sheriff would have to be informed of the attack. There was a slim chance Watson and his deputies might still catch the culprits, even after all the time that had elapsed.

A grim smile curved Morgan's mouth. If Heather's assailants were still in town, they should be fairly easy to spot. All the law had to do was to be on the lookout for one man with a broken wrist and another clutching his balls and singing soprano—and hope Morgan didn't find them first.

"Just a dab of powder here and there, just to cover up the bruises on your face and neck," Ginger insisted. "Honest, honey, nobody will even know your wearin' it, but it will hide a multitude of sins."

"And a smidgen of rouge on her lips and maybe on her cheeks," Joy said. "It'll disguise the purple until her lips are back to their natural color."

Heather looked doubtful. "Are you sure it won't be too noticeable?"

Brandy grimaced. "Anything's got to be an improvement. You look like you tangled with a gorilla and lost!"

Heather finally acceded to their suggestions, knowing they were only trying to help. She was truly touched by their genuine concern for her. Each and every one had offered sympathy and advice, though she hadn't been friendly toward them since her arrival. In fact, she'd been a royal snob! And yet here they were, being so kind and helpful that it made her want to weep with shame. Deep down, regardless of how they earned their living, it appeared these girls were really very nice. Perhaps they weren't as polite and polished as most of Heather's acquaintances, but they were not so awfully bad, either.

When she finally ventured downstairs, Heather was very conscious of the hesitant glances Bob and Angus and Lloyd, the piano player, cast in her direction. None of them seemed capable of meeting her gaze straight on. She understood their predicament, since she was having difficulty facing them as well.

After a trying discussion with her father this morning, Heather didn't wonder that he felt a bit awkward in her presence. She felt the same.

Angus had blustered and bellowed like a bull, pacing back and forth. "Ye should hae waited for Morgan, like ye were supposed to," he'd scolded. " 'Twas witless and careless, wanderin' off on yer oon like that."

"Careless, I'll concede," she admitted with a measure of chagrin. "But I am not witless. And I did wait for a few minutes, but when the other women began to leave the church and Morgan still hadn't come, I accepted their offer to walk partway back with them. With only a couple of blocks to traverse on my own, and Piddles with me, I thought surely nothing dire would happen."

"Ye thought wrong, lass," he pointed out needlessly. " 'Tis plain Dodge is na the place for ye. What I should do is pack ye off to Boston on the next train east." Almost in the same breath, he changed his mind. "Nae, I canna do that, either, at least na till yer bruises fade, for 'twould likely gi' yer ma a terrible fright to see ye like this. B'sides, if Sheriff Watson nabs those two yahoos who attacked ye, ye'll hae to be here to identify 'em and testify agin' 'em in court, so I reckon ye must stay awhile longer, like it or nae."

"I suppose so," she agreed meekly.

Next Angus complained, "Morgan should hae left earlier to meet ye at the kirk." Then he did an abrupt about-face and blamed the Temperance Society for concluding their meeting early. "Those old busybodies canna e'er do anything right."

He went on to praise Morgan for coming to her rescue. "I dinna ken how to properly thank Morgan for savin' ye. And to think he bested both o' those men wi'oot a weapon! Seems to me ye couldn't hae asked for a better champion, daughter. He's a right braw young fella."

Heather replied with a sigh, "I realize we owe him an immense debt of gratitude, Angus, but you needn't exalt him so excessively. Heavens! You make it sound as if he should be nominated for sainthood!"

"At the very least," Angus declared.

Heather merely rolled her eyes and bit her tongue on the retort that threatened to escape.

Throughout his diatribe, Angus cursed a blue

streak, calling her assailants every horrid name he could think of, and some Heather suspected he invented on the spot. Very bluntly, he reminded her just what could have resulted if Morgan hadn't saved her in time. "Ye're lucky ye're not lyin' upstairs wi' the doctor workin' o'er yer broken and bleedin' body, and yer auld pa prayin' for yer recovery and hopin' he would na hae to telegraph sad news to yer ma. Ye could hae been maimed for life, wi' yer future tarnished and tattered. Or worse yet, restin' in yer coffin, whilst we prepared yer cairn at the cemetery!"

"I know," she concurred tearfully. "I realize how close I came to true disaster. It terrifies me anew every time I think of it!"

Feeling like an absolute fiend for having made her feel so awful again, Angus had clumsily apologized. "Och! 'Tis a poor excuse for a father I am, stirrin' up yer fright so badly, when 'tis still so fresh a wound to yer soul. A lashin' would be too guid for me. 'Tis sorry I am, lass, to have been so hard on ye. Can ye find it in yer heart to forgive me?"

She'd managed a wobbly smile. "Of course. But only if you promise not to erect a statue in Morgan's image. A hero, he might be, but he already thinks too highly of himself, if you ask me."

That earlier discussion had been awkward for both Heather and Angus, and it would probably take some time for the pair of them to get over it. Yet, in an odd way, their talk had brought them closer together. For the first time in her life, Heather knew what it felt like to have a father—one who worried about her, chastised her when she needed it, and quite possibly even loved her.

He cares, she marveled, overwhelmed with tender emotion. *It's incredible, but I do believe my father really cares about me, after all this time. Even when he's brusque and scolding, I get this wondrous, warm feeling, just knowing he's concerned for my welfare and my feelings . . . for me, as his daughter. I strongly suspect that beneath all that*

*bluff and bluster lies a sweet, loving man, one I truly would
like to get to know much better.*

As for Angus, he'd gotten his first true taste of what
it meant to be a father, to fuss and fret and harangue
his offspring. To go numb with fear over what might
have happened, and thank God for what hadn't. Now
he was in a ticklish spot, and not a little unsure of
himself, which was why he didn't know how to deal
with her at the moment. Moreover, this attack on her
was an issue men viewed somewhat differently from
women, and suddenly he felt as if he were trying to
tread on quicksand, out of his element, not sure what
to say or how to best handle the situation.

Her ma should be the one to deal wi' this, he thought
miserably. *To be here to comfort her wi' a woman's compassion and understandin', to ask all the right questions
and gi' all the right answers and advice. 'Tis not a man's
place, to discuss such personal subjects wi' his daughter.*

His employees were likewise on the horns of a di-
lemma, preferring to ignore the entire episode, but not
certain how to go about doing that, either.

Of all the men, only Morgan didn't seem anxious
over how to approach her. As she walked up to the
bar, he looked her square in the face and said, "High
time you did something with yourself, Boston. I told
you days ago that you needed some color in your
face. You look much better. Now, if you'd add a slight
tint to your eyelids and darken your lashes some,
you'd be downright stunning."

"That's what I tried to tell her, but she wouldn't
listen," Lacy announced importantly. "It was like
pulling teeth to get her to sit still for the powder and
rouge."

"Even that feels odd to me," Heather admitted
stiffly, her injured lips and cheek muscles making
speech painful. "Besides, I don't believe I want to look
too attractive just now. Men have always tended to
admire me, and that's quite possibly what got me into
this trouble in the first place. I'm only wearing the

face paint until the bruising fades, so I don't look like a freak."

Morgan rolled his eyes heavenward, then said in a loud aside to Gus, "There can't be much conceit in the rest of her family. She's used up the whole allotment."

"Och! Believe me," Gus replied with a martyred groan, "her granny Blair was twice as bad."

"The sheriff will be along in a while," Morgan said, changing the subject again. "He wants your description of the men who attacked you last night, Heather."

She frowned. "Why? You were there, too. Surely you've already done that."

"I've given him a fair account of what the one you said was called Willie looked like, the big fellow with the knife and the busted wrist, but I didn't really get a good look at the other one. You saw him better than I did."

Heather shook her head and began to babble nervously. "It was so dark. It all happened so quickly. I was too scared to notice much about either of them."

"You probably remember more than you think," he insisted. "Voices. Particular odors. A neckerchief. A distinctive mole. The smallest thing might help identify one or both of them."

"Aye," Gus agreed. "And I want those two bastards caught and strung up for what they tried to do to ye. Furthermore, from now on, ye dinna step one foot out o' this place wi'out me or Morgan right alongside o' ye. Is that understood, lass? Nae one foot. I dinna care to write yer ma, notifyin' her that ye've met wi' some dreadful mishap, 'specially since she'd say 'twas all my fault, which it could weel be."

"That's preposterous. Surely there is no need to go to such drastic lengths," Heather rejoined. "As long as I exercise caution, and only go out during the day, and tell you where I'm going—"

"Nay, lass," Angus broke in with a shake of his

head. "Ye're nae to go traipsin' about alone at all."

Heather's chin jutted out defiantly, before she realized the discomfort such an act would afford her. Wincing, she switched to a slight glower. "I do not need a warden, Father."

Angus blinked at her, too stunned that she'd called him "Father" for the first time to form an intelligible response.

Morgan took over for him. "Since the day I met you, it's been my opinion that you need a keeper, princess. You're entirely too clumsy and inept on your own, a danger to yourself and others, even when you don't intend to be. Not that I'm real thrilled to be handed the job, you understand, but I'll do it as a favor to your father."

"I'd rather keep company with a wounded bear," she fired back, forgetting for the moment that she owed him her life. "He'd probably be much more sociable and most likely have better manners!"

He awarded her a taunting smile. "Too bad, lady. All the bears declined the position, so it looks as if we're stuck with each other."

"Isn't that just wonderful!" she mocked. "Do I get any time away from you at all, or do you intend to escort me to the outhouse, too?"

His smile broadened, distinctly wicked to match the devilish wink he gave her. "It will be my pleasure, your High-and-Mightiness!"

All was remarkably quiet and uneventful for the next few days, which relieved almost everyone's mind. Except for Heather, who was straining at her leash, anxious to be rid of Morgan's continual presence and his usual obnoxious attitude, to which he had reverted almost immediately after what everyone now politely referred to as "the incident." Morgan's temper was likewise tried, as he and Heather were practically making a ritual of annoying one another.

As Morgan had predicted, as her residual fear diminished, Heather did recall the attack in more detail.

In the end, however, the only significant clue she could offer that could possibly set one of her assailants apart from the run-of-the-mill drovers who drifted through town was that he smelled of mint.

This memory was triggered quite by accident on the second morning following the assault, just before the saloon opened for business. Jasmine, who originally hailed from New Orleans, or so she claimed, had just wandered downstairs, still half-asleep. Yawning and stretching, she ambled over to the bar and requested her usual cup of cold tea, her choice of a wake-up beverage.

"Put a sprig of mint in it, if you have some, will ya, sugar?" she asked Morgan sleepily.

"Sure thing, Jasmine."

Heather, who had been sitting at a nearby table waiting impatiently for Morgan to finish his bar duties and go shopping with her, looked up with a jerk of her head. "Did you say mint?"

"Yeah, dumplin'. Down South we have what ya might call a passion for the stuff. We put it in tea, coffee, juleps, lemonade, just about any drink you'd care to name. You should try it. It gives your mouth a nice, cool taste that lingers for quite a while. Makes yer breath smell good, too."

Heather's face had lost a fair amount of color, a fact that Morgan was quick to note. "What's wrong, Boston? You look like you just swallowed a gnat."

Her eyes huge in her pale face, her hands trembling visibly, Heather replied shakily, "Mint. He smelled of mint."

Morgan frowned. "Who, Heather?"

"That man. The one who attacked me. I'd forgotten until now, but he must have been chewing mint, because there was a strong odor of it on his breath."

Overhearing her comment, Brandy put in with a snort, "What do you make of that? It don't make a whole lot of sense to me, like he was tryin' to be polite and have clean breath when he planned to ravish you? Hell's bells! What kind of loony does that?"

Ignoring Brandy's interruption, Morgan focused his piercing gaze on Heather. "Which man, princess? The one with the knife? The one named Willie?"

Heather shook her head. "No. The other one. The one who was . . . on top of me."

Later, Morgan relayed this tidbit of information to Sheriff Watson, who didn't think it would do much good. Frankly, neither did Morgan, but there was always an outside chance of catching him, supposing the man was still hanging around town. On the average, however, cowboys and drifters remained in Dodge for only a day or two, especially those cowpokes coming in with a herd of cattle. They stayed long enough to squander a good portion of their earnings on clothes, haircuts, poker, whiskey, and women, and were soon on their way back home until next year's drive. If this was the case with Heather's assailants, no one held out much hope they'd be caught, and so far nobody had seen hide nor hair of anyone who might match the vague descriptions Heather and Morgan had provided.

After several days had passed, with no further developments, everyone came to the conclusion that the attack had been a single, isolated incident that could have befallen any woman passing through that area at that particular moment. It just happened to be Heather who had been at the wrong place at the wrong time, and fortunately escaped mortal injury. All things considered, she was a very lucky lady!

Heather could have argued that point. As could Morgan. To his mind, Heather seemed to draw trouble like a magnet attracted iron. Never had he met anyone so blasted clumsy, impudent, aggravating, and mouthy—or so totally beguiling.

❧ 13 ❧

Arlene didn't put in an appearance until three days after the attack. Morgan informed her that Gus was off at a council meeting. "I'm aware of that," she told him. "I've come specifically to speak with Heather."

Upon first seeing Heather, whose bruises had already started to heal, though they were now more of a rainbow hue than black and blue, Arlene exclaimed, "Goodness! You poor child! If you look this terrible now, I can only imagine what sad condition you were in right after the incident. Still, we must all be thankful you weren't hurt more seriously."

Heather grimaced, but said politely, "Thank you, Mrs. Clancy. I'm feeling much better."

"Oh, I do hope so! I didn't want to intrude too soon, you understand, though my initial inclination was to dash right over and see if I could be of some help to you. After reconsidering, I thought perhaps you would need some time to recover a bit first."

"That was considerate of you."

Arlene glanced around to see who might be listening, then leaned closer to Heather and continued in a confidential tone, "It must have been frightful for you. I'm not at all sure I would be bearing up as well as you appear to be. Not after . . ." She patted Heather's hand in a gesture of mute sympathy. "Well, you know," she concluded with a pitying look.

"Mrs. Clancy, I don't know what you've heard, but

123

I came away with nothing more than an awful fright
and a few bruises, thanks to Morgan's swift interven-
tion," Heather retorted.

"That's what your father said, and I can understand
that you wouldn't want anyone to suspect otherwise,
regardless of what actually occurred. After all, it's really no one else's business, is it? Except your immediate family and the man you marry, of course.
Fortunately for you, your friends and fiancé are back
East, and need never know anything about this unfortunate affair, unless you decide to tell them. What
does it matter what people around here think, anyway? You'll leave in a couple of weeks, and the talk
will die down. Besides, you may never visit Dodge
again, or by the time you do, everyone will have forgotten all about it."

"Mrs. Clancy . . ."

"Arlene," the woman inserted with a smile.

"Arlene," Heather amended reluctantly, "I do not
appreciate your hasty assumptions. Nor are they at
all valid. However, you are correct about one thing. I
don't give a flip what the other local gossips may be
saying about me, except for the fact that it may hurt
my father."

"Oh, dear! Now I've wounded your feelings, and
that wasn't my intention at all!" Arlene insisted in
dismay. "You've misunderstood me, Heather. My
only concern is to help you through this trying time.
Why, in and of itself, the fright you received would
be enough to put many ladies off of men altogether,
and it would be such a pity if you couldn't conquer
your fear of them, couldn't stand to have a man touch
you as a result of all you've been through. Think of
your poor fiancé, and how that would affect him and
your future life together. I so hope you can learn to
deal with the aftermath of such a terrifying experience, and not let your entire life be tainted by it. Or
by any false sense of guilt that might haunt you. After
all, you certainly didn't ask those men to attack you!
It isn't your fault in any way whatsoever."

Morgan, who had been deliberately eavesdropping from his post behind the bar, was aghast, and more than a little furious at Arlene's insinuation. Innocently or not, the widow had just planted a whole field of foolish notions in Heather's fertile mind, and watered them with just enough truth to make them grow. Yes, it would only be natural for Heather to shy away from close contact with men for a time, perhaps even to be afraid of it. But by mentioning this, Arlene was promoting such fears, suggesting that Heather might never recover from them, nurturing the seeds of Heather's confusion and fright and giving them strength and depth. Despite intelligent logic, some small grain of doubt might take root in Heather's mind—lingering, growing like noxious weeds.

He could not let that happen. He could not let this woman instill doubts and fears in Heather that could emotionally cripple her! Instinctively Morgan started toward them, primed to protect his lady.

"I know you mean well, but I really don't wish to discuss this any longer," Heather told the older woman.

Coming alongside her chair, Morgan offered Arlene a helping hand from her seat, informing her frankly, "I think it's time you ended your visit. Heather still needs her rest."

Without further ado, he escorted the widow to the door. "I'll tell Gus you were here."

No sooner had he gotten rid of Arlene than Morgan ushered Heather upstairs into her father's office, completely ignoring her protests and bafflement. Seating her in a chair, he perched on the edge of Gus's desk and stared solemnly at her for several seconds. Finally he spoke. "I hope you didn't put much stock in the drivel Widow Clancy was spouting. I'd like to credit you with more intelligence than that."

"Oh, Morgan, I just don't know!" Heather admitted uneasily. "I'm so confused right now. Logic tells me one thing, but my emotions are all tangled up. Arlene wasn't far off the mark, you know. In a way, I do feel guilty, as if I helped to bring these problems on myself."

"How?" he prompted.

"Well, I deliberately wore one of my prettiest dresses, just to impress or perhaps to irritate the other ladies of the Temperance Society. And I didn't wait for you to escort me home, like I was supposed to. I behaved very foolishly, and now have reaped the consequences of my own stupidity."

"I'll agree that you didn't use good sense, but you did nothing to promote that attack, so don't heap needless guilt on yourself. You have enough on your plate as it is."

She offered a lame smile of gratitude. "Yes, but now I've brought shame, not just upon myself, but to Angus's door, and I really do feel terrible about it. He's earned the respect of this town, and he doesn't deserve to have his daughter's name bandied about, besmirching his reputation as well."

"I think you're making mountains out of molehills, Boston," Morgan told her. "Gus is more worried about your welfare than any gossip. Moreover, I'm willing to bet Arlene Clancy has blown this all out of proportion. Sure, folks are curious and will talk, but I'll wager most of them understand and are genuinely concerned, and maybe even a little embarrassed and angry themselves that a visitor to their town was so brutally accosted. It reflects badly on them, that Dodge is still so crime-ridden that ladies aren't safe on the streets."

Heather sighed. "Morgan, I know you're trying to make me feel better, but the fact remains that there are some folks who will believe the worst no matter what, and there's simply no way I can convince them otherwise. I feel as if I've been branded with a scarlet letter, and no matter how hard I try to wash it off or disguise it, it will still be glaringly visible to everyone. I could wear a sign around my neck and take out an advertisement in the newspaper to the contrary, and it still wouldn't make any difference."

"You're right," he agreed mildly. "People will believe what they want to, and they'll make up their own minds. But I don't think you're giving Gus's friends enough credit, princess. They'll stand by him—and by you because you're his daughter. And those folks who don't aren't worth your time, anyway."

"I hope you're right," she said with a hangdog look.

"There's something else we should discuss as well," he continued, his demeanor both reluctant and determined. "I'm not sure how to word this, so bear with me if I'm a bit blunt." He stopped long enough to draw a fortifying breath. "I think Arlene Clancy was an absolute ass for insinuating that you might feel intimidated by men from now on, and you'll never know how tempted I was to throttle her for that."

"But—"

He held up a hand. "Just give me a minute to finish what I'm trying to say. I realize you had quite a scare, and that it's bound to make you nervous about men for a little while, but it's ridiculous to think it should affect you for the rest of your life. Those men were riffraff, the dregs of the earth, and not representative of the entire male gender. They were intent on violation, not courtship, and therein lies the difference."

"I know that," Heather conceded, "but it still frightens me to think about it. They were so big . . . so strong . . . so rough!" Her voice quavered to a halt.

"It doesn't have to be that way, Heather," Morgan told her in a hushed voice, his eyes holding a soft gleam as he reached out to tilt her head back to meet his gaze. "It shouldn't be that way. Physical intimacy between a man and a woman can be incredibly wonderful and fulfilling."

"For a man, I suppose," she allowed, her face aflame.

"For both parties involved," he insisted. "There's

nothing harmful or frightening about it. Mating is a very natural act. God planned it that way. If He didn't want us to do it, He wouldn't have given us the urges and desires to do so. And sharing such passion can be a beautiful and rewarding experience, certainly nothing to fear.''

"We . . . we shouldn't be talking like this," she stammered.

"I agree," he said, leaning closer, their lips a scant breath apart. "They say a picture is worth a thousand words."

His lips grazed hers lightly. "You're not going to bite me this time, are you?"

"I . . . I'll try not to," she murmured, her breath catching. "But your mustache tickles."

He gave a low chuckle. "I'm glad."

He kissed her again, his lips pressing against her more fully, more firmly. His hand curled around the back of her neck, gently urging her closer. He could feel her mouth trembling beneath his.

"Don't be afraid of me, Heather," he implored on a seductive whisper. "Part your lips for me, darlin'. Let me taste you."

Slowly, tentatively, she did as he requested. His breath mingled with hers. Warm. Sweet. His tongue traced lingeringly over her lips, then dipped between them to lightly touch against hers. He tasted of coffee and cinnamon buns. His tongue slid alongside hers, further invading the dark recesses of her mouth, and she stiffened involuntarily.

He retreated long enough to soothe her fears. "It's all right, sweetheart. Just relax. There's nothing to fear. I promise you."

His voice was low, beguiling, luring her toward him for yet another sample of honey-flavored temptation. This time she welcomed him more readily, even now growing accustomed to the feel of him. His taste. His scent. His tender exploration of her mouth. Her lips softened beneath his, molding to Morgan's, blindly following his lead.

Tenderly he led her on a leisurely voyage of discovery. Along a wandering path of growing desire, where her senses heightened and fear was left far behind. She felt as if she were floating on a billowing cloud, adrift on summer breezes, yet so incredibly alive that she seemed to shimmer with it, her skin tingling, her blood surging. Her insides were quivering delightfully, as if a bevy of hummingbirds were fluttering their wings, trying to get out. On a soft moan, she nestled nearer, her arms twining about his neck, her fingers delving into the crisp dark hair at his nape.

At length, his lips left hers to glide along her cheek, dotting her face with tiny, adoring kisses. "Oh, sweetheart," he murmured. "What you do to me! You're so sweet and smooth, like honey and cream. The more I taste, the more I want."

Her hands framed his face, dragging his mouth back to hers. "Kiss me again, Morgan. Please. Kiss me again."

He did, and a flame ignited deep within her, burning softly at first, then more brightly as her longings grew ever more poignant. His arms cradled her close against his firm, warm chest, their hearts pounding in brisk rhythm. Without haste or menace, his hands charted a course from her nape to her waist, stroking her back, skimming upward again along her rib cage. Gently they brushed the soft outer sides of her breasts.

Lost in a daze of swirling sensation, Heather made no immediate move to stop him. Encouraged, Morgan cupped a hand around each breast, cradling them gently. Holding them, feeling their warmth throb through his palm with each beat of her pulse. His blood pooled low, hot and urgent. He bit back a groan of intense yearning. Almost of their own volition his thumbs searched out the proud twin peaks, nimbly enticing them to loftier heights.

At the first brush of his thumbs across her nipples, Heather gave a start. Sparks seemed to sizzle like Chi-

nese fireworks from her head to her toes, from her
breasts to some secret, sensual place inside her. Hot.
Wild. Vibrant. An intense tremor seized her, making
her whole body tremble.

Slowly, reluctantly, Morgan eased away from her,
careful not to let his lower body make contact with
hers, lest she know the full effect her nearness had on
him, sure that so soon after the attack, the feel of his
swollen manhood, straining insistently against the
front of his trousers, would frighten her. His lips released hers with reluctance, their only remaining contact that of his hands on her shoulders, aiding the
support of her weak, shaken limbs.

His gaze sought hers. Her eyes were wide and
misty, somewhat unfocused, revealing confusion but
not true alarm. Her lips were slightly parted, puffed
and pink. Her cheeks were rosy. Her hair was
mussed. Everything about her bespoke a woman who
had been thoroughly kissed—and was amazed by her
own awakened desires.

"I think we'd better call a halt while we still can,"
Morgan suggested on a husky note. "You're mighty
potent temptation, darlin'. Enough to make me keep
forgetting that you're engaged to someone else."

Heather nodded, trying to sort through the myriad
emotions in which she was still enmeshed. Shock. Desire. Wonder. All this, and now shame as Morgan's
words registered in her beleaguered brain. How could
she have forgotten about Lyle, even for a moment?
How could she have given herself into Morgan's embrace, his kiss, and not allotted a single, solitary
thought to the man who was awaiting her return to
Boston? What kind of fickle female was she, to behave
so erratically? To promise herself to one man, only to
covet another so quickly and intensely?

"You . . . you're quite correct," she stammered. "I'm
sorry. I don't know what came over me. If you'll excuse me, I think I'll go to my room."

As she stepped away and turned toward the door,
Morgan reached out and stopped her. "I think we've

determined that you won't have a problem over-coming any lingering fears of intimacy. That, if you recall, was the main thrust of this . . . discussion."

Heather resorted to arrogance to cover her humili-ation. "I suppose you expect me to thank you?" she asked haughtily.

He laughed. "I think you already have, princess. But if you have any further doubts or questions, I'll be glad to repeat the experiment any time you wish. Meanwhile, should you need to discuss problems or queries of a more involved or delicate nature pertain-ing to physical coupling, perhaps you'd feel more at ease consulting the girls. They're bound to be a good source of information, and not shy about sharing it."

"I'll keep that in mind."

"Do that, Boston. For all their faults, I'd trust any of them to be honest with you about the subject."

Just to be sure, Morgan fully intended to speak with the girls before Heather did, advising them to stress the positive aspects of lovemaking and downplay the bad. He didn't want to leave anything to chance, or to inadvertently foster Heather's fears anew. The whole idea was to relieve her anxiety, to undo any harm and doubts Arlene Clancy had inspired—which just might keep him from wringing the widow's neck!

After that disturbing interlude with Morgan in her father's office, Heather discovered, much to her con-fusion and dismay, that she was ten times as aware of him as she'd been before. Despite all conscious ef-forts to curb her growing interest, and repeatedly re-minding herself that Lyle Asher was the man she was going to marry, Heather's senses now seemed so finely tuned to Morgan that he had only to enter the room and she was instantly alert to his presence. Her skin would begin to tingle and flush, her heart to flut-ter, her breasts and stomach to tighten in acute reac-tion.

Her eyes were constantly drawn to him. Many were the times he caught her staring intently at him, which generally earned her a knowing grin, as if he were reading her lustful thoughts. Embarrassing as this was, she could not keep her gaze from straying to his lips, his hands, his broad shoulders. Lord help her, she even found herself eyeing his trim behind! No matter how hard she tried not to be, she was totally fascinated with the handsome rogue, who took unfair advantage and teased her incessantly.

"You've got to stop making calf eyes at me, darlin'," he warned, tongue in cheek. "Folks are beginning to notice, and my virtuous reputation is in question."

"Oh, go suck an egg, you conceited oaf!"

"I'd rather suckle sweeter fare, if you've a mind to oblige me," he challenged, ogling her bosom.

"Try an orange," she suggested dryly, "if you can find one in this primitive place. I've noticed that the selection of fresh fruits is distinctly limited around here, followed closely by the slim variety of meats offered at each meal. Pork and beef, primarily bacon and steak and stew, all inevitably accompanied by beans and potatoes . . . boiled, fried, or otherwise mutilated. Haven't these people ever heard of lamb and rice?"

He laughed. "You're smack in the middle of cattle country, Boston, where 'sheep' is a dirty word. Besides, I happen to know you had fried chicken for supper last night, and if you'd try venison, you might find it to your liking."

"I think not," she told him, wrinkling her nose in distaste. "But if a lime or an olive should cross my path, or a plump, juicy shrimp or lobster, I'd probably pounce on it like a starving maniac."

"Sorry, princess, but there are no shrimp or lobsters to be found in a freshwater river. The best you can hope for is a nice bass or trout, I'm afraid."

"Even that would be a welcome change," she bemoaned. "Or clam chowder or mushroom soup for luncheon; and for breakfast, scones and marmalade, with fresh melon slices, and a cup of frothy hot chocolate."

"Sounds good, but as the saying goes, 'When in Rome' . . ."

She sighed dispiritedly. "Then it's fortunate that I won't be stuck in 'Rome' much longer, isn't it?"

❧ 14 ❧

Much as Morgan had supposed, most of the townspeople seemed willing to accept on faith Heather's account of what had happened the night of the attack. Only a few ladies shunned her openly. Most went out of their way to lend their support, especially the dozen members of the Temperance Society. Many expressed frank dismay and regret that Dodge had not yet progressed into a civilized state of law and order, in which a lady could safely traverse the streets without fear of being assaulted by some randy drunkard. To their ire, Heather was not the first innocent victim to be accosted, nor would she be the last, despite attempts and promises from a long line of mayors, sheriffs, marshals, and governors.

While Heather was treated with continued respect and cordiality by most folks, opinion was more split when it came to Morgan. Part of the population still viewed him as a criminal who deserved worse than he was presently receiving in the way of punishment. Since he'd saved Heather, he was lauded as a hero by some people who were willing to give him the benefit of the doubt and concede that perhaps he wasn't the blackguard they'd thought. A smaller portion of the townspeople were reserving judgment.

In any case, many of the patrons of Gus's Gurdy now held Morgan in wary regard for an altogether different reason. He was well on his way to becoming renowned for his ability with a bullwhip. While others might be skilled with a gun or knife, Morgan was amazingly proficient with the lash, as many a hapless fellow could readily testify. Since the night of Heather's attack, when he'd faced her two assailants unarmed, Morgan was never without that whip. He wore it attached to a hook on his belt, always accessible when he needed it.

One evening in the saloon, a cardsharp was accused of cheating at poker. A particularly disgruntled player at the table stood up, whipped a previously concealed pistol from beneath his coat, and threatened to shoot the gambler on the spot. Aware of the pending danger, other patrons immediately backed off, not wanting to become involved in a shoot-out in such close quarters, where a wild shot or a ricochet might kill anyone. Morgan calmly unhooked his whip from his belt, waited for precisely the right moment, and lashed out. The whip snaked around the fellow's gun, wrenching it from his grip without ever touching the man's hand. The gunman was stunned, as was everyone else who witnessed the feat.

Another night, Morgan dislodged a man's hat, exposing him as a cheat when several secreted cards fell from their hiding place in the fellow's hat. He then had to curb the resulting fracas. On still another occasion, a drunk was giving one of the girls a hard time, trying to force her upstairs with him. Aware that Joy was not in agreement with this arrangement, Morgan employed his whip as a lasso of sorts, literally jerking the man away from Joy and off his feet. Wisely, the fellow sobered enough to seek his amusements elsewhere. At various other times Morgan quickly broke up brawls, discouraged unruly behavior, and swiftly convinced belligerent drunks to leave. Gus was highly pleased with his newest employee's skill at keeping peace in the bar.

Meanwhile, Morgan was making less headway in his attempt to discover who or where the real bandits might be. Drake was making the rounds of nearby towns, trying to gather information in the surrounding area, with no better success. So far, they'd found no one who was suddenly spending money to excess, or had come into an abrupt unexplainable inheritance, or was bragging about how cleverly he'd duped the law. From all appearances, the robbers and the money had disappeared into thin air.

Although Heather met with no further mishaps of deliberate violence in the days immediately following the attack, she did experience several episodes of clumsiness and bad luck, which Morgan by now assumed was virtually normal for her. For a man not previously prone to superstition, just being in her company made him feel as if he were waiting for the other shoe to drop.

First, she slipped on a glob of face cream on her bedroom floor, nearly falling through a glass windowpane before she caught herself on the framework and saved herself a two-story plummet straight down. Heather swore the cream had not been there before. Moreover, the slick mass was nowhere near her dressing table, but beneath a small rug under one of her side windows facing the alley. The rug was curiously out of place, too, she claimed. It usually lay right beside the bed.

Two days later, she almost swallowed a jagged piece of glass floating unseen in her mug of ginger beer. Several more slivers were discovered in the bottom of the glass. No one had the foggiest notion how they had come to be there, and Morgan was positive they'd not been in the mug when he'd poured the beverage for her. Luckily, she'd barely nicked her tongue, suffering no serious injuries, such as she would certainly have done if she'd actually swallowed the sharp chips.

Next, as if to continue her streak of misfortune, she suffered a dire reaction to some nut bread she ate one morning. Within minutes after consuming the bread, Heather began to break out in huge, itchy welts. Her face and limbs began to swell. In scarcely a quarter hour, her eyes were mere slits, and she was gasping for breath.

"Get the doctor!" Morgan ordered Bob. "Hurry!"

By the time Morgan and Gus got her upstairs to bed and loosened the collar of her blouse, Heather's tongue had expanded to twice its normal size and her throat was nearly swollen shut. Jasmine came running into the room with a length of narrow rubber tubing used for siphoning beer from one vat to another. "Here. Ram this down her throat if ya have to in order to let her breathe."

"Do it, Morgan," Gus commanded. "I'll hold her mouth open and tilt her head back while ye shove it doon."

Heather's face was already turning blue by the time Morgan managed to get the tubing halfway down her throat and give her some small relief. Fortunately, the doctor arrived shortly thereafter, applauding their ingenuity as he set about diagnosing his patient. Some twelve hours later, the physician gave Heather a final dose of medication to further reduce her internal swelling, and finally deemed it safe to seek his own bed.

"She came very close to dying," he informed them somberly. "However, she's responding to treatment nicely now. I expect she'll be just fine, given a couple of days to rest and recuperate. A soda bath will help ease the itching, even if you just sponge it over her. Give her plenty of liquids. Puddings and soups should be soothing to her throat."

By the next morning, Heather could speak in a hoarse voice. "That nut bread we all ate," she rasped. "Was it made with sweet potatoes?"

Gus frowned. "I dinna know, lass. What difference does it make?"

"I've had a severe intolerance to sweet potatoes since I was a little child. I don't dare eat them."

Strangely enough, no one seemed to remember how the two freshly baked loaves had come to be in the saloon. Nobody acknowledged buying, baking, or delivering them, or seeing anyone else do so.

"I dinna recall that they were there when I first came down and unlocked the back door," Gus said.

"Well, I was the second person up and dressed that morning, and those loaves were sitting right on top of the bar, still steaming hot, when I got there," Morgan said.

The appearance of the nut bread, and the identity of its donor, remained a mystery—and from then on, Heather was very cautious about what she ate or drank.

With Heather's scheduled visit nearly at an end, Gus decided to show her his ranch. Though he doubted it would impress her much, it would surely be less disastrous than her time in town had proved to be thus far. Perhaps she would experience fewer calamities and she could return to Boston with a few nice memories of him and the area. Of course, Gus was nearly ecstatic that Heather had deigned to call him Father, which she'd first done unconsciously but now did deliberately, more and more frequently. He walked around as if to burst his buttons, he was so proud.

Gus wanted his daughter to remember him fondly, which was why he decided it would be better if Arlene Clancy did not go along with them to the ranch. Though mutually polite, the two women showed no signs of forming a close friendship. Rather, they seemed to merely tolerate one another.

Gus invited Morgan to accompany them instead. Heather wasn't abundantly thrilled with that idea, but Gus wasn't confident enough in his new role as Heather's father to feel comfortable without a third party along to help ease the strain of keeping the conversation flowing.

And Morgan was especially good at that. With just a word, it seemed, he could set fire to Heather's temper. He teased, he taunted, he tormented Heather to her wits' end. It was vastly amusing to Gus to watch those two light into each other. In fact, people had started coming into the bar just to see the sparks fly between them, as if it were some sort of comic entertainment Gus was providing his customers these days.

They started out early in the morning for the hour's ride to the ranch. Gus had his own horse stabled at the livery, where they rented two more for Morgan and Heather. Since they planned to be back in town in time for a late supper, they packed only enough food for lunch.

Morgan started out by teasing Heather about her riding abilities. "Hellfire, woman! You look like a nervous hen perched on a wobbly nest! As graceful as you are, you're gonna topple off that sidesaddle onto your nose before we hit the town limits. If I'd guessed you weren't going to ride astride, I'd have taken bets on how long you'd last up there, and probably won myself a bundle of cash."

"Just how many ladies do you know who ride astride?" she countered. "Or do you know any ladies besides me?"

"As a matter of fact, I do. But not around here."

"Where?"

"Mostly in San Francisco."

Heather thought about that. "Why there?"

It was on the tip of Morgan's tongue to say that was where Wells Fargo had their main headquarters. He caught himself in time and fabricated a reply. "Uh, that's where the shoe company I work for is located."

"That reminds me, I have yet to see any of those shoes you supposedly sell," she commented. "Don't you carry a sample case or something?"

Morgan caught Gus's half-amused look, which clearly said he was on his own now and would get no help from Gus. "I . . . well, I did, but I haven't seen it since the train robbery. I can only surmise it was stolen."

An incredulous expression came over Heather's face. She started to laugh. "Gosh, imagine thieves

who steal shoes! That should make them fairly easy
to spot, don't you think? Several men who are the
proud owners of new shoes that don't fit quite right?
We must tell the sheriff to be on the lookout for fellows hobbling about in the latest of fashionable footwear and the newest of blisters!"

"Very funny, Boston. Speaking of which," Morgan
added in a goading tone, "did you have your little
conversation with the girls?"

Heather glared at him. "You know darned good
and well I did! You set me up for it. Before the day
was out, each and every one of them had stopped by
my room for a girl-to-girl chat."

"I hope you found it informative," he taunted, his
mustache twitching in amusement.

"My goodness, yes!" she enthused with a sly smile.
"You'll just never know how enlightening it was."

For the rest of the ride, Morgan wondered to himself just what Heather had learned from those female
gab sessions—and how he might convince Heather to
reveal some of the more novel ideas the women had
shared with her.

An old farmhouse and its assorted outbuildings
stood in the center of Gus's property, surrounded by
acres of grassland. Though she'd been warned of its
run-down condition, Heather was appalled at the di-
lapidated state. Each building looked worse than the
next. The house, a small two-story structure of
weather-beaten wood, was in major need of repair.
Windows were broken and boarded over to keep out
the elements, not to mention whatever snakes or ro-
dents might decide to invite themselves inside. The
small front porch was on a definite slant. Half the
shingles on the roof were missing. The floors were so
warped, they resembled waves on the high seas, and
the walls were molding in those places where the
paint and wallpaper had chipped off. Even the old
outhouse stood at a forty-five-degree tilt. All in all, it
was not the most attractive abode.

As if he were seeing it for the first time through Heather's eyes, Gus grimaced and gave an apologetic shrug. "Na Buckingham Palace by any stretch, but I've plenty o' time to fix the place up, and lumber's a mite easier to come by these days, wi' the railroad and all. Back when this place was first built, it came dear, which is why the barn is built half belowground."

Heather had wondered why the building looked so odd. Not that she'd seen all that many barns before, but she'd assumed they usually had four walls. This one had a front, with a wide door, and parts of two short sides which slanted downward, disappearing into a small hillock.

"That makes sense, I suppose," she allowed.

Morgan nodded. "Especially around these parts, where storms can kick up all of a sudden, with nothing to stop the wind."

Just then, a short, rotund man of Mexican descent strolled out of the barn.

"Oh, there ye are, Pedro," Gus called out. "C'mon o'er here and meet my daughter and my new bartender."

As Pedro approached, Gus said, "Pedro watches the place for me and tends to the livestock while I'm in town. He's a fair cook, too, if ye dinna mind settin' yer tonsils afire. He's right fond o' those chili peppers."

Pedro seemed a pleasant sort, though Heather had to wonder how he and her father had ever managed to form an alliance considering Gus's convoluted Scots-western accent and Pedro's broken, Spanish-sprinkled speech. It was a miracle either of them could understand a word the other uttered.

"I glad you come, señor," Pedro told Gus. "Some *cucaracha* cut de fence and we got *tres caballos* out."

"Where?"

"De *norte* pasture. I was jus' gonna try roundin' 'em up, *pero es muy difícil* by myself."

"What did he say?" Heather whispered to Morgan.

"That some cockroach cut the north pasture fence

and three horses are loose, and he's glad your father is here because it's difficult to round them up by himself," Morgan interpreted.

"Oh." She eyed him askance. "I didn't know you spoke Spanish. Isn't that a little unusual for a shoe salesman from San Francisco?"

"Not when you consider that San Francisco was founded by the Spanish. And there's a lot more you don't know about me, princess." He added with a roguish wink, "If you'd like to get better acquainted, I'd be glad to oblige."

"Gee, thanks, but I think I'll decline that offer."

"Well, dumplin', it's your loss."

"I'll live, I'm sure."

A short while later, Heather went along as an interested spectator while Pedro, Gus, and Morgan rounded up the stray horses and drove them back into the pasture. Then she watched the three men mend the cut in the fence. Afterward, Pedro returned to the ranch, while Gus gave Heather and Morgan a quick tour of his land, pointing out the cattle grazing on the open prairie.

"Only the horses are kept fenced," he explained. "O' course, the time's comin' when I'll have to fence the cattle in, too. The farmers hereabouts are havin' fits, claimin' the loose livestock are ruinin' their crops and gardens. Wi' all the fencin' nowadays, 'twon't be long b'fore the open range and the cattle drives are a thing o' the past. Then I imagine Dodge will just dry up and blow away, like all the other cow towns. Don't see how it can survive wi'out the money we make from the drovers."

It was long past noon, and Heather was looking forward to lunch by the time they headed back toward the ranch house. Her stomach wasn't the only part of her anatomy that was starting to claim her attention. Her bottom was also complaining after so many hours in the saddle. She highly suspected she'd be making good use of that brass tub this evening.

With her thoughts thus occupied, it took her some

time to notice that the wind had picked up and a mass of black clouds was gathering to the southwest, gradually darkening the day.

"I hope we make it back before it starts to rain," she said.

"Don't bet on it, sugar," Morgan advised her. "That looks like one helluva storm brewing."

"Ayc," Gus agreed. "Could be we'll be spendin' the night at the ranch and eatin' Pedro's cookin' after all."

They kicked their mounts into a gallop, but Heather soon found herself lagging behind. She simply couldn't keep the pace, and her seat, riding sidesaddle. Finally Morgan noticed that he and Gus were outdistancing her. He turned back and rode to her side.

"Here," he said, reaching out to grab her by the waist and haul her off her horse onto his. He seated her before him, and wrapped one arm securely around her. Grinning, he drawled into her ear, "Hold on, Boston. You're in for the ride of your life."

❧ 15 ❧

The first fat drops of rain were pelting the ground as they raced into the barnyard. Gus held the barn door open for them, then slammed it shut behind them. "The two o' ye tend to yer horses and stay dry. I'll hie up to the house and tell Pedro to make a big pot o' his special firebrand chili. That'll warm ye up some, I reckon."

"Right," Morgan replied. "We'll join you as soon as the rain lets up a bit. No sense in Heather getting soaked. She'd probably look like a drowned rat and scare poor Pedro to death before he could get supper ready. And frankly, I'm too hungry to risk it."

Chuckling to himself, Gus dashed out into what had become a virtual downpour that was rapidly turning the barnyard into a sea of mire. As lightning speared the heavens, followed a scant second later by a loud rumbling of thunder, Heather winced. "Lord, I hope he doesn't get hit by lightning. He should have stayed here with us until this storm settles down some."

By the time they'd unsaddled their horses and wiped them down, the storm had intensified to one of alarming severity. The big wooden doors were heaving in and out, their hinges squeaking a high pitch that grated on the ears. The rain poured down in torrents, hammering on the wooden portion of the roof. Then an even more ominous pounding began.

"What's that?" Heather asked, her voice raised to carry over the din of the storm and the horses stomping and whinnying nervously in their stalls.

Morgan peered out through the slats in the door. "Hail," he informed her with a frown. "I don't like the looks of this. You get back into the far section, while I move the horses to the rear stalls where it's more sheltered."

"I'll help you," she offered.

"No. These animals are getting more fractious by the moment. Just do as I tell you, and let me tend to them."

It took several long minutes for Morgan to relocate the skittish horses back into the part of the barn built into the ground. There, the earth overhead muted the sounds of the storm and the beasts calmed somewhat.

"We'll be safer here, too," Morgan said, his mouth drawn into a tight, worried line. "They say animals have better instincts than people do. In this case, it wouldn't surprise me to find that's true."

Heather gave a jerky nod, her gaze on the front part of the barn, where the board walls were quaking ominously with the force of the wind. "Don't you think it's queer, the way the light has changed? It has a strange cast to it."

She was right. The forward section of the barn, where light and rain filtered in from broken slats and holes in the roof, was now bathed in an eerie yellowish gray hue. "I'm going up to take a look. You stay right here," Morgan instructed.

He came back at a full run. "Holy thunder! The way those clouds are whipping around, I bet we're in for one of Kansas's infamous twisters."

"Twister?" she repeated, her eyes going wide at his obvious alarm.

"A tornado," he told her bluntly.

"Oh, my stars!" she exclaimed, her anxiety growing. "Those are supposed to be terribly dangerous, aren't they? We're not prone to them back home, but

I've heard they can be devastating. Even deadly!" Her voice was shrill with growing panic.

Morgan sat down beside her and drew her into the comfort of his arms. "Hey! Don't get all upset, now. We're probably safer here than we would be anywhere."

"But what about Gus? And Pedro?"

Morgan shook his head. "I suppose they've taken shelter of their own somewhere. Maybe there's a root cellar or something below the house."

"I hope so," she said, cuddling closer to him. The whine of the wind rose to frightening heights, screeching a ghostly tune that sent gooseflesh skittering along her arms and shaking the thick roof rafters along the front of the barn as if they were twigs. Thunder resounded furiously. Lightning lit the interior of the barn with a blinding glare.

Heather gave a squeal of fright, turning more fully in to Morgan's embrace, half burying her face in his broad chest. "Oh, Morgan! Hold me! I'm so afraid! Are we going to die?"

"I sincerely hope not, darlin'," he said, tightening his clasp on her. "Though I can't think of a better way to go than with you in my arms." His fingers tilted her face to his. "Still, I'd hate to depart this earth without first savoring your intriguing delights. It just wouldn't seem fair somehow, as if my life were ending on an unfinished note."

She stared into his mesmerizing gaze. "I know," she murmured. "Oh, kiss me, Morgan. Please. Hold me close and don't let go."

Morgan was glad to oblige. His mouth swept down to cover hers, his kiss hot and urgent. Their lips melded, their breath mingling. At his silent entreaty, her lips parted willingly, eagerly receptive to his invading tongue, her own meeting it in an ardent duel.

There was a loud roaring in her ears, but whether it was the sound of the storm or her own blood rushing to her head, Heather couldn't tell. Neither did she care, for Morgan's hands were stroking her, running a mad course from her head to her heels, sending fiery shivers all along their path. The tips of his fingers brushed fleetingly across her breasts. Her muffled moan was lost in the depth of his mouth.

His lips abandoned hers to dash avid kisses over her face and throat. He caught her earlobe between sharp teeth, nipping lightly, his breath warm and uneven, catching her up in a wild shudder. His tongue dipped inside, painting the small shell with sultry heat.

"God help me, but I want you, Heather," he murmured. "More than my next breath. More than I've ever desired anything. Tell me you want me, too."

"Yes," she hissed, her mouth seeking his.

His mouth seized hers again. Possessively. Commandingly. His hands resumed their exploration of her with renewed determination and daring, boldly staking claim to her breasts and their high, pointed crests. Lightning sizzled through her, leaving her weak and wanting. She shifted impatiently, seeking . . . something she could not define.

"All right, darlin'," he crooned, scooping her up in his arms and carrying her to an empty stall nearby. "I know, sweetheart. I know."

He lowered her onto the fresh bed of straw, his body following hers. Her arms reached out to him, her mouth blindly searching for his, feeling strangely incomplete without the bond he'd created with his warmth and strength. Now it was her lips that came up to capture his, her tongue delving brazenly into the sweet, dark cavern of his mouth. Tasting. Teasing. Exciting him beyond measure, until he, too, trembled with desire.

Her senses awash with the scent, the flavor, the fire of him, Heather was scarcely aware that he'd undone the buttons of her blouse, peeling the panels aside to reveal her scantily clad bosom to his greedy gaze. For comfort's sake, in anticipation of the long ride to the ranch, she'd forgone wearing her corset, opting for the less restrictive cover of a simple chemise. Now this single lace-edged garment was all that shielded her breasts from his view. And that not for long.

As Morgan tugged the thin straps from her shoulders, drawing the cotton top downward, Heather gave a halfhearted whimper of resistance, her hands coming up in a timid attempt to conceal her half-exposed torso.

"No. Don't hide from me," Morgan murmured enticingly. "Don't be shy. Let me see you, love. Let me touch you."

As if under a sorcerer's spell, she acquiesced, yielding to his gentle coaxing. His hands, warm and slightly callused, cradled her breasts, holding them in his palms as though they were the rarest of jewels. His turquoise eyes gleamed brightly with undisguised hunger as his thumbs grazed lightly over her raised nipples. She shivered with delight and the sharp shaft of longing that shot through her at his touch, a low mew issuing from her throat.

"You're so beautiful. All soft and smooth. Your breasts make me think of two tempting mounds of vanilla ice cream topped with the most delectable strawberries. I can't wait to taste them, to wrap my tongue around them and draw their sweetness into my mouth."

His dark head lowered, his mustache tickling over her sensitized flesh as his mouth sought its target. His lips closed moistly over one pert peak. His tongue flicked at it in sensual strokes, and Heather felt her insides melting, simmering, bubbling to a boil. He suckled deeply, and that secret, hidden place between her legs went hot and damp—pulsing with an insistent ache. She moaned aloud, her hands rising instinctively to clasp his head to her breast and hold it there, unconsciously seeking more of the delicious delights he was bestowing upon her.

His hand stroked her hip and thigh in a hypnotic rhythm, lulling her into acceptance of this newest advance before straying lower, where his fingers snagged the hem of her skirt and dragged it toward her waist. His hand slipped under the cloth, fondling her leg in long, sleek motions, inching higher and higher, curving around her upper leg to ease her thighs apart.

"Morgan?" she questioned in a quavering voice.

"Let me touch you, sweetheart. I can make you feel so good, love. So very good."

As he spoke, he loosened the ties of her underdrawers and, with one smooth tug, pulled them off. Before she had time to object, he was kissing her again, one hand kneading her breast, the other intimately cupping her mound, his nimble fingers delving through the sheltering down to caress the soft, velvety cleft hidden there. The heel of his hand rubbed teasingly against the small, sensitive bud that formed the core of her feminine passions. Heather jerked wildly, drawing in a sharp gasp.

"Easy love," he breathed. "There's more. Much more. And it gets better and better. I promise."

With the tip of his finger, he tested her portal, pleased to find her moist there. Slowly, taking care not to startle her, he eased his finger inside the sleek passage. His own body tightened all the more painfully in response to the snug, hot feel of her. A tortured groan escaped his lips. When she arched slightly upward, he nearly died wanting to be inside her, but he forced himself to wait, to prepare her fully for him.

As his fingers stroked and prodded and stretched her, Heather was staggered by the sensations assaulting her. It seemed that every nerve in her body was centered where he was touching her. Her mouth, her breasts, between her legs. And everywhere he touched tingled with ever-growing flames that licked greedily at her aroused flesh. Jagged spears of desire streaked through her, leaving her dazed and yearning for more.

She reached out, stroking his broad shoulders, his chest, her fingers fumbling with the buttons of his shirt until, in acute frustration, she yanked it open, sending several buttons popping. She ran her palms lovingly over his chest, delighted by the soft, springy mat of dark hair growing there. Tugging lightly on it, she urged him down, until the tips of her breasts were nestled in the dense fleece. The delicate scrape against her supremely sensitized breasts titillated in the extreme.

At last, when he could bear the exquisite torment no longer, Morgan unfastened his trousers and mounted her. Honor bade him give her one last chance to preserve her virtue, even as he implored her not to accept his gracious offer. "I beg you not to ask me to stop now, Heather. But I will, if you insist."

"No," she whispered breathlessly. "This might be all I ever grasp of such glorious earthly passion, and I want to know it all."

Her reply stunned him, striking deep into his heart. With their limbs entwined, and their lips clinging in fervent desire, he surged into her, piercing the membrane that guarded her virginity. At her startled gasp, he paused, his blood pulsing, his body screaming with the urge to bury himself deeper within her. Still, he denied himself that pleasure until he felt her quivering muscles relax as her untried passage gradually accepted his intrusion. Only then did he thrust more fully inside her warm, wet chamber.

After that first slight twinge, there was no pain, just the strange sensation of her inner body expanding to admit his. Heather had never felt anything to compare, could never have imagined what such intimacy would be like. To feel him deep inside her, to know that a part of him was gloved within her feminine embrace. Filling. Stretching. Caressing. Touching her in the most profound and wondrous way.

He moved within her, and a wave of sensation radiated outward from the center of her being. Tentatively, instinctively, she began to move with him, arching upward to meet his thrusts and match them with her own. His lips left hers, to murmur words of praise and encouragement in her ear. And all the while he filled her, stroked her body with his, plunging deeper. Faster. Until her head was spinning with a kaleidoscope of colors, and her body seemed to tighten, to gather itself for some momentous occurrence. Her breath came harder, her pulse throbbing to an ancient drumbeat.

Then it happened. A magnificent explosion, within and without, hurtling her spirit heavenward amid a swirl of wind and stars. Every part of her seemed to quake and quiver with the power of it. Brilliance blinded her. The force and splendor of it stole her breath away. And most fantastic of all, Morgan was right there with her. All the way. His cry of ecstasy blending with hers. His arms enfolding her with tender strength, cradling her gently as they descended slowly from the heights of passion to the realm of reality once more.

Awed and breathless, Heather lay beneath him in stunned disbelief. "Goodness gracious sakes alive!" she exclaimed softly.

Above her, braced on his elbows and gazing down at her amazed expression, Morgan chuckled. "You can say that again, darlin'. I can safely say I've never before experienced anything as incredibly marvelous as that."

"Did the earth really move?" she inquired tremulously. "I mean, I've read of such things, in bits of poetry and an occasional romance novel, but I always thought it was fanciful nonsense. I didn't think it could ever actually happen."

"Yeah, sweetheart. The earth really did move. In more ways than one."

❧ 16 ❧

Bestowing one last kiss on Heather's lips, Morgan levered himself off her and cast a cautious look about the barn. "Better get dressed, princess," he advised solemnly. "It looks like we've got some serious work ahead of us."

His abruptly somber mood alerted her. Suddenly she, too, became aware of the changes that had occurred around them while she and Morgan had been so blissfully occupied, oblivious to everything but each other. One look, and she stared in horror. The rear portion of the barn, the part underground, was relatively intact—the stalls still standing, the horses unharmed, though they were still rolling their eyes and behaving jittery. But the front section was . . . gone! Completely demolished. Not a wall was left standing. Or the doors, or the roof. Rain poured down on a gnarled stack of huge beams and planks and bales of hay, which were strewn about in a sodden heap, like toys carelessly broken and tossed aside by some giant, petulant child.

Heather stared at the massive destruction, her mind boggled by it. Automatically, as if in a trance, her hands took up the motions of pulling her chemise and blouse back up, of retrieving her drawers and pulling them on, of straightening her clothing and her tumbled hair. Beside her, Morgan did likewise.

Tucking his buttonless shirt back into his trousers,

he gazed bleakly at the ruined remains of the barn, much of it now blocking their exit. "You sit tight, Boston. I need to find us a safe route through this mess."

"Wait!" she cried, reaching for him. "It's still raining. Is it wise to go out? Are you sure it's over?"

He nodded. "I'd guess the worst of the storm has passed."

She stood and watched anxiously as Morgan picked his way through the tangled mass—shifting debris aside, moving twisted sections of lumber, shoving cautiously at timbers, burrowing through the wreckage. Gradually he worked his way toward the entrance and out of sight. It seemed to take forever before he returned to her side.

"That's the best I can do for now," he told her, wiping his dirt-streaked face on a torn shirtsleeve. "I'm going to lead the way. Hold on to my belt, and try not to bump into anything. God knows, this pile of rubble is settled precariously enough, without you sending it tumbling onto our heads. Watch your step. There are splinters as long as your arm, and nails scattered underfoot."

That was the least of it, Heather discovered, as she tucked her skirts close and climbed gingerly over mounds of posts and planks, snagging her hair and clothes as they traversed the hazardous maze he'd uncovered. At one point they had to crawl on their stomachs, through a tunnel of debris, taking care not to dislodge it atop themselves. Finally, after what seemed three lifetimes, they emerged into the open.

The rain had dwindled to a heavy drizzle. To the west, the clouds were beginning to disperse, and stray beams of sunlight were filtering through. Heather's relieved breath turned to a cry of horror as she gazed toward the house. It, too, had been reduced to a shambles, a huge, twisted pile of kindling.

"Dad!" she screamed, stumbling toward it.

Morgan blocked her path, concern clouding his face. "Let me take a look first, Heather."

Shaking fingers clutched his arm. "Find him, Morgan. Please." Then, her wobbly legs refusing to support her a second longer, she sank to the muddy ground in a sobbing heap.

He found Pedro first. The wiry little Mexican was half-buried under the heavy kitchen table. A large section of roof and wall had collapsed around it, trapping him there. Miraculously, the sturdy table had held, and Pedro, shouting a stream of rapid Spanish, was alive and relatively unscathed.

Once freed, Pedro aided Morgan in the search for Gus. Though they called for him, and strained for even the faintest reply, there came no response. They continued, stepping carefully, sifting through the rubble as quickly and cautiously as they could.

At last Pedro spotted one burly arm sticking out from beneath a fallen jumble of brick that used to be the parlor fireplace. The rest of his body was hidden.

"Ayiii!" Pedro wailed. "*Dios mío*! Poor Señor Gus!"

"Stop that yelling and help me get these bricks off of him," Morgan ordered grimly. "We've got to see if he's still alive."

"I no think so, señor."

"Well, we can't just leave him here and not check."

It took them a quarter of an hour to dig Gus out from beneath the heap of bricks. In all that time, Gus neither moved nor made a sound as they uncovered his battered, bloody body. Morgan was beginning to think Pedro was right. Poor Gus was probably trying on his halo at this very minute. Heather would be devastated.

Finally they dragged him free and Morgan gently turned him onto his back. With little hope, he placed his fingers alongside Gus's neck, feeling for a pulse. To his surprise and relief, he found one. It was weak and thready, but there. "He's alive," he told the anxious Pedro. "I don't know for how long, but he's alive for now at least. Go get Heather. Warn her, though, that her father is not a pretty sight. It's going to be a shock for her to see him like this."

Pedro ran to get her. Heather took one look at Gus

and threw herself to the floor at his side. "Oh, Daddy!" she cried softly, touching his scraped, dirty cheek. "Daddy, please don't die!" Tears streamed unheeded down her face.

"We've got to get him to town to the doctor," Morgan told her. "I can't tell the seriousness of his injuries, but I imagine they're fairly bad. I know his left leg is broken, and God knows what else."

"How?" Heather asked bleakly. "The horses are trapped in their stalls. We could barely crawl out of the barn."

"Pedro and I will get them out. Or we'll round up a couple of quarter horses from the pasture, if they're still there, and hitch them to the wagon if we have to. They're probably not used to hauling wagons, but we'll get by with them."

"If there is a wagon, and it's still in one piece," she reminded him.

Pedro found a couple of blankets, and using them as a stretcher, they carried Gus out of the tumbled house. Oddly, the rickety front porch was still intact, and they laid him there.

"Stay with him, Heather. Tear off a strip of your petticoat and see if you can clean him up some, maybe get that gash on his head to stop bleeding. Pedro and I will go see about the wagon and the horses."

"Hurry, Morgan. Please," she pleaded.

Between them, Morgan and Pedro managed to clear a path through the ruined barn and let the horses out of their stalls. The wagon was another story altogether. It was gone. Nowhere to be seen in the barnyard, though Pedro swore it had been sitting right beside the old chicken coop. For that matter, the chicken coop had disappeared as well, with not a splinter left to indicate it had ever stood there. Yet contrarily, a scant twelve feet away, the old outhouse, flimsy though it was, remained upright and untouched.

Puzzled and frustrated, Morgan tried to form an alternate plan. "I suppose we could rig up a travois," he said. "Maybe tie the blankets to a couple of pieces of wood."

"Wait, señor!" Pedro exclaimed. "Look! Look!"

Morgan stared in the direction Pedro was pointing. His eyes widened in disbelief. There, smack in the middle of the pasture, stood the old chicken coop, from all indications in one piece, with nary a nail out of place. Perched on top of its tin roof was the wagon, which appeared to be in equally good condition.

"I'll be double-damned!" Morgan declared on an awed whistle. "If that isn't the queerest thing I've ever seen!"

"Me, too!" Pedro avowed, hastily crossing himself.

Though it was an awkward, backbreaking process, Morgan and Pedro managed to tie ropes around the wagon and lower it to the ground. From the underground section of the barn they retrieved sufficient tack to harness a pair of horses to it, and enough dry straw to pad the wagon bed. As carefully as they could, they loaded Gus aboard. Heather crawled in next to her father, cradling his head in her lap. Morgan hopped aboard the driver's seat and took up the reins.

"You sure you don't want to come along, Pedro?" he asked one last time.

Pedro shook his head. "*Gracias*, no. I stay here and tend to the animals for Señor Gus. You take him to town quick, now. Not to worry about Pedro. I be okay."

"I'll send back a couple of men with supplies to help you," Morgan promised. "I just hope to God Dodge is still standing."

Though they tried to hurry, they were forced to a sedate pace out of consideration for Gus's injuries. It was dark by the time they finally reached the outskirts of Dodge City. From all indications, the town had not suffered the same fate as Gus's ranch. All the buildings were still standing, and business was brisk in the saloons along Front Street. As Morgan drew the wagon to a halt outside the Gurdy and yelled for Bob and Lloyd, he could only conclude that the tornado had bypassed the town.

Morgan immediately took charge, spouting orders like an army sergeant. For the moment, at least, and considering the gravity of the situation, no one questioned his authority. Within minutes, Gus was ensconced in bed with Doc Jenkins at his side. Morgan took up a stance at the opposite side, ready to issue more directives according to the doctor's needs. Heather hovered near the foot of the bed like a pale wraith, her nerves stretched taut as they awaited the physician's verdict.

Jenkins completed his examination. With a sigh, he said, "I won't lie to you or make promises I can't keep. It'll be touch and go for a while, I'm afraid, and there's no guarantee Gus will pull through. He's pretty beat up, inside and out. And I don't like the fact that he hasn't regained consciousness. That's not a good sign. I'll set his leg and arm, and bind his ribs, and do what I can, but it will be mostly up to Gus and God to decide whether he lives or dies. Still, Gus is an ornery cuss, and willpower itself can do some mighty powerful healing."

The entire staff and many of the regular customers were distraught at the news. Word spread like wildfire, and soon even the street outside the saloon was crowded with folks wanting to know what had happened and how badly Gus had been injured. Naturally, Arlene Clancy soon heard and came rushing over.

Weary as he was, Morgan dispersed the curious crowd, proclaiming that the bar was closed for the evening and assuring them that any major developments would be announced in the morning. "Go home now," he told them tiredly. "Gus is resting as comfortably as possible. Doc Jenkins intends to spend the night, and Miss Blair-Burns is frantic enough without seeing all of you gathered here as if you were attending a wake for a man who isn't even dead. Please. Just go home . . . and pray."

Arlene wasn't so easily deterred. "I need to see him. He would want me to be at his side, to help look after him."

Morgan tried a diplomatic tack. "Mrs. Clancy, I know how close you and Gus are, but there's nothing you can do at the moment. Maybe you can visit with him tomorrow. Hopefully he'll be awake by then."

Arlene's chin quivered, but she stood firm. "I will not leave before I see him for myself, and hear what the doctor has to say. Rest assured that I will do nothing to disturb Angus, but I must see him. Please." Tears glittered in her gray eyes.

Faced with her sincere distress, Morgan gave in. "I don't suppose it will hurt for you to sit with him for a while, as long as Doc Jenkins doesn't object."

The events of the long, emotional day had caught up with Heather, and she was all but asleep on her feet, yet dreadfully afraid to leave her father's side, frightened that if she did so, he would awake and call for her—or worse, that he would die thinking she hadn't cared enough to stay.

"At least go eat something and tidy up," Morgan urged her gently. "It will help revive you, and Mrs. Clancy or I will call you if he stirs at all."

He led her to the door and pushed her gently toward the girls, who were gathered in the hall outside Gus's quarters. "Will one of you look after her?" he asked. "Help her get changed into something clean and comfortable. Get her some hot soup or tea."

"Sure thing, Morgan," Brandy said, hooking a sympathetic arm around Heather's waist. "Come on, sugar. Nothin' personal, honey, but you look like a horse that's been rode hard and put up wet."

Heather gave a mild start, the glazed look lifting from her eyes—momentarily replaced by a stunned, disconcerted expression. "Actually, I believe I have," she murmured enigmatically, more to herself than to anyone else.

It seemed incredible that so much had happened in a few short hours—momentous incidents that had tilted her safe, sane world on its axis, throwing her adrift in a roiling sea of emotions. Was it only this morning that she and Gus and Morgan had set out for the ranch, healthy and whole? Now her father's ranch was half-destroyed by a devastating tornado, and he lay fighting for his life. It was almost impossible to comprehend.

As was the fact that, in the midst of the storm and her fear of perishing in it, she had eagerly forfeited her virtue to a man she'd known for only a couple of weeks—had literally handed him the precious gift that should have been Lyle's to claim on their wedding night. When all was said and done, she might well wish she'd been swept away by those raging winds, rather than by her overzealous passions.

What have I done? she wondered dazedly. *How could I have behaved so impulsively? Whatever will I tell Lyle? Worse, how will I deal with Morgan after this, or face myself in the mirror with any self-respect? Oh, why was I so stupid, so utterly foolish?*

Shame threatened to overwhelm her, even as she recalled the wild elation she'd experienced in Morgan's embrace. Had anything ever felt so wondrous? So . . . right? With a memory of its own, her body tightened and tingled, yearning to recapture the splendor.

Was it only lust? she asked herself tremulously. *Or have I actually fallen in love with him? But how could I have, when I don't even like him half the time? When I can't determine who or what he truly is? On one hand, he's an accused robber, a merchant-cum-bartender, and on the other he's the white knight who saved my life and Dad's. By turns, he's arrogant, kind, aggravating, humorous, teasing, amorous. Altogether, a confusing blend of opposing qualities. Could I possibly have lost my heart to this paradoxical man?*

She had no ready answer to that question. However, in a moment of clarity, she did realize that only the crisis with Gus, following so immediately on the heels of the impetuous intimacy she and Morgan had showed, had prevented a confrontation with Morgan. In truth, it had simply delayed it, more critical matters taking temporary precedence. Sooner or later, she would have to face him, and herself, and the repercussions of their lovemaking.

But not yet, she decided shakily. *Not while I'm still so anxious over Dad and confused about my own feelings about Morgan and what we've done. I need time to think this through, to sort out my tangled emotions and make some sense of them. Perhaps if I avoid mentioning it, Morgan will do likewise. At least until I can resolve it in my mind, and in my heart.*

Angus didn't regain consciousness until early the next afternoon. Then, despite medication, he was in a great deal of pain, which almost made Heather wish he had remained unconscious, if only to offer him blessed oblivion to his numerous injuries and all the agony he was suffering.

"Oh, Daddy!" she sobbed tearfully. "Thank goodness you're awake! We've all been so dreadfully worried about you."

A ghost of a smile flittered over Gus's face. "Feels like I been stomped by a herd o' longhorns, but 'tis worth it to hear ye call me Daddy, lass. What the divil happened, anyway?"

"There was a tornado. The house blew down, and the chimney fell on you."

Angus frowned in an attempt to pull his thoughts together. "The storm. At the ranch."

"Yes."

"Are you a'right? Was anyone else hurt?"

"I'm fine, Dad. You were the only one injured. Morgan and I were in the barn, way back in the part that's underground, and Pedro hid under the kitchen table, which probably saved him. The ranch is a wreck, though. But Pedro stayed to tend the livestock, and Morgan is looking for a couple of men to help him get the place in order again. You're not to worry about a thing, except getting well."

Angus lay quietly, his eyes shut, for so long that Heather thought he'd drifted off to sleep again. Then he murmured, "Will ye stay, lass, till I'm on my feet again?"

"Of course I will," she assured him, lightly patting his bruised hand. "I'll stay as long as you need me. Between Dr. Jenkins's care and my nursing, you'll be as good as new in no time."

Gus nodded. "The saloon. I need ye to run it for me while I'm laid up."

Heather was aghast. "Gus . . . uh . . . Dad . . . don't you think that's a job better left to someone else?"

"Nae. Ye're my daughter, and I want ye to do it. B'sides, 'twill be good for ye. 'Tis high time ye learned the value o' a dollar, and how t' earn yer own way in the world, like ordinary folk."

"I really don't think this is a very good idea," she warned him. "After all, I am an upstanding member of the Temperance Society. It just wouldn't look right for me to operate a saloon, even temporarily and for a reason as good as this."

"Ah, ye disappoint me, lass." He groaned on a weary sigh. "I was hopin' I could count on ye to do this one wee thing for me, out o' the goodness o' yer heart."

Heather grimaced. "Oh, Dad! Don't! I feel bad enough already. Furthermore, I don't have the foggiest idea how to run a saloon, let alone the inclination to do so. I'd probably completely ruin your business within a week or two."

"I'm willin' to take that chance," he informed her weakly. "I'm also willin' to give ye full rein to run the place the way ye see fit."

"You are?" she inquired dubiously. Suddenly, out of nowhere, a spark of inspiration took form in her brain. "What if I decided to make a few changes? To enhance profit?"

"I'll leave that to yer own judgment, good or bad.

'Twill be worth the risk to see ye givin' it a try, workin' for yer keep for once in yer life."

"All right, Dad. I'll do it, as long as you promise not to interfere. I want to do this on my own, to try to prove to you that I can."

"One more thing, lass," he muttered, groggy now with pain, his body seeking the relief of sleep. "I canna keep an eye on Morgan, like I promised Nels I would, so I'm turnin' custody o' him o'er to yer dainty hands. He's yers to handle now."

❧ 17 ❧

"**Y**ou're *what*?" Morgan bellowed in disbelief.

Heather smiled sweetly. "I'm now your boss, Morgan. Your custodian. Your keeper. Your overseer. Your warden. Call it whatever you please, but it amounts to the same thing. While Dad is recuperating, I am in charge of both the saloon and of you."

"Oh, no! There is no way on God's green earth I'm going to agree to such an asinine arrangement," Morgan informed her, shaking his head.

"I don't believe you have much of a choice in the matter," she replied smugly. "Dad has made his decision, and that is that."

"Judge Swanson might have something to say about it, especially considering that Gus's mind is dulled with pain and medicine."

"Dad was very lucid, which Dr. Jenkins can verify. He was in the room at the time."

"Swanson will never agree to this," Morgan predicted.

"Oh, but he already has. I sent him a note, and he responded affirming the transfer of custody. He'll be visiting Dad a little later, if you'd care to confirm it with him."

"You can bet your sweet ass I will!"

"You needn't resort to vulgarity, Morgan, simply because you're peeved at having to abide by my orders now."

"Sweetheart, I'm more than peeved," he assured her. "I'm downright pissed! Furthermore, I will not take orders from you, or trail around on your imaginary leash like a trained puppy! Is that perfectly understood?"

She met him glare for glare. "Want to bet? From what I gather, it's either me or Sheriff Watson. Take your pick, buster."

Morgan stomped off grumbling. "Damfool females! Give 'em an ounce of power and it goes straight to their silly heads! Turns them into monsters in the blink of an eye! One minute all sweetness and light, and the next, Genghis Khan in a corset!"

"It must be the moon," Morgan groused to his friend Drake a couple of nights later. "That's the only thing I can think of to explain why the whole blasted world seems to have gone haywire at the same time."

Drake chuckled with a distinct lack of commiseration. "Hey, count your blessings, Stone. You could be pushin' up daisies on Boot Hill right now."

"That's right, Drake. Laugh. You're not the one saddled with a female Attila the Hun for a boss. I still can't believe Gus would do this to me, after I busted my butt to save his life."

Drake shrugged. "Maybe the laudanum pickled his brain. At any rate, you're stuck with it, so you'll just have to do the best you can, old buddy. Meanwhile, we have more important problems afoot. The bank in Wichita was robbed two days ago. Sounds like the same bunch who hit the train. Only this time, the teller was killed. Shot in the head."

"Yeah, I heard. I figure that's why Sheriff Watson has decided to set up permanent camp at one end of the bar. If he whipped out a pair of binoculars and trained them on me, he couldn't be more obvious. He's waiting to see if I try to contact my old gang, I suppose, or if any of them wander in for a drink. I'm just lucky I had an alibi for the afternoon of the robbery, or he'd be inviting me for another chat in the local calaboose."

"Well, you can't blame him for being a little on edge. The bandits couldn't cover their tracks as well this time around. It had rained, and the ground was soft, and it looks like they might have been headed for Dodge. So keep a sharp eye peeled and an ear to the ground, Morgan. Oh, and if you chance to spot a horse with an oval chip in his right forehoof, give a holler."

"Sure, Drake. I'll make it a practice to run out to the hitching post and check all the horse hooves at least once every hour," Morgan scoffed. "You don't think that would look too suspicious or obvious to anyone, do you?"

"Morgan! There are three new customers waiting to be served at the other end of the bar," Heather called out imperiously, cutting into the men's conversation.

Drake laughed in midswallow and nearly choked on his beer as Morgan sketched a subservient bow in Heather's direction and tugged on his forelock. "Yes, mistress. Right away, Your Highness. Royal Pain in the Arse!"

Though he'd regained consciousness, Gus's recovery was slow and painful. His injuries were numerous and quite serious. In addition to three broken ribs, a broken leg and arm, and a concussion, he also had a cracked cheekbone and a bruised lung and kidney. It would be several weeks before he was up and about again.

Everyone pitched in to aid in his recovery, to fetch and carry, and to sit at his bedside. Arlene volunteered as his primary caretaker, and Gus was happy with that arrangement, since Heather would be busy running the saloon. Still, whenever she wasn't occupied with other duties concerning the business, Heather made it a point to spend as much time with Gus as she could. It was terrifying to think that, after meeting her father at last and coming to love him, she'd almost lost him.

Though she'd never attempted to run a business before, hadn't even dreamed she ever would, Heather was determined to prove to her father, to Morgan, and everyone else that she could operate the saloon successfully. She threw herself into the project with more enthusiasm than knowledge, and a great deal of bossiness. It quickly became apparent that she had a termagant's talent for ordering subordinate employees around, and assigning tasks to all and sundry—reserving the position of overseer for herself, naturally.

"I've made a list of chores that need to be done," she announced imperiously, shuffling a sheaf of papers.

Morgan eyed the thick stack with trepidation. "Darlin', if all those were tied together and rolled up, they'd look like the Egyptian scrolls. It must have taken you hours to think up that many chores, let alone write them down. Surely you have better things to do with your time."

"Oh, this is just the beginning," she assured him and the others she'd called together for the meeting. "Now, suppose we get started. Who wants to be in charge of washing the windows, especially those facing the street? It would be nice to be able to see out of them for a change, don't you think?"

All eight of the girls and the three men stared at her as if she'd lost her mind.

"No volunteers?" she questioned. "Fine, then I am assigning the job to you, Lloyd. Take care not to break the glass, please. It would most likely take weeks to get it replaced. And don't forget to do the mirrors."

The task of cleaning, polishing, and filling the oil lamps that ringed the walls and hung from the ceiling fell to Morgan. "Make sure to trim the wicks properly so they don't smoke so badly," she reminded him in a brisk, businesslike tone.

Bob was put in charge of making a complete inventory of the stockroom, including formulating a list of needed supplies.

The girls did not escape her dictatorial mandates, either. They were summarily issued dustcloths, lemon oil, brooms, and an array of other cleaning articles. Each grumbled irritably at the extra assignments.

"This ain't my normal line o' work," Jasmine groused. "If I wanted to scrub and dust, I'd have gotten married."

"Are we gonna get paid extra for this?" Velvet wanted to know. "If not, I have a recommendation as to where you can stuff this dustrag, sugar."

"You will receive compensation," Heather assured them, "though I wonder that Dad didn't have you doing these tasks all along. I suppose men don't pay much mind to such things."

"Neither did you, the last time I got a look at your rooms," Morgan pointed out. "Or is this a case of 'do as I say, not as I do'?"

"Yeah, I sure hope you don't expect us to clean your rooms for you, 'cause you'll be barkin' up the wrong tree, honey," Joy injected with a sour face.

"My own rooms are perfectly clean, thank you. I did them myself," Heather informed the girl tartly.

"That I gotta see!" Lacy declared. "Did you do all that dirty laundry?"

Heather was momentarily taken aback, but recovered swiftly. "That reminds me. I intend to contract with a local laundress to contend with the weekly wash, so please gather up your soiled linens and have them ready for her to pick up."

Morgan's grin was snide. "You certainly have a knack for wiggling out of something you don't want to do, don't you, princess? Tell me, if Gus wasn't laid up, what would you have done for clean clothes?"

She offered him an unruffled smile. "I would have been on the train home in a couple of days, and wouldn't have had to concern myself with it, of course."

"Of course," he repeated dryly. "I should have guessed."

Turning once more to the girls, she said, "I want to see a shine on those tables and that bar when you've finished. And a gleam on the staircase railing. I imagine it was once beautiful wood, but it's been sadly neglected. The floor is probably beyond redemption, but at least it can be mopped and waxed."

She glanced around with a critical eye before adding, "Oh, and, Morgan, when you've finished with the lamps, apply some of that brass cleaner to the footrail along the bar, will you please? It's tarnished beyond belief."

"And what'll you be doin' while we're all workin' our fingers to the bone?" Ginger inquired of Heather.

Morgan gave a derisive laugh. "Sitting on her fanny and making more lists of chores for us, no doubt."

Heather glared at him. "Just for that, you can have the task of aligning all those liquor bottles behind the bar into some sort of attractive sequence. I suggest arranging them according to height, or perhaps placing the tall ones in the center and tapering outward, with the shorter ones at the ends."

He gaped at her in disbelief. "You've got to be joking, princess. It may not appear so, but those bottles are already exactly where they belong, conveniently located so that both Bob and I know exactly where they are and don't have to waste time trying to lay hands on them. If we change them around, it will make filling the orders go more slowly, and irritate the customers."

"You'll both adjust, I'm sure," she said pompously, boldly testing her newborn authority.

Morgan awarded her a mocking salute. "Aye, aye, Captain. But before I get started, are you sure you don't want those bottles put in alphabetical order?"

As was her habit, Heather checked in on Angus after the bar closed for the night. Then, looking forward to some peace and privacy at last, she headed for her own room. With her mind on her plans for further renovation of the saloon, Heather absently began to undress as she walked through her sitting room to her bedroom. Consequently she had her sash undone and her dress unbuttoned by the time she glanced up and saw Morgan casually reclining on her bed, his back propped against the headboard. He was obviously waiting for her—and enjoying the view she was allotting him, if the avid gleam in his eyes was any indication.

" 'Do come in,' said the spider to the fly," he intoned airily. "By the way, you've tidied your quarters considerably. Quite an improvement, darlin'."

"What in blazes are you doing here?"

"Why, waiting for you, naturally," he replied calmly. "I certainly wasn't trying on your hats, love."

"Kindly remove yourself from my bed and my rooms this instant," she snapped back.

"Not until we get a few things settled, Miss High and Mighty."

Heather heard a strange, muffled noise, though she failed to immediately locate its source. "What was that? Did you hear an odd sound?"

Morgan gave a nonchalant shrug. "Oh, that's just Piddles. He was making a nuisance of himself, so I stuffed him in your wardrobe. He's probably gnawing on your shoes as we speak."

"Drat you for a fiend, Morgan Stone!" Heather headed for the wardrobe, but Morgan leapt from the bed with the speed and ease of a panther and grabbed her arm to stop her.

"No, you don't, princess. You can let him loose later, after we've conducted our business. I don't trust that mutt any farther than I can throw him, though the thought of seeing how far he'd soar is truly tempting."

His knuckles brushed the side of her breast, and his attention veered to the gaping bodice of her dress. "My, but you do know how to provide a distraction, Boston," he drawled.

She drew away from him, her tone haughty as she said, "Say what you came to say, and then get out of here, Morgan. I am not amused by your antics this evening."

"Yeah, well, I haven't been too amused by yours lately, either, sweet thing. You've been running around for two days now, acting like some sort of female potentate, throwing your weight around and barking orders right and left. Frankly, my dear, it's disgusting, and I for one have had quite enough of it. Don't get me wrong, Heather. I don't mind doing my share of the work around here, but you've become a little dictator, and if you don't ease up, you're going to find yourself trying to run this place all by yourself. Even the girls are getting fed up with your high-handed ways."

"Really," she crooned, looking down her nose at him, though she had to crane her neck to do so, which rather ruined the effect. "Well, I suppose I have been a bit brusque at times, but you have been equally obnoxious. Any other employer would have dismissed you long ago for your disrespectful attitude."

"Ah, but there's the rub, sweetheart," he said jeeringly. "You can't fire me, can you? And I can't quit. We're going to have to come to an equitable agreement, however, or I just might lose my temper one evening and paddle your little rump in front of everyone in the saloon. And wouldn't that be embarrassing? Especially when I toss your skirts over your head to do it."

"You wouldn't dare!" she snarled, her eyes spitting dark flames at him.

"Oh, but I would. And while we're on the subject of bared posteriors and such, I find it very odd that since our intimate interlude in that barn, you've been acting as if nothing happened between us. While I didn't expect you to shout it from the rooftop, I didn't expect you to ignore the affair, and me, altogether either. Unless all the sniping you've been doing lately is your way of venting your anger on me, which in itself would be baffling, since you seemed to enjoy yourself immensely while we were ... shall we say, *involved*. As I recall, you voiced your pleasure quite loudly, in fact."

"You are an uncouth cad, to remind me of such a thing!" she hissed. "Damn you, Morgan! Haven't you figured out that I don't want to be reminded what a fool I made of myself? It was a mistake, and would never have happened if I hadn't thought we might both die that day. Further, it only served to complicate matters, when my life is already in turmoil. I wish I could wipe the memory of that day from my mind and forget it ever happened."

"You can try, princess," he told her wryly, "but that won't change anything. It won't mend what's been broken, or make you all pure and chaste again. And how will you explain that particular fault to your rich Boston beau, who will no doubt expect a virgin bride in his marriage bed?"

With no conscious forethought, her hand arced toward his face. But before her palm could connect with it, his fingers clamped around her wrist, stalling the movement. She raised her other hand to strike him, and he grabbed that wrist, too. His eyes glittering dangerously, he yanked her close, pulling her arms behind her and locking them there with one strong hand.

"You might be able to get away with slapping the faces of your mild-mannered Boston gentlemen, but I don't hold with such actions, princess. I wouldn't advise trying it again."

"Let go of me, you ... you vile beast! You ill-bred barbarian!"

His answering smile had a ruthless quality. "I think not. I rather like holding you hostage, your breasts crushed against me this way. Would you care to bargain for your freedom?"

She glared up at him. "You are despicable! And if you don't release me this instant, I am going to scream the roof off, and then I'll have you arrested."

"Scream away, darlin'," he told her with cool indifference.

But as she opened her mouth, his lips swooped down to cover hers, his tongue thrusting past her parted teeth. Her intended shout emerged as a muffled moan. With her hands bound behind her, and her back slightly bowed over his arm, Morgan had thrown her off balance, forcing her to rely upon his strength for support. In this precarious position, she couldn't even move her head far enough to elude his marauding mouth.

Her first thought was to fight him; her second to simply lie limp in his embrace and endure the kiss until he tired of getting no reaction from her. But that was not to be, and somewhere deep inside herself, Heather had known that tactic would not work with him. Especially now, when his touch was so familiar, the taste of him like an addiction in her bloodstream. Within seconds, she was responding to the urgent demands of his lips, her tongue sparring with his, her mouth clinging with desperation, hungrily yielding to his domination.

When he finally released her mouth, only to trail hot, moist kisses down her arched throat, she moaned again, this time with fervent desire. His lips wandered lower still, his tongue sweeping out to trace the full upper slopes of her breasts, exposed to his touch by her gaping gown and the low-cut bodice of her chemise. Then his wet, probing tongue dipped deep into the shadowed valley between her breasts, as if in search of more delicious fare hidden there.

Heather felt her breasts swell, her nipples harden in unspoken request, one Morgan was quick to answer. He mouthed the stiffened crests through the fabric of her chemise, wetting them, suckling them, sending violent quivers through her. It was not enough—for him or for her.

Dimly she heard her own voice, sultry with longing, begging him. "Please, Morgan. Please."

"Tell me, sweetheart," he replied huskily. "Tell me what you want."

"More," she said breathily. "Closer."

How he managed, with his one free hand, to rid her of her clothing, Heather could not discern. By now her mind was clouded with desire, her body aching with alarming intensity, and Morgan was spreading warm kisses all along her pulsing flesh. Before she was aware of what was happening, she was standing amid a puddle of fallen garments, completely naked. And she became alert to that fact only because Morgan seemed to be caressing her bare flesh everywhere at once. Her back, her buttocks, her trembling thighs. Planting lingering kisses along her shoulders, her breasts, her stomach. Making her melt and burn and yearn as she'd never imagined possible.

He suckled her breasts until she could scarcely endure the intense craving that washed through her, pooling low in her belly and between her thighs. Then, still holding her hands behind her, he sank to his knees before her and nudged her legs apart. Shocked, she felt his warm breath whisper over her most intimate place, his mustache brushing the inner curve of her thigh.

"Morgan? Oh, God! What are you doing?"

"Adoring you, love," he murmured. "Every lovely, dewy inch of you."

Then his lips touched her there—his tongue like a firebrand—and she went up in flames. If not for the support of his arm around her hips, she would have sunk to the floor. But he held her there, and the exquisite torment went on and on and on—until, with a hoarse cry, she found that final, climactic release that made her mindless of anything but the fantastic waves of emotion rippling through her.

When, some moments later, she came to herself, she was lying on her bed. Morgan, divested of his own clothes, was leaning over her, propped on his elbows, a smug male smile curving his mouth as he watched her surface slowly from the depths of desire. Then he bent down and kissed her, leisurely and thoroughly, and she tasted the essence of her own passion on his lips.

"Someday I'll teach you to do the same for me, but not tonight," he promised huskily. "Tonight my need for you is too strong to wait any longer."

His lips melted over hers once more, muting her sharp gasp of pleasure as he raised her legs and joined his body to hers in a long, smooth plunge, seating himself deep within her. With each successive thrust, their desire grew hotter, brighter, until they found themselves consumed by the blazing splendor that burst upon them, enraptured by the blinding ecstasy. Their joyous cries blended in harmonious accord, fading slowly away like dying embers.

Still over her, Morgan gently kissed her love-blushed lips. "You're mine, Heather," he whispered gruffly. "Mine in a way you'll never belong to any other man as long as you live. I hope you realize that."

She nodded weakly, her energies spent, too tired to argue the point and knowing it would be futile. "I know."

"I'll put up with your high-handed ways, and your pompous prancing, but I won't let you continue to ignore me or what has passed between us. You won't get rid of me that easily, love, because I intend to be right here every night to remind you just how much you want me, to reinforce the passion we feel for each other."

She sighed. "I won't pretend to understand why you hold such allure for me. At this point, the reasons are far too complex for my poor, baffled brain to fathom. But right or wrong, I can't fight it anymore. I haven't the strength or the will to resist you. I do hope we can at least be discreet about our alliance, however. I really would prefer that our private affairs not be broadcast to the entire town."

"Afraid you'll be ridiculed for bedding a common shoe salesman, princess?" he mocked.

"Actually I hadn't thought of it in those terms. I'm more concerned with being labeled a tart, and shaming myself and my father before all his friends."

"Fine. We'll keep it confidential for now. As long as I don't catch you flirting with other men or otherwise trying to maneuver me out of your life or your bed."

"You don't own me, Morgan," she stated flatly.

"I will," he vowed quietly. "Oh, and while we're on the topic, it might be best if you write your former fiancé and inform him that he has been replaced."

"Anything else, before you sneak off to your own bed and leave me in peace?" she inquired tartly.

"Yeah," he chuckled. "Don't forget to let Piddles out of the closet before he hikes his leg on your clothes."

❧ 18 ❧

The next morning, Heather had to run several errands. Morgan escorted her, as usual, though now he positively reeked of male arrogance, at least in Heather's estimation. They'd just come out of the mercantile when they noticed a commotion in the street ahead of them. Several cowboys were circling around another individual, laughing and hooting and totally engrossed in taunting him. At first Heather thought their victim was a child, or perhaps an old woman, but as she and Morgan drew closer they saw it was a small, odd-looking man with slanted eyes. He was attired in some sort of black outfit that resembled pajamas, with a funny little hat on his head and a long braid hanging down his back.

"A Chinaman," Morgan said, noting her curiosity.

"Oh. What do you suppose he's done to make those men so riled?"

"Probably nothing. Some folks just can't resist tormenting anyone who is different from them. For some reason, they seem to think all foreigners are either suspect or stupid, or both. At any rate, the Chinese are a particular target, since they were imported as cheap labor on the railroads and took a lot of jobs American men wanted or needed. Of course, that was the fault of the railway officials, who wanted the task done as quickly and inexpensively as possible, and didn't care who got hurt or cheated in the process.

But the average working person doesn't see it that way, and the Chinese are bearing the brunt of their anger."

"It's not fair," Heather said, frowning at the men, who were now tugging on the Chinaman's braid, yanking him this way and that.

"No, it's not," Morgan agreed calmly.

"Well, do something about it, Morgan!" she insisted, staring at him with her hand on her hip. "Go rescue that poor man before those idiot cowboys hurt him."

"What do I look like? A universal savior?" he grumbled. "It's not our fight, Boston."

"It is now," she informed him, dumping her parcels on the boardwalk and stalking toward the fray.

"Heather! Get back here! It's none of your concern!"

She ignored him and kept on walking.

"Damn it to hell!" he muttered. "Sometimes that woman is more trouble than she's worth." Unhitching the bullwhip from his belt, he started forward, calling to her. "All right! You win! Just step back out of the way and let me handle it."

By now a crowd had gathered to watch the sport, but as Morgan advanced, whip in hand, they made way for him—some with wary looks and others with gleeful anticipation.

"Okay, break it up, fellows," he warned. "You've had your fun. Let the man go."

Only one of the five hecklers paid any heed; he'd had previous contact with Morgan in the Gurdy and wasn't eager to repeat the experience. He left the group, and quickly melted into the crowd of onlookers. The other four afforded Morgan little notice, not even bothering to turn around and see who had spoken to them.

One fellow did reply over his shoulder with a laugh, "Not until we cut his pigtail off. These slant-eyes think they won't get to heaven without it, so we're gonna make sure he don't."

At this, the Chinaman became more anxious, spouting a stream of Chinese and prancing about in a panic, trying to tear his hair loose of the man's grip.

"Whoa!" another of the cowboys exclaimed in delight. "Look at him dance! I ain't seen footwork that fancy since ole Charley stepped on that rattler last year!"

Realizing that he was getting nowhere with peaceful measures, Morgan uncoiled the whip and snapped it into the rowdy cluster with a loud crack. All eyes turned his way, several pair narrowed in distinct displeasure.

"Maybe you didn't hear me, boys. I said turn him loose."

"Yes, maybe you should pick on someone your own size," Heather jeered from the sidelines.

Morgan bit back a silent groan. With support like hers, he was liable to get the tar beat out of him. He couldn't help but wonder, after last night, if that wasn't her main objective. She probably didn't care a gnat's ass about the Chinaman's fate, as long as he, Morgan, got his comeuppance.

"Maybe we ought to do just that," the larger of the group replied with a nasty grin. He gestured toward Morgan. "This fella seems bent on pokin' his nose in where it don't belong, and he seems about the right size to me."

He took a menacing step toward Morgan, seemingly unconcerned about the whip Morgan held. It was a tactical error. His next step landed him flat on his back in the dirt, compliments of Morgan and the lash, which had wound neatly around the man's foot. He landed with a thud that made two horses tied nearby start in fright as the earth vibrated beneath their hooves. His head hit a clod of mud that had dried to the hardness of petrified wood. He was out cold, never knowing what had hit him.

"Next?" Morgan invited with cool disdain.

His second opponent decided to better his odds by drawing a knife from its sheath. Morgan dispatched him and the knife with equal swiftness. When he withdrew the whip, the knife came with it. The cowboy was left nursing a badly wrenched wrist.

Morgan turned his attention to the man still clutching the Chinaman's pigtail. Fast as a striking snake, the whip sang out, biting into the cowpoke's hand, cutting a long, bloody gash. Freed, the little Oriental dashed quickly away before the last of his tormentors could grab him.

Wisely, the lone remaining antagonist abruptly decided that discretion was the better part of valor and gave up the cause. Collecting his wounded friends, he helped them down the street toward Doc Jenkins's office.

Morgan heaved a sigh of relief, thankful that none of the men had worn guns, and that no one else had decided to join the fight. He turned to Heather, who was gazing at him with open admiration. Despite the pride that swelled in his chest at her adoring look, he adopted a stern glower. "Are you satisfied, Miss Meddler? Can we get on with our shopping now?"

An hour later, as they were strolling back to the saloon, their arms loaded down with packages, the Chinaman popped out from the shadows of an alleyway. He executed a respectful bow toward both of them and said in broken English, "I much hoppy you save poor Ching Yung from those men. Thank belly much."

"You're welcome," Morgan replied. "Just try to avoid that sort in the future, if possible, or you might lose that queue yet."

"Oh, Ching Yung be belly careful. You betcha. Now I carry packages, yes? I jolly good servant."

"It's very nice of you to offer, but not at all necessary," Heather answered politely. "We have only a short distance to go with them."

The Chinaman nodded. "To Gus place. I know. I carry for you." He reached out and plucked the packages from Heather's arms, then trotted swiftly toward the saloon on silent slippered feet.

Heather was nonplussed. "Have I just been robbed

in broad daylight?" she wondered aloud.

Morgan chuckled. "On the contrary, I think you just gained a devoted slave."

She shrugged. "Well, if not devoted, he's certainly determined."

"More than you imagine, I suspect."

"What do you mean?"

He grinned down at her. "If I'm not mistaken, there is an old Oriental custom which states that if you save someone's life, you become responsible for that person's life forever. It would not surprise me in the least if Ching Yung has claimed you as his savior and is fully prepared to repay that debt for the rest of his days on earth—while you provide for his basic needs, of course, as you would any household servant."

Heather stared in stunned disbelief. "You must be joking."

Morgan shook his head. "Nope."

"But you're the one who saved him, not me."

"A matter of opinion. You initiated the venture. Evidently Ching Yung is aware of that, though I expect he'll allot me a fair measure of respect as well, for helping you achieve it."

"This is preposterous!" she scoffed. "I can't have saddled myself with two stubborn men within the span of twelve short hours!"

Morgan's prediction proved correct. Ching Yung declared that he would serve his new mistress long and well. He refused to consider any other option, regarding himself as Heather's property now. It seemed that nothing short of a stick of dynamite would dislodge him from his chosen path. After arguing until she was almost blue in the face, Heather admitted defeat, much to everyone's amusement.

"Oh, all right. You may stay," she told him. "I'll have one of the girls make up one of the spare rooms for you."

"No need, missy," Ching Yung told her. "I no trouble. I sleep in hall outside your room. Guard you good!"

"No," Morgan stated firmly. "Absolutely not. You can arrange a cot in the storeroom, if you want, but if anyone is going to guard Missy Heather at night, it will be me.

"Which reminds me," Morgan said, turning his attention to Heather, "have you written that letter to your erstwhile fiancé yet?"

"I haven't had time."

"Well, I suggest you make the time, darlin'. Also make it short and sweet and to the point. It can't take that long to write."

"I'll do it when I get darned good and ready," she countered huffily.

"Don't press your luck, princess, or I'll take a full-page notice out in tomorrow's newspaper, and have them announce your disengagement in big bold print."

She snarled at him, baring her teeth. "I suppose you want to read the letter when I've finished, just to make sure I haven't misspelled any words?" she replied sarcastically.

His taunting grin was back, making Heather itch to rip his mustache off!

"An excellent idea, sugarplum. I'll do just that."

In the end, Heather took the cowardly route and addressed the letter to her mother instead, as Morgan discovered when he read it. She'd written:

Dear Mother,

I am extending my stay in Dodge City for several reasons, the most compelling being that Father has had a serious accident and needs my help. We were visiting his ranch when a tornado hit, causing the most awful devastation you can fathom. The house and barn were demolished, and Father was badly injured when the chimney crashed down on him. For-

tunately, no one else was harmed. I am perfectly well and very busy trying to keep Father's business going.

Can you imagine me trying to operate a saloon? I did tell you in my previous letter what a shock it was to learn that Gus owns a barroom, didn't I? And me, a member of the Temperance Society! By the way, I've joined the local chapter here in Dodge, and met a lovely group of ladies. I just hope they don't kick me out of their circle now that I am temporarily in charge of running this tavern. I do have special changes in mind for it, however, in the hopes of turning it into a more respectable establishment. Wish me success, Mother. I'll certainly need it.

One last item, and this I write with some regret, if only because I lack the courage to do it myself, and am therefore asking your assistance and understanding. It would mean a great deal to me if you would inform Lyle that I have decided I cannot marry him after all. If he asks why, please just tell him that I've simply changed my mind and concluded that we would not suit one another all that well. I'm sorry to sound so fickle, but he would do better to find a woman who truly loves him, which I have discovered I do not. In this instance, absence did not make the heart grow fonder. Rather, the opposite occurred.

Therefore, if you would please break this news to him as gently as possible, I will be forever grateful, Mother. I hope you will both find it in your hearts to forgive me, but it is for the best. Farewell for now. I will write again soon and keep you informed as to how matters are progressing here and when I might be heading home again.

Your loving daughter,
Heather

P.S. Quite by chance I recently acquired a new servant to replace Etta. He is Chinese, and his name is

*Ching Yung. He is much more devoted to me than
Etta ever was.*

"I see you made no mention of me in your letter,"
Morgan remarked after reviewing it.

"What would you suggest I tell my mother?"
Heather retorted. "That I'm conducting a clandestine
affair with a shoe salesman who, coincidentally, is
suspected of train robbery? That I'm no longer her
innocent little daughter, but a scarlet woman?"

"You told her about Ching Yung," he pointed out.
"You could at least have said something about me, if
only to mention that I tend bar here and follow orders
fairly well."

Heather let loose an inelegant snort. "That will be
the day, Morgan Stone."

"I follow them better than you, evidently. You were
supposed to write this letter to your fiancé, this fellow
named Lyle."

"I reconsidered and decided that such an announcement would be better delivered in person
rather than by letter. Mother is very tactful. She'll
break the news to him gently, I'm sure."

"That is beside the point, Heather. The man was
your fiancé, and it's your duty to break off with him
yourself. If you respect him at all, you owe him that
much. Furthermore, you have a nasty habit of pushing your obligations off onto other people, like a fractious child who shoves her spinach onto someone
else's plate. There comes a time in life when, as a ma-
ture adult, you must outgrow such infantile tenden-
cies and learn to shoulder your own responsibilities.
Therefore, I strongly suggest that you march back upstairs and write another letter, addressing it to Lyle."

"And if I don't?" she challenged.

"Then I'll find a way to write to him myself," Morgan warned, his calm tone making his threat all the
more convincing. "And believe me, dumplin', I won't
be nearly as diplomatic as you would be."

* * *

Ching Yung soon proved to be worth his puny weight in gold, and Heather was delighted with his performance. The man literally coddled her, waiting on her hand and foot. He served her breakfast in bed. He insisted on personally laundering and pressing her clothes. He doted on Piddles, bathing him and feeding him and taking the dog on his daily outings. Contrarily, while Piddles still snarled at Morgan, he accepted Ching Yung with reserved regard.

The diminutive Chinaman was also an excellent cook, and was soon concocting the most tantalizing dishes, both Chinese and American fare, on his portable brazier. Soups and meats and fresh vegetables— all irrefutably delicious, for which Heather was boundlessly grateful. In addition, he cleaned Heather's rooms, ran numerous errands, and with the aid of his abacus, was a veritable genius at accounting.

His only irritating qualities were his absolute subservience and his penchant for shadowing Heather's every step in anxious anticipation that she would require some duty of him. Before long, his constant attendance was driving Heather batty and fraying Morgan's limited patience.

"It's bad enough the man is coddling you silly," Morgan complained one night when they were finally alone in her bedroom. "But does he have to cling to your skirts while he does it? Good grief! I half expect to find him hiding under the bed, or lurking beneath the sheets!"

"Jealous, dear?" she taunted, though she'd thought the same thing herself.

"Of a Chinese lapdog?" Morgan retorted. "I'd sooner envy that miserable mutt of yours."

"I've tried to get Ching Yung to accept that I don't need him hanging about all the time, that I prefer a bit of privacy from time to time, but we seem to suffer a lack of communication in that area," she told him. "However, if you would care to try convincing him, have at it. Just don't wound his pride. I understand it's very important for an Oriental not to lose face."

"I'll explain it very gently and thoroughly to him," Morgan assured her. "Then maybe I'll stand a chance of cornering you in the supply room now and again. Or in the linen closet."

"My stars! Was ever a woman so pursued by so many?" she declared dramatically. "Why, it's enough to turn a girl's head!"

"I'll show you pursuit, sweetheart," he vowed with a roguish leer. "And it's not your head I intend to turn, but your saucy little bottom!" With that, he grabbed for her and quickly flipped her over onto her stomach. His mustache grazed lightly over her bare buttocks, followed by his lips. "This is merely to ensure that you can't ever claim I've never kissed your behind," he informed her.

"Morgan Stone!" she exclaimed on a giggle. "What will you come up with next?"

He proceeded to demonstrate that, too. And by the time he was done, they were both thoroughly reduced to a languid state of bliss.

❧ 19 ❧

Within a few short days, Heather set about renovating Gus's Gallery to better suit her own standards. Many of her ideas met with frowns and doubt and dismay—others with outright disapproval. She began by ordering Gus's "artwork" removed from the walls, replaced with pictures she considered more proper.

As he reluctantly hung the new paintings, complaining all the while, Morgan queried, "Where did you get these god-awful pictures, Boston?"

"I recruited the help of my fellow Temperance ladies, and we scoured the town in search of them. It wasn't easy to find a dozen large paintings of decent depiction here in Dodge, let me tell you."

He grimaced at the one he'd just put up. "I don't doubt it. I'd never have guessed you'd find so many pitiful pastoral scenes in one small cow town. You do know, don't you, that you're inviting trouble if you insist on displaying the one with all the sheep in the midst of cattle country?"

"Oh, twaddle!"

Morgan gave in with a shrug. "Okay. Just don't say I didn't warn you, when someone decides to deface it—not that it wouldn't be an improvement, mind you. I'm tempted to do the deed myself. Furthermore, I think that homely shepherdess at the well would look much better with a mustache and beard and a big hat."

Heather narrowed her eyes in warning. "If I find her sporting them, I'll certainly know where to look for the guilty party, won't I?"

The new artwork was only the first of the changes Heather initiated, and perhaps the least absurd, when all was said and done. The flowered chintz curtains she requisitioned from a local seamstress were not at all in keeping with typical tavern decor. The barstools were more of an inconvenience than anything, as those men who didn't choose to sit at one of the tables preferred to "belly up" to the bar. But when Heather added tablecloths and decorated the bar and staircase with ruffled bows, she'd gone beyond the pale, at least in Morgan's estimation.

"Are you deliberately trying to put your poor father out of business?" he inquired, eyeing the feminine frills with distaste. "Our customers are going to take one look at this place and run screaming and laughing to the nearest suitable saloon, one that isn't all gussied up to resemble a spinster's parlor. Men don't like lace doilies and candles on the tables in a barroom. All they want is a place to relax, get drunk, and enjoy a game of cards and the company of their friends. Throw in some music and a pretty barmaid or two, and they're as happy as pigs in a puddle."

"An apt analogy of our usual clientele," Heather agreed wryly. "But all that is going to change. Henceforth, we will be catering to more discerning tastes. We'll also be abiding by state law, which means that liquor will no longer be served here. I've ordered one of those new soda water fountains, with a nice variety of flavorings, which should arrive any day now. In addition, we'll offer coffee, tea, lemonade, and sarsaparilla, with a selection of cookies and biscuits. Later, if all goes well, we may expand the list to include soups and light luncheon fare."

Morgan groaned aloud. "No liquor? Drovers drinking flavored soda? Are you deranged? What does Gus say about all this, or have you even bothered to in-

form him that he is soon to be the proud owner of a
blooming tea parlor?"

"Dad has given me full rein to do as I see fit. Not
that it's any of your business," she added in that superior tone that never failed to grate on his nerves.

"What about Bob, and Lloyd, and the girls? Do they
have any idea what you're up to?"

"As a matter of fact, I've already informed the girls
that they will no longer be entertaining in their rooms,
and that I will aid them in altering their attire to make
it more appropriate for our new image."

"I'll bet that went over like a curse in church."

"Don't be so crass, Morgan," she replied sternly.

He offered an insincere apology, accompanied by a
crooked grin. "Do pardon my vulgarity, princess. We
lowly serfs aren't up on royal demeanor, though I do
see how such talk is not in line with the oh-so-proper
impression you want to project these days." He
wagged his eyebrows at her and taunted further,
"And wouldn't everyone be surprised to learn that
Miss Prim and Proper has been doing a good bit of
entertaining in her own room at night?"

"You say one word about our . . . our . . ."

"Affair?" he supplied helpfully, still grinning.

"Liaison," she said curtly, "and if you tell anyone,
I will see that Judge Swanson hangs you from the
highest tree, at which time I will personally place the
noose around your blasted neck!"

Clasping a hand over his heart, he feigned a love-
lorn look. "Such honeyed words from such sweet lips,
my dear! Why, it's almost enough to make a grown
man swoon."

"Do so on your own time, please," she commanded
with a tart smile. "Just now I want you to clean out
the storeroom."

The girls shared Morgan's dubious opinion of
Heather's scheme. Velvet quit on the spot and went
to work across the street at the Longhorn Saloon. "I'm

sorry, Heather, but I make most of my money on my back, not serving drinks."

The remaining girls echoed that sentiment, but out of loyalty to Gus, decided to stay on awhile and see how things panned out. They discussed it among themselves at some length.

"Maybe it won't be as bad as all that," Joy said hopefully. "If it doesn't work out, Heather might give up and change everything back the way it was. Besides, Gus isn't going to be laid up forever. Then he'll be back in charge, and business will return to normal."

"Lord, I hope so!" Brandy declared in disgust. "It's plain as the nose on your face that Heather doesn't know the first thing about runnin' a saloon."

"Ah, but that's the gist o' the whole problem," Jasmine pointed out. "She doesn't want to run a bar. She wants to run a refreshment parlor, all refined and respectable like."

"In Dodge?" Pearl scoffed. "She'd have better luck sellin' ice to Eskimos. And in the meantime, our best customers are gonna be spendin' their coin elsewhere."

"Not necessarily," Morgan put in. Leaning casually against the bar, where he'd been openly eavesdropping, he added in a confidential tone, "You could still keep your clientele happy, and your earnings coming in. There's always the back stairs, and what the little princess doesn't know won't hurt her."

Several pair of eyes lit up with eager anticipation. "Yeah, but what about the booze?" Crystal asked. "Those thirsty cowpokes are gonna want to wet their whistles with somethin' stronger than tea and soda water."

Lacy nodded. "I agree. Most of them are still gonna go somewhere else to drink and play poker, and like as not, take up with some other woman for pleasure."

Morgan gave a devilish wink. "Well now, suppose we serve those fellows some of our infamous Baptist lemonade and Presbyterian punch? Moreover,

Heather doesn't know poker from pinochle, and unless someone enlightens her, how's she to guess the difference? Add to that the fact that she intends to continue the dancing, and what you've got is a glorified gurdy, merely primped up to look more proper."

"Oh, you wonderful, wicked man!" Ginger squealed. "And they claim women are devious! Why, if I didn't think Heather would pitch a fit, I'd climb over this bar and kiss you."

Morgan's brows rose. "What makes you think she'd mind if you did?"

"Oh, c'mon, Morgan," Ginger gibed. "We all know what's goin' on between you two."

Seven heads bobbed in accord. "You really should oil the hinges on her hall door," Jasmine advised him with a saucy grin.

"And avoid those squeaky floorboards between your room and hers," Brandy suggested. "God forbid Gus should ever find out you've been dallyin' with his daughter on the sly. But don't worry, we won't tell him, especially now that you've come up with a way to save our primary means of income."

"Or the bother of havin' to set up shop elsewhere," Lacy added. "Still, you really should be more cautious, what with Arlene wanderin' about at all hours. If anyone would spill the beans, she might."

So it went. Heather continued to think up new innovations, and her employees continued to secretly circumvent them, or to put up with what they couldn't avoid. For her part, Heather soon learned how to compromise, something she'd rarely had to do before. No one said much when she decided to rename the place Gus's Social Salon. But when Heather wanted to change the hours, opening at nine in the morning and closing at nine each night, the girls flatly refused to start work before noon. After heated debate, Heather relented. The salon would operate from noon to midnight, offering beverages and light snack foods, music, dancing, cards, and billiards.

Heather remained adamant on some points, however. She was determined that the Social Salon would be a respectable establishment, serving both men and women customers, and that the girls would have to reform their mode of attire and behavior accordingly. Thus, she set out to teach all seven of them the art of refined manners, a task that the men seemed to find highly amusing, Morgan most of all. For days, he went around with a perpetual grin on his face, while Heather and the girls suffered his wry comments and skewed sense of humor.

"Give up, Boston," he said, chuckling as Heather monitored her would-be ladies while they marched up and down the room with books balanced atop their heads. Three volumes toppled to the floor in quick succession, and Heather stifled a weary sigh. "It's hopeless, darlin'. Like trying to turn a flock of colorful parrots into snow white swans."

"Piffle! They can do it if they'd just set their minds to it."

"Precisely your problem. Perhaps they were content the way they were and don't want to convert. Have you thought of that?"

"They'll learn eventually, if only to get me to quit harping at them," she insisted stubbornly. Directing her next comment to Lacy, she snapped, "That book would remain balanced if you would remember to hold your head up and stop trying to watch your feet. That applies to you, too, Brandy."

"Hell's bells, Heather!" Brandy griped. "I don't know about you, but I ain't seen my feet while I'm standin' since I was fourteen and grew breasts! The thing is, it just ain't natural to go around with your nose poked into the air like this."

Morgan laughed. "Heather doesn't seem to have any problem with it. Of course, that might explain why she's so habitually clumsy."

Heather wrinkled her nose at him. "Very funny, Morgan." Then, to Brandy, "I've told you repeatedly, *ain't* is not a proper word. Please make an effort to say *isn't* or *is not*. Also, ladies do not utter curses."

"At least not aloud or in public," Morgan agreed with a smirk. "I can attest that privately it's another matter."

Heather speared him with a chilling glare. "Mr. Stone, kindly desist with your mocking commentary. If you've nothing better to do, which I'm sure you do have, please do it elsewhere, or curses will be the least of your worries."

"Yes, ma'am." He saluted smartly and sauntered off, still chuckling.

Heather's attention returned to her reluctant apprentices. "Jasmine! Lose that wiggle on your backside! Crystal! Shoulders back! Ginger! Step lightly. You're not stomping bugs, for crying out loud! Glide, ladies. Glide."

Yet another argument ensued when it came to the matter of how the girls should dress, now that Gus's Gurdy was being transformed into a more respectable enterprise. Heather had in mind a serving uniform of sorts, similar to those that the Harvey Girls were required to wear. Gus's girls had other notions entirely.

Confronting Heather in force, they informed her bluntly, "We've taken a vote and decided we wouldn't be caught dead in those drab gray dresses and white aprons and caps you want us to wear."

Heather sighed loudly. "I suspected you'd feel that way, but it was worth a try. Still, your usual attire simply will not do, most especially to serve the ladies of Dodge City society. No doubt, members of my Temperance group will be stopping in for tea, as might the pastor's wife, or even the mayor's wife. Why, I can only imagine their shock should you appear in such short skirts, with garters and stockings showing, not to mention displaying your other . . . uh . . . assets above such low-cut bodices. You must see how inappropriate that would be."

"Course, we do," Jasmine announced peevishly.

"We're not a bunch o' witless ninnies, like some folks seem to think we are. We're not a pack o' mules, either. Meet us halfway, and we can be real reasonable."

"Then you're willing to discuss alternative measures?" Heather inquired hopefully. "Somewhere between prudish and provocative?"

Jasmine shrugged. "That depends on what you have to suggest, and how well we like it."

Heather took a deep breath and plunged in. "All right, ladies. Let's hash this out. First, your skirts must be longer, no more than a couple of inches off the floor, and no ruffled petticoats showing beneath the hemline."

After a quick consultation among themselves, the girls agreed. "On the condition that we can wear our choice of undergarments beneath them, including net hose," Jasmine qualified.

"And we wear our own shoes, not those fuddy-duddy black clodhoppers most women wear," Joy inserted.

"And bright fabric for the dresses, with ribbons and ruffles and lace and such," Pearl put in, garnering a round of affirmative nods from her cohorts.

"Pastels or prints," Heather countered. "At least for daytime attire. With a modest décolletage and tasteful trim. No excess of ornamentation, including jewelry or hair ornaments such as ostrich plumes."

"Not even feather boas?" Ginger moaned.

"Not so much as goose down," Heather replied firmly. "Furthermore, you will forgo wearing face paint."

"Whoa!" Lacy exclaimed. "Now, I can see where we might ease up on it a bit durin' the day, with just a dab of rouge and powder and whatnot, but there's no way I'll go completely bare-faced in public. That'd be like goin' naked!"

Heather frowned. "No offense, but considering your choice of occupation, I fail to see why feeling exposed would bother you excessively."

Seven fierce scowls met that statement. Jasmine took up the gauntlet, responding waspishly, "Don't go throwin' stones at us, sugar. Your laundry ain't exactly lily white either these days."

Heather blinked in confusion, her cheeks flushing. "I beg your pardon? What, pray tell, do you mean by that comment?"

Brandy's smile was sly. "She means, dearie, that we're well aware o' what you and Morgan are up to at night, when y'all think everyone else is asleep."

The flush turned into a blaze, turning Heather's face bright red. "Oh," she muttered. "I see. Morgan's been telling tales out of school, I suppose."

"Now, don't go climbin' Morgan's frame," Lacy said. "He didn't say a word, and neither will we."

"Then how did you know?" Heather asked, mortified.

"Squeaky doors and floors and odd noises in the night tell their own story," Crystal explained, not unkindly. "That, and I guess we're just used to such goings-on. Maybe most folks wouldn't catch on right off, but we're more alert that way."

Heather winced in dismay. "Does anyone else know?"

"Like yer pa, for instance?" Joy suggested. She shook her head. "I reckon not, since he hasn't torn Morgan's head off yet. But I'd be a mite more careful if I were you."

Noting Heather's distress, Jasmine threw a friendly arm across her shoulders and gave her a quick hug. "No need to fret, sugarplum. We can keep a secret . . . if you can. Just remember, one good turn deserves another. We help you, and you help us, which is only right." She slanted a wink at Heather, adding, "Now, you and Gus do intend to pay for these new dresses you want us gals to wear, don't you?"

❧ 20 ❧

To everyone's surprise, and to Heather's delight, business remained as brisk as ever. Gus's Social Salon was a novelty in Dodge, and curiosity alone lured many new patrons through the doors. After the initial shock of seeing their favorite tavern transformed, and the relief of discovering that they could still indulge in their usual pleasures and pastimes, though more discreetly, most of the regular customers continued to frequent the Salon. They even abided by Heather's strict directives that they wipe their boots clean on the nail scraper before entering, that no weapons of any kind were allowed inside, that no cursing or quarreling would be tolerated, and anyone who did not employ the spittoons and ashtrays for their proper purposes would be ousted.

Some fellows grumbled at the changes, but most seemed to take it in stride and even enjoyed being included in the conspiracy to proceed with their customary diversions while Heather remained innocently oblivious to their trickery. For the most part, local folks were pleased with Heather's innovations, claiming it was high time Dodge started shedding its old title as "the wickedest little city in America" and began exhibiting a more sophisticated and dignified demeanor to the outside world.

When Heather's new soda machine arrived, the Social Salon held a grand opening, to which Heather formally invited all her Temperance friends and several prominent ladies of Dodge society. By early afternoon, the salon was packed with chattering women, all of them eager to investigate this formerly notorious tavern to which they'd heretofore been banned, both by order of their husbands and by social edict.

"Good grief!" Morgan complained as he prepared yet another raspberry soda. "I've never seen such a gaggle of giggling geese. It'll be a wonder if any self-respecting male sets foot in here again."

Heather sent him a smug smile. "Don't delude yourself. Those ganders will be swarming in here by the dozens, attracted by the presence of these refined ladies, if only because it may be the first time some have had an opportunity to rub elbows with an actual gentlewoman."

Contrary to all Morgan's expectations, Heather's claim proved true. Before long, a motley assortment of men had ambled in—a number of cowboys and drovers, a couple of old miners, a drifter or two, several town merchants and councilmen. All were trying mightily to appear nonchalant, though it was apparent from their scrubbed faces and slicked-down hair that each had made a deliberate effort to improve his appearance. Amassed, they resembled a flock of peacocks prepared to preen before a gathering of hens.

"If this doesn't beat all!" Morgan declared, shaking his head in amazement.

"Personally, I think it's disgustin'!" Jasmine complained. "Just look at those yahoos, drooling over those prissy gals, like they've never seen a woman before."

"Oh, get off your high horse, Jas," Crystal said with a laugh. "They're just shoppin', lookin' at what they can't afford. Come sundown they'll be pantin' after us like always, all worked into a lather, and I won't be shy about taking their money for all o' ten minutes' work."

Jasmine gave a disgruntled snort. "I reckon you're

right, but it still burns my buttons. It's like those other women are somethin' special, straight out o' the Monkey Ward catalog, and we're cast-off hand-me-downs at a rummage sale!''

"Well, one man's trash is another man's treasure, so they say," Crystal reminded her with a wink. "I'll keep waitin', and I just know someday some nice, lonesome fella is gonna take one look at me and think I'm sweeter than candy. Then I'll just hafta give in and marry the poor man, I guess, hard as it'll be to give up this glamorous life I'm leadin'!"

Jasmine had to laugh. "Crystal, I swear you're three bricks shy of a full load, but I'll sure miss you if your prince charming does show up and takes you away with him."

While the Salon was turning out to be an unexpected success, with the ladies coming in during the day for tea and conversation, and the men crowding in at night for dancing and drinking, life still doled out its disappointments. Gus's recovery was erratic at best. The doctor was as puzzled as the rest of them, for one day Gus would be bright-eyed and almost cheerful despite his lingering pain, and the next he'd be out of his head, rambling incoherently.

"I just don't understand it," Doc said, shaking his head. "He doesn't have a fever, and there's no sign of infection setting in. His wounds are healing much better than I'd anticipated, yet he has these strange mental lapses."

"Could it be the medication?" Heather asked worriedly.

"I've pretty well ruled that out," Doc told her. "I treated Gus with the same drugs a couple of years ago, when his horse threw him, and he didn't have any adverse reaction to them then."

"He has such drastic changes in his moods, too, often within mere minutes," Heather continued with concern. "One minute happy, then so awfully depressed, and yesterday he went into a frothing rage for no apparent reason. Has he been prone to such unpredictable behavior before?"

Doc shook his head. "Not in the ten years I've known him. For the most part, Gus has always been congenial and even-tempered. However, though he's slow to anger, he can be a mean old cuss when he's finally riled."

Heather nodded. "Only now it doesn't take much to light his fuse. You never know if he's going to be as sweet as apple pie or as testy as a panther with a sore paw."

The physician patted her shoulder consolingly. "Just keep a close watch on him, and send for me if you need me. I'll be back to check him again in a couple of days. With luck, this odd malady will pass soon. In the meanwhile, bear with him. In addition to the pain, he's not used to being bedridden, and that alone takes its toll on a man's temperament."

Despite learning that the girls knew about their midnight trysts, and Heather's concern that others might discover the same, Morgan was disinclined to curtail their ongoing affair. He went so far as to oil the hinges on her door, and to memorize the creaky boards in the hall, but flatly refused to cease visiting her room each night.

"Why must you be so obstinate?" Heather argued. "I'm merely suggesting a temporary suspension of our clandestine activities, until Dad has improved enough that Arlene is not constantly prowling the premises. I vow, that woman has the eyes of an owl and the ears of a bat! And she'd run blabbing to Dad at the first hint of suspicion. I just know she would. Why can't you be more reasonable on this issue?"

Morgan grinned at her. "No one's ever accused me of being particularly malleable, and I don't intend to start at this late date, sweetheart. So you might as well stop trying to change my mind. However, if you insist on flapping your tongue, put it to better use."

"Are you about to suggest something lewd?" she

queried warily, noting the wicked sparkle in his eyes.

His smile was diabolical, tipping his mustache upward at the edges. "Very," he drawled. "But I'm willing to bet you'll enjoy it every bit as much as I will. Come, princess. Let down your hair and be my wanton wench once more. Wallow with me in carnal delight, and I'll show you such splendor that royal jewels will pale by comparison."

The cattle drives were in full force now, and would continue through late summer. Thousands of tons of beef, on the hoof, were gathered together on the plains to the south of the city, awaiting transport by rail. Fortunately, few herds were driven through town, since most arrived from Texas and other points south or west of Dodge. Occasionally, however, a herd from the north would be routed through the city streets.

The first time this occurred, Heather viewed the event with awe and apprehension. Such a sight was never beheld in Boston, and she was nearly dumbfounded at both the size of the herd and of the longhorns themselves, which paraded slowly past the front doors of the Salon. The choking clouds of dust stirred up by churning hoofs hung in the air as thick as fog, and the noise of the bellowing beasts was positively horrendous.

Noting her wary fascination, Morgan sidled up and commented, "Listen to that, darlin'. Isn't it just music to your ears?"

Heather cast him a curious glance. "Are you crazy? Or simply tone-deaf?"

He laughed. "A little of both, I suppose, but if you listen real close, it sort of sounds like those cattle are singing opera, doesn't it?" he suggested teasingly.

She shook her head at him. "Morgan, you're paddling with one oar. I swear it."

His eyebrows quirked over mischievous turquoise eyes. "C'mon now, Boston. Surely you remember our first kiss, aboard the train. As I recall, you told me I'd get my grubby hands on your frilly underwear when cows sang opera. Well, sugar dumplin', they are, and have been for some time. Or haven't you noticed how, when the town settles down in the wee hours of the morning, you can hear the herds out there on the prairie, singing their hearts out?"

"Oh, I've heard them, all right," she conceded dryly, "but I wouldn't exactly call the sound music, let alone opera."

"But it has to be, honey," he taunted sweetly, " 'cause I've been playing in your lacy britches since they first started. Fact is, I've come to think of it as *our song*."

Heather rolled her eyes. "How romantic," she sighed with feigned ardor.

"I thought so, too," he retorted. "Actually, I get extremely aroused every time I hear that lilting tune. Would you care to accompany me upstairs for a little afternoon delight, darlin'?"

"Morgan Stone! You're absolutely incorrigible!"

He winked. "Yeah, but I'm cute and cuddly . . . and horny as hell!"

She had to laugh, despite herself. "What's new?" she inquired drolly. As she sauntered off, her own smile was impish, and her hips swayed with deliberate seduction—actions specifically designed to torment him further.

A short while later, Heather accompanied a couple of her Temperance compatriots outside, where they all stood on the walkway, impatiently watching the last of the cattle pass by. The visiting ladies had been effectively trapped in the Salon for most of the afternoon, compliments of the massive, milling herd. Now the pair were eager to get home and begin muchdelayed supper preparations for their husbands.

"I'm afraid Herbert is going to have to settle for hash and eggs this evening," Anita White said with an exasperated sigh. "The poor man is going to think I've forgotten how to cook."

"That's better than never having learned at all," Heather told her friend. "Like me."

Anita and Sue Barton wore identical looks of astonishment. "You can't be serious."

"I'm afraid so," Heather admitted. "My grandparents had a cook, among other household help, and Mrs. Brimby loathed having anyone in her kitchen. Not that I really wanted to invade her domain, mind you, but now I wish I'd learned the basics at least. Until Ching Yung happened along and began fixing my meals, I was a steady patron at Vern's restaurant."

"Dear girl, why didn't you say something sooner?" Sue chided. "I would be more than happy to instruct you."

"That's very ki—" Heather's reply broke off abruptly, suspended by a sudden spate of gunfire.

On a chorus of alarmed shrieks, the trio watched in amazed fright as the startled steers bellowed and broke rank. Just that quickly, crazed cattle were running amok, racing in all directions at once, butting and gouging each other with sharp horns, clambering onto boardwalks, crashing into storefronts. Panicked townspeople ran for cover, even as others peered anxiously from doors and windows.

As one, the three women turned to make a dash for the Salon entrance. Intent on flight, Heather didn't even see the man behind her until it was too late to avoid colliding with him. Abruptly her face was mashed against a solid chest. Before she could regain her balance, rough hands gripped her arms. Then, without warning, the man thrust her away from him, literally pushing her into the street.

She was too stunned to cry out, even when she tumbled awkwardly off the boardwalk amid the stampeding herd. As sharp hooves struck all around her, Heather instinctively rolled onto her stomach, hunching into a ball, her arms wound around her head. In the next instant, something hard and heavy landed on her back. Dimly she wondered if one of the steers had fallen on her. Then, draped over her elbow, she recognized Ching Yung's black braid, and realized that he'd thrown his own body protectively over hers.

Even in the midst of the bawling, thrashing herd, she could hear people shouting. Piddles was barking frantically. Ching Yung gave a grunt of pain as a steer stumbled into them. Heather stifled a frightened whimper. Overhead, a loud cracking noise resounded again and again. Firecrackers. Or gunshots.

Suddenly Ching Yung's weight was gone, and Heather, still cringing, was yanked off the ground. Next she knew, she was clasped tightly against Morgan's chest, both of them safe inside the Salon, within a circle of concerned faces. Completely disoriented, Heather lay quivering in Morgan's embrace. Perhaps it was only her own befuddlement, but it seemed Morgan was trembling, too, his heart thudding as rapidly as hers.

Her shocked gaze met his. "M-Morgan?" she stammered. Then, before he could utter a word, she promptly began to sob.

Still holding her, Morgan sought a chair and eased both of them into it. Gently he rocked her back and forth, cradling her head to his chest. Finally, when he could wait no longer, he said gruffly, "Stop that caterwauling, Boston. We need to know if you're hurt or just scared simple."

"J-just scared," she wailed.

"Good. Then I won't feel too badly when I blister your behind for giving me such a fright and several gray hairs."

"H-how's Ching Yung?" she asked between hiccups.

Jasmine spoke up. "Don't worry none about that wiry little fella. He's gonna be fine. Just a couple o' crushed fingers, near as I can tell. Lloyd's gone for Doc Jenkins."

"Again," Lacy added. "Hellfire, we'd do better just to give Doc a room upstairs and have done with it. He's here half the time as it is."

"Lord in Heaven, Heather!" Brandy put in excitedly. "I thought for sure you were gonna be trampled to death. Probably would've been, too, if it hadn't been for Ching Yung throwin' himself on top o' you, and Morgan poppin' that whip o' his to run those steers off. They really saved your bacon out there, sweetie."

"Again," Lacy repeated. "Seems like rescuin' you is gettin' to be a regular habit around here."

"One I'm heartily weary of," Morgan stated tersely. He speared Heather with a sharp look. "What do I have to do to keep you safe, woman? Shackle you to my wrist?"

Drawing herself upright on his lap, Heather announced shakily, "It wasn't my fault. I didn't start that blasted stampede, you know. And I would have made it inside just fine if that dratted man hadn't shoved me off the walk."

Morgan's eyes widened, then narrowed dangerously. "What man?"

"The one I ran into . . . or who ran into me. Accidentally, I suppose. He pushed me, and I fell into the street."

"What did he look like? Do you know who he was?"

Heather shook her head. "It all happened too fast. I didn't get a good look at anything but the front of his shirt. It was red plaid, rather soiled . . ." Her voice trailed off, her own eyes growing wide as she abruptly recalled something she'd been too upset to remember until now, something she hadn't even realized she'd noticed. "He . . . Morgan! He . . . his shirt . . . the pocket . . . It smelled of mint!"

❧ 21 ❧

Days later, they were still pondering whether Heather had encountered the same assailant twice, or if it was all just a curious coincidence. Then Drake popped in for a visit, and he and Morgan began comparing notes. Naturally, Morgan mentioned Heather's accident. Drake was immediately on the alert.

"I'll be damned!" he declared. "If that isn't peculiar. One of the customers who was held up in that last bank robbery said the same thing. Past the bandanna he wore, she couldn't see the face of the bandit who stole her purse and jewelry, but she swears his breath smelled strongly of mint."

The two friends shared a long look. "Do you suppose the man who attacked Heather, then returned to push her into the middle of a stampede, is one of the train robbers we're after?" Morgan said.

"Could be," Drake replied. "Stranger things have been known to happen."

Morgan nodded. "True, but if that's the case, it means the fellow frequents Dodge every so often between robberies. He, and perhaps a couple of his cohorts."

"Or maybe one or more of them live somewhere around here—if not permanently, then temporarily," Drake contributed. "You know, I think maybe I'll just mosey over to the hotel and rent me a room for a while, stay in Dodge and snoop around a bit longer."

"Good idea," Morgan agreed. "I don't think our culprit comes in here to do his drinking, so you might hang around the other saloons. And check some of the boardinghouses while you're at it. Folks might open up to you more than they will to me. Some of them still think of me as a suspect and don't trust me enough to talk."

This drew a chuckle from Drake. "Small wonder. After all, I still have a sterling reputation, while you're just a dirty jailbird."

Morgan glared. "Go ahead, old buddy. Rub it in. Amuse yourself while you can, because we both know that what goes around comes around, and I for one will be tickled spitless when your turn comes up."

"Don't I know it. You always have been the vengeful type." Drake drained his mug. "Say, this punch stuff wasn't half-bad. Does your boss lady know you're lacing the drinks with liquor?"

"Bite your tongue, Drake. She'd have my head on a platter if she thought we were serving anything remotely related to alcohol. She's a banner-waving Temperance teetotaler."

Drake laughed and rose to leave. "Well, we all have our faults. Still, I'd keep a close watch on her from here on, if I were you. For some reason it looks like our mint-loving outlaw is intent on doing her harm."

"Believe me, now that I suspect all these mishaps of hers aren't caused by her blasted clumsiness, Heather isn't going to be able to draw a single breath, day or night, that I haven't breathed first."

Drake grinned. "So that's the way the wind is blowing. Last I noticed, she was tearing strips off your hide. Sure didn't take you long to clip her claws."

Morgan chuckled. "Don't make me laugh. She still scratches and hisses when I rub her the wrong way, which is most of the time. That lady is one temperamental tigress. The crazy thing is, I'm not sure I'd want to see her tamed. She's utterly fascinating just the way she is."

* * *

Heather's body was so thoroughly sated by love-making that she felt as if her bones had melted. She lay with her head pillowed on Morgan's shoulder, his arm curled around her, his hand lazily stroking the curve of her hip. Drowsy and relaxed, she murmured huskily, "Don't forget to let Piddles into the bedroom when you leave. He's used to sleeping with me and whines incessantly if he's confined to the parlor at night."

"I'm sorry, darlin', but he's going to have to get used to it, because from now on I'll be sleeping in your bed," Morgan replied softly.

"Mmn-hmmn," she mumbled. It took a moment for his comment to register in her fogged mind, but when it finally did, she sat bolt upright in bed. "What did you just say?"

"I said I'm staying right here with you," he repeated calmly. "I'm tired of sneaking back to my room in the wee hours."

"Well, that's just too blooming bad!" she retorted, fully alert now and ready to fight. "We had an agreement to be as discreet as possible. I fail to see how we can continue that policy if you go traipsing out of my room in broad daylight. So you can just get yourself up and return to your own quarters right now, and I don't want to hear any more about your spending the entire night in my bed. I didn't invite you into it in the first place, if I remember correctly."

"Oh, you invited me, all right," he rebutted. "Maybe not with words, but you certainly were hot to have me between your sheets . . . and your thighs."

She whacked him in the chest with her doubled fist. "That does it, Morgan! Get out! Now! And don't bother to come back."

He remained where he was, though he did reach out to capture her wrists in his hands. "For someone so adamant about not getting caught bare-ass naked, you're getting awfully loud, darlin'," he informed her quietly, reminding her that she was nearly shrieking at him.

"Out!" she hissed.

"No. And it's not just my own convenience I'm concerned about. It's your safety. It appears that someone is out to do you harm, sweetheart, and I'm just as determined to see that they don't. From now on, I'm going to be as close to you as your own shadow, day and night. If they want you, they'll have to get past me first."

Caught off guard, Heather ceased trying to free her arms and froze in place, half over him. Even in the dim bedroom, Morgan saw her eyes go wide as she contemplated his words.

"I . . . I was hoping it was all some strange coincidence," she whispered faintly. "Otherwise, it means someone really is trying to hurt me. Those incidents . . . the attack in the alley, getting pushed into the street, perhaps even those slivers of glass I nearly swallowed. Do you truly suspect they're connected somehow?" Her voice quivered with her rising fear.

"I think it's safer to assume so, at least for now, and to stay alert in the days ahead. Just in case," he told her. "Forewarned is forearmed."

He wanted to say more, but the need for secrecy prohibited relating his recent conversation with Drake, or divulging his and Drake's true profession and mission. It occurred to him that she might feel more secure, more comforted, to know that she was being guarded by a trained agent who was well-versed in defense tactics. For now, at least, she would have to be satisfied with her itinerant shoe salesman-cum–reformed bartender—her undercover lover.

He pulled her more fully into his embrace, twining his long fingers in her tumbled hair and urging her head against his chest. "Go to sleep, love," he said softly. "I'll keep you safe."

She sighed. "I know. It's what you're doing to my reputation and my morals that has me worried."

Though Heather had come to value Ching Yung and his numerous services immensely in the past weeks, she now feared that she was about to lose his aid. Initially his loyalty had stemmed from the fact that she had helped save his life. Now Ching Yung had returned the favor in kind, and the scales were evenly balanced once more. When she approached Ching Yung about his future plans, he was stunned to learn her concerns.

"No, no, missy!" he assured her excitedly. "Ching Yung no go. I stay. Much hoppy here."

"And I'm happy to have you, Ching Yung. But you needn't stay out of any misguided sense of obligation, if you would prefer to go elsewhere. You saved my life the other day, at much risk to your own welfare, and any debt you feel you owed me has been repaid tenfold. Words cannot express my gratitude for your selfless rescue."

He executed a gracious bow, his long queue swinging. "I most grad to do so. I stay. Attend you and boss. He save Ching Yung two time now."

"Boss?" Heather echoed. "I take it you mean Morgan."

"Just so, missy."

Heather's lips twitched in a half smile. "Well, that certainly puts me in my place, doesn't it?" she commented wryly.

Again Ching Yung's head bobbed. "Just so, missy."

It was therefore ironic that Ching Yung brought near-disaster upon Morgan's head the very next day. It happened in the early afternoon, when the Salon was packed with patrons. As luck would have it, Sheriff Watson was also in attendance, with a front row seat to the unfolding drama.

Morgan and Bob were dashing back and forth behind the bar, trying to keep up with drink orders. Morgan had also effectively blackmailed Heather into serving tables along with the other girls, by threatening to make Ching Yung stop indulging her every whim if she didn't start doing her fair share of work around the Salon. Even Arlene had volunteered to help out for a short while. Ching Yung, despite his broken fingers, was everywhere at once, it seemed— clearing tables, washing glasses, replenishing supplies from the storeroom.

Heather approached the bar with yet another order, just in time to see Ching Yung stoop down and retrieve an item from the floor near Morgan's feet.

"Hey, boss," he said. "You drop this, maybe?" He held out his hand, from which was suspended a lady's gold pendant watch.

Heather's heart lurched into her throat. She stared at the dangling timepiece with disbelieving eyes. "Oh, my stars!" she exclaimed softly. "That's my watch!"

At her startled declaration, several heads turned toward her, their faces displaying a variety of expressions—from mild curiosity to frowns of concern. Just two seats down, Sheriff Watson perked up and leaned forward with avid interest, his gaze shifting swiftly from Morgan to Heather and back to the watch. Arlene hurried toward the bar, as if sensing something momentous was afoot.

Morgan reached out to casually take the pendant from Ching Yung, holding it out toward Heather. "You really ought to be more careful with your baubles, princess," he commented lightly.

Before Heather could claim it, stunned as she was to behold the very watch the robber had taken from her on the train, Arlene stepped forward and took the pendant. "My goodness, Heather! Didn't you tell us your watch had been stolen? However did it get here, do you suppose?"

Morgan's gaze locked with Heather's, both filled with a hundred unvoiced questions. Queries that neither of them asked or answered aloud, but upon which so much depended.

"Let me see that," the sheriff demanded. Arlene immediately relinquished the timepiece to the lawman, who examined it closely.

"Is this your watch, Miss Burns?" he inquired.

"Yes," she answered, for once not bothering to correct his alteration of her surname. Her gaze clung to Morgan's, intent and searching.

"The same one that was stolen during the train robbery?" he prodded.

For a heartbeat, she hesitated. Then calmly and surely, her eyes never leaving Morgan's, she said, "No. This one is a spare I packed with my luggage."

The sheriff glowered. "Are you sure?"

"Quite certain, Sheriff."

Watson's interrogation turned abruptly to Ching Yung. "You found this on the floor? Just a few minutes ago?"

Ching Yung nodded miserably, by now aware that all was not well with his boss and beloved mistress.

"What made you think Mr. Stone had dropped it? Did you see it fall from his pocket?"

"No. It by boss's foot. It not there rast night when Ching Yung sweep. Just be here now."

"Well, that's very interesting." Watson sneered at Morgan. "And what do you have to say about all this, Mr. Stone? Was Miss Burns's watch in your possession?"

"Oh, for heaven's sake!" Heather interrupted. "Of course it was!"

Morgan's eyes flared in surprise.

Heather ignored him and swiftly rounded on the lawman. "I gave it to him last evening. The latch on the chain was broken, and Morgan offered to fix it for me. I was simply surprised that Ching Yung had found it on the floor, where it might have gotten stepped on, that's all. Hardly enough to make a federal case out of, or to harangue my employees, Sheriff." She speared the man with her haughtiest glare. "I demand that you apologize to both Morgan and Ching Yung, and that you refrain from such rude behavior in future, or I shall be forced to ban you from the premises."

Watson's face reddened from the neck up. His eyes narrowed angrily. Aware, however, that he'd made enough of a fool of himself in front of half the town, he grudgingly growled, "My mistake, fellas. It won't happen again."

His statement was deliberately double-edged, both apology and warning.

Afterward, it was some time before Morgan and Heather found a moment alone together. Finally, during the lull in business that signaled the supper hour, Morgan cornered her in the storeroom, where she was making a list of supplies to reorder. Her back was to him, and if she noticed him enter the room and shut the door quietly behind him, she gave no indication, keeping on with her task. For some minutes he stood silently observing her. Then he spoke up softly, careful not to startle her.

"I didn't have your watch, Heather. I don't know how it came to be on the floor behind the bar, but until Ching Yung handed it to me, I'd never touched it."

She sighed audibly, her shoulders slumping. "Just between the two of us, and to set the record straight, it *is* the same watch the thief stole from me during the train robbery. Also, I'd made up my mind that I wasn't even going to ask you about it, Morgan. I guess I was afraid to hear your answer. Afraid you might say something I didn't want to hear." She turned to face him, her eyes glistening with unshed tears.

"Oh, baby!" he murmured. "Do you really have so little faith in me, after all this time?"

She shook her head, and two fat tears escaped to trace wet tracks down her cheeks. "It's not that. I trust you with my life. With my body. With my entire being and every possession I own. It's my heart I feel the need to defend. You could break it so easily, Morgan, without even trying. With no effort at all, and without meaning to do so."

Wordlessly he held his arms open to her, and she rushed into his embrace. "I won't hurt you, kitten," he promised, stroking her bright hair. "Never. Your heart is safe within my keeping. Always. Don't you know that by now?''

A sob caught in her throat. "I didn't want to fall in love with you, Morgan. I tried my hardest not to, but it happened anyway." In frustration, she beat her small fist on his shoulder. "Damn it all! Why did it have to be you?"

He threw back his dark head and laughed. "God, but you batter my pride, lady! It's not as if I'm an ax murderer, or a snake-oil peddler."

"For which, I suppose, I should be eternally grateful," she muttered into his shirt. "Mother is going to have a seizure when she learns I threw Lyle Asher over for you. A bartending shoe salesman, for pity's sake!"

He chuckled louder, the sound rumbling through his chest beneath her ear. "Look on the bright side, darlin'. With me, you'll always have shoes and sarsaparilla."

❧ 22 ❧

Later that day, thinking back on their conversation in the storeroom, which was cut short when Bob arrived to tell Heather that Gus was awake and wanted to talk with her, Heather realized something very significant—at least to her. While she had poured out her innermost feelings, admitting her love to Morgan at last, he had not reciprocated. Not once, she recalled with growing anger and dismay, had he mentioned his feelings for her, let alone any desire to marry her. Oh, he'd told her he'd never hurt her, or break her heart, but he hadn't professed undying love, or given any hint of his intention to spend his future with her.

The more she thought about it, the more morose Heather became. For all she knew, Morgan might consider their romance just a temporary interlude, an amusing way to pass the time until he was cleared of all suspicion and free to leave Dodge City. The mere notion that he could regard her as a short-term dalliance made her temper simmer. By early evening, she'd worked herself into such a frothing state that she couldn't glance in Morgan's direction without glaring at him, could scarcely speak without snarling.

"What in tarnation is wrong with you?" he inquired, frowning impatiently across the bar at her. "You're behaving like you ate a pile of prunes and someone locked the privy door."

"Spare me your quaint analogies, please. They're so invariably crass."

Morgan's brows shot up. "Oh, the princess is really in a royal snit tonight, isn't she? Thinking she's so high and mighty. And what brought this on? Your talk with Gus?"

"It has nothing to do with Dad."

Before Morgan could question her further, Jasmine strolled up and requested a Gentleman's Ginger. "Heavy on the ginger, please, sugar pie," she drawled, batting her long lashes at him.

Morgan responded with a wink and a teasing grin. "Only the best for our fragrant flower."

By now Heather was familiar with the often ribald repartee that was routine among the girls and the bartenders. Usually it didn't bother her much, for she knew it was harmless jesting. But tonight the banter grated on her raw nerves and too sensitive feelings.

"Speaking of scents," she put in waspishly, "yours is rather overwhelming, Jasmine. You're supposed to apply it with discretion, not bathe in it."

Jasmine rolled her big eyes in droll amusement. "Here we go again with the lady lessons! Why can't you just let it rest? If it ain't broke, don't fix it."

"Meaning?" Heather inquired.

"The girls and I have been at this business a lot longer than you have, honey. We know what works for us, what gets the best results from a customer."

Heather's chin rose haughtily. "Only if that customer is a man," she said pointedly.

Jasmine laughed. "Sugar, as far as we're concerned, there is no other kind."

When Jasmine had left with her order, Morgan commented lightly, "She's right, you know. It's fine to act all prim and proper during the day, when the ladies come in for tea. But at night, when the men have the place to themselves, they prefer a little friendlier service."

Heather sniffed. "In other words, they expect tarts in short skirts hanging all over them."

He gave a careless shrug. "Basically, yes."

"Don't you find that attitude highly hypocritical?" she asked bitterly. "The same fellows who seek the company of trollops in the evening would have a conniption if their wives were to behave so brazenly, while on the opposite side of the same coin, they would never dream of marrying a hussy."

"Oh, I expect some would," Morgan replied with a chuckle. "Many a man has wished he could have both types of women rolled into one. A lady in the parlor, and a harlot in the bedroom. It's a perfect combination."

"Is that so?" Heather mused acidly. "Well now, that certainly puts an interesting slant on things. Gives me an entirely new perspective, so to speak."

She flounced off, more furious than ever. "For two cents, I'd make him eat those words!" she grumbled to herself. Pearl passed by with a tray full of drinks, and Heather promptly claimed one for herself.

Pearl stopped dead in her tracks. "Heather!" she squealed. "That was for one of my customers!"

"Get him another one."

Pearl's eyes widened in dismay as Heather tipped the glass and drank deeply. This particular beverage was liberally laced with liquor. Pearl waited in tense anticipation as Heather slowly lowered the mug and licked her lips.

"I don't believe I've tried this particular drink before," she stated contemplatively. She took another sip. "What's it called?"

"Uh . . . a Christian cordial," Pearl stammered. Gathering her courage, she asked hesitantly, "Do you like it?"

"It has an unusual tang to it. Some flavor I can't quite identify."

"Orange?" Pearl suggested hopefully.

Heather smiled. "Yes, that's it. Orange. Quite tasty, actually. I'll have to remember this, and order it more often."

Pearl returned Heather's smile with a rather lame

one. "Not too often, I hope," she said ambiguously, and hastily made her way back to the bar.

Not long afterward, Heather was feeling much more relaxed, if not more cheerful. She was still in a pique over Morgan's irritating male opinions. Now, however, her viewpoint was becoming slightly skewed.

"That man deserves to be taught a good lesson," she mused fuzzily. "And I'm just the woman to do it." She giggled to herself. "So he wants a harlot, does he?"

Passing close by, Lacy stopped to inquire, "Did you say somethin' to me, Heather?"

Heather waved a languid hand. "No, no. Just talking to myself."

Lacy bent closer and peered into Heather's flushed face. "Great garters! You're a wee bit sloshed, ain't ya?"

"Pardon me?" Heather asked, staring up with glazed eyes.

"Nothin', sweetie," Lacy replied quickly. "Just wondered if you were feelin' all right."

"Just dandy," Heather answered.

"If you say so." Shaking her head, Lacy started on her way again, only to be brought up short when Heather tugged at her sleeve.

"Lacy, you want to do me a big favor?" Heather said, wondering why it took such effort to enunciate her words properly.

Lacy hesitated. "That depends on what you have in mind."

Heather pulled the woman closer, and whispered something that made Lacy's jaw drop. Minutes later, Lacy was helping Heather up the stairs, the two of them giggling like schoolgirls.

The last customers left the Salon, and Morgan gratefully locked the door behind them, drew the curtains shut, and began turning down the lamps. It had been a long day, fraught with pitfalls, and it wasn't over yet. Unless Heather had passed out from her inadvertent encounter with alcohol, he would probably have to deal with her before he could call it a night. Her moods today had been erratic at best, swinging wildly like a pendulum on a too tightly wound clock. He could only hope she had run down by now, and was not in a tantrum.

He dragged his fingers through his hair in a gesture of weary frustration. Egad! What a day! First that watch turning up when and where it had. Then having to assure Heather that he'd had nothing to do with either its absence or its untimely reappearance. Not that he'd had to do that much convincing. She'd been ready enough to believe him, and even when she hadn't been sure of his innocence, she'd lied to protect him. Then, to add icing to the cake, she'd taken him completely by surprise by announcing that she was in love with him.

She'd caught Morgan off guard, shaking him to his soul, thrusting his own emotions and intentions forward for self-examination—something he wasn't quite ready to do. He had sufficient problems to deal with already. The train thefts, with the crafty outlaws still on the loose. Sheriff Watson eagerly grasping at any excuse to hold a necktie party, with Morgan as the guest of honor. Heather's numerous so-called accidents, and the more direct attacks aimed at her. Gus's slow recovery. Morgan had more than enough on his plate at present, without Heather adding to the fare by expecting some sort of declaration from him, which he highly suspected she did.

He really didn't want to deal with this now, didn't have time to probe into all the whys and wherefores, to sort through his feelings and examine them in depth and detail. If Heather would just agree to let sleeping dogs lie for a little while longer, until he got some of the other aspects of his life and his job straightened out, it would certainly be more convenient.

Not that he didn't adore her. Even at her haughtiest, she was cute and funny and beautiful, and so desirable that Morgan walked around in a perpetual state of arousal. Even when she made him mad enough to spit, he wanted her. Moreover, he'd never before felt so protective about any woman, or so possessive. No doubt about it, the little redhead with the big brown eyes had him in a dither—first wringing him dry, then filling him up again, with an improbable blend of laughter and lust, tenderness and fury, passion and frustration.

But love? The everlasting, do-or-die, till-death-do-us-part, faithful-ever-after type of love that poets wrote and troubadours sang about? The kind that set strong men trembling in their shoes, changed cowards into heroes, and vice versa? Morgan simply didn't know. He supposed he was going to have to sit down and analyze his feelings sometime soon. To ask himself some extremely important and soul-searching questions, and to answer as honestly as he could.

For instance, could he give up his footloose ways, and probably his lucrative employment with Wells Fargo as well, if that's what it took to keep Heather? Did he really want to? If not, how would he feel, deep down where it counted, if she went off and married someone else? Morgan suspected he already knew the answer to that one. He'd feel miserable—and murderous! What about children? Would Heather be a good and loving mother? And what sort of father would he be?

Suddenly, as if someone had walloped him aside the head with a hammer, Morgan realized that parenthood might be more a reality than a fantasy at this point. The way he and Heather had been mating like minks every night, they might already have conceived a child together. The thought stunned him. More amazing, it intrigued him. For a moment he allowed himself to imagine a miniature version of himself, or perhaps a tiny replica of Heather, and found himself grinning like an idiot at the idea, though he had trouble picturing Heather, with her trim, enticing figure, all plump and round with child.

"That would be a sight to behold!" he muttered to himself with devilish humor.

"What would?"

Heather's voice called him back from his private pondering. Morgan glanced toward the stairs, blinked twice, and had to quell the urge to rub his eyes in total disbelief. There, midway down, stood the object of his musings, though certainly not the way he'd ever thought to see her.

As he gaped in dumbfounded astonishment, she started toward him, her gait somewhat wobbly. Whether it was the amount of liquor she'd previously consumed or those ridiculously high-heeled shoes that made her unsteady, he could only guess. She stumbled, the crimson ostrich plume in her coiffed hair waving wildly, and Morgan shook free of his stupor to dash forward and catch her as she tripped down the steps and into his arms.

Not at all concerned that she'd just risked breaking her neck, she gazed up at him with adoring eyes and crooned, "Oooh, Morgan! You're sooo strong! So chiv . . . chiv . . ."

"Chivalrous?" he supplied huskily, his eyes scanning the provocative cleavage displayed by the low-cut gown.

"Yes. Handsome, too."

"And you're tipsy," he informed her.

"C-can't be," she hiccuped. "Only had that Chris . . . Chrisss . . . Oh, drat! You know what I mean!"

"Yeah, Pearl told me," he said with a grin. "It must have gone down real smooth and hit you darned hard for you to come waltzing downstairs in that getup."

He stood her on her feet and held her at arm's length to get the full effect of her efforts. Her dress was bright red satin, trimmed in yards of ebony lace, with a décolletage that dipped halfway to her navel and revealed a shocking expanse of creamy white flesh. Her arms were bare from shoulder to elbow, then sheathed in dark lace gloves. Below the flounced hem of her skirt, a ruffled black petticoat showed, the left side of both articles hitched up in a huge bow at her hip to expose her long leg and the beribboned garter riding high on her net stocking. Jet beads dangled from her earlobes, and her hair had been caught up in a tumbled mass of curls. Her face sported rouge on lips and cheeks, and kohl shaded her eyelids, deepening their color to that of rich dark chocolate.

"What's your game, princess?" he asked in a voice raspy with desire.

She tossed her head, and her earrings jangled merrily. "Darling, I thought this was the way you wanted me to look. I dis . . . distinctly recall you saying I'd look fetching in a dress of this sort."

Morgan drew a deep breath and slowly let it out, reminding himself that she was as drunk as a skunk and therefore not wholly responsible for her actions. "So you are, love. Quite fetching. I must say I'm glad you waited until we closed up before coming down to display your new look. If our customers had seen you like this, they'd have stumbled over their tongues, and I would have had to bash a few heads."

"Would you really?" she asked in a velvet voice that sent desire lancing through him. "You're so gal . . . gallant, Morgan."

He shook his head and gave a wry grin. "That's me. Gallant to a fault. Now, what do you say I take you upstairs and put you to bed before you fall on your backside?"

Her painted lips pursed in a pout. "No. I want another one of those drinks first."

"Sweetheart, you'll regret it if you do," he warned.

"I don't care. I'm thirsty."

He reluctantly relented. "Okay, but don't say I didn't warn you, when you wake up and everything including your hair hurts." He towed her along to the bar, Heather clinging to his arm, and attempted to seat her on one of the barstools.

"Wait," she told him, holding his hands to her

waist. "I wanna sit on the bar, the way the girls do sometimes."

"All right, but try not to topple off on your nose, will you?" he agreed, hoisting her up.

She gave an elated giggle. "Ooooh, I like it up here. It's rather like sitting on a raised throne, surveying everyone and everything below you."

His crooked smile appeared again. "Actually, there's a fairly fantastic view from here as well," he said, peering up her skirt.

She wagged a gloved finger at him. "How naughty, Morgan!"

His hand wandered up her thigh, his fingers looping through the band of her garter to give it a tug. "How nice, my dear," he replied. "Warm, and smooth, and tempting. Shall I go on?"

"With your words or your actions?" she teased in that sensuous tone that reminded him of smoke and silk.

In reply, he touched his mouth to her thigh, letting his lips linger lovingly before they wandered upward, his mustache raising gooseflesh. She moaned in delight, and he lifted his head to spear her with a challenging gaze.

"Just how daring do you feel tonight, darlin', in your fancy feathers and your besotted haze?"

She slanted him a beguiling look, her tongue sweeping out to wet her lips. "As bold as brass."

"What if I said I want to make love to you here? Now?"

"On the bar?" she questioned, arching a delicate brow.

"The bar, the floor, maybe even atop the billiard table."

She laughed, low and lusty, her eyes glinting with mischief. "The billiard table? Wouldn't that be a bit risky, sweetheart? It really wouldn't do to get the wrong balls stuck in the corner pocket. Bad form, you know."

He burst out laughing. "Ah, Boston, you enchant

me! Tyrant or trollop, you are utterly bewitching."

Clamping his hands around her waist, his eyes shimmering with passionate promise, he lowered her slowly onto her back—following her descent onto the hard, polished surface of the bar . . .

❧ 23 ❧

The next morning, Heather's head felt as if it were about to fall off. In fact, she wished it would, if only to rid her of the pain. Her stomach was queasy, her tongue felt as if it had been coated with fur, and it was all she could do to crawl out of bed.

Even her eyes throbbed, and they were so sensitive to light that she had to squint to look at herself in the mirror. Upon viewing her reflection, she winced. Merciful heavens! She looked like a hag! No, maybe a rabid raccoon was a better description, now that her eye paint was smeared in dark rings beneath her eyes and her hair was standing on end. All told, she looked like warmed-over death, and didn't feel much better than that.

Ching Yung, bless his heart, brought up a tray of biscuits and weak tea, but it was still nearly noon before Heather felt recovered enough to venture downstairs. She regretted it instantly, for Morgan took one look at her and went into spasms of laughter.

"You look a bit worse for wear, princess," he told her unsympathetically.

She sneered at him. "Brilliant deduction, Mr. Stone. Maybe you really ought to be a detective."

She lowered herself gingerly into a chair and cradled her aching head in her hands. "What was in those orange-flavored drinks I had last night, anyway?"

Morgan adopted an innocent demeanor that didn't quite suit him. "Nothing special. Why?"

"Because I feel as if a locomotive is running through my head, and my stomach is threatening to stage a revolt."

Morgan mustered a look of concern. "Could be you're coming down with some sort of ailment."

She skewered him with a glare. "Or perhaps you doctored my drinks," she suggested.

"Now, how could I do that, when the first one wasn't even meant for you?"

She shook her head—another bad move—and groaned aloud. "I don't know, and I'm too frazzled to figure it out right now. I just want to sit here and expire quietly."

Her wish was not to be granted. Not only did she live, but when the Salon opened for business, peace was but a remote recollection. Between the clatter of cups and glasses and the relentless chatter and laughter of the customers, Heather wanted to scream, except that would only make a bad situation worse, of course. When Lloyd sat down at the piano and began to pound out a merry tune, she promptly stalked over and threatened to slam the keyboard lid on his fingers if he did not desist.

He eyed her warily. "Kinda testy today, aren't you? What did you do, get up on the wrong side of the bed?"

Morgan chuckled and answered for her. "Naw, she probably just laced her corset too tight again, and it's cutting off the flow of blood to her brain."

Before Heather could summon a suitably scathing retort, one of the gentlemen engaged in a round of billiards held up an object and queried loudly, "Hey! Which one of you gals lost your garter?"

One glance at the red satin garter rimmed with lace, and Heather wanted to crawl in a hole and pull it after herself. Drat! Then she brightened a bit. It wasn't as if her name were on the blasted thing, or she had to publicly claim it, after all. Moreover, she was supremely grateful more intimate items hadn't been found lying around—like her corset, or stockings, or, God forbid, her underdrawers. Suddenly she had the urge to rush upstairs and account for the rest of her clothes.

At the bottom of the stairs, Lacy waylaid her with a wink and a giggle. "My lands, girl! That must have been some game of billiards!" she whispered.

Her face flaming, Heather dashed up the steps, disregarding her headache in favor of speed.

As she neared her quarters, she could hear Piddles growling and scratching at the closed door. "I'm coming, sweetums," she called out. "What's the matter? Do you need to go for a walk?"

Scarcely had she entered the parlor than the dog began barking and running in circles around her legs, almost as if he were trying to herd her back out again. "Hold on a minute, you impatient pooch!" she admonished. "Let me get your leash. And stop that infernal yapping, before my head explodes!"

She nearly tripped over him twice on her way to the small table near the divan, where she'd left the leather tether. She was reaching toward it when she caught a slight movement from the corner of her eye, a shifting of the throw pillow in the corner of the sofa. She watched for a moment, and when nothing happened she gave a shrug.

"My poor red eyes must be playing tricks on me," she muttered to herself.

Again she reached for the leash, and this time the pillow most definitely moved, the action accompanied by a strange rustling sound, similar to that of dry leaves. Backing slowly away, she stared warily at the pillow, fully expecting a mouse to poke its head out from under the fringe. With a low snarl, Piddles edged between Heather and the divan, his ears and ruff raised and his gaze riveted on the pillow.

The arrow-shaped head that emerged a few seconds later belonged to a much more sinister creature. Its forked tongue flicked rapidly back and forth. Its yellow eyes seemed to glow with evil intent. Heather stood rooted to the spot, then fled the room so rapidly that she didn't recall her feet actually touching the floor. By the time she reached the head of the stairs, she was shrieking at full volume, screeching Morgan's name again and again.

Her screams turned every head in the Salon, and so startled Morgan that he dropped a full bottle of gin on the floor, where it shattered. He left it there, taking time only to make sure his whip hung from his belt before he bolted up the stairs.

"What is it? What's wrong?" Thinking she was in shock when she didn't reply immediately, he shook her by the shoulders. "Dammit, Heather! Answer me!"

"Sn-snake!" she exclaimed breathlessly, her eyes dark with fright. "In my s-sitting room!"

Knowing how every woman since Eve detested snakes of any kind, Morgan would not have been surprised to find a teeny little garter snake not much bigger than a fishworm. He was therefore taken aback to find Piddles practically nose to nose with a fair-sized rattler. The reptile was coiled on the sofa cushion, head raised and fangs bared, ready to strike. Though growling menacingly, Piddles sat motionless, some inborn instinct warning him to remain still.

"Stay, Piddles," Morgan commanded quietly. "Don't move, boy."

As he spoke, Morgan advanced slowly, cautiously, loosening the whip as he went. When he was near enough for a clear attempt, he lashed out, the leather hissing through the air toward its target. The thong passed inches from Piddles's snout, caught the snake just behind the jaws, and cut deep, instantly severing head from body. In its death throes, the reptile's muscles twitched violently, its rattles vibrating rapidly for several seconds longer. At last the creature lay still.

Re-coiling his whip, Morgan snapped his fingers at the dog. "Come, Piddles. Let's go find Heather."

Upon hearing his mistress's name, the Pomeranian

left off investigating the remains and trotted into the hall, content that all was well at last. On his own way out, Morgan shut the door before following Piddles in search of Heather.

He found her where he'd left her, sitting on the topmost step, shaking like a leaf and snuggling the pup in her lap. "I'll have Ching Yung clean up in there," he told her, nodding toward her rooms.

"Is . . . is it dead?" she asked fearfully. "It didn't bite you or Piddles, did it?"

He offered a comforting smile. "Yes and no, in that order." Then he thought to qualify his answer. "At least I don't think Piddles got bit. You might want to check him out, just to be sure, though with all that fur, it might be hard to locate any puncture wounds unless they're bleeding. If you don't find any, just keep an eye on him for a while, in case he starts acting sluggish."

She gazed up at him with wide brown eyes. "Could you do it? Please, Morgan?"

He frowned down at her. "Aw, Heather! You know that blasted dog hates me! If I even look like I'm going to touch him, he bares those sharp little teeth at me and snarls fit to beat the band."

"Please?" she pleaded prettily.

Morgan heaved a huge sigh. "All right. I'll examine him, but only if you hold his head and keep him from biting me. I don't trust that mangy mutt for a minute."

A grin broke through and curved her lips. "Gee, for a big bad hero, you sure do have some peculiar qualms about one small dog, Morgan," she teased.

"That," he said, pointing at the animal in question, "is not a dog. It's a four-footed menace masquerading as one."

Heather refused to enter her quarters until Ching Yung had removed all evidence of the rattlesnake. Even then, she shivered as she walked past the divan, and was sure she'd never be able to convince herself to sit on it again. Realizing this, Morgan and Ching Yung removed the sofa, replacing it with another from Gus's office. The pillow went into the trash.

Gus was livid when he heard about this latest danger to his daughter. He was also extremely grateful to Morgan for taking care of the situation before anyone was hurt.

"I owe ye a debt, laddie," he said earnestly. "And I'm na a mon to forget a guid turn." Gus's brow wrinkled again as he considered the matter once more. "I'm still wonderin' how that rattler got into Heather's room, though. I canna ken a'tall how the creature managed to slither all the way to the second floor. 'Tis right odd, I'm thinkin'."

"More so than you realize," Morgan confided. "You see, we found a burlap bag behind the pillow where the snake was hiding. It's my guess someone carried the snake upstairs and put it on the divan, then propped the pillow over the sack and left— knowing the rattler would soon seek its freedom and perhaps lodge in the sofa cushions waiting for the first victim who happened to sit down there."

"That bein' Heather, most likely," Gus deduced with a dark frown. " 'Tis clear, then, that someone is tryin' his darndest to hurt her. I'm thinkin' it might be time for the lass to go back to Boston, where she'll be safe from harm."

Morgan nodded. "That would be one solution, provided her would-be killer doesn't follow her home. Another answer would be to catch whoever it is and put a stop to these attempts on her life. I'm willing to watch over her for you, Gus, for as long as it takes to nab the culprit."

"That's right braw o' ye, Morgan. I appreciate it. But do ye think we can catch him b'fore Heather comes to real harm?"

"I hope so, Gus. I'll protect her with my very life if need be."

Gus's shaggy brows rose. "Sounds like ye're plenty fond o' my wee lass."

Morgan feigned a careless shrug. "You could say that, I suppose. At any rate, I'll do my utmost to keep her safe until you're on your feet again. You have my solemn word on it."

"Speakin' o' which, have ye heard anything about those train robbers?"

"Not much. Word has it they might be in the area, but they seem to be lying low for the time being."

"Weel, sooner or later, they'll slip up, and then ye can get on about yer business. Course, then I'll have to hire another bartender to take yer place," Gus commented, his words beginning to slur. His eyelids drooped over glazed blue eyes. "Damnation! A new bairn can stay awake longer than I can these days, and most likely has more strength. 'Tis highly irritatin', bein' bed-bound for sae long."

Morgan, too, thought it odd that Gus should be so slow to regain his strength, but he merely shook his head and said, "It takes time and rest, Gus. Try not to worry. We'll look after things."

"Hmph!" Gus snorted. "Arlene tells me we're running a salon now. Gettin' a tad fancy for my blood."

Morgan held up his hands in a gesture of self-defense. "Hey! You're the fellow who turned Heather loose to run this place as she saw fit," he reminded the older man. "You've got nobody to blame but yourself. But I will say, it's all turning out much better than expected, with the help of a little treason in the ranks. Still, I don't look forward to the day when your daughter discovers our deceptions."

Gus smiled drowsily. "She's got my temper, she has. Aye. A chip off the ol' block."

Morgan chuckled softly. "I suspected that's where she got it, but I didn't want to get you riled by pointing out your daughter's faults so bluntly."

" 'Tisn't a fault, lad," Gus murmured, his eyelids drifting closed. " 'Tis a Scots virtue."

It was early Sunday morning, and though she'd gotten to sleep late the night before, Heather was up and dressed and almost ready to leave for church. Morgan, grumbling like a bear roused early from hibernation, insisted he accompany her. True to his word, he was intent on making sure she was as safe as possible.

He was standing behind the bar, sipping coffee and watching as Heather, perched on a barstool, finished the bowl of oatmeal Ching Yung had cooked for her. "How can you stand to eat that stuff?" he asked with a grimace.

She grinned at him. "It's delicious, especially if you sweeten it with brown sugar or maple syrup. And if you slice a peach into it, it's absolutely divine!" She licked her lips at the mere thought of fresh peaches, her eyes closing in remembered ecstasy of the last time she'd eaten some.

Gazing at her rapt expression, Morgan would have sold his soul for a peach tree. He was instantly aroused as he envisioned the two of them in bed, dripping the sweet nectar over their naked bodies, then licking one another clean.

His sensual daydream was rudely interrupted by a loud rapping on the locked main door. Morgan and Heather exchanged a frown. "Who on earth can that be, so early?"

The knocking came again, harder this time. "Whoever it is, he's damned determined," Morgan pointed out irritably.

As he started around the bar, a voice shouted from outside. "Open up, in the name of the law!"

Heather gave a groan and rolled her eyes heavenward. "Oh, misery! It's Sheriff Watson again! Whatever can he want this time?"

Morgan slanted her a mocking look. "Three guesses, darlin', and the first two don't count. He wants my neck in a noose."

She went with him to the door to greet the scowling lawman. To her surprise, Watson had his gun drawn and ready.

"You're under arrest, Stone," the sheriff said.

"Come along peaceable, or you'll be takin' up space at the undertaker's instead of a jail cell."

"Would you mind telling me what the charges are first?" Morgan inquired wryly.

"Same thing as before. Train robbery."

Morgan's brows rose in surprise. "Haven't we already done this vaudeville routine? Why the repeat performance?"

Watson poked the barrel of his pistol forward, butting Morgan in the chest with it. "Cut the wisecracks, Stone. You know darned well the train was held up again this morning. You were there, and you're not gonna get away with it this time. I have a witness who has described you right down to your back teeth."

Morgan glared back. "How much did you pay him, Watson?"

"You'll live long enough to regret that remark," the sheriff promised nastily. He poked Morgan again. "Let's go."

"Just a minute, Sheriff," Heather put in. "I don't care how many witnesses you have, or who they claim they saw. It could not have been Morgan. He was here the entire night and all morning."

Watson gave a smirk. "How would you know that? He probably snuck out after everyone went to bed, and was back in before anyone got up. You run a loose ship here, girlie. You're supposed to be keepin' a closer eye on this yahoo."

"Oh, believe me, I do," Heather assured him, matching him sneer for sneer. "And I know for a fact that Morgan hasn't set foot off this property since yesterday afternoon. I'll swear to that in court, if it comes to it."

"What do you do, lock him in his room at night?" the lawman scoffed. "Chain him to his bedpost?"

Heather's reply dripped with sarcasm. "Nothing quite that drastic."

"Then like I said, he could have snuck out with no one the wiser. Through a window, if he had to."

Heather heaved an irritated sigh. "Why must you

be so obstinate? Why can't you simply take my word for it?"

Watson leveled a hard look at her. "Because I strongly suspect you lied to me about that watch of yours, Miss Burns. You made a fool of me, and I tend to hold a grudge against such things. So, unless you can convince me that Stone really was here when the train was being robbed, you'd better plan on hirin' a new bartender right quick."

"But he *was*!" Heather declared in exasperation.

She shared a look of frustration with Morgan. "Apparently there's only one way to convince him, Morgan," she said softly, despair shadowing her eyes.

"No, Heather," he advised dismally, guessing what she was about to do. "Don't tell him. For your own sake, not mine."

"Don't tell me what?" Watson demanded.

Heather dragged in a deep breath. Her color was high as she announced quietly but firmly, "Sheriff, Morgan could not have helped hold up the train because he was with me all the while."

❧ 24 ❧

Morgan closed his eyes and groaned aloud.

Watson stared at Heather in mute disbelief for several seconds before finally commenting, "Are you sayin' what I think you are? That you spent the entire night with Stone? Alone?"

Heather nodded miserably, knowing she'd just shredded her reputation with her own tongue. "Yes, Sheriff, that is precisely what I am telling you."

"I don't believe it," the lawman said, shaking his head. "You're lyin' just to save his hide."

Heather glared at him. "Do you honestly think I would blacken my own name, and my father's, unless it was the truth? Come now, Sheriff, even you can't be so stupid."

He peered down at her, still contemplating her revelation. "I don't suppose you have any real proof of the matter?"

"For God's sake, Watson!" Morgan exclaimed with disgust. "We didn't exactly sell tickets, you know. It *was* rather an intimate get-together."

"Yeah, I imagine it was at that," the sheriff conceded. "But it's still your word against that of my witness."

"Then I suggest you talk to your informant again, and get a better account of things," Morgan told him. "Meanwhile, if you don't mind leaving, Heather and I were on our way to church."

Watson was nonplussed. "Church?" he echoed. He holstered his gun with a shrug and waved them toward the door. "Be my guests, folks. And don't forget to confess all your sins while you're there."

Almost as an afterthought, he added slyly, "Meantime, I think I'll just mosey upstairs and have me a little chat with Gus. What do you suppose he'll have to say about his daughter's nighttime activities?"

"You lousy bastard!" Morgan advanced on Watson with doubled fists, only to have Heather catch him by the arm and stop him.

"No, Morgan. It's not worth it. Dad was bound to find out sooner or later anyhow, and it might as well be now, while he's still laid up and can't do much about it."

"Such as beat the living crap out of me and send you to a convent?" Morgan supplied with dry wit.

Her sense of humor revived enough for her to offer him a weak smile. "Well, that's certainly better than the other way around. Somehow, I can't picture you in a wimple and a long black gown."

Out of respect for Gus, Watson agreed to wait downstairs while Heather and Morgan personally broke their shameful tidings to her father. "Mind you, if you two don't tell him, I will," he threatened. "So you might as well get it over with as painlessly as possible. Maybe he'll take the news a little better if it comes from you."

Fortunately, Arlene was not in attendance just then. Gus was alone and awake. He was also lucid this morning, which meant he understood everything they were telling him, with no chance of misinterpretation.

"Ye *what*?" Gus bellowed, literally rattling the windows. This, immediately after Morgan had assumed the lead and frankly admitted that he'd been bedding Heather. "Why, ye young rapscallion! I ought to see ye horsewhipped! And after I warned ye not to trifle wi' my daughter!''

"You did?" Heather put in with wide-eyed surprise.

"Aye, for all the guid it did," Gus said, turning his burning blue gaze on her. "And you, ye canny hizzy! Sneakin' round b'hind yer ole pa's back, lettin' this rascal b'neath yer skirts! 'Tis ashamed o' ye, I am. Hae ye no honor, lass?"

She drew herself up proudly, her back stiff and her face flaming. "Is the pot calling the kettle black, Dad?"

"Ach! Now ye're throwin' my own affairs in my face, are ye? Weel, let me tell ye, hinny. I'm a tad aulder and wiser than you, and not accountable to anyone but myself. Furthermore, 'tis na likely I'll ever find myself wi' a bun in the oven, which is more than ye can say."

She had the grace to hang her head. "I'm sorry, Dad. My only excuse is that I love Morgan. As for the other . . . I . . . I don't know."

Morgan jumped back into the fray. "I believe it's too early to tell if Heather is pregnant, sir."

Gus's eyes shot blue daggers at him. "Mayhap so, but the odds are good ye've gotten her wi' child. Moreover, 'twas a grave mistake makin' light o' my warnin' to ye, and now yer bound to pay the piper."

Gus released an angry sigh and shook his head in weary dismay. " 'Tis truly a sad day when I find myself grateful to that fool o' a sheriff, but if na for him, I'd yet be ignorant o' all this, wouldn't I? Neither o' ye had any intention o' tellin' me what was goin' on right b'neath my own nose, did ye?"

"In time, sir, yes," Morgan replied stiffly.

"B'fore or after the bairn arrived?" Gus inquired cynically.

Heather winced. "Now, Dad, don't get all worked up. You know now, and frankly, it's a relief to me that you do."

"I wonder if ye'll be as cheered when ye're standin'

b'fore Nels Swanson, daughter," Gus responded dryly.

Heather's head snapped up so quickly that her neck cracked. Her eyes questioned his, wide and pleading. "Whatever for?" she asked. "Surely you can't intend to press charges against Morgan for this, when it was both our faults. Or do you intend to renege on your agreement concerning Morgan's employment?"

"Neither, lass. Ye're barkin' up the wrong tree, as usual."

Heather frowned in bafflement. "Then why would I need to go before Judge Swanson?"

Morgan knew the answer before Gus uttered it, but he held his tongue and let the older man have his minor revenge, as was his due.

"Why, so he can wed ye to this four-flushin' scoundrel ye're so fond of, o' course," Gus informed her. "Ye dinna think I was gonna let the pair o' ye off scot-free, did ye now?"

"But . . . Dad," Heather stammered, not knowing what to say—afraid to even look at Morgan for fear of what she might see on his face.

"But nothin'," Gus stated, his jaw set as stubbornly as hers often was. "Ye'll marry him, if I have to hold both o' ye at gunpoint to see the deed done."

He threw a sharp glance at Morgan. "Do I hear any objections from ye, lad? Not that it'll make a tad o' difference."

"No, sir," Morgan responded politely. "But I do have one small request."

Gus's mouth quirked upward at the corners. "A blindfold, perhaps? Or a last meal for the condemned man?"

Morgan struggled to keep a straight face. "No, but I would like to formally ask both you and Heather for her hand in marriage. You see, Gus, I prefer to do my own proposing. In my own words and my own time, though you do seem to have me backed neatly into a corner."

Gus waved a hand, indicating for him to continue. "Weel, get on with it then."

Very properly Morgan intoned, "Sir, I would like your permission to marry your daughter. I promise to provide for her to the best of my abilities, to honor her, to keep her safe—"

"Permission granted," Gus broke in impatiently.

Morgan bit back a grin at the older man's irascibility. Turning to Heather, he took her hand in his, knelt down on one knee, and asked softly, "My dearest Heather, would you please do me the great honor of becoming my wife?"

Tears welled up in her eyes, turning them to liquid chocolate. "Yes. If you're sure that's truly what you want, and not just a result of guilt, or a sense of obligation, or because of my father's threats."

"Believe me, darlin', threats or no, I wouldn't have asked if I didn't want to marry you."

"Then I'm thrilled to accept your offer, Morgan, and I pledge to be the best wife you could ever want."

"Dinna make promises ye canna keep, daughter," Gus grumbled. "Ye're right bonny to look at, but a pampered, bossy lass wi' more arrogance than sense, and I dinna imagine marriage is suddenly gonna turn ye into a bloomin' saint."

"God forbid!" Morgan exclaimed with a broad grin. "I've just about gotten used to her the way she is."

"Now that we've all agreed on what's to be done, it's time to get Nels over here to seal the deal all legal like," Gus said. "Heather, send Ching Yung over right away with a note, and then ye'd best go get yerself gussied up for yer weddin'. Morgan, ye go inform the others, and tell Bob I need to see him. Wake 'em all up, if need be."

Heather's eyes went round with alarm. "Dad! When you insisted on a wedding, I didn't know you meant so soon! We can't possibly make all the arrangements so quickly."

"Why not?" Gus challenged. "As I see it, the sooner the better."

"But I need time to write to Mother, and time for her to travel to Dodge. And I don't have a proper wedding gown or anything!" she wailed.

"Ye should hae thought o' that b'fore ye let this scoundrel sweet-talk his way into yer bed, daughter. Now, get goin', 'cause I mean to see ye wed b'fore the day is out. Ye'll not be sleepin' t'gether another night under my roof till ye are, and that's final."

At a nod from Gus, who had been carried downstairs to the main room of the saloon and was now ensconced in an overstuffed chair near the stairs, Lloyd pounded loudly on the piano keys to alert the throng of spectators to the start of the wedding. Judge Swanson took his place at the foot of the steps, next to Morgan and Bob, who had been drafted as the best man. A hush fell over the crowd, all eyes turned expectantly toward the upper balcony as Lloyd launched into the beginning chords of the "Bridal Chorus."

First came seven of the most distinctive bridesmaids the residents of Dodge had ever been privileged to see. Lined up in alphabetical order, for lack of a more democratic system, they presented a vibrant picture as they preceded the bride down the stairs. Except for their too elaborate hairstyles, an excess of face paint, and glimpses of black net stockings beneath their rainbow-hued skirts, a stranger to town might never have guessed that they were barmaids and harlots by trade.

Finally the bride appeared. She wore a cream-colored satin gown with a matching lace mantilla draped over her bright tresses. The dress was trimmed at bodice, cuffs, and hem with silver-blue lace. Pearls modestly adorned her ears and throat, and in her hands she carried a bouquet of bluebells and lily of the valley.

The flowers were from Morgan, compliments of Margaret Hinkle's garden. The gown was one Heather had brought from Boston, but hadn't worn yet. The pearls had belonged to her grandmother Elise. Lacy had lent her the mantilla. Hence, even on such short notice, Heather had managed to fulfill the fabled prerequisites of "something old, something new, something borrowed, something blue." Arlene had even presented her with a brand-new penny for her shoe.

As she stood at the head of the stairs gazing down at Morgan, Heather was almost overwhelmed with emotion. How vastly her life had changed since coming to Dodge, just a few short weeks ago. And it was about to change even more, for within minutes she would become Morgan's wife, assuming a new role and a new name.

The thought was exhilarating—and just the tiniest bit scary, too. Morgan still hadn't said he loved her, and regardless of what he claimed, she fervently hoped he wasn't marrying her because he felt he had to. She loved him so dearly that she feared it would break her heart if he didn't return that affection in full—or learn to love her, if he didn't yet.

As his eyes held hers, warm and admiring, Heather's doubts dissolved. For better or worse, for richer or poorer, it would all work out somehow. Slowly, surely, she stepped forward, toward her destiny.

Morgan had always considered Heather lovely, even with dirt on her face or her hair tousled, but he'd never seen her as beautiful as she was at this moment. He'd heard it said that a woman glowed on her wedding day, and now he knew it was true. His lady . . . his bride . . . was positively radiant.

As he met her on the lower step, taking her trembling hand in his, he murmured in a voice filled with awe, "Princess, you're absolutely glorious. Have I told you yet how very much I love you?"

At his words, those very words she so longed to hear from him, tears rose to her eyes. "Oh, Morgan! That's the best wedding gift you could ever give me!"

With his free hand, he brushed a crystal tear from

her lash. Then, as one, they turned to face their guests and Judge Swanson.

A lady and gentleman, both carrying traveling bags, entered the crowded Salon and gazed about inquisitively. It seemed odd that the place was so quiet, when every chair in the place was filled, with an overflow of customers standing on every available inch of floor space. Moreover, everyone seemed to be enthralled with something that was happening toward the rear of the room, though the newcomers couldn't see beyond the throng in front of them.

Curious, the lady leaned over and tapped the man nearest to her on the shoulder. "Pardon me, sir," she said in a low tone. "Is something special going on here?"

"Sure is," the fellow replied. "Gus's only daughter's gettin' herself married today."

The woman's eyes went wide, her hand flying to her chest. Next to her, her traveling companion stiffened on a gasp. Just then, from near the foot of the stairs, they heard a man intone, "If anyone knows of any reason why these two should not be united in holy matrimony, let him speak now, or forever hold his peace."

The lady let out a muted squeak. Her friend opened his mouth as if to utter a rebuttal. Neither accomplished the task soon enough, as the woman fainted into the gentleman's arms, both of them sagging slowly to the floor. By the time the man assured himself that she had merely swooned, the crucial moment in the ceremony had passed.

Lyle Asher felt Betsy Blair-Burns stir in his arms and regain consciousness just in time to hear bride and groom pronounced man and wife.

❧ 25 ❧

To the delight of the onlookers, Morgan gave his new bride a kiss that threatened to melt her corset stays. Matilda Hershey was heard saying to her husband of thirty years, "Hank, you old geezer, why can't you kiss me like that?"

Hank replied drolly, "I would, honey pot, if you'd keep your teeth in for more than five minutes at a stretch."

Immediately following the ceremony, knowing the crowd would soon get rowdy, Heather climbed up a few more steps and called out, "Girls! Gather round! I'm going to throw the bouquet now."

At least a dozen and a half hopeful maids pushed their way to the front, shoving and laughing good-naturedly. Turning her back to them, Heather tossed the flowers over her shoulder. As the ladies vied for the coveted prize, believing whoever nabbed it would be the next to wed, squeals erupted, followed by several disappointed groans.

Eager to see which of them had caught her bouquet, Heather spun quickly around. The sight that met her eyes nearly had her stumbling down the stairs. She stared in disbelief. There, not twelve feet from her, and clutching the bouquet in her arms, was her mother—and at her elbow stood Heather's glowering ex-fiancé.

It took Heather a moment to recover from the

shock, but when she did, she dashed down the steps and threw herself into Betsy's embrace. "Mother! I'm so happy to see you!" she cried. "What a surprise!"

"I believe that should be my line, dear," her mother replied, kissing Heather lightly on the cheek. Backing off a step, Betsy peered into her daughter's glowing face, her own eyes shadowed with concern. "Oh, my sweet, impetuous child, what have you done?" she asked solemnly.

Before Heather had a chance to answer, Ching Yung came rushing up. "Missy! Photoglapher ready. He say come now!"

"In just a moment, Ching Yung. First I want you to meet my mother."

"Oh, blessed saints!" Betsy exclaimed faintly as she gazed at the diminutive Chinaman. "Is . . . is this your new husband?"

Heather blinked in confusion, then burst out laughing. "Oh, Mother! Whyever would you think such a thing?"

"Your letter, Heather. You mentioned this fellow in your letter, right after telling me you were breaking off your engagement to Lyle. Naturally, the two subjects linked themselves in my mind, and the more I thought about it, the more worried I became, until I simply had to come and see for myself that everything was well with you."

"And, just as understandably, Lyle decided to come with you," Heather added, reluctantly turning to face the man she'd once promised to marry. She held out her hand to him. "Hello, Lyle. I do hope you had a pleasant journey."

He frowned down at the bright gold wedding band on her finger. "Actually, it was quite harrying. Our train was held up near a little town east of here, which is why we did not arrive earlier in the day."

Heather's eyes widened as she recalled Sheriff Watson's disagreeable visit that morning. Somehow, with all that had happened since, she'd pushed the incident from her mind. A grin tilted the corners of her mouth. "You're in good, albeit unfortunate, company. My train, too, was robbed on my way to Dodge. In fact, that's where I met Morgan, my husband."

As if by mentioning him, she'd conjured him up, Morgan appeared at her shoulder. "Did I hear you bandying my name about, princess?" Even as he bent to brush his lips across her cheek, his turquoise gaze curiously examined the man and woman who'd held Heather's attention for several minutes now.

"Oh, Morgan, I'm so glad you found me. You simply won't believe it. Mother and Lyle arrived just in time for our wedding, and Mother caught my bouquet!"

Recognizing the flowers in the lady's hands, Morgan gave her a courtly half bow. "Mrs. Blair-Burns, I presume?"

Betsy nodded politely. "And you are?"

"Morgan Stone, ma'am. I'm pleased to make your acquaintance, and also grateful that you chose this day to arrive. Heather was distraught that you wouldn't be here for our wedding."

"As you probably know, it's quite by chance, since I hadn't an inkling that my daughter was romantically interested in anyone here, let alone planning to marry so abruptly." Betsy addressed her next comment to Heather. "I suppose we left Boston before your last letter arrived."

Heather blushed. "Actually, I haven't had time to write our news yet. There wasn't even time to send a message by telegraph."

Betsy's brown eyes, mirror images of Heather's, widened appreciably. "Why not, pray tell?"

"Most likely because I only proposed to her this morning," Morgan explained bluntly.

"Oh, dear!" Betsy looked as if she might swoon again, and Lyle rushed to grab her arm for support. "Why such a rush?" she inquired weakly. "Couldn't you have waited a while, like everyone else? Why, this must be the shortest engagement on record."

"It's positively outrageous!" Lyle agreed pompously.

"Not done in the better circles, I'm sure," Morgan commented wryly. "But this isn't Boston, and better circles are hard to find in Dodge."

Heather smothered a chuckle. "Actually, it's a little more complicated than that, but we needn't go into that here and now. After all, it's my wedding day, and we must celebrate both it and your timely arrival."

"Heather, aren't you going to introduce me to your mother's companion?" Morgan asked suddenly.

Heather's smile was more of a grimace as she replied, "Of course, darling. How remiss of me. Where are my manners?"

"You probably left them in your other shoes," Morgan informed her with dry wit, well aware of the identity of the man before him and Heather's discomfort.

"Morgan, behave yourself!" she admonished in a side whisper. In a more normal tone she said, "Darling, I'd like you to meet Lyle Asher. Lyle, I am proud to present my husband, Morgan Stone."

The two men eyed each other warily, like dogs sniffing the same bone. Morgan broke the tense silence first. "Ah, the other man. My predecessor. I must admit, I was curious about you."

"You have the advantage on me there," Lyle responded stiffly, "since I knew nothing about you. Still don't, for that matter. Nor does poor Betsy, which in my opinion is totally reprehensible."

Morgan replied with deliberate nonchalance, "Well, what can I tell you? I was a traveling shoe salesman . . . before I came to Dodge and was falsely arrested for train robbery. Consequently, I am currently on temporary probation with the court until my name is cleared. Gus took me on as a bartender. Of course, that was before Heather revamped the place into this Society Salon. Now I'm just a glorified soda server." He paused dramatically and added with a false smile, "And Heather's husband, of course. We mustn't forget that . . . you most of all, Asher."

In an effort to change the course of the conversation before the two men came to blows, Heather put in quickly, "Mother, have you and Dad greeted one another yet?"

It took Betsy a moment to collect her wits. If her renewed pallor was any indication, she was still trying to assimilate all Morgan had just told them, and trying to decide whether or not he was serious or merely jesting at her and Lyle's expense. Finally she responded weakly, "No, and I can't say I'm looking forward to seeing Angus again after all these years. But I suppose I must."

Leaning closer, Heather murmured confidentially, "I should caution you, he has a lady friend, a local widow by the name of Arlene Clancy."

Betsy nodded. "I appreciate the warning, dear. I'll do my best to be gracious, though under the circumstances that may be promising more than I can deliver."

As reunions went, this one was awkward at best. Angus was thoroughly shocked to see his former wife standing before him for the first time in eighteen years. She'd been so young, so lovely, the last time he'd seen her. Now there were a few streaks of silver glimmering in her dark hair, and tiny lines fanning out from the corners of her eyes. But those eyes were still as big and bright as ever, and her mouth still held its Cupid's-bow shape.

"I'd hae known ye anywhere, Bets," he told her, his own gaze lingering on her face. " 'Tis kind the years hae been to ye, lass."

"It's generous of you to say so, Angus," she replied with a slight quiver in her voice, "though not altogether true." She offered a slight smile. "I always did say you should have been Irish instead of Scottish, with all that blarney you spew."

"Bite yer tongue, woman!" he retorted. "Them's fightin' words!"

"Heather wrote to me about your accident. I hope you're recovering nicely."

"Not as quickly as I'd hoped, but Heather's been helpin' out round the place."

"Do you always do such a brisk business, or does today's wedding account for all the people here?" she inquired politely.

"Truth o' the matter, this be the first I've been out o' my bed since the mishap. Nearly didn't recognize my own bar, Heather's gussied it up so much."

"My, yes," Arlene spoke up, insinuating herself into the discussion and laying a proprietary hand on Gus's shoulder. "Your daughter has been busy lately."

Betsy's brow arched in an arrogant gesture so reminiscent of Heather that Morgan was hard put not to laugh. "So it would seem," Betsy commented crisply. "I don't believe we've been introduced. Are you one of Angus's employees?"

Arlene puffed up like a ruffled hen. Gus's face grew red. "This is my friend Arlene Clancy. She doesna work here, but she's been helpin' take care o' me while I'm laid up."

"I see. I hope she isn't overcharging you for her services, Angus. For all your frugal ancestors, you never were a wizard at finances. At least not when I knew you," Betsy qualified.

By now, Arlene looked as if she'd swallowed a prune pit that had lodged somewhere between her throat and her stomach.

"People change, Bets," Gus commented lightly, his blue eyes taking on a twinkle as he recognized the instinctive rivalry between the two females.

Betsy readily agreed. "Some sooner than others. You simply cannot imagine my surprise upon arriving and discovering that our daughter was getting married today. She was never prone to such impulsive behavior when she was with me in Boston. Therefore, I must assume this sudden transformation has something to do with the atmosphere here in Dodge City. Could it be that she's been unduly influenced by those she's been associating with lately? Perhaps persons of looser morals than the friends she has back home?" She speared both Angus and Arlene with a sharp glare.

"Now, don't ye go pointin' yer finger b'fore ye know the whole story, Bets. Course, that'd be just like ye, wouldn't it? Ye wouldn't know the truth if it bit ye on the nose."

"And you wouldn't know how to reveal the truth if your life depended on it," she countered tartly. "But do go on. I'm simply dying to hear your account of how and why all this came about so abruptly."

Heather was as uncomfortable at the turn of the discussion as her parents and Arlene were. "Mother, wouldn't you rather get settled in first?" she suggested. "We'll all have plenty of time to talk later, and more privacy."

"An excellent idea," Morgan concurred. "Besides, you really should put those flowers in water before they wilt, Mrs. Burns. And when you've freshened up a bit and had some rest, you can rejoin us for the remainder of our nuptial celebration."

"I suppose so, since you all seem so bent on evading the issue," Betsy allowed. "At the least, it will give me more time to sharpen my wits. By the way, Lyle and I left our luggage with the gentleman behind the bar. Could someone kindly retrieve it for us and direct us to a decent hotel nearby?"

"But, Mother! I . . . well . . ." Heather's gaze ricocheted back and forth between her mother and father. "I just assumed you'd want to stay here. There are rooms upstairs, and it wouldn't take more than fresh linens and a tad of dusting to make one ready for you. I can have Ching Yung see to it right away."

"Unfortunately, there is only one spare room at present," Morgan inserted hastily, lying through his teeth and refusing to meet Heather's eyes. "Lyle, old boy, I'm sure you'll agree that Heather's mother should be the one to occupy it. The hotel is only a few blocks distant. Why don't I have someone show you the way?"

"Egad! What an eventful day this has been!" Morgan exclaimed, not even bothering to pull down the coverlet before collapsing naked onto the bed. "I'm so tired I could sleep for a week." He gave a yawn. "You won't be too disappointed if we don't make love tonight, will you, darlin'?"

Heather bounced onto the mattress beside him. "Oh no you don't, Morgan Stone! If you think I'm going to let you doze off, you're crazy. You've kept me awake enough times for fun and games, and turnabout is fair play." She leaned over to nip his left earlobe.

"Ouch!" He grabbed for her, pulling her down on his chest, her breasts poking into the dark mat of hair. "I suppose if you insist, I can dredge up the energy," he teased with a broad grin.

She grinned back at him. "Oh, I'm sure you'll be up to the task before long."

"Have a little decorum, Boston," he declared in mock dismay. "Your mother is just down the hall, you know."

"So is my father, but that's never stopped you."

"Mothers are different," he insisted.

"How so?"

He chuckled. "If you don't know that by now, sweet thing, you're hopeless."

She playfully nipped the tip of his nose. "Speaking of my parents, isn't it odd that Mother caught my bouquet, and then Dad caught my garter when you threw it? Wouldn't it be strange if they actually got together again after all this time?"

"More like a miracle, considering their reactions to

each other today. So don't get your hopes up, my pet, only to have them dashed on rocky shoals."

She shrugged. "I suppose you're right, but it was a nice thought while it lasted. As for miracles, I still can't believe Mother turned up in Dodge just in time for our wedding."

"*I* can't believe we managed to evade her inquisition all evening," Morgan added.

"We wouldn't have if she hadn't been so travel-weary, and if Dad hadn't retired early, and if it weren't our wedding night," Heather replied. "Tomorrow she'll be fully recovered, and we'll really be in for it."

Morgan grimaced. "I thought she was in fair form today. For a minute or two, I felt downright sorry for Arlene."

Heather pushed herself up and swiveled around until her bare toes were near his face. "Massage my feet, darling. I've been walking around on that new penny Arlene gave me, and it rubbed a sore spot."

Obligingly he took her foot in his hands and began to prod the aching muscles. "Good grief, girl!" he exclaimed. "You have a perfect imprint of the coin on your big toe!"

"I shouldn't wonder." Heather gave a groan of pleasure. "Oh, Morgan! That's pure bliss! Don't stop."

He let her get totally engrossed and relaxed before he planted a wet kiss on the arch of her foot.

She jumped like a scalded cat and squealed, "Oh, you rotten devil! That tickles! Especially with that ratty mustache of yours!"

"You think that's bad?" he asked. "It's mild compared to this, sugar." With that, he popped her toe into his mouth and began to suckle it.

"Oooh! Stop!" she wailed in exquisite torment. "Morgan!"

His mouth wandered up her calf to the back of her knee, where her warm flesh was redolent with the scent of vanilla.

"You smell delicious," he murmured. "Good

enough to eat. Come to think of it, in certain lights your hair does resemble a red hood, my dear." He raised his head to waggle his brows at her in a lascivious leer.

She laughed in delight. "And you, my love, are definitely a ravenous wolf."

He grinned, twirling the end of his mustache like the villain in a vaudeville play. "Ah, we're made for each other, my sweet. The perfect pair. Now, let me show you what big teeth I have."

"Not to mention your eyes, your tongue, and your ears," she added. She gave another shriek as he bit her playfully on the tender inside of her thigh.

"Will you hush?" he chuckled. He soothed the small wound with a kiss, his lips exploring higher still. "Your mother will be beating down the door in a minute, sure that I'm killing you."

"Oh, you are! You are!" she moaned, feeling his warm, teasing breath where his mouth would touch next. "I'll surely die if you don't stop tormenting me so."

Her fingers dug into his dark hair, tugging his head closer to that supremely sensitive place she wanted his mouth to be. "Kiss me," she whispered. "Love me."

He did, with his tongue and teeth and lips, while she writhed wildly beneath him. Finally, when he'd brought her release with his mouth, he moved up over her, his lips trailing moist kisses across her belly, her breasts, her throat and face. Laving every inch of her fragrant flesh. Caressing it. Marking it as his.

Her lips sought his, their tongues mating eagerly. Her arms stroked the smooth muscles of his shoulders, his back. Lower still, her fingers wrapped around his hard, hot tumescence, fondling and tantalizing with covetous care. By her own hand, she led him to her portal, wrapped her thighs high over his hips, and arched upward.

Their bodies joined, moving in perfect rhythm, and their blood sang a sensual duet as they sped together toward the summit. Then they were soaring into sun-splendored heavens on golden wings, tumbling through silver-laced clouds, sliding gently down a rainbow, melting in replete rapture.

"I *do* love you, you know," he whispered into her tousled tresses. "I think I've been falling in love with you since you first stumbled into my arms. I'll make you happy, Mrs. Stone, or die trying. I swear it."

"Don't perish on my account, darling, because I'm already deliriously delighted just to be your wife."

He chuckled softly. "Lands, but you're easy to please!"

"Treasure that thought, Morgan, faulty as it may be." Her contented smile lingered on her lips far into the night.

❧ 26 ❧

Ching Yung was sent to fetch the newlyweds at the ungodly hour of eight o'clock. Due to the late working hours at the Salon, Heather usually preferred to sleep in until at least ten. Naturally, both she and Morgan were somewhat grumpy at being awakened so abruptly.

When Morgan tripped over her discarded shoe, he growled irritably, "I wish you'd put your shoes away, instead of letting them lie in the middle of the floor. I almost broke my neck."

"Then stay out of them and wear your own," she sassed back. "That, or watch where you plant those big feet of yours."

With a sigh, he picked up the shoe, wondering what she would do if he decided to lob it at her. The direction of his thoughts altered as a bright new penny dropped onto his stocking-clad foot. "Perhaps our luck is about to improve. At least the penny landed right-side-up."

"Pardon me?" she inquired.

"Haven't you heard it said that if you find a penny lying tails-up, let it lie or it will bring bad luck, whereas the other way around is good fortune?"

"I'll have to remember that."

He tossed the coin into the air and caught it in his palm. Then something about it drew his attention. Something odd, niggling at the back of his mind. Sud-

252

denly the missing piece of information popped forward, and Morgan stared at the one-cent piece in amazement.

"Heather? Did you say Arlene gave you this penny?"

"Yes. It was for good luck, you know. A bride is supposed to wear something old, something new, something borrowed, something blue, and a brand new penny in her shoe. Why?"

"This coin isn't just new. It's also quite unique."

"How so?"

"It's part of a batch that was misprinted and has been recalled to the mint to be melted down and recast. Only a few hundred went out before the mistake was discovered, and nearly all had been accounted for. The last lot was being shipped back on the train in a specially marked bag. The very train we were riding when it was held up. I'd forgotten all about it until I saw this penny."

Heather's eyes lit up. "Do you mean to say this penny might have been stolen in that robbery? The very one in which you were accused of being a participant?"

Excitement edged Morgan's voice. "Precisely. And if that's the case, it would appear that the thieves didn't realize that these coins are so exceptional that they can be easily traced, or they'd have kept them out of circulation. I wonder how Arlene came by this coin."

Heather shrugged. "My guess would be that she received it as change for some purchase she made at a local store."

Morgan nodded. "You're likely right, which means we should make a special effort to watch out for any more of these coins that might show up around town, especially in the Salon, because I'd bet my bottom dollar that if one of these mismarked pennies has surfaced in Dodge, more will follow. Which would also substantiate the theory that one or more of the outlaws is either a frequent visitor in town or an actual resident."

Heather came closer and peered at the penny in his palm. "What's so special about it, anyway? How can you tell it's one of those that are misprinted? It looks perfectly ordinary to me."

"Look closer, Boston. All United States coins are imprinted with the words 'In God We Trust.' This one reads—"

" 'In Dog We Trust'!" she exclaimed with a brusque laugh. "Good heavens! No wonder they wanted them out of circulation! How embarrassing to the government!"

"And the mint," Morgan agreed. "If they'd just misprinted the date, or made an error of less significance, chances are they would have let it go without comment. But this was too disgraceful to ignore."

Heather's brow furrowed thoughtfully. "How did you know about all this anyway?"

For a moment, Morgan was stymied. He certainly couldn't tell her that Wells Fargo notified all its agents as a matter of routine policy on anything concerning currency. After a moment he said simply, "I happened to overhear a conversation between a banker and one of the officials at the train station when the coins were loaded aboard at St. Louis. It caught my interest, since misprinted money and stamps are somewhat rare and usually become collectors' items."

"Obviously Arlene wasn't aware that this particular penny is so unusual, or she'd have kept it. Wouldn't she be perturbed to learn that the one simple cent she gave away could someday be worth a fortune? Do you think I ought to give it back to her?"

"Maybe later, but for the time being I'd prefer to keep this information just between us. You see, darlin', Arlene has unwittingly handed us our first real clue in this confounding case."

Heather blinked in surprise. "Goodness! I guess she has at that. But what are we going to do about it?"

"You and I are going to keep our eyes peeled, and

see if any more of these coins are discovered. We're going to examine every penny that crosses our palms, and be especially alert to any that might come into our own till downstairs. Any one of our customers who gives us one in payment could be a suspect. Then again, they might come across it the same way we would, by casual monetary exchange. It's a long shot, but if we're attentive, we might get lucky and catch ourselves a thief."

"What about the girls? And Bob? Shouldn't we alert them to be on the lookout, too?" she asked.

Morgan shook his head. "No, darlin'. As much as I like all of them, we just can't trust anyone else with this knowledge. Not even Sheriff Watson."

Heather snorted. "That goes without saying. He'd immediately assume you'd gotten the blasted penny in the holdup. But I think you're wrong not to tell the others. It's going to be like looking for a needle in a haystack, and we could certainly use a few more pairs of eyes."

"I know, but we can't chance it, sweetheart. Though it pains me, we've got to consider everyone a viable link to the bandits. For all we know, the culprits could be some of our regular customers, people we talk to nearly every day."

Heather shivered. "What a horrifying thought!"

He draped a comforting arm over her shoulders and pulled her close for a quick hug. "I know. So be very circumspect, my love. You're in danger enough as it is."

She tilted her head to look up at him. "It's strange, Morgan," she commented lightly, "but during this entire conversation you actually sounded as if you might truly be a Wells Fargo agent, just as you originally claimed."

He forced a smile, even as his heart lurched in his chest. "*Now* who's building castles in the air, trying to make me more than a footloose merchant? You've got an active imagination yourself, princess."

"Maybe with the part about you being an agent,"

she agreed. Spearing him with a sharp look, and poking her finger into his chest for emphasis, she concluded, "But your days of being footloose and fancy-free are over, Mr. Stone. You're a married man, now. And don't you forget it!"

"Weel, it took ye two lovebirds lang enough to join us," Gus remarked sourly, shifting uncomfortably in his desk chair. The family meeting was being held in his office, in order to provide more privacy.

One look at his face, and Heather was immediately concerned. "Dad, should you be up and around again so soon? You don't look at all well."

He gave a tight smile. "Aye. All the excitement yesterday took some o' the starch out o' me, all right, but yer mama flat-out refused to come to my bedroom." He turned his eyes on Betsy. "Afraid I'll ravish ye, Bets?"

"No, Angus," she replied. "I was foolish enough to fall for your false charms when I was young, but I'm older and wiser now, and I try to make it a point not to make the same mistake twice. Now, may we please get down to the business at hand? I want to know how it is that my daughter came here just a few short weeks ago and suddenly decided to break off her engagement with Lyle and rush into marriage with Mr. Stone."

Gus shot a glance at Heather and Morgan, who were seated side by side on the divan—the same one on which Morgan had killed the rattler. Gus could only assume that Heather's distress over this morning's topic had made her temporarily forget her aversion to that particular piece of furniture.

"Do the pair of ye want to start this confession, or should I?" he asked dryly.

Heather took a fortifying breath and leapt into what she was sure would be a difficult discussion. "Regardless of all else involved, it all comes down to the fact that Morgan and I love each other very much.

That's the most important thing to remember, don't you think?"

"Of course," Betsy agreed, "but why on earth did you have to marry so quickly? Surely a few months to prepare a proper ceremony wouldn't have been unreasonable. And I don't mind telling you that I'm extremely hurt that you would even consider getting married without first telling me and inviting me to the wedding."

"That was my doin', Bets," Gus said, generously assuming his share of the blame. "Not that I didn't want ye here, or respect yer right to be here to see yer daughter wed, but it seemed a case of urgency." At her inquiring look, he continued, "Ye see, when it came to light that Heather and Morgan had been . . . makin' a habit o' anticipatin' the weddin' night, so to speak, I thought it best to correct the situation as soon as possible. Especially since they'd been carryin' on that way since my accident. And b'fore ye say anything, let me remind ye that I've been in no position to monitor matters round here since then."

Dismay filled Betsy's face. "I was afraid it was something like that." She shook her head at her daughter. "Somehow, this all sounds so distressingly familiar, as if you are treading in my earlier footsteps. I suppose the fruit doesn't fall so far from the tree after all, but I prayed you would have better sense than I did at your age." Sudden apprehension clouded her eyes. "Please tell me you haven't been conducting yourself in such an improper manner with other men, some of your suitors back in Boston perhaps."

"Mother! How can you even suggest such a thing?" Heather squealed, mortified.

"I should think that would be evident, dear," Betsy informed her sternly. "After all, you evidently had no qualms where Morgan was concerned."

"That's different. I love him."

"You loved Lyle, too," Betsy was quick to remind her. "Or thought you did, at least."

"No, Mother. I felt genuine fondness for Lyle, and perhaps mistook it for love. Maybe because I wanted to love him. After all, I'd known him nearly all my life, and everyone kept telling me he was the perfect catch. Rich, refined, well educated, from a distinguished family, all the things a girl is supposed to want in a husband. And for a while, I assumed that was what I wanted, too. Until I met Morgan, and he taught me the difference between love and affection."

"It seems he taught you more than that," Betsy replied. "Somewhat prematurely."

Morgan decided it was time to try to mend the breach he'd helped to rend between Heather and her mother. "Mrs. Blair-Burns, I accept full responsibility for that, and for any repercussions that may result. If you need to place blame on anyone's shoulders, place it on mine. It was evident to me from the outset that Heather was new to passion, whereas I knew precisely what I was doing when I seduced her. My only excuse is that I was overcome by her charm and beauty, which she obviously inherited from you. Also, please believe that I love your daughter deeply, and will devote my life to making her happy."

Betsy frowned. "Seems I've heard those same claims somewhere before, but I suppose you deserve the benefit of the doubt. Until you prove otherwise, I'll try not to paint you and Angus with the same brush."

"That's most generous of you, Mrs. Blair-Burns."

" 'Tis na," Gus put in with a glower. "B'sides, I never once claimed ye got yer charm and looks from yer ma, Betsy. Ye can't hang that on me."

She glared back at her former husband. "Do pardon me, Angus. You're correct. As I recall, you despised my mother with a passion."

"Aye, and wi' guid cause, so it turned out. She was the most overbearin' ornery old shrew ever born. B'tween her and yer pa, they made a pack o' badgers look tame!"

Heather saw an opportunity to make good her escape, and took it without remorse. While her parents continued haranguing one another, their rapidly heating argument rendering them oblivious to all else, she grabbed Morgan and urged him silently into the hall.

Once there, the door shut firmly behind them, Heather heaved a sigh of relief. "With luck, it will be a good hour before either of them misses us. By then, perhaps they will have vented all their anger and leave off lecturing us."

Morgan checked his pocket watch and gave Heather a lustful grin. "Meanwhile, we still have time for a quick romp before the Salon opens." He swooped her into his arms and began walking rapidly toward their rooms. "Come on, you sly minx. I'm in a mood to let you seduce me."

Drake arrived late in the afternoon. He'd been out of town most of the previous day, trying to get a lead on the latest train robbery. "I'll sure be glad when this job is done and we can get onto something else," he grumbled. "I'm plumb wore out chasing these outlaws. We did get one small break this time, however. One of the bandits let his neckerchief slip in front of several witnesses. Though none recognized the culprit as anyone they knew, they might be able to identify him if they ever see him again."

"Glad to hear it," Morgan commented. "With luck, only a few of them will say he looks exactly like me. Watson was in here early yesterday morning, bound and determined to arrest me because, according to him, some idiot described me perfectly."

Drake frowned. "That's odd, 'cause the descriptions I heard didn't resemble you at all. Of course, by the time six individuals finish trying to recall what one fellow looks like, the suspect ends up having four different shades of hair, three eye colors, and is short-average-tall, all wrapped into one. A local artist has volunteered to help work up a sketch, combining the various descriptions into a single reasonably accurate drawing. Maybe that'll give us a little more to go on."

"Along with this," Morgan added, pulling the newly minted penny from his pocket and handing it to Drake. "Recognize it?"

Drake puzzled over it for a moment, then exclaimed softly, "This is one of those defective coins, the ones they're calling back to the mint to be melted down."

Morgan nodded. "A whole bag of them was aboard that first train that was robbed, the one we were on. Remember?"

"Holy Neds! You're right! Where did you get this, Morgan?"

"The Widow Clancy gave it to Heather, more than likely not aware of what she had."

"Where did Clancy get it?"

"I don't know, and I'm not about to ask. For now, this is just between you and me—and me and Heather. Arlene probably received it as change somewhere in town, and my theory is that more of these pennies might soon surface if we keep still about it so the thieves don't get wise to us."

Drake handed the penny back to Morgan. "I'll keep my eyes peeled and an ear to the ground."

Morgan chuckled. "Good way to get your head stomped on, old buddy."

Just then, Heather stepped up to the bar. "Darling, could you fix Mother and me a couple of those orange-flavored drinks? I was telling her how delicious they are, and she wants to try one."

"It'll be a couple of minutes, sweetheart. Why don't I bring them over to your table when they're ready?"

"Thank you, love."

As Heather walked away, Drake stared after her in bafflement, then swiveled to face Morgan. "Darling? Love? Sweetheart? What in Hades is going on here? Last time I was here, the two of you were fighting like two cats in a bag, and now the Shrew of the West is acting like Little Miss Sunshine."

Morgan grinned. "Yeah, well, newlyweds tend to

get along better, at least until the honeymoon is over."

"Newlyweds? Honeymoon? You telling me she got married, and that's why she's so sweet? Who'd she marry, anyway?"

"Me."

Drake's mouth fell open. "You?" he squeaked in a voice he'd outgrown years ago. "How? When? You're joshin' me, aren't you?"

"It's the gospel truth, Drake. To make a long story short, Heather saved my bacon yesterday by telling Watson I couldn't have been in on this latest holdup because I'd spent the entire night in her bed, which was also true. As a consequence, we ended up having to tell Gus, who insisted on an immediate wedding. Judge Swanson did the honors."

Drake shook his head in wonder. "Shoot, Morgan! I don't know whether to congratulate you or offer condolences!"

"I'm content with the arrangement," Morgan admitted, his eyes taking on a special gleam. "It's time I settled down anyway. I was just waiting for the right reason, and Heather is it."

"I'll be danged! You really love her, don't you?"

Morgan laughed at his friend's amazement. "Surprised the hell out of me, too!"

"What about your job with the company? Does this mean I'll be losing a partner?"

"I'm not sure, yet," Morgan said. "I'd really miss all the excitement and challenge if I quit. I'm thinking of asking if they can assign me to cases in and around San Francisco, so it would cut down on so much of the travel. If not, I could always go into the trading business with Dad."

"Does your new wife know all this? About you working for Wells Fargo?"

"No. She isn't aware of any of it. I simply told her to be on the lookout for more of those pennies so we can find the real outlaws and get me off the hook."

"She still thinks you sell shoes for a living?" Drake

chortled. "And she married you anyway? The woman must be crazy in love with you."

Morgan grinned. "It's like I've told you all along, Drake. Some of us fortunate fellas were just born with natural appeal."

"And with more bull than a Texas ranch," Drake agreed with a lopsided smile. "Which is why most of you wear boots."

❧ 27 ❧

Morgan hobbled through the back door of the Salon, a thunderous expression on his face and one boot held aloft in his hand. "Heather Elise Blair-Burns Stone! I want to see you! Now!"

His booming command rang from one end of the hall to the other. Patrons and personnel alike came alert in avid expectation of the entertaining confrontation that was sure to ensue.

Heather emerged from the storeroom with a frown on her face. Marching up to him, hands on hips, she said, "All right, you're looking at me. Now, stop bellowing. I'm not deaf."

He glowered down at her and waved his boot past her nose. "Can you still smell, Boston? Can you identify this mess I stepped in by its offensive odor?"

Heather grimaced and hastily backed away. "Offhand, I'd say you walked through a pile of dung."

"Good guess, darlin'," he shot back. "Can you also surmise whose pet left that particular deposit in the back lot, and several more like them, for some unsuspecting soul to land in?"

Her expression turned contrite. "Piddles?" she suggested weakly. "I'm sorry, Morgan. I'll have Ching Yung see to cleaning the yard immediately. We've all been so busy lately that—"

"Oh, no," he said, with a shake of his head. "Not this time, Lady Despot. You're not going to shove this delightful chore off onto him or anyone else, as you are so inclined to do. You'll perform it yourself, as you should have all along. Piddles is your dog, pathetic excuse for one that he is, so you can just get a shovel and trot your sweet little butt out there and attend to the problem personally. And when you're done with that, you can clean and shine my boots!"

She speared him with a malevolent look. "Well, I guess the honeymoon is over. You're back to being your normal, overbearing self!"

He dropped the boot at her feet. "If the shoe fits, Cinderella."

Morgan wondered if he ought to take lessons from Betsy, for somehow the woman seemed to walk in and take over running the saloon without even a peep of argument from her daughter. It was a neat trick, and one that defied his reasoning. On the other hand, he wasn't sure he'd want Heather all that amenable where he was concerned. In truth, he rather enjoyed her sassy mouth and sharp wit. It was a good part of what had attracted him to her in the first place, and made life with her utterly fascinating, both in bed and out of it.

Betsy decided to take Heather's original ideas for the Salon and expand upon them. "I suggest we charge a quarter a dance, at the least," she said. "These wranglers are bound and determined to squander their pay as fast as possible anyway, so why not take advantage of their spendthrift ways? Also, since they have a penchant for gambling all their money away at cards and billiards, we should charge a fee for the use of the tables, since they occupy them for such lengthy periods. Perhaps half a dollar per game would be reasonable. After all, if they didn't have the money to spend, they wouldn't be in here every evening, and it would increase our profits nicely."

Unlike Heather, Betsy soon caught on to the fact that the girls were entertaining after hours in their rooms, and that liquor was still being served to the male customers. But instead of abruptly curtailing these clandestine activities, she tried a more diplomatic approach in her efforts to further enhance the image of the Salon and its employees.

"I've noticed that many of the gentlemen who frequent this establishment are lonely, and come to enjoy the company of the women here, as well as that of their fellow men. That being the case, we should offer them a chance to compete with each other in more than cards and billiards. Suppose we install several comfortable sofas in the back area, around the dance floor, and soften the lighting with a few shaded lamps? Maybe add a carpet and a few plants and flowers to make it more resemble a meeting parlor, where these roving cowboys could enjoy the illusion of being in a private home. I'm sure many of them miss that family atmosphere, while others might never have had the pleasure of experiencing it."

"That may be true, but where does the competition you mentioned come into play, Mother?" Heather wanted to know.

"Not counting you and me, of course, there are currently seven available companions for all these men. Now, if we were to instate a new policy, at least during evening hours, that required everyone to purchase refreshments at the bar and convey them to the tables themselves, it would free the girls to do more entertaining in the back room. They would no longer be waiting tables, you see. They'd be acting solely as partners for dancing and conversation and such, for which each gentleman would pay a nominal fee."

She continued to expound on her idea. "Now, suppose the men had to vie for the women's attention, much as a suitor has to outmaneuver others for the favors of his favorite lady. Soon they'd be arriving with bouquets and candy and small gifts, the better to entice a particular partner away from the others, would they not?"

Catching Betsy's enthusiasm, Heather added, "Most likely they'd also be shaving and bathing and taking more care with their appearance as well, which was one of my objectives at the start. Too many of our male customers arrive smelling like the cows they herd."

"Precisely. Also, this arrangement might encourage the men to view the girls in a more favorable light. Those fellows who come in regularly will become more fully acquainted with our ladies, perhaps grow to appreciate more than their bodies and realize what a pleasure it is to simply converse with a woman in comfortable surroundings."

"As a beau might," Heather deduced, finally catching on to the gist of Betsy's scheme. "Mother, you're talking about starting a courting parlor! Where the girls and the men can get to know each other well enough to—"

"To contemplate marriage," Betsy finished for her with a satisfied nod.

Morgan felt obliged to point out, "Your strategy has one major flaw, Mrs. Blair-Burns."

"Oh?"

"If the men propose, and the girls marry, you've depleted your dance partners."

"Yes, but once the idea catches on, other women with little hope or opportunity for catching husbands will apply for positions here, and the cycle will continue. I should imagine we'll have more aspiring companions than we can accommodate, and be turning them away."

"Or making lists of those next in line for employment," Heather submitted eagerly.

"You might be on to something, Mrs. Blair-Burns," Morgan conceded. "I have to admire your nose for enterprise, especially for someone who has never competed in the business world before."

Betsy smiled. "I'm beginning to think you have potential as well," she quipped. "As for my business acumen, it doesn't take a genius to know that there is a world filled with lonely men and women in search of someone with whom to share their lives. I simply see a need, and a means of fulfilling it."

"And make a tidy profit while you're at it," Morgan said. "If I was wearing a hat at the moment, I would tip it to you. You are one smart lady, Mrs. Blair-Burns."

"Betsy," she corrected smoothly. "After all, we are family now, Morgan, and needn't be so formal with one another."

"As long as we're going to do all this work, it wouldn't cost much more to redecorate some of the rooms upstairs," Heather suggested.

"Such as yours, for instance?" Morgan surmised cannily. "I swear, woman, you're as easy to read as a dime novel."

Heather scowled at him. "They're your rooms now, too, Morgan. And you needn't make me sound so self-centered. The girls might want to fix their quarters up a bit as well. Nothing elaborate, you understand. Just a fresh coat of paint or wallpaper, perhaps. A lampshade here, a rug there, a colorful throw cover for a worn divan."

"How generous of you," he mocked. "Especially considering the money will not be coming out of your pocket."

Heather's chin came up. "How much can a few small frills cost? It's not as if the paltry selection of available material and merchandise in this squalid cow town extends to anything remotely elegant or tasteful. If there is a stitch of Belgian lace or fine French silk in all of Dodge, I'll eat it."

Morgan gave up the argument—for the moment. "Just try to keep the expense to a minimum, darlin'. You don't really want to send your poor, sick father to the poorhouse, do you?"

Lyle was less than thrilled with the entire situation—Heather's marriage, Betsy taking so readily to

Morgan and vice versa, and this latest venture of Betsy's. Under the circumstances, however, he could comment on only one of those factors without appearing foolish and spiteful.

"Betsy, dear, I realize what you are trying to do, of course, and it's highly commendable. But this endeavor is also naive. You can paint a privy any color you want, but it will remain a privy."

"Is that your way of saying that trollops, reformed or otherwise, are not good enough to be taken to wife?" Heather said, inserting herself into the conversation. "I would say that is bigoted of you, Lyle."

"Perhaps narrow-minded would be a more generous term," Betsy allotted. "I'm sure Lyle doesn't intend to come across as such a prejudiced prude. He simply isn't accustomed to dealing with the lower classes of society."

"And you are?" Lyle inquired skeptically.

Betsy smiled weakly and admitted, "I've had my moments, I suppose. I did marry Angus, after all."

"Mother! Really! Dad might be a little rough around the edges, but he's still a fine man."

"Rather like an unpolished gem?" Betsy suggested. "Far be it from me to disillusion you, but don't be too disappointed when all your efforts to buff him to a high gloss gain you naught but a fake jewel, daughter. The man is a charlatan, born and bred."

"Yet you intend to attempt a similar transformation with these Jezebels," Lyle told her pointedly. "Quite idealistic, if you ask me."

"Funny, but I don't recall anyone soliciting your opinion," Morgan commented with a mocking grin.

"All that aside, these women are young yet, and perhaps not as irredeemable as some people might suppose," Betsy maintained. "I should think they're at least worth an effort to set them on the path to a better life."

Lyle was also put out that Betsy was throwing herself into this new project and could not give him any indication of when she might want to leave Dodge City. Their original intent had been to collect Heather and return to Boston immediately. Now their plans had completely unraveled.

"I'm sorry, Lyle," Betsy told him. "I want to see this project off to a good start and visit with Heather for a time. Her plans are rather up in the air now, too, so I gather, with Angus still recovering. So you see, I can't even estimate how long I'll want to stay. If you feel you must return now, don't let me keep you. I can take the train back myself when I'm ready. Surely the odds of it being robbed again while I'm aboard are next to nil."

"I'll wait a bit, I suppose," he decided reluctantly. "If all we've heard is true, perhaps Stone will soon be arrested and hanged, and Heather will be free again."

"Lyle! What a perfectly horrid thing to say!" Betsy exclaimed.

Looking only slightly abashed, Lyle replied, "I know, but I can't help how I feel. The man stole Heather from me, after all, and I resent him for it."

Betsy patted his hand in a consoling gesture. "I understand, dear. It's perfectly natural to be bitter, but do try to retain some perspective and self-esteem, if only to remind yourself that, despite your loss, you are still an honorable gentleman."

Shortly thereafter, in another conversation with Heather and Morgan, Betsy mentioned Lyle's distress. "If only he had something to take his mind off his troubles. While the rest of us are busy, Lyle has entirely too much time to dwell on his loss. I wish there were some project in which he could involve himself while he's here."

"Why doesn't the man simply return to Boston and be done with it?" Morgan inquired peevishly.

Amusement lit Betsy's brown eyes. "Beyond his role as my escort on this trip, I assume his sense of obligation extends to Heather. He probably feels he should remain at hand, in case you turn out to be a cad. He's waiting in the wings, so to speak."

Heather shook her head and sighed. "You're correct, Mother. Lyle does need something else to occupy his time."

"Like what?" Morgan wanted to know. "Does he have any particular talents, other than being a nuisance?"

"Don't be nasty, Morgan," Betsy admonished. "Lyle is a very educated man, and undoubtedly most adept, or his father wouldn't be putting him in charge of their publishing company."

Heather's eyes lit up. "Mother, you're a marvel! You've just hit on the very thing." She went on to explain. "When he first learned that I was traveling to Dodge, he expressed regret that he couldn't come with me. Of course, it wouldn't have been at all proper for the two of us to travel together, and his father had some special assignment he wanted Lyle to finish just then. Anyway, Lyle told me that he envied me this chance to see the West, because it was one of his goals to someday explore it and write about a real western town, complete with trail drives, and gamblers, and saloons and such. This could be his golden opportunity to do some in-depth research for his story, though I suppose he hasn't yet realized it, with everything else on his mind."

"What a fantastic idea!" Betsy agreed. "You simply must tell him right away."

Morgan frowned. "I don't want to sound like a jealous husband, but wouldn't it be better for you to make the suggestion, Betsy? The way I see it, the more contact he has with Heather, the more he'll be reminded of her rejection of him, like pouring salt into an open wound. The sooner he comes to accept things the way they stand, the better for all parties concerned."

"Perhaps you're right, Morgan." Betsy gave him a

shrewd look. "You're very astute, if somewhat proprietary."

He shrugged in an offhand manner and offered his mother-in-law an impish grin. "Even as a boy, I never liked sharing my toys, and I don't intend to start now."

"Uh-oh!" Jasmine prodded Ginger and pointed toward Morgan, who stood behind the bar wearing a distinct scowl. She waved a hand toward Heather, who was speaking with Lyle Asher, blithely ignoring her husband's displeasure. "Someone ought to warn that gal not to pull the tiger's tail."

Ginger scoffed. "Knowing Heather, do you think it would do any good?"

"Probably not," Jasmine decided. "She does pretty much as she wants most of the time."

"Well, I got a feelin' this ain't gonna be one of those times." Ginger chuckled. "And we've got front-row seats when the fireworks start, which should be any minute now."

Indeed, the longer Morgan watched his bride conversing with her ex-fiancé, and apparently enjoying herself immensely if the bright smile on her face was a proper indication, the more annoyed he became. Drat that woman! He'd made it perfectly clear that he didn't care to have her associating with Asher any more than was absolutely necessary. What did he have to do, imprint it on her forehead?

Without so much as a backward glance in Morgan's direction, as if she couldn't care less how he might react, Heather placed her hand in the crook of Lyle's arm and began strolling casually toward the staircase with him. As Morgan watched her walk away, her seductively swaying backside seemed to taunt him, much like a cape waved before a raging bull.

Almost instinctively, his hand reached to uncoil the whip at his side. It took a moment longer for a couple of passing customers to clear his intended path, but his target was still well in range as the lash sang out.

With the proficiency of a master bullwhacker, Morgan whisked the leather thong neatly around Heather's trim waist—his skill such that, while she was securely bound, she wasn't hurt in the least. As she gave a startled yelp, Morgan reeled her in like a fish on a line. Leaping agilely over the bartop, he met her halfway, his eyes flashing a turquoise warning, which she promptly disregarded.

"Blast you, Morgan Stone! What game are you up to now? Get this thing off me at once!"

"Believe me, I'm beyond playing games, princess. We're down to the real issues here," he informed her tautly. "One of which is, I distinctly remember saying I didn't want you hanging around Asher, let alone clinging to him like a monkey to a banana."

She blinked up at him, silent for all of half a second. Then she lit in to him. "Oh, for pity's sake, Morgan! I was just taking him upstairs—"

"I'm well aware of that, which makes me all the more—"

"—to speak with Dad," she finished. "Lyle is interested in interviewing Dad for his book."

"The man has two good legs and all his wits, at least for the time being," Morgan pointed out heatedly, darting a furious glare toward Lyle, who was standing nearby regarding them curiously, as if uncertain whether or not to interfere. "As near as I can tell, he's perfectly capable of finding his own way to Gus's quarters."

Heather heaved an exasperated sigh. "I was only being polite, Morgan."

"Oh, really! From where I stood it looked as if you were being a tad more than merely polite, Miss Propriety. You were obviously having a delightful time, smiling and laughing, and batting your lashes like a two-bit tart."

Her eyes flashed dark flames. "Don't be more of an ass than you normally are, Mr. Stone."

He glowered back. "Now that you've mentioned

that particular part of the anatomy, I also recall warning you what I would do to yours if I ever caught you flirting with another man. Do you remember that conversation, *Mrs.* Stone?"

Her eyes widened, then narrowed in seething indignation. "You wouldn't dare!" she hissed.

"Is that a challenge, or an invitation?" he taunted.

"Now, see here," Lyle butted in. "This has gone quite far enough."

Both Heather and Morgan rounded on him. "*You* stay out of this!" they intoned as one.

Just as quickly, the two of them squared off again, brown eyes locked to turquoise, matching one another glare for glare, much to the delight of their spectators, who were eagerly placing bets on which of them would win this marital dispute.

"Gus was right," Morgan alleged. "You definitely have more sass than sense."

"And you have more brawn than brains," she countered recklessly. They were eye to eye, nose to nose— with Heather standing on tiptoe in her attempt to match his height.

"Well, then, why don't I put a little of that brawn to good use?" he suggested.

Bending abruptly, he snaked an arm around both her legs and hefted her upward. She landed facedown over his broad shoulder. "Morgan! You beast! Put me down this instant!"

He smacked her lightly on the bottom with the flat of his hand. "Bob, take care of the bar for a while, will you? The little woman needs my attention."

Amid laughter and ribald remarks, he carried her through the crowded Salon and up the stairs, with Heather beating on his back all the while, and shrieking fit to burst his eardrums.

Behind them, Lyle called out, "Heather! Do you want me to tell your father you require assistance?"

"Nooo!" she wailed, bumping along upside down

on Morgan's shoulder, her face hidden in a cascade of red-gold curls.

Morgan chuckled. "Get your own girl, Asher. This one's mine."

❧ 28 ❧

Lyle did, indeed, get his own girl, and without
wasting much time about it. Of course, he didn't have
to look far for his companionship. By early the next
afternoon, he was escorting Ginger around town,
while she pointed out to him various spots of local
interest. The expedition, which in Heather's estimation should have taken all of fifteen minutes, turned
into an all-day event.

"Mother," Heather complained to Betsy, "why
didn't you set a time for Ginger to be back? She's
supposed to be waiting tables, and now we're short
of help."

"Under the circumstances, I thought it might be
wise to get Lyle out from underfoot for a while,"
Betsy said, casting a look in Morgan's direction.

"Be that as it may, I doubt he needed Ginger's assistance, and certainly not for so long."

"Perhaps they got lost," Betsy suggested.

"In a town this small?" Heather scoffed.

Betsy studied her daughter closely. "After breaking
off with him so abruptly, and with such little finesse,
you aren't going to begrudge Lyle the company of
another woman, are you, Heather?" she inquired re-
provingly.

"Certainly not."

"Good, because that would be petty of you. Just
remember, dear. You tossed him over. You have no

room to complain if someone else grabs him up."

Ching Yung put a halt to their conversation as he walked up and handed Heather an apron. At her questioning look, Ching Yung nodded toward Morgan. "Boss say we busy, you work now."

Heather's gaze swung toward her spouse, a sharp retort on the tip of her tongue. His steady, challenging gaze made her reconsider. With a muttered oath, she yanked the apron around her waist, tugging at the ties so angrily that she nearly ripped them off.

"That man is really starting to rile me," she grumbled.

Betsy gave a wry chuckle. "Husbands have a way of doing that, I'm afraid. That's one reason I never remarried. I've never found a man I enjoyed fighting with as much as I did with your father."

It was another one of those hectic shopping expeditions, inspired by Betsy's renovation plans, that had Morgan gnashing his teeth. Because he still wasn't willing to let Heather traverse the streets without him, Morgan was forced to accompany her and her mother, and somewhere along the line they'd gotten the impression that he was a beast of burden. At scarcely eleven o'clock in the morning, he was loaded to his eyebrows with packages, nearly staggering beneath their combined weight, with more purchases yet to be made.

"Ladies, please! Have a little mercy, will you? My arms are going to be four inches longer when we're done than when we began."

Heather laughed and playfully wagged her eyebrows at him. "The better to hold me with, my dear," she quipped. "Now, try to bear up for just a little while yet. We're nearly finished."

"I should hope so. By the way, does Gus know you two are out spending all his money on lampshades and birdcages and silly whatnots?"

"We didn't want to trouble him with trivial details," Betsy replied. "After all, he's recovering slowly enough as it is, and we wouldn't want to be held responsible if he suffered a relapse."

"Well, when he does find out, just remember that I had nothing to do with it. It was all your idea."

"Oh, no, Morgan," Heather corrected. "By carrying the goods, you have become an accessory, and are just as guilty as we."

"Devious brat!" he grumbled, trying in vain to see his feet past the packages in his arms. "At least guide me along here, will you, darlin', before I fall off the walkway and break a leg."

She took his arm. "Watch your step, love. We're going to cross the street here. I'll try to route you around the worst of the potholes."

"This should be good for a laugh, Miss Graceful," he muttered. "Like the blind leading the blind."

They were midway across the street when Heather stumbled, causing Morgan to trip and bump into Betsy. All three wobbled precariously, like a trio of bumbling actors in a comedy production, as parcels fell like raindrops. Together they stooped to retrieve their bundles. Only then did they hear gunshots, and the screams of several frightened townspeople.

Morgan heard a bullet whiz past his head, so close it sounded like a bee buzzing in his ear. He glanced up in time to see Betsy's bonnet tilt sideways, the top blown off by the blast. The package closest to Heather exploded as a bullet tore into it.

Parcels forgotten, he grabbed each lady by the arm and rushed them toward the nearest store. "Come on! Run!" he urged.

A few steps away, four horses stomped and neighed nervously at a hitching rail. Morgan yanked Heather and Betsy into their midst, using the animals as temporary shields. "Duck under the rail," he yelled. "Hurry!"

More shots rang out, one thudding into a post to Morgan's immediate left. One of the horses jerked violently and gave a pained whinny. In her panicked rush, Heather caught her skirt on the rail. The material ripped, leaving a sizable piece behind. Disregarding modesty, she ran on.

Morgan all but threw the women through the doorway of the barbershop, tumbling in after them just as the glass in the big front window shattered into a thousand slivers. "On the floor!" he commanded unnecessarily.

Heather and Betsy were already huddled together in a quivering ball, unable to stand a moment longer. Walt Finch, the barber, was crouched down behind his swivel chair. His half-shaven customer was hunched under the counter, looking for all the world like Saint Nicholas with a bad case of the mange.

"What in thunder is goin' on out there?" Ray Burger grumbled. "Walt here nearly slit my danged throat!"

"Did not!" Walt declared. "You're the lily-liver who jumped halfway to the ceilin'!"

The barrage stopped as suddenly as it had begun, an unearthly silence taking its place. Warily Morgan crept to the door and peered out. "I think it's over now, but if you don't mind, we'll just camp here until we're certain."

Walt nodded. "The more the merrier. When you see Sheriff Watson out here, you can be pretty sure it's okay to go. He never leaves his office until it's safe to poke his nose out."

"More's the pity," Heather mumbled shakily.

Morgan crawled over to the two women. "Are both of you all right?"

Cautiously Heather and Betsy raised their heads and gazed around with wide brown eyes, like a pair of does sniffing for danger.

"Are either of you hurt?" Morgan repeated.

"I . . . I'm not sure," Betsy replied unsteadily, raising trembling fingers to her hat. Her face paled even more as she removed it and stared at the large hole in it. "Oh, my gracious Lord! Is . . . is that a bullet hole?"

"Mother!" Heather gasped. "You . . . you nearly had your . . ."

"Hair parted," Morgan supplied. He reached forward and gently felt her head for any sign of a wound, breathing a sigh of relief when he encountered none. "Maybe a few strands missing, but nothing more," he stated thankfully.

Mother and daughter echoed his sigh. "Hopefully it yanked only the gray ones, but I doubt it," Betsy commented weakly.

"What about you?" Morgan inquired, addressing his wan-faced wife.

"Just my shoulder. It stings a little, but not badly."

He nudged her around to get a better look, and winced at the needle of glass protruding from her upper arm. A stream of blood soaked the back of her sleeve. "Try not to move your arm, honey. The glass is still in there. As soon as we can, we'll get Dr. Jenkins to remove it."

"Not until I can get back and change into fresh clothes," she told him.

"Darlin', Doc won't care if your dress is rumpled. Besides, it'll be a bit difficult to get you out of it until he takes that splinter out."

"I'll manage somehow," she insisted. "What I don't know is how I'm going to get from here to the Salon without the entire town seeing my backside," she added on a whisper. "I ripped half the back of my skirt off!"

Morgan gaped at her, bemused. "If we both live long enough, maybe to age one hundred or so, perhaps I'll fathom the workings of your brain. Never mind that we nearly got killed. You're worried about showing your petticoat!"

Betsy gave him a sympathetic pat on the shoulder. "Don't wear yourself out trying to understand it, Morgan. It's a 'woman thing.' "

As it turned out, Dr. Jenkins was already at the Salon making one of his periodic checks on Gus, so they didn't have to track him down. With Betsy's help, Heather changed her clothes, and the physician successfully removed the sliver of glass and bandaged her shoulder. Afterward, they discussed Gus's condition.

"You know," Jenkins said pensively, stroking his beard, "if I didn't know better, I'd swear Gus has been taking heavy doses of some sort of opiate, but the amount of laudanum I've been giving him for his pain is too low to account for such exaggerated symptoms."

"You mean his lethargy?" Betsy inquired.

"That and his lack of appetite, and the constricted pupils."

"But he's not like that all the time," Heather noted.

"No, and that's what has me so confused. It's as if he's getting a high dose of opiates at odd intervals, often with enough time between to partially recover from the drug. Then his pupils dilate, and he gets aguelike symptoms. Chills, diarrhea, sweating and shaking, irritability, all of which are also signs of withdrawal from a narcotic drug, particularly if the patient is not running a fever. Frankly, I'm at a loss to explain it."

"Doc, you mentioned opiates," Morgan put in. "Is that the same as opium? The kind that comes from Oriental poppies?"

"Yes, or a derivative thereof, such as morphine or laudanum. Why?"

Morgan shook his head, though his brow remained furrowed in thought. "Nothing, really. I just wondered. Back in San Francisco, in Chinatown, they smoke it in what they call opium dens. I've never been inside one of those places, but I've heard of them."

The doctor nodded. "Opium dens are prevalent in the Orient, where the poppy originated, though the flower is grown elsewhere, of course. Right here in America, as a matter of fact. The people who practice the Shaker religion almost always include it in their medicinal herb gardens, though the average person would not be aware of its pharmaceutical properties and would consider it nothing more than an attractive addition to a flower bed."

"But an Oriental would know what the poppy's true nature is, wouldn't he?" Betsy asked. "And the various effects of opium?"

"I would assume so," Jenkins replied. A dawning awareness crossed his face. "Ching Yung!" he declared softly. "Of course! Why didn't I think of him sooner?"

"Now, wait just a minute!" Heather demanded. "Just because he's Chinese doesn't make him guilty of dosing Dad with more than what you've prescribed. That *is* what you were about to claim, isn't it?"

"Well, yes. It would make sense," Doc said.

"That's preposterous! I'd trust Ching Yung with my life! Which, by the way, he has already saved at great risk to his own. Furthermore, we don't have a garden, or any flowers except those we've recently purchased elsewhere, and Ching Yung doesn't give Dad his medication anyway."

"She's right, Doc," Morgan concurred. "As much as Ching Yung can be a pest at times, I'd wager that little fellow is trustworthy to the bone. He's totally devoted to Heather. Hell, he's even taken a shine to that ankle-biting mutt of hers. I can't see him doing anything to hurt her, or anyone she loves. Besides, what possible motive would he have?"

Jenkins shook his head. "I wouldn't know. For a moment it seemed a likely explanation to a puzzling problem, but I'm probably grasping at straws. Still, I'd keep a keen eye on the amount in that laudanum bottle, just in case."

The doctor pushed himself out of his chair and picked up his bag, preparing to leave. "Sometimes I wish I'd taken up something more predictable than doctoring," he admitted with a weary sigh. "Like forecasting the weather!"

* * *

"I simply cannot believe this day," Betsy exclaimed. "Or this town! It's like a bad dream! First there's that gun battle right in the middle of town, and now this. I tell you, Heather, if I'd had any notion that life was so perilous here, I would never have allowed you to come. And at the moment, I'd love to have ten seconds with my hands around Etta's throat. To think the woman abandoned you to face this place alone."

"There is just as much crime in Boston, Mother," Heather insisted.

"Yes, but at least no one is deliberately plotting to kill you there," Morgan pointed out.

"Are you alluding to Dad's condition or those shots fired at us earlier?" Heather asked.

Morgan grimaced. "Mostly the shooting."

Betsy's distress grew. "Then you think those shots were intentionally aimed at us?" she queried, wide-eyed.

"I would assume so."

"Oh, dear! It was bad enough when I thought we were simply caught in the middle of a shoot-'em-up feud, or hapless victims of a rampaging drunkard! But to suppose that we were the actual targets is simply too frightful!"

"You've been reading those wild western tales, haven't you?" Heather put in with a wry grin.

"Angus had one or two lying around, and I was curious," Betsy admitted sheepishly. "I judged them to be a bit exaggerated. However, with all that's happened, they seem more fact than fiction now. But why would anyone want to kill us? And what's all this about Ching Yung saving your life, Heather? You certainly didn't mention that to me before. If you had, perhaps I wouldn't have been so quick to suspect the man."

Heather chose to respond to Betsy's second inquiry, offering a drastically abbreviated version. "Someone pushed me into the midst of a cattle drive, right outside the Salon. Without concern for his own well-being, Ching Yung bravely threw himself on top of me, using himself as a shield so I wouldn't be trampled. Fortunately, Morgan rescued both of us before we could be badly injured. That's how Ching Yung's fingers came to be broken."

Heather paused in thought, then posed a question to Morgan. "Was that before or after the episode with the rattlesnake on my sofa?"

"Before," he replied. "And after the incident with the broken glass in your drink, and the attack in the alley."

"Heavens to mercy! This is all too alarming!" Betsy declared. "But why? Why would anyone want to harm Heather?"

Morgan ran his fingers through his hair in a gesture of frustration. "That's what has us going in circles. At first it seemed like a series of unconnected accidents, but after a while it became fairly clear that someone is out to harm Heather. Now this thing with Gus, and the shooting today, are just muddling matters all the more."

"Perhaps not," Betsy said thoughtfully. "If someone wants to hurt Heather, it wouldn't necessarily have to be confined to physical abuse, would it? Harming Angus, or you, or me, or anyone she cares for, would achieve a similar result."

"That's an angle I hadn't considered, but it stands to reason," Morgan agreed. "Yet it still leads back to our original query. Why is Heather the primary target?"

"What are the usual motives behind such attacks?" Betsy posed, then proceeded to list a few possibilities. "Anger. Envy. Greed. In the case of the assault on her person, I'd suggest animal lust."

"That pretty well covers most of the deadly sins, Mother, unless you'd care to add gluttony and laziness and false pride to the list," Heather commented.

Betsy glowered. "Don't be facetious, daughter. This is nothing to joke about."

"Sorry, Mother, but at this point, I either laugh or

cry . . . or lose my mind with worry. Now, to top it off, I may be putting all of you in danger. All because of some offense I may or may not have committed, toward someone I may or may not have met! Or, for all we know, maybe the undertaker is simply having a slow month and needs to boost his business.''

❧ 29 ❧

To be on the safe side, Betsy decided she would take over nursing Gus. The first thing she did was to mark the level on the laudanum bottle, so she would be instantly alerted if it altered drastically. She also monitored Ching Yung when he entered Gus's quarters to clean or bring meals. Despite Heather and Morgan's claims that the man could be trusted, Betsy was taking no chances.

Of course, in the process of all this, Betsy practically had to shove Arlene Clancy aside, and the widow was not at all pleased. Nor was she hesitant to voice her objections, very loudly and clearly.

"You have a nerve!" she shouted at Betsy, disregarding the fact that Gus was dozing just a few feet away.

"I have more than one, Mrs. Clancy, and you are fast irritating them," Betsy warned. "Now, kindly lower your voice, or leave this room. My patient is trying to sleep."

"Since when did Angus become your patient?" Arlene demanded angrily. "After the accident, he specifically asked me to tend to him, and until he tells me otherwise, that is precisely what I intend to do."

"Think again," Betsy advised. "Since my conversation with Dr. Jenkins, I have concluded that Angus is in no condition to make such major decisions. Therefore, I am taking matters into my own hands.

You may continue to visit him on occasion, when he is feeling up to having company, but in all other aspects pertaining to his health, I am relieving you of your duties."

"We'll just see about that!" Arlene huffed. "You see, I know all about you, Mrs. Blair-Burns, and I know how much Gus despises you. He'll never agree to allow you to do this."

A gruff voice growled from the bed, "Hellfire! Would ye yakkin' biddies pipe down? For a scant minute's peace, I'd let the divil himself nurse me. Now, clear out o' here, both of ye, and let me be."

Arlene marched to his bedside, her lips pursed as if to argue the point further, then changed her mind and kissed him on the cheek. "I'll be back later, dearest. Don't let that harridan overstep herself while I'm gone."

Gus waved her away and mumbled to himself, "Why those Turks would want more'n one wife is beyond my reckonin'. All those lips flappin' in a fella's ear, all the gripin' and groanin', and petty squabblin'. 'Twould be enough to drive a man skirly!"

Along those same lines, Morgan said to Heather, "I'll bet Gus feels like a pasha, with Arlene and your mother all but dueling for the right to cater to him."

"Mother is simply trying to make sure Dad gets the best care possible."

"Why?" Morgan wondered aloud. "Is this her way of atoning for tossing him out on his ear when you were a baby?"

Heather gaped at him. "Morgan Stone! Where did you ever hear such an asinine lie!"

Brought up short, Morgan frowned. "Right from the horse's mouth, of course. Your dad told me about it weeks ago, and I got the distinct impression he was telling the gospel truth."

"Perhaps as he remembers it," Heather allowed. "But that's certainly not the way my mother recalls what happened."

"Oh? She didn't show him the door, then?"

"Absolutely not! Dad walked out of his own free will, while Mother was still in bed after delivering me. She wasn't even aware he was gone until my grandparents broke the news to her. From what I've learned, Mother was so heartbroken that if it weren't for having to tend to me, she might have gone into a permanent mental decline."

"You know, darlin', something doesn't add up here," Morgan said. "Gus is sayin' one thing, Betsy another, and from all accounts, each is most sincere. Now, how is that possible, unless they have both misunderstood the situation?"

Heather stared back at him in dismay. "Oh, Morgan! Wouldn't it be simply tragic if they've been separated for all these years over what amounts to a terrible misunderstanding? But how could two people who truly love each other let that happen?"

"Lack of communication, I presume," he offered. "Which brings up something else I've been meaning to ask you. Why haven't you ever visited your father before now? Wouldn't your mother agree to let you see him?"

"She might have, if we'd known he was alive."

"You thought he was dead?"

Heather nodded. "Yes. That was my grandparents' doing. Their way of getting Mother to accept that Dad was gone forever and to get on with her life, I suppose. You see, even though the annulment had been final for nearly three years, Mother still wasn't displaying any interest in other suitors. It was then, I believe, that Grandfather told Mother he'd read in the newspaper of an Angus Burns being killed in a tavern brawl. Mother was devastated. She mourned him all over again . . . for years."

"How did you learn the truth?"

"The family attorney informed us after Grandmother died early this spring. Until then, neither of us was aware that Dad was alive and had been supporting us since Grandfather's death, and that Grandmother accepted the money he sent and never said a word to anyone. It came as a shock to both Mother and me."

"I can imagine," Morgan said. He shook his head. "No, actually, I don't think I can. Your grandparents sound like a devious pair. Small wonder Gus doesn't have much good to say about them."

Heather sighed. "They never did care for Dad. The Blair lineage dates back to the landing of the *Mayflower* and beyond, and they simply could not fathom what their daughter saw in a lowly Scots immigrant who could barely speak proper English."

"Sounds vaguely familiar, with a few revisions," he drawled. "I take it they condoned the alliance in the end?"

"Only when it was a choice between allowing the marriage or having their daughter bear a child out of wedlock. You see, Morgan, I was already on the way by then."

Morgan considered this for a moment, then suggested gravely, "If those two tyrants despised Gus so much, and went so far as to claim he was dead when he wasn't, what's to say they didn't scheme to break up the happy couple once you were born and carried your father's surname?"

Heather was flabbergasted at the notion. "But . . . how?"

"Well, you've said Betsy was still confined to bed. Perhaps they prevented Gus from seeing her for a while. Maybe they took it upon themselves to relay messages back and forth between your parents. False messages, designed to create a rift that might never have developed if Gus and Betsy had been able to communicate face-to-face."

"It's possible, I suppose," she admitted, after mulling it over. "Perhaps even probable." She turned troubled eyes up to his. "Morgan? Do you think it's also possible to correct a mistake made so very long ago?"

He kissed her lightly on the tip of her nose. "I'd say that's up to Betsy and Gus to decide."

"How can they, when they never stop arguing long enough to compare notes?"

Morgan chuckled. "Give them time, darlin'. I'm sure they'll get around to discussing the important issues. After all, they've had tons of bitterness bottled up inside them for years. The cork holding back all that pent-up resentment is bound to pop sooner or later. More than likely, with a terrific bang."

Drake showed up as soon as the Salon opened the next day. He brought a newly printed copy of a Wanted poster, depicting the artist's rendering of the train robber whose mask had slipped. "Here it is, Morgan. I just *happened* to be hanging around the printer's office, and grabbed this fresh off the press. The sheriff hasn't even seen it yet."

Morgan chuckled, reaching for the poster. At his first glimpse of the robber, his smile melted, instantly replaced by irate recognition. "This looks like one of the men who attacked Heather in that alley! The one she claims smelled of mint. Probably the same man who shoved her into the street during the cattle drive."

"Are you sure?" Drake asked.

"Fairly certain, but Heather got a better look at him than I did. Let's see what she says."

Morgan called Heather over. "Mr. Evans was just showing me this poster that's being passed out around town. Take a look at it, and tell me if you've ever seen this fellow before."

One look and Heather's face went pasty white. "That's him!" she squeaked in disbelief. "Morgan! That's Mint-Breath!"

Morgan echoed Drake's query. "You're sure?"

Heather gave an involuntary shudder. "Positive. If I live to be a thousand, I could never forget that face!"

Morgan grabbed her hand. "C'mon, darlin'. We're gonna pay another visit to our friendly sheriff, and this time he'd do well to pay heed."

"But, Morgan! We have customers!"

Towing her toward the door, Morgan called out over his shoulder, "Bob, if you need any help, enlist Mr. Evans until we get back."

Behind his back, Drake grumbled, "Thanks a heap!"

Sheriff Watson was just leaving his office when they arrived. "Hold up, Sheriff. It's about this Wanted poster."

Watson jeered, "Yeah, Stone? You gonna surprise me and tell me you know the fella?"

"In a manner of speaking. I don't know his name, but Heather and I are certain he's the same man who attacked her in the alley."

Watson became instantly alert. "Well, now! This ya-hoo's been real busy. He's also wanted in connection with those train robberies. Matter of fact, I was just heading down to the stockyards to bring him in for questioning."

Heather gaped in surprise. "You know who he is?"

Watson nodded. "I do now, thanks to that drawing. Recognized him right off. His name's Clem Beemus, and he works at the stockyard, loading cattle onto the railcars."

The sheriff tipped his hat toward Heather. "So if y'all will excuse me, I'd like to nab this culprit before he finds out I'm lookin' for him and hightails it out of town. If you have any other vital business with me, you can either come back later or relate it to Deputy Arnett. Dave's mindin' the jail while I'm gone."

"I'm coming with you," Morgan said. "I want a piece of this animal who tried to molest my wife."

Watson shook his head. "Nothin' doin'. You're too likely to kill him, and I want Beemus alive and squealin' like a stuck pig." The lawman sneered. "Thing is, Stone, I want to see if your name comes up durin' the questioning, and if it does, I'll be comin' for you next. So you and the little missus just mosey on back to Gus's place, and be sure to stay put. I'll give a holler when I want you."

"We'll be waiting, Sheriff," Heather told him in a haughty tone. "And while you're busy prying information out of your prisoner, try to get the name of his cohort, that Willie person who was with him the night the two of them dragged me into that alley. Assault might be a lesser offense to you, compared to robbing a train, but it ranks pretty high on my list of crimes, and I intend to see that they pay for it."

Two hours later, Watson strode through the swinging doors of the Salon. "Looks like you're off the hook for the time being, Stone," he said. "Clem Beemus seems to have a lack of memory when it comes to recalling the names of his train-robbin' partners."

"I suppose he has a similar block when it comes to remembering the attack on Heather," Morgan surmised as Heather interrupted her work to join them.

"Funny thing, but his recollection improved some on that issue, though his side of the story is a mite different. According to him, he and Willie Short were walkin' along mindin' their own business when Miss Burns came by and offered her . . . uh . . . services."

Heather gave an outraged gasp. "That's a bald-faced lie!"

Watson shrugged. "So you say, but it boils down to your word against his. Rather, against his and Willie Short's, that is. I've sent Deputy Arnett out to fetch Willie from his farm, just to confirm Clem's claim." He let loose a mocking laugh. "Could be I'll have you up on charges next, Miss Burns, for solicitation. If you're real nice, maybe I'll let you share the same cell with your husband."

"That's *Mrs. Stone* to you, Watson," Morgan informed him curtly. "And I'll see you in hell before I let you arrest my wife."

The lawman chuckled. "That's big talk comin' from the likes o' you, Stone. Rest assured, I'll get back with you two later, after I've had a chance to chat with Mr. Short, and then we'll see who eats his words."

* * *

When Willie arrived at the jailhouse for questioning, he broke down almost immediately and confessed to the attempted assault on Heather. "It was all Clem's idea," he whined. "That's why he got to go first. And I didn't get my chance at all, 'cause this fella came along and everything went haywire. Anyway, I don't see what all the fuss is about. She didn't get hurt none, not like Clem an' me. My wrist is still sore as a boil. Can't hardly hold a pitchfork to get my work done round the farm."

When Sheriff Watson reluctantly related this tale of woe to Heather and Morgan, it was Morgan's turn to gloat. "Looks like you've got some words to eat, or maybe a small helping of crow. How would you like that served up, Sheriff? With or without the feathers?"

As it happened, no one was laughing for long. That night, while Watson was at home asleep in his bed and Arnett was guarding the prisoners, the two criminals somehow managed to knot strips of their blankets together and hang themselves in their cell—all without alerting the dozing deputy. Dave Arnett didn't notice anything awry until nearly sunrise, and by then it was too late. Neither of the culprits would be offering further information about the train robberies or any other subject.

Watson was livid, as was most everyone else in town.

"How in Hades could you let that happen?" Morgan shouted at Watson. "Damn it, man! The first solid lead you get on these bandits, and you let it slip right through your fingers! Talk about incompetence!"

Judge Swanson was inclined to agree. "George Watson, I've seen a lot o' stupidity in my day, but you beat all! Just remember, when you lose the next election, you've got no one to blame but yourself."

"I wasn't guarding the prisoners. Dave was," Watson was quick to point out. "B'sides, how were we to know they'd go and hang themselves? And with their blankets, of all things? It's not like we gave 'em ropes, all tied up in a nice neat noose, and instructions on how to go about it."

Swanson shook his head. "Wouldn't surprise me if you had, the way you've been handling matters lately."

"Do you want me to fire Dave?" Watson suggested.

"And who would you get to replace him?" the judge asked in turn. "Some equally unqualified nincompoop? No, just try to keep a keen eye on things from now on, George. You're making every one of us connected with the law look bad."

In a more private conversation, Drake and Morgan exchanged opinions.

"Something smells fishy here," Morgan told his friend. "It's awfully convenient that the only man arrested in connection with those train robberies, the only one who could identify the others in his outlaw band, suddenly hanged himself before he could report anything of significance."

Drake agreed. "Especially when, as far as we know, he hadn't even confessed to the holdup. In fact, he didn't confess to anything except assaulting your wife, and that only after his cohort informed on him. Now, why would two men go to such fatal lengths to avoid an attempted rape charge that they might have beaten in court anyway, given a proper defense?"

"Maybe because there is no such thing as a proper defense in this town," Morgan suggested. "Or . . . it's possible they were more afraid of their fellow gang members getting wind of their confessions concerning Heather and concluding they would soon leak information about the holdups as well."

"Or those same gang members might somehow have arranged to dispose of two blabbermouth prisoners before they blew the whistle on the whole operation," Drake supplied.

"That's my guess, too," Morgan said. "But how, with the deputy sitting not twenty feet away?"

"Maybe they slipped a sleeping draft into Arnett's coffee," Drake suggested. "Could be why he couldn't stay awake, and why he didn't hear anything."

"That's one possibility," Morgan conceded. "Or Arnett could have been in on the whole mess."

"Watson, too?"

"Maybe. Maybe not. The trouble is, Drake, all we have are wild suppositions and gut instincts, and not a shred of proof."

"And that puts us right back where we started."

❧ 30 ❧

As if to make up for disappointments on one side of the scale, matters were looking up on the other end. The "Courting Salon" notion was catching on extremely well.

"I suppose it's the novelty of it all," Heather commented to Morgan one evening as they watched several would-be suitors trying to outbid each other for the next dance with the girls.

"Honey, there's scarcely anything new about it. Your mother has simply come up with a legal way to run what constitutes a brothel."

"With one major exception," Heather hastened to point out. "The girls are no longer doling out their favors for monetary gain."

"If you say so, darlin'," Morgan said, amazed that she was still so blind to what was going on upstairs after closing time.

"This is the third time this week that Walt Finch has been in to dance with Crystal," Heather went on. "I do believe there is a romance blossoming between those two."

"Maybe so, but unless I miss my guess, there's trouble brewing for Brandy. Bob looks as if he'd like to dismember that cowboy she's flirting with."

"Then he should stop waffling and admit that he cares for her," Heather declared. "If he's serious, he should tell her. If not, he has nothing to whine about."

"You know, the strangest combination I've noticed so far is that farmer who is drooling over Lacy," Morgan commented. "Can you imagine her slopping hogs and milking cows, her feather boa dragging along behind her and her shoes coated with animal dung?"

"No more than I can picture Joy shoeing horses with that big blacksmith who is making calf eyes at her. Or Pearl matched up with that timid telegraph operator," Heather admitted.

"Maybe he's teaching her Morse code," Morgan suggested with a roguish grin. "Could be all those little dots and dashes intrigue her."

Heather laughed. "All right then, what is so attractive about the hotel clerk who is conversing so intently with Jasmine?" she challenged.

"Why, sweetheart, it's perfectly obvious. All those beds in all those hotel rooms, and he has the keys to every room. Imagine the variety the situation offers."

Heather's gaze strayed to Ginger, and her smile wavered. "I do hope Ginger isn't setting herself up for a fall. I'd hate to see her get hurt. Comforting Lyle is one thing, falling for him is quite another."

Morgan considered her comment. "Is it Ginger's feelings you're worried about, or your own?" he asked solemnly.

Heather blinked at him. "Pardon me?"

"Could it be you still care about Asher, and seeing him with Ginger is stirring up some latent jealousy on your part?"

"Oh, Morgan! That's pure drivel!"

"Is it?"

"Don't be a ninny! Of course it is! Lyle was mine for the taking, had I wanted him, but I chose you. Though at times like this, you truly make me doubt my judgment."

"Just wanted to be sure, Mrs. Stone," he stated gravely. "You did sound a little 'dog in the manger' for a moment there, you know. As if you might not want him, but you don't want anyone else to have him either."

"I couldn't care less who ends up with him," she insisted peevishly. "Now, may we please drop the subject? I'm sorry I even brought it up. Had I known you were going to be so sensitive about it, I would have kept quiet."

"That would be a rare phenomenon," he said. At her questioning look, he explained with a wry grin, "You keeping your mouth shut, love."

"Well, if it bothers you so much, I needn't speak to you at all, ever again," she told him huffily.

"Promises, promises," he intoned with exaggerated delight.

She glared at him. "You're asking for it, Morgan Stone!"

He gave her a ribald wink. "Yes, but am I going to get it?"

"In spades," she promised with a fiery glint in her eye.

He laughed aloud. "In that case, I really think we ought to retire to more private quarters, sweetheart. We wouldn't want to embarrass anyone. You most especially, my lusty bride."

"Me?" she asked, batting her lashes at him in feigned innocence. "Darling, I'm not the one standing here with my tongue hanging down to my knees, making a lecherous spectacle of myself."

He wagged his brows at her in playful deviltry. "Then, by all means, let's give our spectators the show they expect."

With no more forewarning, Morgan snaked an arm around her waist and yanked her close. With theatrical flair, he bent her backward over his arm. His lips sought the exposed arch of her throat, while the fingers of his free hand delved into her upswept hair, freeing her copper curls from the restricting pins. Her tresses tumbled down in a shimmering cascade, the ends brushing the floor.

Faking a French accent, he crooned, "I want you, *chérie*. I need you as ze boot needs ze heel. Your eyes glow like two wet seals in ze sea. Come wiz me now, and be my petite pet, and I will stroke you until your fur falls out. Zis I promise."

By the time he swept her into his arms, she was weak with laughter, barely able to loop her hands around his neck to help support herself. Their avid audience was likewise convulsed with mirth.

"Morgan Stone, you are a complete loon! Now, put me down, and behave yourself!" she giggled.

"*Non, ma chérie*. We are on ze land now, and seals are not so graceful zare. I would not have you waddle, my precious one, and perhaps bruise your dulcet derriere."

Still spouting nonsense, to the amusement of all, he carried her swiftly to their rooms, leaving a trail of hairpins in their wake.

"Angus, you cantankerous old Scot!" Betsy stood over his bed, hands on her hips. "It's high time you had a bath, and I don't need all this false modesty or foolishness out of you!"

"Woman, take yer soap and stick it in yer ear!" he advised churlishly. "I'm na a wee bairn, nor so feeble that I canna manage the job myself, and even if I were, Ching Yung could aid me. Why don't ye jest call him up here, and make the both o' us happy?"

"Ching Yung is busy, and you are being ridiculous. After all, Angus, you haven't anything under that nightshirt I haven't seen before."

His eyes narrowed as he glowered up at her. "Aye, and precisely how many bare male backsides have ye seen, I'm wantin' to know?"

She returned his glare and answered frostily, "That is none of your business, Angus. It ceased to be your concern when you walked out on me eighteen years ago."

That brought him immediately upright, flames leaping from his blue eyes. "'Tis me ye're talkin' to, Bets, na someone who wasna there and doesna know better, so ye can drop the pretense and tell it like it really happened."

"That is what happened, you dolt! I was there, too, and having your husband abandon you and your newborn daughter is not something a woman is bound to forget!"

"Saints, ye've gone daft!" Gus claimed in exasperation. "I didna desert ye, Bets. 'Twas the other way round. Ye made it plain ye had nae further use for me, and all but showed me to the door yerself. But then ye'd have had to face me, and 'twas a lot easier to let her ma and pa do the dirty deed for ye, wasn't it?"

"You're a raving idiot!" she shouted back. "I didn't even know you had left until Mother came upstairs and broke the news to me. God alive, Angus! It would have been kinder if you'd ripped my heart from my chest and been done with it!" Remembered pain brought tears to her eyes, and they streamed unheeded down her cheeks.

"Betsy, my lang-lost love, I swear to ye, I would niver hae left if I'd thought ye still wanted me. How could ye believe such a thing, lass?"

"How could you believe I'd ever want you to go?" she countered with a sniffle.

His brow furrowed, his own eyes clouded with painful memories. "B'cause after Heather was born, when all I wanted do was to see ye, yer ma told me ye didna want me near ye ever again. Ye wouldna even agree to speak to me and explain why ye were suddenly behavin' so strange."

"Dear Lord, Angus! I'd have sold my soul to have you with me then," Betsy declared.

"And I'd hae fought the divil himself to stay. But I couldna fight you, lass. I loved ye too much, and if ye wanted me gone that badly, that's what I was bound to do, though it broke my heart to leave ye."

"Merciful heavens! What did we do, Angus? What did we allow my parents to do?" Betsy knelt at the side of the bed and laid her head alongside his. "If what you are saying is true, then my parents must have deliberately separated us. But why?"

Gus rested his hand atop her head, stroking her hair, his gaze solemn. "No doubt b'cause they loved ye and wanted better for ye, Bets."

"Loved me?" she echoed on a sob. "That's not love, Angus, it's selfishness. Love doesn't deliberately wound. It doesn't set out to cripple your soul and break your heart. It isn't used as a weapon against all your most precious dreams. It's supposed to be kind and sweet and giving."

"All the things we once were t'gether," he added sadly. "All we could hae had for all these years. Ye know, Bets, even wi' the annulment, I've always felt married to ye in my heart."

"When Father told me you'd died, I wanted to die, too. I mourned you terribly, Angus. I want you to know that. And though our marriage had been officially dissolved, I felt like a widow."

"I had no idea ye thought I was dead, Bets. Not until ye wrote, askin' me if I was yer own Angus Burns. I am, lass. I always hae been, and I guess, deep down, I always will be."

Betsy sighed and brushed a tear from her lash. "So much needless anger and resentment. So much loneliness and lost love. All those years when we could have been raising our daughter together."

"Ye did a guid job o' it, hinny. She's a fine young woman, and I'm right proud to be her pa."

"She has a lot of you in her, Angus. Not merely the color of her hair, either. She's stubborn to a fault, quick to anger and to judge, but just as swift to admit her own failings. And if she feels justified, she can hold a grudge longer than anyone I know. Of course, she might get a lot of that from my side of the family as well, poor child. Lord knows, I've loathed you long enough."

"Do ye still?" he asked gently.

"No, and even when I did, I still loved you. That doesn't make much sense, does it?"

"Aye. To me it does, love. I've been doin' likewise

for years. Hatin' ye. Lovin' ye. Missin' ye till I thought I'd go mad."

Betsy turned soft brown eyes to his and asked hesitantly, "Angus? Is it too late for us to begin anew? To make up for all that was stolen from us?"

He smiled, and leaned close to brush his lips across her forehead. "I'd like that, Bets. A fresh start. But 'tis just like ye to propose to me when I'm practically on my deathbed."

"Don't say that!" she exclaimed, fear etching her face. "You're going to recover, my dearest. I'll not let you do otherwise, when we've just found each other again. Promise me, Angus. Promise you'll get well again."

"I'll do my best, darlin'," he pledged. "And when I'm on my feet again, we'll have another weddin', just to make it legal once more."

Her smile was tender and bright. "I've always been your wife, Angus, with or without the lawful documentation. But I think a second wedding is a wonderful idea, and maybe even a second honeymoon."

Gus thought it only proper that he should be the one to break the news to Arlene. Betsy was equally determined that she would be present when he did. The result was a shouting match that could be heard for two square blocks.

"What do you mean, you intend to marry your ex-wife?" Arlene screeched. "Thunderation, Angus! Just last week she was the bane of your life, and now you want her back? I knew I shouldn't have left you alone with her! She's warped your mind somehow, hasn't she?"

"Nae, Arlene. Betsy has but helped me, as only she could. I'm right sorry if I've hurt ye, but 'twasn't as if what you and I had was a permanent arrangement. I niver made ye promises o' that sort, though I did care for ye a guid deal."

"You cared enough to eat at my table nearly every Sunday, and set your boots beneath my bed whenever it suited you, you jackanapes! You led me on, with actions as well as words, and you darned well know it! You owe me, Angus Burns! I deserve better than this, after all the time and attention I've devoted to you!"

"He owes you only an explanation and an apology, both of which he has already tendered," Betsy inserted curtly.

"You call that an explanation? An apology?" Arlene shrieked. " 'Sorry, sweetheart. It's been great fun, but it's all over, because my wife has been feeding me a line of bull manure a mile long, and I lapped it up like it was honey'?" she misquoted spitefully.

"Really, Mrs. Clancy, there is no need to resort to vulgarity," Betsy snapped. "I regret that you have been wounded by our decision to reunite, but as Angus said, he made you no promises, no declarations of undying love. He did, however, make those vows to me, and I'm happy to say he is honoring them."

"Forgive me if I don't leap for joy or offer congratulations!" Arlene replied.

Gus sighed. "We didn't really expect ye to, but I was hopin' we might part as friends."

"Friends do not stab one another in the back, Angus! Nor do they switch alliances at the drop of a hat. No, blast it all! We cannot be friends after this. We shall be mortal enemies from this day forth."

"It saddens me greatly to hear ye say such things, Arlene. Perhaps wi' a bit o' time, ye'll change yer mind."

"That is highly unlikely, Angus." She gathered her purse and parasol and prepared to leave. "Mark my words, you'll come to rue this day. Both of you."

Heather was ecstatic over the news of the upcoming wedding, and Morgan shared her delight.

"Do you think I'm too old to be the flower girl?" she asked giddily.

"I think you'd be better suited as the matron of

honor, now that you're an old married lady yourself," he teased.

She poked out her tongue at him. "I am not old. And I'm only a lady when it pleases me to be so."

"I'll vouch for that!"

"Did you see the look on Arlene's face when she came flouncing down the stairs? Gracious, but she was livid! Not that she didn't have just cause to be angry, and I do pity her, but Mother and Dad getting back together is such a marvelous miracle. Dad is positively elated."

"And your mother is absolutely radiant."

Heather sighed contentedly and snuggled into Morgan's welcoming embrace. "It's love," she murmured. "The most glorious glow in the world."

❧ 31 ❧

Drake was becoming a regular customer at the Salon these days. Fortunately, Heather didn't see anything odd about the friendship that seemed to have developed between Morgan and Mr. Evans, never realizing the two men had known each other long before. When he stopped in a few days following the suspicious jail cell hangings, she thought nothing of it. Nor did she question the fact that he brought more news of import to her and Morgan. To her, it all seemed mere coincidence.

"Did you hear about the gambler they found dead in an alley over in Cimarron?" Drake asked Morgan.

Morgan shook his head. "No. Why? Is it somehow significant?"

"You might say that. Seems this fellow was caught cheating at cards, and a while later just happened to get robbed and have his throat slit. When the marshal investigated his hotel room, looking for money to pay the undertaker, no doubt, what do you suppose he found there?"

"A deck of marked cards?" Morgan guessed.

"Nope."

"A lady of the evening?"

"Try again," Drake suggested with a cat-that-ate-the-canary grin.

"Dammit, Drake. Just spit it out, will you? I haven't got the patience for this guessing game."

"A bag of coins," Drake announced smugly. "Pennies, to be more precise. Brand-new, slightly mismarked pennies."

Morgan's mustache tilted upward. "I'll be danged."

"That's the good news," Drake said. His face sobered considerably as he added, "The bad news is that the man's dead, and therefore unable to tell anyone where he got those coins. Furthermore, like most of his ilk, he was just passing through Cimarron, and apparently didn't have any friends there who might enlighten us."

Morgan let loose a grunt of disgust. "One step forward, and two steps back. Blast it! When is this case going to break?"

"Soon, I hope," Drake sighed. "Much more time hanging around this Salon your wife runs, and I'm going to turn into a stumbling drunk."

Morgan threw up his hands. "Hey! Don't blame me for your inherent weaknesses, old chum. All you have to do is say the word, and I'll serve you a teetotaler's special. You can have your choice. Rum punch without either the rum or the punch that usually hits you afterward, or a Gentleman's Ginger, minus the gin, of course."

"Would that be a Gentleman's Ger, then?" Drake joked. "And the Methodist cocktail? Does that come without the cock ... or the tail portion of the drink?"

Morgan answered devilishly, "Depends on who's ordering it, pal. A lady or a man. We aim to please everyone here."

Drake chuckled. "Has anyone ever told you you're a real smart-ass?"

"Yeah," Morgan replied. "Between you and Heather, I hear it on a regular basis. If the two of you don't stop flattering me so much, I'm gonna get a swelled head."

"I'm very pleased with your progress since Betsy took over your care, Gus," Dr. Jenkins said. "If you continue to improve at your present rate, you'll be up and hobbling about on crutches before long. Then poor Ching Yung will no longer have to lug you from bed to chair and back again whenever your linens need to be changed." Doc laughed and shook his head. "That little fella is stronger than he looks, but he still resembles an ant trying to move a buffalo."

"It canna be too soon for me," Gus said. " 'Tis weary I am o' spendin' all my time abed, feelin' more like a limp dishcloth than a man."

Jenkins nodded. "I'm also taking you off the laudanum altogether, which should make you even more alert. You shouldn't have much pain now, if you continue to take it easy."

"I'll see that he does, Doctor," Betsy assured the physician as she handed him the bottle containing the laudanum he'd previously prescribed. "The sooner he recovers completely, the sooner we can remarry."

"Aye." Gus sighed contentedly, his blue eyes glowing with love. "We've a lot of time to make up for, my Bets and me."

Jenkins's smile was wide. "I've heard the glad news. The two of you have my warmest best wishes. Is it going to be a private affair, or a big to-do? I was rather hoping for an invitation."

"Rest assured, whichever we decide upon, you'll be invited, Dr. Jenkins," Betsy promised. "After all, if not for you, Angus might not be alive today."

Jenkins shook his head and grinned at Gus. "I can't take all of the credit. It was probably pure orneriness that pulled him through the worst of it."

"Aye," Gus agreed jauntily. "And don't either o' ye be forgettin' it."

Arlene stormed through the entrance of the Salon and toward the staircase like an Indian on the warpath, her face set in tight lines and her gray eyes blazing.

"Uh-oh!" Heather said. "'Trouble's brewing again." She watched as Arlene trooped up the steps on a direct course for Gus's rooms. "Do you think we should intercede?"

"Not unless we're invited to do so," Morgan decided. "If either of your parents wants or needs our aid, I'm sure they'll let us know."

Heather's gaze remained on the upper door through which Arlene had disappeared. "What do you suppose was in that bag she was carrying?"

Morgan shrugged. "As long as it isn't a gun, it's none of our business until someone tells us otherwise."

She glowered at him. "It's simply not normal to be so devoid of curiosity."

Morgan grinned. "Curiosity killed the cat."

"And satisfaction brought it back," Heather reminded him.

"Later, darlin'," he told her with a mischievous leer. "I'm too busy to entertain you now."

Meanwhile, upstairs, Arlene barged into Gus's sickroom and slung her bundle on the foot of his bed. At the sudden intrusion, Betsy gave a start and spilled some of the tea she was pouring for herself and Angus.

Frowning, Betsy grumbled, "You might have had the courtesy to knock, Mrs. Clancy. These are, after all, Gus's private quarters."

Ignoring her, Arlene glared at Gus, indicating the satchel with a curt wave of her hand. "I am returning all the gifts you've given me over the years, Angus. They mean less than nothing to me now, without the caring I thought came with them. Perhaps you'll want your *wife* to have them. Or burn them. I really don't give a hoot."

Gus sighed. "Ah, Arlene, why'd ye go and do this? I wouldna hae given ye these things if I hadna wanted ye to keep 'em."

Resentful at this blunt reminder that her husband had shared an intimate part of his life with another woman, and not wanting even the smallest glimpse of the gifts he'd given Arlene, Betsy quickly excused herself. "I need a cloth to mop up this tea." She speared Arlene with an icy look. "I'll be back in a moment, but while I'm gone I would appreciate it if you would promptly conclude your visit with Angus, Mrs. Clancy. He needs rest, not constant upheaval."

Left alone, Arlene and Gus stared at one another, her expression bitter, and his full of pity. " 'Tis sorry I am that I've hurt ye, hinny. I do care for ye, as much as I've ever been able to feel for any woman other than my Betsy."

"Oh, Angus!" Arlene wailed miserably. "Why did she have to come back into your life now?" She fumbled for a handkerchief and sank into the chair next to his bed. "I know you never mentioned marriage between us, but I guess I always hoped for it in the back of my mind. At the least, I thought we'd go on the way we were, with nothing to interfere. Keeping company, enjoying Sunday dinners together. Now all of that is suddenly past, and I'm having a difficult time accepting it."

Blindly she reached for his hand. In the process, she knocked the satchel from the bed. It fell, opening as it went, the contents scattering across the floor. "Oh, drat! Now see what I've done!"

She knelt to scoop the small treasures back into the bag. "I always loved this," she told him tearily, displaying the dainty shepherdess she cradled in her hand. "Now just look! The lamb's head is broken off!"

"Mayhap 'tis not beyond repair, if ye can find the pieces," Angus said in an awkward attempt to comfort her.

Arlene searched the immediate area, even peeked beneath the bed, but could not locate the missing part. "I can't find it, Angus. Could it have rolled to the far side of the bed?"

He scooted over and cautiously peered over the opposite edge, into the cranny between the mattress and the wall. "I dinna see it here," he announced after a moment.

Arlene sniffled, retrieved the rest of the items from

the floor, and resumed her seat. "Oh well, it probably couldn't have been mended properly anyway." She placed the broken figure on the bedside table next to his teacup and gazed at it forlornly. As if the thought had only then occurred to her, she attempted a weak smile and asked softly, "Do you think we might share a bit of tea, Angus? A sort of farewell toast between the two of us, before Betsy comes back? I'd really like that."

"To be sure, hinny," he agreed, relieved that she seemed to be recovering somewhat.

Quickly she topped off the two cooling cups with hot tea from the pot. "You don't think Betsy will mind me using her cup, do you?" she inquired hesitantly.

"Not to fret," he assured her. "She'll get another."

Arlene handed him one, and extended her cup toward his. "To us, Angus Burns," she said solemnly. "To the past, and whatever the future holds for each of us."

Angus clinked his cup to hers, the china chiming a clear tone. "Bottoms up, lass!" he intoned with a wink.

When they set their cups aside once more, Arlene retrieved her precious mementoes and rose to leave. "I'll be going now, Angus. I'll miss you."

Betsy carefully balanced the supper tray Heather had just helped her prepare. "I hope Angus is awake and ready to eat," she said worriedly. "He seemed totally drained after Mrs. Clancy left, but it's unlike him to sleep the entire afternoon away now that he's regaining his strength."

"He probably just needed the rest, Mother," Heather told her. "Emotional trials can be just as wearing as physical ones."

Scant minutes later, Betsy's frenzied screams echoed through the upper hall. Heather and Morgan nearly bowled each other over in their rush toward the stairs. They were halfway up when Betsy bolted from Angus's room. "Get the doctor! Oh, God! He won't wake up! I don't think he's breathing!"

The next hour would remain chaotic confusion in Heather's memory. Everyone shouting at once, people dashing around, she and her mother hovering anxiously at the foot of the bed as Morgan and the doctor worked frantically to save Gus's life.

"Lift his head! Press on his chest! Not that hard! Like this!" Doc Jenkins demonstrated, then went back to poking at Gus's throat. "No obstructions," the physician noted, almost to himself. He ceased his prodding, placed his mouth over Gus's, and breathed into it. Gus's chest rose and fell in rhythm with the doctor's ministrations. Finally Jenkins pulled back, panting. "Thank God! He's breathing on his own now, though barely. His respiration is sporadic, and his pulse is weak."

"What . . . what's wrong with him?" Betsy gulped through her tears. "Why won't he wake up?"

Jenkins threw her a quick glance, then went back to monitoring his patient's vital signs. "In the medical profession Gus's condition is termed as comatose, Mrs. Blair-Burns. Which in layman's language means that he is in a deep sleep, one that is usually a prelude to death."

Heather whimpered. "He . . . he isn't ever going to wake up again? Is that what you're saying?"

"Possibly not," the doctor replied. "He may just drift off, deeper and deeper, until his heart finally stops."

"Is he in pain now?" Betsy needed to know.

"No, and for that alone we can be thankful."

"What brought this on?" Morgan asked with a frown. "Why now, when it seemed he was recovering so well?"

"Under other circumstances, I might suspect a stroke," Jenkins said, his eyes glinting angrily as he looked up. "But unless I'm sorely mistaken, someone has given Gus a large dose of opiate. He's flushed, and his pupils are mere pinpoints and don't respond to light, which are both indicators of the drug."

"But . . . how?" Betsy inquired in confusion. "You took his medication with you when you left this morning. There's none here for anyone to give him."

"That, my dear lady, is a very good question. One to which I wish I knew the answer. Further, I think we need to ask ourselves who would want to kill Gus, and why, because this is undoubtedly a deliberate attempt on his life. One which may yet be successful." The doctor paused, then added firmly, "Given his Oriental background, Ching Yung would be first on my list of suspects. Do you know if he was in this room today?"

"Yes, but so were half a dozen other people," Betsy said.

"Then I suggest you alert the sheriff and initiate an immediate search of the premises," he advised gravely. "Someone has a stash of laudanum, or morphine, or paregoric, or some such opiate hidden somewhere. Unless our murderer has given poor Gus the entire lot in one final, lethal dose."

"Finding it is not going to help Dad much now, though, is it?" Heather lamented. "Oh, Dr. Jenkins! Isn't there something else we can do? Some way to bring him back to us?"

The doctor shook his head. "You can watch, and wait, and pray. Beyond that, if he stops breathing, you can do as I did. Breathe for him. Share your own breath with him. Just remember to pinch his nostrils shut when you do, so the air goes down into his lungs. And if his heart stops, you can try applying rhythmic pressure to his chest, though it probably won't help much."

"Do people ever pull out of this sleeping state?" Morgan inquired.

"Some. With luck, they recover with all their faculties and everything in working order. Others are not so fortunate, a few so badly damaged mentally and physically that it might have been better for all concerned if they had died." At Betsy's sharp gasp of distress, he said, "I'm sorry, Mrs. Blair-Burns, but I don't believe in sugarcoating the truth. You need to be prepared for the worst."

❧ 32 ❧

While Heather and Betsy were practically in a state of shock, nearly everyone else who knew Gus and heard the latest awful news was likewise stunned. Not that Gus hadn't made an enemy or two in his time, but it was hard to imagine anyone trying to kill him in this vile, underhanded manner. Moreover, courtesy of the local grapevine, Ching Yung appeared the obvious culprit, and sentiment was running high against him. In light of all this, and the gravity of Gus's condition, Morgan took it upon himself to close the Salon for the remainder of the evening.

Doc Jenkins provided even more help by aiding them in the search for the opiate, since he would more readily recognize it in its various forms. One by one, despite some indignant protests, each room of the Salon was thoroughly searched. Bottles, jars, and various containers in the storeroom, kitchen, and bar were investigated to make certain they contained their labeled contents—sugar, salt, whiskey, syrup, gin. Nothing remotely suspicious was found, though several interesting items of a sensual nature were discovered in the girls' rooms.

Ching Yung was openly grieved to learn that he was top on the list of possible suspects. "I no hurt Gus!" he insisted, his black braid swinging as he shook his head in denial. "Gus good to Ching Yung.

Missy good to Ching Yung. No give Gus poppy juice."

"But you are aware of the effects of opium and what it can do," Dr. Jenkins pointed out.

Ching Yung nodded. "Opium good or bad. Got to use wisely." He studied the physician solemnly. "Gus gonna be okay, Doc?"

"I don't know. I've done about all I can. Now it's up to God, I suppose."

"And Ching Yung," the Chinese man asserted resolutely. "I know of this dream sleep. I help."

"How?" Heather asked, ready to grasp at anything that would save her father.

"Old Chinese way, missy." He paused, his forehead wrinkled as if mentally attempting to translate his thoughts into English. "Poke pins in skin," he tried to explain. "Make yin and yang go back as they should be."

Her slight hope deflated. "Oh. Some sort of Oriental magic?"

"Not magic. Ancient medicine," Ching Yung corrected with quiet dignity.

"I've heard of such methods," Jenkins admitted. "Not that I'd put much stock in it, but in the Eastern countries, it is quite common, and supposedly effective to some degree."

"Then it's worth a try, isn't it?" Morgan put in. "At this point, what harm could it do?"

"None, I reckon," the doctor concluded.

The three men turned to Heather, awaiting her assessment of the idea.

"Does it hurt?" she asked.

"No, missy," Ching Yung assured her. "Make better."

It took some persuasion to get Betsy to agree to the odd treatment. Even then, she insisted that she and Dr. Jenkins remain on hand while Ching Yung employed the procedure. Unlike Heather, she was still not convinced that Ching Yung hadn't been the one to administer the opium to Gus in the first place.

Pulling her mother to one side, where they could debate the issue without being overheard, Heather said, "Mother, what possible reason would Ching Yung have for doing something like that?" Heather pointed out. "It's not as if he stands to gain anything if Dad dies."

"Perhaps his motive lies in some strange Oriental rite that we would never begin to understand," Betsy argued. "Who knows? But you must admit that you haven't been acquainted with him for long and know very little about the man. Where he is from. Why he came to Dodge when he did. Also, it is curious that Angus never had any problems of this sort before Ching Yung arrived on the scene."

"No." Heather stood firm. "I can't believe it of him. He saved my life, Mother. It doesn't stand to reason that he would turn around and deliberately harm Dad."

"All right, Heather. Trust him if you must, but for your father's sake, I'm keeping an eye on him just in case you're wrong."

As Heather watched Ching Yung implant dozens of sharp needles into Gus's skin, she had cause to doubt her own judgment. Thankfully, there was no blood drawn, and Gus didn't seem to feel any pain. Still, he did look dreadful, with all those pins sticking out of him, as if he were some sort of human pincushion.

"How long until we know if this is doing any good?" she whispered to Morgan, not wanting to distract Ching Yung.

"According to Ching Yung, it may take several tries for Gus to respond to the treatment. We should know in a day or two, at most, if it will help at all."

"If Dad even lives until then," Heather responded softly. She turned toward the door. "This is too much for me to bear watching any longer. I'm going downstairs."

Morgan followed, tugging her against him for support. "Wouldn't you rather go lie down for a while? It's going to be a long night, darlin'. You ought to rest while you can."

"I'm too worried to sleep," she told him.

"What about having a bite to eat, then?"

"You can, if you want. Frankly, I don't think food would settle too well just now. My stomach is tied in nervous knots."

"I'll fix you some soda," he offered.

Neither of them made it as far as the bar, for their attention was drawn instead to the noisy crowd gathering in the street outside the Salon. Bob and the girls were clustered near the windows, peering cautiously past the curtains.

"What's going on out there?" Morgan asked.

"I'm not sure, Morgan, but it's lookin' more and more like a lynch mob," Bob answered worriedly.

"A lynch mob?" Heather echoed. "Why?"

"For the usual purpose. Hangin' someone, sugar pie," Jasmine replied mockingly. "Namely, Ching Yung."

Heather's eyes went wide. "But . . . they can't do that! It's against the law!"

"I don't think they care much about that right now," Brandy pointed out. "They're too mad, and gettin' more worked up by the minute."

"Well, we simply can't allow it!" Heather announced with all the naïveté of a city-bred lady. "Where is that blasted sheriff when you actually want him? Why doesn't he put a stop to this nonsense and send those people home?"

"He's probably too busy twiddling his thumbs to be bothered," Morgan guessed. "That takes immense concentration, you know. Looks like we'll have to find a way of dealing with this ourselves." He eyed the others with an assessing gaze. "Do any of you know how to handle a gun?"

Bob and four of the girls nodded assent, and Morgan began spouting orders.

"Heather, get the keys to your dad's gun cabinet and alert your mother and the doctor to the situation. Bob, you issue the weapons and the ammunition."

"Should I bring one down for you, too?" Bob asked.

"Yeah," Morgan decided. "Guess this is one of those times when you act first and explain later. I just hope Judge Swanson sees it that way."

"What about Ching Yung?" Heather queried shakily. "Should we tell him what's afoot? Perhaps hide him somewhere?"

"He's probably safest where he is now. Even if that mob does storm the place, if they have as much respect for Gus as they claim, I doubt they'll invade his sickroom," Morgan reasoned. "Besides, that's the last place they'd expect Ching Yung to be."

Even as they prepared for possible violence, it was decided that they should try to reason with the crowd, attempt to convince them to disperse quietly. Rather than unlock the front doors and all but invite the angry horde inside, Morgan suggested they speak to them from the relative safety of the second-floor balcony that ran along the front of the building.

Morgan tried first. "Folks! Please! Go home. The best thing you can do for Gus is to stop upsetting his wife and daughter. They already have enough to bear, without all of you adding to their worries."

"You want us gone? Then send out that slant-eyed snake!" one fellow called out loudly, eliciting a rousing cheer from the others.

"That's not the way to handle this! What happened to the notion of being innocent until proven guilty?" Morgan retorted.

"How *is* Gus?" someone else in the crowd asked.

"He's hangin' in there." The reply hadn't cleared his mouth when Morgan winced at his poor choice of words. Nothing like reminding this rowdy bunch why they were clamoring at the door.

"Which is exactly what we plan to do with the Chinaman!" came the answering shout, accompanied by loud agreement. "Quit stallin', Stone, and turn the little weasel over, or we'll come in after him!"

"Someone's bound to get hurt if you try," he warned, his hand hovering over the pistol in the holster he now wore.

Realizing that the mood was getting uglier instead of better, Heather stepped out onto the balcony to stand next to Morgan. "Please! Can't you leave us in peace?" she cried, her voice filled with anguish. "Where is your respect? For Gus and his family, and for yourselves? There's nothing you could do tonight that can't be done tomorrow, or the next day, when we've all had time to think this through properly. Wait until we know more about Dad's condition and who is responsible for this horrid deed."

A number of those gathered below seemed willing to consider her plea. A few began to mumble and drift toward the outer edges of the crowd, ready, it seemed, to heed her advice and go home. Many, however, were as riled up as ever.

"That yellow devil's the one who did it!"

"Yeah," another man hollered, holding up a length of rope. "And we mean to see him pay!"

Morgan murmured to Heather, "This isn't getting us very far, I'm afraid."

She nodded wearily. "Too bad we can't call in the cavalry."

"We'll just have to rely on our own troops, darlin'," he said with an encouraging wink. "I think it's time to institute the second phase of our battle plan."

He and Heather stepped back into the upper hall. Seconds later, they reemerged, along with all seven girls, each of them bearing a large pot. Before the throng below them could determine what they were about to do, or move to get out of the way, they were being deluged with gallons of sticky, flavored soda syrup. It cascaded down in a thick, honeylike rain, splashing and coating the unsuspecting crowd.

While the hapless swarm was still wondering what had hit them, milling about and trying to brush the goo from their heads and clothes, the organized crew overhead launched a second volley. As Heather and Lacy and Brandy ripped open pillows and shook a storm of feathers down on them, Morgan and Jasmine and Ginger dumped the contents of several chamber pots over the railing. Pearl and Crystal and Joy hurled a barrage of brimming spittoons.

Immediate havoc ensued, at the height of which Judge Swanson put in a timely appearance. Flanking him were the sheriff, a deputy, and a handful of Dodge City's more civilized, levelheaded citizens. Among the new arrivals were Lyle Asher, Drake Evans, and several wives of the would-be lynchers.

As a means of getting everyone's attention, Watson fired a shot into the air. The clamor died instantly, followed by a silence so intense that Heather could hear her own heart beating.

"Well, well!" Swanson chuckled with undisguised glee. "Lookee what we have here! Looks like you fellas got a good dose o' tar and feathers, and a little extra to boot! Phew! If you ain't ripe!"

Watson, prodded by the judge more than by a sense of duty, took up the call. "Y'all go on home now, b'fore I have to arrest the lot o' you. The party's over."

"This one might be, but mine's just startin'!" one of the wives declared, marching into the mob to grab her husband by the ear. "Harold Digger, you should be ashamed of yourself! Now, git on home, and don't even think about messin' up my floors until you get clean o' that muck you're wearing!"

A second woman brandished her fist at her shame-faced mate. "You too, Marv! You can strip down and wash up outside at the pump. Then you can sleep in the stable with your horse, since you smell so much like him. Saints! What a mess!"

"And tomorrow you can all come back and clean up this filth in the street, or I'll fine you for litterin', as well as disturbin' the peace and half a dozen other charges," Judge Swanson instructed as the disgruntled crowd began to disperse. "We aim to run a clean town here, not a pigsty."

❧ 33 ❧

"**I** see you're back to wearing your gun again," Drake commented the next day.

"Yeah," Morgan said. "After last night's near-fiasco, Judge Swanson thought it might be a good idea."

Drake grinned. "I'll bet that set Sheriff Watson on his ear. Furthermore, I just learned another piece of interesting news that will have him scratching his head and rubbing his behind."

Morgan's brows rose. "Do I have to guess, or are you going to come right out and tell me this time?"

"You remember our friendly train conductor, Hal Hunt by name, the same man who helped apprehend you and who testified at your trial?"

Morgan nodded. "Yeah, and he still owes me twenty-four dollars to boot, which he seems to have conveniently forgotten."

Drake continued. "That's the least of it. Seems old Hal isn't paid well enough by the railroad, so he had to sell off a few items of jewelry a couple of days ago up in Kansas City. Trouble is, the baubles weren't his, and the jeweler was astute enough to recognize their description from one of the flyers listing stolen property from that train heist. Not wanting to tip off Hunt, he asked the man if he could come back in an hour or so, to give him time to evaluate the worth of the items. Hunt agreed, and when he left, the jeweler notified the authorities."

Morgan's eyes lit up. "The conductor was in on it all along?" he exclaimed. "They got him? Did he confess?"

"Oh, they got him, all right. Too well. He ran, and was shot while trying to elude his pursuers. He didn't live long enough to hit the ground breathing, let alone inform on his companions in crime."

"Well, hell!" Morgan cursed, his mustache drooping. "Same old song and dance. Damn it, Drake! Everyone we've come close to nabbing is either stabbed, shot, or hanged before we can get anything out of them."

"I've noticed that," Drake concurred wryly. "The question is, is it purely a coincidence? Or have a few of our outlaws been given a helpful push along the path to Hades by their greedy comrades?"

"Probably a bit of both," Morgan suggested. "I never did buy that tale about the first two hanging themselves in their cell. Now, I have to wonder about the gambler in Cimarron. Was he killed by someone he cheated at cards, or by one of his worthless friends?"

"So far, that makes four dead men directly connected to the holdups," Drake stated. "The two who attacked Heather, the gambler, and now the conductor. How many do you suppose that leaves?"

"You're forgetting about 'Blackie,'" Morgan pointed out. "The man they arrested with me and hanged. Counting him, that's five dead."

"I'd say that leaves maybe two or three still roaming around loose," Drake guessed. He began counting those he recalled at the robbery. "You were holding two at gunpoint inside the mail car, and there were two more outside loading the money onto the horses. At least one was collecting loot from the passengers."

"Or more," Morgan said.

"I don't think so. I could swear I only tracked five

away from the holdup that day. Blackie and Hunt make seven for sure."

Morgan grimaced. "Blast! It really boils my blood to think Hunt got the drop on me like that! A lousy conductor!"

Drake's grin widened. "Oh, I don't know. I thought he was a pretty good conductor. Prompt. Conscientious. Surly enough to keep the rougher passengers in line. Light of foot, so he wouldn't wake anyone at night, and could sneak up on unwary Wells Fargo agents."

"Very funny, Drake," Morgan groused. "You'll notice I'm not laughing. Moreover, the man might have had a soft tread, but he also had very sticky fingers."

Lyle Asher stopped by later that afternoon to check on Gus and Betsy and Heather—and to chat with Ginger. "I thoroughly enjoyed last night's impromptu performance," he told them. "I'll wager there are still a number of men dashing around with feathers stuck to their ears."

"Tickled pink?" Ginger suggested with a giggle.

Lyle laughed, then added soberly, "On a more serious note, I'm glad everything turned out so well, without anyone getting hurt. It's bad enough that Angus is so seriously ill. For a while, I feared I would actually witness a lynching." He paused and shook his head in disbelief. "To think they really still resort to such measures out here in the West. It's both fascinating and barbaric."

"How is the research for your book coming along?" Heather inquired politely.

"Very well, as a matter of fact," he said. "I'm pleased with the vast amount of information I'm gathering. Despite being settled a mere decade ago, Dodge has an interesting history, filled with some very unique events and characters. I just wish Mr. Earp and Mr. Masterson were still around. An interview with one of them would be positively riveting, and a wonderful addition to my book."

"You hang around long enough, you might get that wish," Ginger informed him. "Wyatt and Bat and Doc Holliday all get back this way from time to time, and when they do hit town, things usually start poppin', like somebody lit the fuse to a keg of dynamite."

Lyle considered this. "I suppose I could extend my visit for a while yet," he said, offering Ginger a warm smile. "After all, I should stay to see if Angus makes it through this terrible ordeal, and to support Betsy in her time of need." His gaze swept toward Morgan, his smile turning sour. "I presume offering comfort to Heather is out of the question altogether, especially now that her husband is sporting a pistol."

Morgan's answering grin was smug. "You've got that right, Asher. One thing I'll say for you. You catch on real quick."

Heather lost count of the number of times they had to revive Gus by breathing for him and thumping his chest. Then, following the third needle-pricking session, his respiration and pulse became more steady. Everyone but Ching Yung was genuinely amazed, including Doc Jenkins.

"He's not out of the woods yet, however," the physician warned, not wanting them to build their hopes too high. "He's still hovering in a dream state, somewhere between life and death."

Ching Yung blandly ignored the dire assessment and continued the treatment, serene in his confidence that the ancient Oriental practice was working.

"Is there anything else we can do to help?" Heather asked.

Ching Yung nodded. "Talk to him, missy. You and others got to let Gus know you here, that you want him to wake up."

She eyed the little man curiously. "Do you really think he can hear us?"

Ching Yung smiled. "If you asleep, and someone whisper in your ear, you gonna hear it, huh? Same with Gus. You call him back from sleep. Soon he wake."

Though still doubtful that Gus could hear or understand what they said, Heather and Betsy took turns watching over him and talking to him—about anything and everything. How much they loved him and wanted him to get well. How the Salon was doing. Delivering messages of hope and faith from Gus's friends around town. Relating various occurrences, both present and past. On Doc Jenkins's advice, they also began massaging Gus's limbs and regularly rolling him from side to side.

"It's just a theory of mine," Jenkins told them, "but I believe it helps keep his blood flowing, his muscles in good form, and helps prevent a patient who is bedridden for so long from getting such severe bedsores."

Long, fretful days passed, while Gus lay seemingly oblivious to all. In the wee hours of the fifth night, Betsy suddenly burst into Heather and Morgan's bedroom, waking them with a start.

"Heather! Morgan! Come quickly!" she shrieked in a panic-laced voice. "Angus is having some sort of fit!"

Taking time only to yank on his britches, Morgan dashed after her. Heather followed, stuffing her arms into the sleeves of her abandoned nightgown. They found Gus thrashing wildly on the bed, his facial features contorted into a grotesque mask, his limbs twitching uncontrollably. Ching Yung lay across Gus's chest in a vain struggle to hold the larger man still.

Morgan immediately lent his own strength to the effort, while Heather and Betsy each grabbed one of Gus's legs, pressing them to the mattress as best they could.

"He's having a seizure of some sort," Morgan deduced. "Betsy, have you sent for Doc Jenkins?"

"Yes," Betsy panted, "but Ching Yung claims there isn't much point to it."

By now, Ching Yung had managed to wedge a portion of one of Gus's leather belts between his teeth. "This keep him from biting tongue," he explained shortly. "Must hold him on bed so Gus not hurt self till fit done."

The convulsion seemed to last forever, though in reality it was only a matter of minutes. Finally Gus's muscles relaxed, and his whole body appeared to melt bonelessly into the mattress.

Breathing heavily, the four attendants tentatively released their hold. "Is it over?" Betsy asked fearfully. "Is he still alive?"

"Done for now," Ching Yung assured her. "Maybe more come. Not be upset, missus. Gus much alive."

"What was that seizure all about?" Morgan inquired. "Is it some type of reaction to the needles?"

"Not to needles," Ching Yung replied. "To opium. I see this many time. Body wanting more poppy juice, but no can have. Would be most bad."

When he arrived, Dr. Jenkins concurred with Ching Yung's evaluation. "Convulsions are a common result of an overdose of opiates. The body is battling itself as it withdraws from the hold of the drug."

"Does this mean that Dad is getting better?" Heather wanted to know.

"Possibly," Jenkins said, still not wanting to arouse unrealistic expectations. Examining Gus's eyes, he added, "His pupils are starting to respond and dilate. That, and his other symptoms, indicate that he's fighting the effects of the opium, and displaying signs of coming out of his coma. I should also warn you that if he continues to regain consciousness, in addition to the convulsions, Gus may have spells of delirium, which can also be frightening to someone who hasn't witnessed them. He may rant and rave incoherently."

"I don't care," Betsy claimed tearfully. "At least he'd be talking, which is more than he's doing now."

"True, but as his system tries to adjust, he might also become nauseous," the physician warned. "If that happens, you must make sure someone is near to aid him, or he could choke to death."

"On what?" Morgan put in. "We've barely managed to get enough broth down his throat to hold body and soul together. I can't believe the amount of weight he's lost in so short a time."

"Then it's a good thing he carried a few pounds to spare," Jenkins claimed.

As the doctor and Ching Yung had predicted, Gus experienced additional seizures and periods of unconscious ravings. But with each passing day, he seemed to be pulling out of his drugged state. Upon hearing this encouraging news, the townsfolk were almost as heartened as the girls and family. Business picked up again, with many people stopping in to hear the latest word on Gus's improvements.

During this time, Arlene Clancy was conspicuously absent. It was several days before Margaret Hinkle happened to mention that Arlene had packed up and left town.

"She was out in her flower bed the other afternoon, and gone the next morning, and never said a word about moving or having any travel plans. You'd think she would have, wouldn't you, since I'm her neighbor and her landlady?"

"Did you speak with her that day?" Heather asked.

"Yes. After being such close friends with Gus, I thought she might like to know that he was doing much better and likely to regain consciousness soon. I hope you don't think I was carrying tales."

"Not at all," Heather assured her friend. "It was a kind, Christian gesture on your part."

"She left most of her furniture behind, but little else," Margaret said. "I was wondering if some of it might belong to Gus, and if he might want it back if Arlene doesn't return to Dodge."

Heather's brow furrowed in thought. "I have no idea, Margaret. We'll have to wait until Dad wakes up to ask him. At any rate, don't you suppose we should leave everything as it is for the time being? It wouldn't be fair to remove her furniture while Arlene is gone, only to have her return from visiting relatives or something, and think she's been robbed."

Margaret looked slightly abashed. "You're right, of course, and her rent is paid up until the first of the month. I guess I'm a bit irritated with her, for more reasons than one. When I realized she was gone, I went over to check the house, to make certain everything was all right, you see. I'm glad I did, because there was a pile of trash still smoldering in the fireplace, with no screen in front to keep sparks from flying onto the rug. It's a wonder the place didn't burn down and take my house with it."

Margaret shook her head and went on, "That woman must be too distraught over Gus to think straight these days. She actually tried to burn weeds in that fireplace, on one of the hottest nights we've had this summer. Later, I recalled smelling something strange in the air coming through the bedroom window that night. The odor even made me slightly nauseated and light-headed, and here it was Arlene burning flowers, of all things!"

Morgan had been only half listening from his post behind the bar, but now his ears perked up. "Mrs. Hinkle, do you happen to know what kind of flowers Arlene tried to burn?"

The lady frowned. "I'm not certain, but I think it was a clump of those pretty, big red blossoms with the long stalks. I don't know what they're called, but she grew them next to the house, where the wind wouldn't blow them over."

"Poppies, perhaps?" Morgan suggested with an expectant expression.

"I'm sorry, but I can't recall her ever telling me what those flowers were. I just thought they were so bright and unusual. I'd never seen any quite like them before."

"Are they still there?" Morgan persisted.

"I don't know about the ones outside. I had no reason to check. But those in the fireplace should still be there, unless they've finally burned down to ashes."

"Thank you, Mrs. Hinkle."

Morgan strode to the other end of the bar for a hasty exchange with Bob. On his way out the door, he stopped to give Heather a parting peck on the cheek. "I'm off to find Doc Jenkins, darlin'. You stay here and hold down the fort, and I'll be back soon."

"Is this something to do with Dad?" she questioned anxiously.

"In a way," he replied. At her worried look, he added, "It's all right, Heather. Don't fret."

Morgan was back within minutes, carrying a charred bunch of flowers. Doc Jenkins was with him. Without a word, the two men hurried upstairs into Gus's room. Curious, Heather traipsed after them.

She arrived in time to hear Morgan ask, "Can you tell us what type of flowers these were, Ching Yung?"

The servant took a close look at the seed pods, which were now burned bare of petals, sniffed at them, and nodded. "That opium poppy," he said.

"You're sure?" Jenkins chimed in.

"I show you, Doc." Ching Yung chose the least damaged of the pods, one that had scarcely been scorched. He retrieved a small knife from inside his shirt and made a series of slits in the pod. White, milky sap oozed out of it. "This soon become sticky and brown. Then scrape it off pod. Opium."

"Raw opium," Jenkins echoed. "I'll be damned! And it was right under our noses all the time."

"Are you telling me that the flowers Margaret was talking about, the ones Arlene grew and tried to burn, are full of opium?" Heather questioned in dumbfounded amazement.

Betsy was similarly astonished. "Then . . . was Arlene Clancy the one who tried to kill Angus?"

"That certainly looks like a distinct possibility," Doc stated, his face drawn into grim lines.

"But why? She loved Dad." Heather's question was directed to anyone who might have an answer.

"Mad jealousy, first of you and then of Betsy? Revenge? A case of if she couldn't have him, nobody would? Take your pick, darlin'," Morgan told her. "They're all strong motives."

"Oh, my gosh!" Heather exclaimed softly, seeking the nearest chair before her knees gave out beneath her. "Here she was nursing him all that time!"

"Even more damning, as soon as your mother took over his care, Gus began to improve dramatically," the doctor stressed. "Until this last episode."

Betsy's eyes grew wide. "She was here that day, Dr. Jenkins. Mrs. Clancy came to return some gifts Angus had given her."

"Was she alone with him for any length of time?"

"Lord, yes!" Betsy looked stricken. "I spilled some tea and went to fetch a rag to wipe it up. She was leaving just as I came back upstairs, and she still had her bag of gifts with her, except for one broken figurine which she left on the bedstand. Angus told me they'd talked things over between them while I was gone, and Arlene seemed much more calm. They even drank some tea together."

Jenkins's brows drew together. "Out of the same cup?"

"No. She used my cup. I remember Angus teasing me about having to wash it or get a clean one, rather than drink after her."

"Did Gus start behaving oddly after that?"

"I don't think so. He just seemed terribly tired. He napped for the remainder of the afternoon. Then, when I took his supper tray up, I couldn't wake him. We sent for you immediately, and you know the rest."

Jenkins inhaled deeply and let his breath out in a gush. "Folks, I think we just solved our mystery."

Morgan voiced the thought that occurred to all of them.

"Yes, but the Black Widow has fled her web."

❧ 34 ❧

Three days later, Gus finally opened his eyes for the first time in almost two weeks. The first thing he saw was Betsy's tear-streaked face as she knelt at the side of his bed in prayer. He reached out a trembling hand to touch her cheek, and in a voice rusty from disuse, said gruffly, "Bets, don't cry. I hate it when ye cry, my bonny Betsy."

Still weak, still enduring the aftershocks of the potent drug, Gus took some time to assimilate all that had gone on while he'd been in the coma, to learn how Arlene had tried to poison him, and how Ching Yung had saved his life.

"Hae they found her yet?" he asked.

"Sheriff Watson's still looking for clues to her whereabouts," Morgan told him. "The search would be easier if she'd taken the train. At least then they'd have a starting point. But she lit out on horseback in the middle of the night, and no one has any idea where she's gone, or even in which direction she headed. One thing's for certain, though. If she ever dares show her face in Dodge again, she might as well provide her own rope, because they'll hang her. You have a lot of good friends here, Gus. Folks who have prayed for your recovery and are mighty riled at what Arlene tried to do."

* * *

Heather was overjoyed that her father was awake and apparently going to recover fully from his ordeal. Doc Jenkins had warned that Gus would experience various aches and pains, perhaps some lingering nausea, shaking, sweating, and chills; as well as bouts of nervousness, anxiety, insomnia, and irritability. But the worst was past, with no perceivable permanent damage to his body or mind.

As Gus continued to recover with remarkable speed during the next couple of weeks, Heather's own health suddenly began a decline. At first she tried to ignore the symptoms, thinking she was having sympathy pains for her father. Soon, however, they became too much to disregard, especially when Morgan caught her losing her breakfast for the third straight morning.

Considering their recent ordeal with Gus, Morgan was instantly alarmed. "How long has this been going on? When did it start? Have you eaten anything different in the past few days? Why didn't you tell me you weren't feeling well? Where do you hurt? What are your symptoms?" He fired the questions at her so fast that Heather couldn't begin to answer them.

"Morgan, please! If you'll just calm down. You're making me dizzy with this fast-draw interrogation of yours."

"Dizzy?" he echoed. "And nausea? You're going to see Doc Jenkins. Today," he insisted.

"Oh, for pity sake, Morgan! The man is going to think he's been adopted by the sickliest family he's ever met!"

"I don't care what he thinks. I'm concerned about how you feel."

"I'm sure this will pass in a day or so. I'm really not all that ill."

"Stop arguing. I've made up my mind, and that is that. I don't want to run the risk of losing you. What if Arlene put some of that opium in the tea, or the coffee, and we failed to find it during our search?"

Heather threw up her hands in defeat. "All right.

You win. I'll see the doctor when he comes to check Dad this afternoon. Is that soon enough to suit you, Master?"

For the first time that morning, Morgan grinned. "Say that again. I rather liked the sound of it. I suddenly got a mental image of you decked out in a sheer gown and veil, eager to obey and serve me."

She chortled and reached out to test the temperature of his forehead. "Maybe you should be the one to see the doctor, Morgan. You seem to be hallucinating."

As it turned out, there was a very simple and natural explanation for Heather's malaise.

"You're pregnant, young lady," Jenkins announced with a fatherly smile. "About two months along, I would surmise. Which would make the baby due sometime in the early spring, along about March, give or take a bit. The first ones tend to arrive early or late, but rarely on schedule."

When she relayed the glad tidings to Morgan, he was both relieved and elated. Moreover, he couldn't believe he'd leapt so hastily to the wrong conclusion. "I should have known," he told her with a sheepish grin.

"If I didn't, how could you?" she inquired, still wearing the giddy smile that had claimed her face the moment the doctor had told her she was going to have a baby.

"I'm older. I've been around more, and learned a few things. I should have realized our lovemaking has yet to be interrupted by your . . . uh . . . monthly visitor."

"Oh. I wasn't aware . . . that you were aware . . . of such feminine habits," she stammered, her face turning a fascinating shade of pink.

He chuckled. "Yes, well, I do have a mother, you know, and a sister. Besides, I was a very precocious lad."

"I can well imagine," she said. Then she frowned.

"With so much happening at once, I hadn't realized until now just how close-mouthed you've been about your family. Of course, you did mention your parents once or twice. They live near you in San Francisco, don't they?"

"Yes."

"You don't live with them?"

"No. I've had a place of my own for several years now."

"Why?"

Morgan shrugged. "Mostly for my own privacy, and to keep Mom from harping at me every hour of the day that I should find a nice girl and get married. She's a sweet, lovely lady, but very determined, you understand."

Heather grinned. "I see. Well, now you won't have that problem, will you? What about your father? What does he do for a living?"

"Dad works at the docks. You'll like him. He's a wonderful person. Hardworking, good husband, great father. If I can be half the man he is, I'll have done well."

"Any brothers?"

"No, just a younger sister, who is about your age."

"Is she married, or is your mother constantly lecturing her, too?"

"Sara married this past spring. For all I know, I may be an uncle before I get back to San Francisco."

"Have you written to them about us?"

"Not yet. After all the nagging Mom's done, I want the pleasure of seeing her face when I present you to her in person."

"What's your mother's given name? And your father's?" she inquired suddenly. "All you ever call them is Mom and Dad."

"Helen and Everett. Why?"

"Because we're going to have to consider names for our baby," she told him shortly, as if he should have already figured that out for himself. "I was wondering if you would want to name him or her after one of them. Or after yourself, if we have a son."

Morgan shook his head. "No. I hate it when a child is made to go through life being called Sonny, or Junior, or Little Johnny, or Little Mary. Lord knows, the kid could grow up to be as tall as an oak and twice as wide, and he'd still be Baby Harold, or Louis the Sixteenth, or some such nonsense."

Heather giggled. "Don't let Lyle hear you say that. He's terribly proud that he bears the title of Lyle Asher the Third."

Morgan grimaced. "I never thought I'd say this, but the man has my sympathies."

After locking the Salon for the night, Morgan went upstairs to join Heather, who had retired to their rooms earlier in the evening. He suspected she was tired again, as a result of her pregnancy, and fully expected to find her sound asleep in their bed. Thus, he was totally stunned by the sight that greeted him upon entering their bedroom.

His wife must have collected every throw pillow in the place and piled them all atop the bed. She was currently lazing amidst their colorful array in the most diaphanous gown Morgan had ever hoped to see. Sleeveless, the bodice crisscrossed over her breasts and banded beneath them, swathing them in a soft, peach-hued haze so sheer that her nipples were visible through the gossamer material. Likewise the copper patch of curls at the juncture of her thighs was provocatively shadowed as the fabric of the skirt sheathed her shapely limbs. Her long, penny-bright tresses were drawn up in a sort of horsetail effect, bound there by a gauzy scarf, the length of which was artfully veiled across her lower face. A rope of pearls was twined in her hair and left to drape across the crest of her forehead. One slim ankle sported a gold chain, from which tiny bells dangled. She presented the perfect image of a pasha's pampered slave girl— and every man's secret fantasy.

Her smile behind the veil was bewitching—as she

intended it to be. Her eyes glittered like dark jewels. "Welcome, Master. I've been waiting to serve you," she purred in a sultry voice that sent shivers of anticipation tripping up Morgan's spine. "What is your pleasure, my lord?"

He had to swallow twice before he could speak. "You, darlin'. You're my pleasure."

She held out her arms to him. "Then come get me," she said. "I'm all yours."

He walked to the side of the bed and stroked one hand down the sleek length of her, from shoulder to ankle. She smiled up at him and gave a little quiver of delight. "Princess, you never cease to amaze me," he told her, his voice gone gruff with desire. "You are my every dream come true."

She rose to her knees before him, her fingers going to the buttons of his shirt. "You're terribly overdressed for the occasion, sire. Allow me to remedy that."

With nimble fingers, she swiftly divested him of his shirt, then slid to the floor and tugged off his boots and stockings, while he removed his gun belt and set it out of the way. Her knuckles teased at his swollen manhood through the thick denim of his Levi's as she pushed the buttons from their holes one by one, taking her own sweet time about it. Her nails lightly raked his bare buttocks as she peeled the trousers from his legs.

"Your bath is ready, my love," she informed him in that low, intimate tone. "Shall I bathe you while you relax in the hot water?"

"Relax?" he repeated wryly. "Honey, I doubt that's within the realm of possibility right now." He waved a hand toward his turgid member. "As you can see, you have my full attention."

Still, he let her lead him to the tub she'd prepared for him, and lowered himself into steamy, sandalwood-scented water. Leaning back, he grinned at her. "You'd better be careful, Miss Meek and Helpful. I could get used to this, you know."

When she knelt at the side of the tub, her breasts rested on the curved edge, mere inches from his face, like two ripe melons awaiting his delectation. Unconsciously his tongue swept out to wet his lips.

She laughed, her veil fluttering with her exhaled breath. "See something you like, sweetheart?"

His eyes twinkled like sunlit ocao. Without a word, he leaned forward to suck her nipple deep into his mouth, cloth and all, his mustache brushing sensually over the slope of her breast. He tugged, long and hard, and she couldn't contain her moan of desire as fire raced through her veins on a direct path to her womb.

"Two can play this game, darlin'," he murmured, when at last he released her.

"I'm counting on it," she replied shakily.

Taking up the soap, she began laving his chest with loving strokes, working a rich lather into the dark mat of hair that so intrigued her, running her fingers lovingly through the swirling strands. "I adore your chest," she told him softly. "So broad and furry and strong. Have I mentioned that to you before?"

He sighed blissfully. "I don't mind hearing it again."

Her nails scraped his nipples, and he twitched reflexively. But that was nothing compared to his reaction when her hand delved beneath the water and caressed him in a much more intimate manner. "At this rate," he warned her breathlessly, "the water is going to boil before I get clean."

Her smile widened, her laugh tinkling as merrily as the bells on her ankle. "All right. I'll stop teasing . . . for the moment."

By the time she had him completely scrubbed, they were both wet, her gown soaked and clinging to her in transparent folds. She made a tantalizing production of drying him off, and by the time she was done tormenting him with the towel, he was so hard, he swore he could have driven nails with an upstanding part of his anatomy.

A few seconds later, she had him ensconced in the center of the bed, atop a mass of fluffy pillows, and was seated at his side. "Now a little snack to revive your energies," she told him. "And I'll have you know that Ching Yung searched all of Dodge for this treat."

She retrieved a bowl of fresh fruit from the nightstand and plucked out a wedge of peach. Touching it to his mouth, she invited him to partake of the succulent slice. When he'd accepted it, she unhooked her veil and placed her mouth on his to lick the nectar from his lips.

"Delicious," she murmured. Before he could deepen the caress, she straightened and selected a bright red raspberry. This she rubbed over her own lips, just firmly enough to make the juice stain her lips with a ruby sheen. Again she bent, offering him the tidbit from between her teeth. Their lips met and clung—sipping, tasting, savoring the tangy flavor of the berry and their building ardor.

As his arms reached out to enfold her, she drew back once more. This time she chose a plump blueberry, which she promptly popped into her own mouth. "It's yours if you can take it from me," she taunted, as if daring him to try.

His gaze held hers, his eyes gleaming a brilliant turquoise as his hand snaked up to coil her hair around his fist. With a light tug, he drew her down to him. "Never challenge a famished beast unless you intend to be the feast," he growled.

Before she could remark on his poetic phrasing, his mouth claimed hers with devastating command. His lips parted hers. His tongue swept into her mouth, deftly stealing the morsel from her. His mouth lingered to ravish hers, until they both came up panting. "Purloined fruit always tastes sweeter by far," he drawled.

She wriggled, and he reluctantly acceded to her demand for freedom. "Now, the *pièce de résistance*," she announced smugly. From the bowl she picked a cluster of opalescent white currants. Gazing intently into Morgan's eyes, she dangled them over his torso. Then, slowly and deliberately, she squeezed them in her fist, letting the tart liquid trickle drop by drop onto his chest and stomach.

His eyes widened in eager anticipation, their color deepening to a mysterious shade of aqua that betrayed his mounting lust as he watched her tongue sweep across her lips and the sharp edges of her teeth. As he knew it would, her head lowered, the silken swath of hair and veil brushing his thigh in a sensual prelude to the touch of her hot, wet mouth on his yearning flesh.

Though he knew what to expect, his muscles automatically tensing, the sensation was still akin to being stamped with a hot branding iron. He sucked in his breath and gave a spontaneous lurch as her moist tongue laved his heated skin.

Leisurely Heather applied herself to her self-appointed task, licking at the sticky sap with long, lingering strokes. Sipping, nipping, lapping languidly like a lazy sun-dazed cat cleaning its coat. Her mouth traced his heaving rib cage, her nose nuzzling the dark fleece on his chest, his pulse throbbing heavily against her lips. Lower, across his taut stomach, her tongue darted into his navel for the single bead of nectar nestled there.

She rose away from him slightly, just far enough and long enough to squeeze the last of the juice from the clump of currants still clutched in her hand. Dewy droplets rained down on his rigid shaft, coating it in glossy streaks that drizzled downward to pool upon the twin globes at its base.

As her mouth closed around him, sucking, pulling, drowning him in waves of pleasure, Morgan was sure he'd died and gone to purgatory. This was too glorious to be hell, and too much torment to be Heaven. On and on it went, until his teeth were grating together in an effort to keep the dam from bursting.

Employing his superior strength, which was fast

waning, he pulled her up to straddle him. He aided her in guiding him into the welcoming shelter of her passion-misted body. One long, sweet plunge, and he was sheathed to the hilt, her inner muscles contracting around him like a silken mitt. His groan was echoed by hers, as they plunged headlong into a whirlpool of splendor, spinning dizzily through a pulsating, rainbow-hued spiral that surged and swelled about them—until at last it curled gently over them, washing them up on star-dusted shores.

Weakened and replete, he cradled her to his chest. "Lady, when I said you had a wicked tongue, I didn't know the half of it."

"You still don't," she assured him smugly. "Though I'll wager this is the first time you've heard bells." Her statement was accompanied by a series of metallic chimes as she gave a little shake of her ankle.

He laughed. "You do realize that we're going to have to wash up again, or we may be permanently stuck to one another by morning."

She stifled a yawn. "I suppose I can stay awake that long."

His answering chuckle was low and devilish. "Oh, I can guarantee it, sweetheart, because now it's my turn to bathe you."

❧ 35 ❧

An irritating noise was insinuating itself into his dreams. A dog. Barking. Growling. Clawing at something. Morgan shifted restlessly, wanting the clamor to cease but unable to control it from within his unconscious mind. Slowly he began to come awake, and still the racket persisted. It dawned on him then that Piddles was scratching at the closed door between the sitting room and their bedroom, alternately snarling and yapping.

"Dratted mutt!" Morgan complained sleepily. "Shut up, dog!" he hissed loudly.

Beside him, Heather stirred. "What is it? Does he need to go out?"

"How should I know?" Morgan grumbled. "I don't understand Pomeranian."

Groaning, she tossed back the sheet and sat up, her eyes still closed. "I'll see to him." She fumbled in the dark for her robe and slippers. Suddenly she went perfectly still, sniffing at the air. "Morgan? I smell smoke. Like something's burning."

"Probably just somebody's trash pile smoldering," he muttered.

"Most likely," she agreed. Because of the summer heat, the windows were open to let in the cooler night air. "I'll bet that's what has Piddles so agitated."

She stumbled to her feet and into the next room, shushing the rambunctious pup. "Hush, now, before you wake everyone." Groping along the mantel, she found matches and a candle, not trusting herself to locate one of the oil lamps without knocking it over in the dark.

"C'mon, Piddles, let's go visit your papers. It's too late to go outdoors. Or too early," she amended, squinting at the hands on the mantel clock, which read a quarter after two in the morning. It was when she glanced down at the dog that she noticed the thin wisps of smoke drifting up through the boards where the area rug didn't cover the floor. Piddles was sniffing at the acrid tendrils and growling menacingly, as if to make them retreat.

"Oh, my gosh!" she breathed. "Morgan! Morgan! There's smoke coming through the floorboards from downstairs! I think the building is on fire!"

Morgan leapt from the bed as if he'd been shot from a cannon, all remnants of sleep fleeing at her panicked cry. Snatching up his jeans, he stuffed his legs into them, not even taking time to button them. Nor did he bother with belt or socks as he hobbled into his boots.

"Let's go!" he ordered, grabbing her arm and ushering her toward the hall door.

He had presence of mind enough to feel the panel before yanking the door open and pulling her into the hall with him. Piddles was fast on their heels.

The smoke was thicker here, drifting up from the larger rooms downstairs, but as he glanced over the banister, he could detect no sign of flames. "You start waking the others," he told her. "I'm going down to see how bad it is, and how far it has spread."

"Morgan!" Heather tugged at his arm. "Don't forget about Ching Yung." The Chinese man had set up a cot for himself in the back storeroom rather than taking one of the upstairs bedrooms. "And be careful."

"You, too," he said, giving her a quick kiss. He dashed off before she could delay him further, and Heather began making her way down the hallway, rapping on doors and calling out to her parents and the girls.

Despite the fact that he was still recovering his strength and had just been awakened from a sound sleep, Gus took charge immediately. "Lacy, run ring the fire bell! Brandy, start rousin' the neighbors! Crystal, grab that dog b'fore he trips someone. Joy, Pearl, Jasmine, are we all accounted for here?"

Pearl glanced hastily around through the thickening haze. "Where's Ginger?"

Supporting her father on one side, while Betsy helped prop him up on the other, Heather said, "I knocked on her door. Didn't she come out?"

Jasmine frowned. "I'll go get her. She's probably trying to gather her clothes to keep 'em from burnin'. Heather, you hurry on outside. Right now. Pregnant ladies shouldn't be swallowin' all this smoke."

Between them, they managed to get Gus—crutches, brace, and all—down the stairs. Morgan met them at the bottom, Ching Yung lying slack in his arms. "Hurry, folks! Out the front door. You can't get out the back. It's all aflame."

Coughing, eyes watering, in various stages of dress and dishevelment, the small party traipsed out into the street. They were met immediately by members of the Dodge City Fire Company and a throng of other volunteers, some of whom were still in their sleepwear. A bucket brigade was already operating, forming a long line from the water tower at the railroad depot, a block and a half down Front Street. Others began dipping their pails into horse troughs along the street.

Gazing around her, it seemed to Heather that the whole town had turned out to fight the blaze. There were familiar faces everywhere. Bob, Drake Evans, Mr. Hinkle, Lloyd, and Lyle in the bucket battalion. Even Judge Swanson and Sheriff Watson were helping out. Fortunately, Dr. Jenkins was also on hand, and Morgan promptly turned Ching Yung over to the physician's care.

"I'm not sure, but it looks like he's been stabbed in the back, Doc," Morgan told him. "So far, he's still alive, and if you can keep him that way, I'd be much obliged."

"I'll do my best," Jenkins pledged. "Is anyone else hurt?"

"Not that I know of, at least not yet." Morgan's reply was voiced a moment too soon, for just then Jasmine burst from the front entrance of the Salon, tears gushing down her face. Behind her, one of the firefighters emerged, carrying Ginger's limp body. Ginger's head lolled over his arm, her tawny hair streaked with blood. A long red gash banded her neck, gaping like an obscene vermilion smile.

Doc Jenkins rushed forward, but it was too late. There was nothing he could do. Ginger was already dead, her pale throat slit nearly ear to ear.

Bile rose in Heather's throat, and she burst into sobs, her wails of grief adding to those of the other girls. "Merciful Jesus! Who would commit such an atrocious act?" Heather cried.

"That poor girl," Betsy groaned. "She was such a friendly little thing. And so pretty!"

Abandoning his pail and his place in line, Lyle ran past them, his face nearly as waxen as Ginger's. He stopped before the fireman, gazed down at the mutilated body before him, and slowly held out his arms. "Give her to me," he choked out sorrowfully. "I'll take care of her . . . of everything. She . . . she was my friend." As if in a trance, his face a portrait of agony, he turned and staggered down the street toward the undertaker's office, hugging Ginger's bloody corpse to his heaving chest.

"How awful!" Betsy cried. "I do believe he really cared for her." She turned to Gus, who stood beside her on his crutches. "I've got to go to him, Angus. For just a while. He shouldn't be alone at a time like this."

Gus mustered a weak smile. "Go, hinny. There's nothin' ye can do here anyway."

She reached up on tiptoe to kiss his bristled cheek.

"I'll be at the undertaker's. Send for me if you need me."

Heather was grateful for her mother's kindness. In another time, another place, she might have done the same for Lyle. Now, however, it seemed that all she was capable of doing was stand rooted to the spot she stood upon, quivering with shock despite the suffocating heat of the fiery night. Through eyes glazed with tears and the bright reflection of the flames, Heather watched the dozens of townsmen fight the blaze that threatened her father's livelihood.

To Heather's surprise, through group effort, the fire was extinguished within the span of half an hour, though trails of black smoke still rose from the rear of the building. Morgan came out to report on the damage.

"The fire was limited to the kitchen, storeroom, and rear parlor, which will all have to be repaired before we can use them again. But the rest of the structure sustained more water and smoke damage than anything. It's messy, but inhabitable."

"What about the main supports to the second story?" Gus asked worriedly. "What about the floors and the stairs?"

"The front part of the building and the central staircase were virtually untouched. The lower half of the back stairs will have to be rebuilt, as will much of the rear wall. But the main beams are still sturdy enough to support the upper level. The floors upstairs are waterlogged, but solid. Of course, the ceilings below them are scorched and charred. Nothing that can't be rectified, though we'll be breathing the stench of it for some time, I imagine."

"At least we'll be breathing, which is more than poor Ginger can do," Heather murmured, her voice hitching on a sob.

"Aye," Gus agreed, surreptitiously wiping a tear from his eye. His weary gaze returned to the damaged Salon. "How did the fire start? Does anyone know?"

"As near as we can piece together at this point, someone poured kerosene across the floor and furnishings of the kitchen and parlor, and tossed a match to it. You can guess that much by the path the fire took and the lingering oil fumes."

"But what about Ginger and Ching Yung? Who stabbed them, and why?" Heather asked.

Morgan shook his head, dislodging a rain of ashes from his dark hair. "I don't know. Jasmine found Ginger still in her own bed. I took a quick look in there, to see what I could find, and from the amount of blood soaked into the bedding, I'd venture to say she was killed right where she lay."

"Oh, God!" Heather gasped, covering her face with her hands. "I hope she was asleep when it happened. Do you suppose that's possible, Morgan? That she never felt the pain?"

"I'd like to think so, darlin'. It is possible, since I didn't notice any signs that would indicate a struggle."

"But why would the arsonist have to kill her?" Heather persisted. "And why Ginger? Why not any of the rest of us? Why only her and Ching Yung?"

"Assuming our killer is a man, perhaps he was one of her customers," Morgan suggested.

"That would stand to reason," Gus agreed. "No one gets inside unless one of us, or the girls, unlocks the door at the back stairs."

Heather stared at the two men in disbelief. "But I thought . . . I mean . . ."

Morgan grimaced. "No, Heather. They all still had nightly visitors. Everyone knew it but you. Even your mother knew. I'm sorry."

She mulled this revelation over for a moment, then said, "Even so, Ginger was seeing Lyle on a regular basis. I wouldn't think she'd have much time for anyone else." Suddenly an awful thought made her eyes widen and her mouth sag. "Holy Moses! You don't suppose Lyle . . ."

Morgan blinked in surprise that she would even

think to suspect her former fiancé of such a dastardly act. "I don't believe even Lyle would be that stupid, Heather. First to make such an obvious display of keeping company with Ginger, and then to set himself up as her murderer."

She breathed a sigh of relief to have him logically defeat her supposition. "You're right. I just leapt to a hasty conclusion since I can't begin to think who else could be responsible. Surely not Arlene this time."

"I rather doubt it," Morgan agreed. "As your father can verify, women tend to use more cunning and tidy methods of disposal, such as poisons. Besides," he added in a brief flash of humor, "I have trouble picturing her in bed with Ginger, though some women do lean toward that persuasion."

Heather's eyes went even more wide.

Gus made a choking sound, and quickly steered the discussion in another direction. "Do ye suppose Ching Yung caught the fella dousin' the place wi' kerosene and got 'imself stabbed for the effort?"

"No. Like Ginger, Ching Yung was still in bed when I found him. It appears he was lying on his stomach, asleep, when someone crept in and stabbed him in the back. We'll have to wait until he regains consciousness to be sure, but I don't imagine he got even a glimpse of the arsonist."

Gus shook his head in despair. "Ach! What a tragic tangle we hae here. Puir wee Ginger, as bonny a lass as ever there was. And Ching Yung, who ye tell me was blamed for poisonin' me, then turned right round and saved my life. Someone seems bent on harmin' everyone close to me, but for the life o' me, I canna fathom why. I can half understand Arlene flyin' off in a fit o' jealousy, but everything else that's happened—those men attackin' Heather, somebody shootin' at ye two and Bets, this fire—'tis purely a riddle, as if the wee kelpies and fairies are workin' o'ertime in our lives."

* * *

With their thoughts centered on Ginger's demise, and the manner in which it had been brought about, none of the residents of the Salon was eager to reclaim his or her bed for what little remained of the night. Therefore, though thoroughly disheartened and weary to the bone, they set to work trying to make the establishment more presentable. By lamplight, they began swabbing down floors and walls, scrubbing away as much of the grime as they could, with Gus directing their efforts.

Some time had passed, and the eastern sky was just beginning to lighten, when Gus commented to Heather, "I wonder what's keepin' yer ma, lass. I dinna think she'd be this long consolin' yer friend."

Heather frowned. "You're right, Dad. It's been hours. Perhaps I'd better go check on her."

"I'll do it," Morgan offered.

Heather sighed. "Morgan, it's ridiculous for you to behave like this. Lyle is too distraught to attempt to lure me away from you, and I'm too tired to cooperate if he did try."

Morgan let loose a snort of disgust. "As charming as you are with your face all smudged, that was the least of my worries, princess. Might I remind you that there is a killer lurking out there somewhere, and I'm not all that enthused about becoming both a bridegroom and a widower in the space of a few weeks."

Heather was nonplussed. "Oh. I suppose it would make more sense for you to fetch Mother, after all. She might require protection as well."

"Check in on Ching Yung while ye're about it, won't ye?" Gus asked.

"If Doc's still up, I will," Morgan said.

The doctor's office door was unlocked, and when Morgan entered he found the physician sound asleep in a chair at his patient's bedside. Relieved to see that Ching Yung seemed to be resting easily, Morgan slipped quietly out again without waking either of them.

Next, he stopped by the undertaker's place, but it was closed up tight, with all the windows dark and shaded, and no one in sight. The only other logical spot to search was the hotel where Lyle was staying. He and Betsy had most likely gone there to talk and grieve for their lost friend.

The desk clerk was not happy at being roused from his doze, nor was he much help. "If Asher came back in, he probably went right up to his room without stopping at the desk. He usually keeps his key on him."

"Then you didn't see or hear him? Or Mrs. Blair-Burns with him?"

"Nope, but that don't mean he ain't here. He could'a snuck right by without my takin' notice."

"Being awake usually makes it easier to observe things," Morgan replied sarcastically. With some irritation, he swiveled the registry book around and scanned the listings for Asher's room number, then bounded up the stairs to his room.

After several minutes of Morgan's persistent knocking, Lyle finally answered the summons. The usually impeccable gentleman's fair hair was mussed, his eyes were bloodshot, his shirt was rumpled and hanging half out of his pants, and he reeked of whiskey.

"Wadda ya want?" he mumbled groggily.

"I've come to get Betsy."

"Bets . . . Betsy's not here. Why'd ya think that?"

Morgan's patience was already running thin, and there was nothing more trying than attempting to converse with a drunk. "Because she followed you to the undertaker's office in order to console you, and she's been gone so long, Gus is starting to worry."

"No, she didn't," Lyle said, his brows drawn together in concentration. "Last I saw her was in front of the saloon, er, Salon, during the fire."

Morgan's eyes narrowed. "Are you sure?" he questioned with a snarl. Grabbing Asher by the front of his shirt, he pulled until they stood face-to-face. "Are you absolutely sure you haven't seen her since then?"

Lyle reared back, trying to focus his bleary gaze. He swung an arm outward, indicating the room. "See for yourself, if you don't believe me. Check the wardrobe. Hell, check every room in this flea-trap of a hotel, for all I care. I'm telling you, I don't know where she is."

"Hell and damnation!" Morgan swore. "Where could that woman have gotten off to? Listen, Asher, if you see her, tell her we're looking for her. Tell her to come home immediately. Gus is going to be worried sick if Betsy doesn't return soon. So will Heather and I, for that matter."

"Do you think something's happened to her? That she met with foul play?" Lyle asked, sobering at the thought.

"Lord, I hope not! But the way our luck has been running, I wouldn't doubt it."

Lyle sighed, dragging his fingers through his hair. "Look, Stone. Let me get properly dressed and grab a cup of coffee, and I'll help you hunt for her. If Betsy was on her way to join me last night, then I feel partially responsible that she's missing."

"Meet me back at the Salon," Morgan told him. "Unless she's turned up since I left a while ago, I imagine we're going to have to institute an immediate all-out search. And pray to God we find her alive."

❧ 36 ❧

Betsy hadn't returned to the Salon, and Gus was nearly beside himself with worry. It didn't take long to organize a search party. As they'd done when the fire had broken out, all Gus's friends and neighbors volunteered their help. Fanning out, they covered the entire town in a few hours. They checked homes and businesses, even the train depot. Every street, every alley, every outhouse and pothole, was investigated. By the time they were finished, every person in Dodge knew Betsy Blair-Burns was missing, but no one had seen her.

"Do you suppose she fell in the creek or the river?" Drake suggested. That seemed the only place left to look, though they had searched along the banks.

"Only if someone took her out there and dumped her in," Morgan said. "She wouldn't have any reason to go wandering around out there in the dark by herself."

"At least we haven't found a . . . body," Heather stammered, her face tight with worry. "I suppose we can be thankful for that much."

Neither Morgan nor Drake was sure of that, but they didn't say so aloud. "If Asher is telling the truth, which I believe he is, then we're back to our original theory. Someone waylaid Betsy somewhere between here and the undertaker's office," Morgan figured.

"Which means she's been gone for over six hours, and could be miles from Dodge by now."

"Or right here under our noses," Drake put in. "Either way, it's time to widen our search to the outlying area and get that lazy sheriff off his butt."

"It's also long past time for me to give up this asinine charade of being a shoe salesman, and go back to doing what I'm best at," Morgan said decisively. "If we've calculated correctly, there are only a couple of bandits left to be caught, and they'll probably turn up dead somewhere like their fellow train robbers. There's no reason for us to continue working undercover."

Drake nodded. "I'll wire the office and tell them we're going to conduct the remainder of our investigation in the open. I'll also inform them that we're involved in the search for your mother-in-law, just to deter them from any ideas about pulling us out of here and giving us a new assignment before we're ready to leave Dodge."

"Good thinking. I really appreciate your help, Drake."

"And I'd appreciate being told exactly what the devil you're talking about," Heather injected, her dark eyes snapping. "If you're not actually a shoe salesman, then what in Hades are you? And I'd advise you to tell me the absolute truth this time, Morgan Stone. *If* that's even your real name. It would be convenient to know such things, seeing as we're married and expecting a child. As far as that goes, are we even legally married?"

Morgan's hand came out to cover her mouth and curb her flow of words. "If you'd stop long enough to take a breath between sentences, I might be able to answer some of those questions, Boston," he informed her with a wry grin. "To start with, I *am* Morgan Stone, and we *are* legally married, so you can get down off your high horse as far as that is concerned. And, if you'll recall, I told you at the very beginning what I did for a living. Before Drake and my superiors decided I should pass myself off as a peddler."

Heather gaped at him and pushed his hand away from her lips. "You truly are an agent for Wells Fargo?" she asked hesitantly.

"Yes, and so is Drake. Since before we met on the train to Dodge, he and I have been working undercover to investigate that string of train holdups."

Heather frowned. "How do I know you're not lying now?"

"Ask your dad, or Judge Swanson. They've known since my arrest, when Watson and his cohorts stupidly jumped to the conclusion that I was part of the outlaw gang and gave me that lovely welcoming party at the jail."

With no forewarning, Heather doubled up her fist and slammed it into Morgan's stomach with all the strength she could muster—hard enough to drive the air out of him in a gush and almost double him over. "Blast you, Morgan! You might have told me all this! No, I correct that! You *should* have told me, you deceitful varmint! You low-down rat! You—"

His hand clamped over her mouth once more. "I get the picture, princess. No need to belabor the point." He rubbed his sore stomach. "Dang, woman! You sure pack a hefty wallop!"

Drake had doubled over, too—with laughter. "Maybe we should teach her to shoot and take her along with us on our jobs," he said with a chuckle.

Morgan's eyes expanded in horror. "My clumsy wife with a gun?" he exclaimed. "Good grief, Drake! Do you want us all killed?"

Heather made a noise that sounded suspiciously like a snarl. "Will you two please keep to the topic at hand? I want to know how much of what you've told me about yourself and your life is pure fabrication. Do you actually live in San Francisco and have family there?"

"Everything else is the absolute gospel, darlin'. The company's main office is in San Francisco. Mom and Dad and my sister all live there, too. I do have my own house, and when all this is over, I intend to take you there and prove it to you. After all, it will be your home, too."

"You swear, Morgan, on sacred oath?"

He raised his hand, as if being sworn in at court. "So help me, God."

She heaved a disgruntled sigh, shooting him a final dark glare. "All right. I suppose I'll have to accept your word on it. But don't you ever lie to me like that again!"

In his own defense, he noted, "I didn't so much lie, sweetheart, as stretch the truth. Besides, I couldn't tell you. No one other than your dad and the judge, and Drake, of course, was supposed to know. The fewer people who knew, the less chance there was that someone would accidentally spill the beans. Even Watson still thinks I'm guilty, and you've seen what problems that has caused us, but it was essential to our investigation, the only way to give us some small advantage over the real robbers."

As if mentioning his name had magically made him appear, Sheriff Watson strode into the Salon, Lyle Asher right behind him. "Gus, this note was delivered to my office. It's addressed to you. And before you ask, I don't know who dropped it off, or when. I was out trying to get a lead on where your wife has disappeared to, and when I got back, this paper was on my desk."

With trembling hands, Gus accepted the letter. As the others watched, he unfolded it and began to read. Moments later, he let out a huge sigh, his body sagging.

Startled and afraid, Heather rushed to his side. "Dad! What does it say?"

"She's alive," he declared softly. "Thank God! Yer ma's still alive!"

Heather was baffled. "Where is she? Why did she write instead of coming home?"

Morgan had silently retrieved the note from his father-in-law and perused it himself. He answered her query. "Your mother didn't write this, Heather. Someone has abducted her, and is asking a huge sum of money for her safe release."

"Who? How much?" she asked without stopping to consider her words.

Despite the gravity of the situation, Morgan gave a wry smile. "The note isn't signed, love. I don't imagine her kidnapper wants to advertise his name for all the world to know. As to the amount, he's demanding a hundred thousand dollars."

A united gasp echoed through the Salon.

"That's preposterous!" Heather exclaimed. "Where would Dad come up with that sort of money? Even if we sold the Salon, which will bring much less in its present condition, it would never total that much."

"Dinna worry about the funds, lass. I'll pay it, and gladly, to get my Betsy back. The main problem is, turnin' the money o'er to this divil won't assure her release. Chances are, he cuid kill her anyway. Still, what else can I do?"

"When and where is the exchange to be made?" Drake inquired.

"Two days from now, at sunset. Gus is to leave the money in the hollow of a triple-trunked tree along the river four miles west of town. He's to drop the money off and return directly to Dodge. The next morning, at sunrise, he is to return to the same spot. Betsy will be there, supposedly alive and well."

Drake grimaced. "Not a direct trade, then. The bandit will have the money, and we'll be left to hope he follows through with his end of the deal. That's not the best arrangement for us, is it?"

"Isn't there any other way?" Lyle put in. "Some means of assuring Betsy's safety?"

"Only if we can somehow figure out where she's bein' held," Watson told him. "And arrange to rescue her without anyone gettin' hurt, except maybe the yahoo who took her. That's a mighty tall order for the time we have."

"Speaking of which, why wait two whole days?" Heather inquired. "You'd think the man would want his money right away."

"I reckon 'tis to allow me time to get the money t'gether, daughter. Ye might hae noticed, Dodge doesna hae a regular bank, though plans are in the works for one to be built next year. The mercantile handles most o' our needs, like makin' small loans and holdin' our weekly profits in their safe until we can transfer 'em to the bank over in Wichita."

"Can you send a wire from here and have the money sent by train, or do you have to go in person?" Morgan asked.

"Nae. The bank manager knows me weel enou," Gus said. "And we hae a secret signal b'tween us, to let him know 'tis really me wirin' for the funds." Gus hitched his crutches under his armpits and started slowly toward the door. "Guess I'd best get over to the telegraph office and get things rollin'."

"Do you need a loan, Gus?" Morgan offered. "I can wire San Francisco immediately."

"I can help out too, sir," Lyle added graciously.

Gus turned, the corners of his mouth twitching in a sad smile. "Nae, but thank ye, lads. I've enough put away, though I niver thought to use it this way. Nae that I'm complainin', mind ye. I'd gladly spend every cent to free my bonny Betsy."

Lyle's surprised expression was echoed by Heather's, and a number of other bystanders' who'd had no notion that Gus was worth much more than the property he stood upon. To learn now that Gus, whom they'd known for years and who was as common as an old shoe, had accumulated that much money in his lifetime was truly astonishing.

"How, Dad?" Heather asked softly. "Where did you come by such wealth, when you left Boston with little more than the clothes on your back?"

"The mines, lass. If I did nothin' else right back then, I headed west at the best time. And it seems I had a nose for sniffin' out precious ore. Gold and silver, mostly, buried in the ground and just waitin' for me to dig it out."

His face turned reflective. "I used to dream o' goin' back to Boston and flauntin' my riches b'neath yer ma's nose. Thought maybe if I offered her enou money, she'd want me back." His gruff laugh lacked humor. "Guess I'll still end up payin' for the pleasure o' her company, won't I? After she's a'ready taken me back, askin' for nothin' more than my love."

Ginger's funeral was held late that afternoon. Given the girl's occupation, Heather expected the number of mourners to be limited to employees of the Salon, and perhaps a few close friends. She was both surprised and pleased when many other people attended. Lyle was there, of course. In fact, he'd insisted on paying the burial expenses, confirming his depth of feeling for Ginger. Also in attendance were Drake Evans, Judge Swanson, most of the ladies in Heather's Temperance Society, and numerous regular patrons of the Salon, both men and women.

Following the short service, Lyle arranged with Margaret Hinkle for a rosebush to be planted on Ginger's grave the following spring, and for the site to be tended regularly.

Heather was touched to tears. "I'm so sorry, Lyle. We'll all miss her terribly, if that's any consolation to you."

"Not much, I'm afraid," he admitted with a sorrowful sigh. "It's crazy, but I think I loved that girl. For all her obvious faults, she was wonderful. Her smile, the way she had of tilting her head when she was listening to something I said, her unique outlook on life. When I first met her, I assumed I was so superior, but in the final analysis I probably learned more from her than she did from me, and I'm richer for knowing her, if only for this short time. I just wish it could have been longer."

"So do I," Heather said. "I know she would have

liked that, too. Did you tell her how you felt about her?"

He shook his head sadly. "No, and that's something I'll regret for the rest of my life. If I had spoken up, perhaps she wouldn't have taken other men to her bed. And maybe she'd be alive today."

Heather touched his arm in sympathy. "You can't blame yourself, Lyle. We don't know for sure that one of her lovers killed her, though it does look as if it was someone she knew."

"Either way, it's too late to go back and change anything now," he lamented. "What's done is done. I just hope they nab the bloody bastard who did it and hang him from the highest limb."

"So do I," Heather agreed with a shudder. "It's scary to think of him walking around, free to commit similar atrocities."

"I considered going back home now that Ginger is gone, but I changed my mind. I want to stay on for a while, do some more research on my book, and see if they catch Ginger's murderer and your mother's abductor. And to see your mother safely returned. You know, Heather, it's funny, but when that mob was out to lynch Ching Yung, I couldn't fathom how folks could actually look forward to such a gruesome event. Now I'm feeling much the same anticipation. I suppose there's a bit of beast lurking in the most civilized of us. It just takes something like this to bring it out."

The ransom money arrived safely from Wichita on the morning train, in itself a blessing. They'd all had nightmares of the train being held up, and wouldn't breathe easily until the cash had been collected by the kidnapper and Betsy returned. The long hours of waiting took a toll on everyone's nerves. Heather lost count of the number of times she snapped at someone, mostly Morgan. No sooner would she apologize than she did it again. They were all on edge, and Morgan was especially frustrated that they couldn't devise some sort of workable plan to catch the culprit when he came to collect the ransom at the tree.

"I know it's risky, but I can't see what other choice we have. Otherwise, we're trusting to blind luck."

"Nae, 'tis too chancy," Gus said, firmly disagreeing with the plot. "I dinna care 'bout the money, as lang as Bets comes to nae harm. What if this man isna workin' alone? His partners might kill her if anything goes awry. E'en if there is but one fella, what if somethin' happens and he gets killed b'fore he can tell us where he's stashed Bets? She could starve afore we found her. Nae," he repeated, shaking his head. "We canna chance it wi'out knowing where she's bein' held."

Meantime, while delving for research material in the basement of the newspaper office, Lyle stumbled across an old newspaper article. He came rushing into the Salon with it and thrust it at Morgan. "Look at this!" he demanded. "Read it, and tell me if I'm losing my mind or if the description fits someone we all know."

More to keep peace than anything else, Morgan read the article. Into the third paragraph, his eyebrows shot up. "Holy Hannah! This sounds like Arlene Clancy! Right down to her gray eyes!"

"What does it say, Morgan?" Heather asked.

Morgan gave a sharp laugh. "Unless I miss my guess, it says she's an outlaw. Wanted for armed robbery. She's part of a gang of roving bandits who hit several western banks a few years back, and possibly held up a few trains while they were at it."

"What!" Heather's cry was echoed by the others, including Drake Evans.

"How old is that article, Morgan?" he questioned.

Morgan checked the date on the newspaper. "It was printed nearly four years ago, in October."

"Jest afore Arlene came to Dodge," Gus supplied. "I recall 'twas right before the first snow that year."

Drake and Morgan shared a contemplative look. "What do you want to bet the Widow Clancy is one of our elusive train robbers?" Morgan suggested. "So close to us that we couldn't see the forest for the trees. Or the widow for the weeds."

"And laughing all the while we were chasing our own tails. I'm just glad she didn't know either of us were agents. That would have been the ultimate humiliation."

"How were we to guess that a woman was involved?" Morgan pointed out. "I just wish she was still in town, so we could put this information to good use."

"We still can to some extent," Drake said. "If I can borrow that article for a spell, Mr. Asher, I'd like to use it when I send a wire to Wells Fargo headquarters. I'm sure they'll be most interested and appreciative. In fact, if we catch her as a result of this lead you've given us, there might be a sizable reward in it for you."

❧ 37 ❧

Drake was on his way out the door as Sheriff Watson came in. "Just a minute, Evans," the lawman said. "You might as well stay and hear this firsthand."

"Hae ye found Betsy?' Gus asked anxiously.

"No, but I think I might have stumbled onto something that will help us. Or maybe not. I just can't believe Dave would be in on something so foul."

"Dave Arnett? Your deputy?" Morgan questioned.

"If what I suspect is true, yes." Watson turned to Gus. "Do you still have that ransom note handy? Could I have another look at it?"

Gus retrieved it from his shirt pocket and handed it to the sheriff. "What's this all about, and what does it hae to do wi' Dave?"

Watson walked over to the bar and spread the note on the bar top. Then he took another piece of paper from his own pocket and laid it next to the ransom note. Slowly he shook his head. "I'm not much good at this sort of thing, but I could swear Dave wrote both of these. Which could only mean that he is our kidnapper, or one of them, at least."

Morgan drew closer and studied the two sheets himself. The second paper was an official police report written and signed by Arnett. "Good God, I think you're right, Watson," he declared. "The handwriting looks identical." He motioned Drake over. "Take a look and see if you don't agree."

Drake, too, saw the startling similarity. "Have you said anything to Arnett about your suspicions?" he asked.

"Not yet, but you can be sure I intend to. And I'll damn well get some answers."

"Let's not get too hasty here, and shoot ourselves in the foot," Morgan said. "This might be one of those times when it pays to play our cards close to the vest, and only produce our ace when the moment is right."

"Set a trap for the unwary prey?" Drake guessed.

Morgan nodded. "As we all agree, the primary objective is to find Betsy and free her from her captor, or captors as the case may be. Now, if Arnett doesn't know we're on to him, maybe we can find a way to get him to lead us to her, without his being aware of it, of course."

"We might have a problem with that," Watson put in. "When I first realized that the handwriting resembled Dave's, I started trying to piece this puzzle together, and it dawned on me that Dave has been right here in Dodge most of the time. I don't think he's left at all in the past three days, which either means he's holding Betsy someplace close by, or he has an accomplice who is watching over her while Dave attends to his duties."

"But we searched Dodge from one end to the other," Heather noted in confusion. "We would have found her."

"Not if Arnett made it a point to search the one place she's being held," Morgan stated. "Which would have been nearly as easy as planting that note on his boss's desk. Real handy for him, not to mention that he's in a prime job to pick up all the latest developments on the case."

"Let's assume for the moment that Arnett has someone else working with him," Drake suggested. "If they're keeping Betsy in Arnett's private quarters, we would be none the wiser. It certainly wouldn't look odd for him to enter his own home, or even to be carrying a supper plate in with him. On the other hand, if she's being held elsewhere, all we have to do is tail Arnett and see where the trail leads, inside the city limits or out."

"Easier said than done," Morgan grumbled. "The man probably enters dozens of different establishments and homes in the course of a day, calls both private and business related. Or he might be avoiding the area where Betsy is altogether, just to ensure the finger of suspicion doesn't point in his direction. We'll have to set up a situation in which he must contact his partner, again assuming that he has one."

Watson jumped in with a comment. "Dave rents a room over at Cara Johnson's boardinghouse, so I doubt they could be holding Mrs. Blair-Burns there. It would be too easy for Cara to catch on."

"Unless she's in on the deal," Lyle said, thinking of the article he'd found concerning Widow Clancy's shady past. "It seems we men make a drastic error in assuming that the fairer sex is incapable of committing crimes."

Morgan agreed, and proceeded to inform the sheriff of their recent discovery about Arlene.

"Well, I'll be a horned toad!" Watson declared. "Still, I doubt old Cara is involved. But just to be sure, I think I'll pay her a call. Maybe say I'm lookin' for an important document Dave left in his room, and get her to let me in for a look-see."

Morgan nodded. "Just don't tip our hand, Sheriff. This might be the last good lead we get before time runs out on us."

Gus grunted his agreement, and added, "If Bets isna there, we still hae to figure a way to get Dave to lead us to the right spot. Any ideas, lads?"

"What would be important enough that he'd need to inform his partner immediately?" Heather inquired thoughtfully.

Morgan's eyes lit up. "What if Watson here let it slip that when Gus got to counting the money, it amounted to only half the ransom demand? That, having no way to contact Betsy's abductor, his only recourse is to drop off the lesser amount, along with a note stating that the rest of the money will be in hand by the following day . . ."

"But that he'll turn it over only after he knows for sure that Betsy is still alive," Drake finished, quickly catching on to Morgan's idea.

Gus perked up. "That jest might work, and it gives 'em reason not to harm her. At least nae till they hae the last half o' the money."

"Yes, but if he's her sole abductor, he wouldn't need to pass the message along to anyone," Lyle said. "What then?"

Morgan offered the answer. "If he is alone in this, she's likely tied up somewhere, or he'd chance having her escape. She'll require the basic necessities—food, water, and such—and if he's the only one to provide them, we can still try trailing him to her."

"Assumin' Bets is still alive to be needin' such care," Gus said softly, voicing aloud their most awful fear.

Cornering Morgan for a moment of private conversation, Heather said, "When you were drafting your plans, did you deliberately exclude me, or was that merely an oversight?"

"Darlin', there's nothing you can do to help except stay here with the girls and your dad and keep praying that everything works out," he told her.

She shook her head. "There must be something more I can do, if only to follow Arnett around town while I pretend to shop."

"No. If he spotted you, you'd be putting your mother in worse jeopardy, not to mention yourself. Arnett might take a notion to grab you, too, and then we'd have two women to rescue. Besides which, we still don't know if he has a partner or not, which makes it even more dangerous for you to be out there."

"But you'd be with me, and I must do something!"

she wailed. "This is my mother's life we're talking about, Morgan!"

"And I'm talking about yours, and that of our unborn child. If you think I'd put you both at such risk, or allow you to do so, then you don't know me very well at all, sweetheart. Moreover, you might give me a bit more credit. I'm used to this sort of investigative work, and I'm very good at it. I know what I'm doing."

"I'm glad to hear it," she told him stiffly, "but I can't just sit here and fret. I won't!"

"You can and you will," he ordered sternly, "if I have to tie you to a chair. I'll be busy enough without having to monitor your welfare and whereabouts on top of everything else."

Her eyes were dark pools of resentment, prompting him to add, "Don't defy me on this, princess. You wouldn't like the consequences."

She tried once more to convince him. "If you let me go, I promise I'll be careful. A couple of the girls could go, too. Surely I'd be safe enough with them along, and you could tend to business without having to concern yourself about me. We'd stay in the main business district, if that puts your mind at ease."

"Absolutely not. Anything might happen. Shots could be exchanged, and there you would be in the thick of it. You could wear a suit of armor, and I still wouldn't agree."

Tears misted her eyes as she thumped his chest with her fists. "Damn you, Morgan!"

He caught her arms and pulled her close, pillowing her head on his chest. "Do you feel my heart beating, Heather?" he asked gruffly.

She gave a stiff nod.

"If anything happened to you, it would cease to beat. I love you that much. I won't take risks with your life."

"Yet you'll risk your own," she replied dejectedly.

"It's my duty, as your husband and as a Wells

Fargo agent. Just as it's your obligation to safeguard our baby and do as I ask."

She heaved a frustrated sigh, her head coming up so she could look him in the eye. "Then ask, blast you!" she exclaimed. "For once, just ask me, instead of issuing commands!"

A smile teased at his lips, but his eyes were solemn. "Will you please stay here in the Salon until I get back?"

"Yes," she told him, her own gaze somber. "As long as you promise to come back alive and intact."

"You have my word on it," he vowed. "How could I not? You are my life."

The rescue plan, as weak and hastily contrived as it was, was put into motion immediately. The women, and Gus with his splinted leg, were relegated to waiting it out at the Salon, while Morgan, Drake, Lyle, and the sheriff performed the more active roles. For once, luck was with them, and Watson played his part perfectly. As planned, he informed Arnett of the blunder the bank had made, and of Gus's intentions. Then, thanking the deputy for all the extra hours he'd put in lately, he offered the man a few hours off duty.

Watching unobserved from various posts along the street, the other men saw Arnett exit the sheriff's office and make a beeline for the livery stable. Within minutes, he led his horse out and rode off, heading west out of town. Collecting their own mounts, which were already saddled and tied to nearby hitching posts, the small, makeshift posse followed. They kept far enough behind him that Arnett would not be able to spot them, but close enough to follow the cloud of dust kicked up by his horse.

A few miles out of Dodge, Watson told the others, "I'm guessing he's headed for Willie Short's farm."

"The fellow who hanged himself in his jail cell?" Lyle asked.

"Or who had help hanging himself," Morgan suggested cynically.

"It's startin' to look as if you might be right about that," Watson conceded.

"But that would possibly link Arnett to the train robberies, as well as the kidnapping," Drake deduced.

"We couldn't be that fortunate, to tie all the loose ends up in one nice, tidy package, could we?" Morgan questioned with raised brows.

"Time will tell," Drake said. "And Arnett, if we can keep him alive long enough to confess."

The sheriff was correct in anticipating their ultimate destination. Staying to the cover of the trees along the river, the posse watched as Arnett drew his horse to a halt in front of the little farmhouse. To their surprise, the door opened and a woman came out to meet him.

"Criminy!" Drake exclaimed softly. "That's the Widow Clancy!"

"Well, I'll be switched!" Watson declared, echoing Drake's astonishment. "Do you reckon we're about to bag two birds with one stone?"

"Not right this minute, and probably not with one shot," Morgan said. "Our best bet is to wait until Arnett is gone and it gets dark. One less gun to deal with, and we can always arrest him afterward, since he has no idea we're on to him. Besides, Arlene has to sleep sometime, and it would be safer for Betsy if we strike then, and catch her captor unawares."

"What about the dog?" Watson said, pointing out a major flaw in their scheme. "He barked his head off when Dave rode up. He sure ain't gonna let us walk up to the house unannounced."

"Yeah, if we'd known, we could have brought along a nice juicy bone to bribe him with," Drake added. "We sure can't shoot him."

"I've got a ham sandwich and a couple pieces of cold chicken in my saddlebag," Lyle announced blithely. As the others turned to stare at him in mute disbelief, he explained hastily. "Well, I didn't know how long we'd be out riding, so I packed it just in case we got hungry. What's wrong with that?"

Morgan gave a low chuckle. "Not a thing, except for the fact that we three westerners should have been smart enough to do likewise." He shook his head and laughed again. "God bless greenhorns and city slickers!"

The lights had been out for over an hour, and the dog was happily gnawing on a chicken leg as the four would-be rescuers crept up to the house. Watson started for the front door, but Morgan pulled him back and whispered, "If Clancy is as smart as I think she is, she'll have that door rigged. If not with a shotgun, at least with something that will make a lot of racket and wake her up. We'd do better to use a window, and hope it doesn't squeak. And watch out for traps just inside those, too. No telling what you might step in."

They chose a side window off the parlor, and were fortunate enough to get inside with no problem, after Morgan deftly pried the lock with the blade of his knife. Guns drawn, the men headed down the short, dark hallway toward the two rear bedrooms, doing their best to avoid creaking floorboards. Silently Morgan gestured to his companions, indicating that he and Watson would invade the left-hand bedroom, while Drake and Lyle took the other. At his signal, they simultaneously burst through the two doors.

His eyes became accustomed to the gloom, and by the weak rays of moonlight streaming through the window, Morgan saw the shadowed figure on the bed jerk awake and start to sit upright. In the next instant he caught the metallic gleam of a pistol barrel.

"Watch out!" he shouted. "She has a gun!"

Both he and Watson dived for the floor, their own weapons shooting flames as their adversary got off two quick shots. Watson gave a muted grunt, but it was drowned out by a loud feminine shriek of pain, followed by a dull thud as their foe's gun hit the floor.

"Quick! Get the gun!" Watson yelled. "I've got her covered."

Morgan kicked the weapon across the room as he made a leap for the bed, catching Arlene by the hair just as she tried to scramble off the other side, nearest the window. She turned on him like a cornered wildcat, scratching and clawing in a fevered bid for freedom. With little regard for the fact that he was manhandling a female, Morgan fought to subdue the wiry woman, who was much stronger than she looked. Finally he managed to fling her onto the bed, facedown, and pin her arms behind her.

Meanwhile, Watson had lit an oil lamp, and stood ready with handcuffs. Noting the thin red stream coursing down the sheriff's cheek, Morgan took the cuffs and secured them himself.

"You okay?" he bellowed over the din of Arlene's continued shrieks.

"Just nicked my cheekbone," Watson assured him. He pointed to their fuming captive. "What about her?"

"One of us winged her upper arm," Morgan replied, viewing the torn, bloody sleeve of Arlene's nightgown. After scanning for any other visible wounds and finding none, Morgan flipped Arlene onto her back. She kicked out at him, barely missing his manhood. With an angry hiss, she spat at him.

"Otherwise, she's none the worse for wear," Morgan concluded, wiping the spittle from his shirt and glaring down at the raging widow, who was cursing him to hell and back.

"Find something we can use to gag this wild woman, will you, Watson?" Morgan requested. "Before we both learn words our mamas would soap our mouths for using."

Watson complied, grinning all the while. "She's already used half a dozen I've never heard before." To Arlene he added, "Settle down, Clancy! Wouldn't want you to suffocate before we get you to that nice cozy jail cell waitin' for you."

Prisoner in hand, they joined Lyle and Drake in the other bedroom. Betsy was sitting in the center of the bed, sobbing and rubbing the abrasions on her wrists, where the ropes had been tightly tied. She still wore the clothes she'd had on when she'd been abducted, and there was a livid bruise on her left cheek. Lyle was trying to comfort her, while Drake guarded the doorway.

"Is Betsy all right?" Morgan inquired softly.

Drake nodded. "A little battered is all. And plenty scared."

"Is she well enough to ride?"

"Ye-yes!" Betsy hiccuped. "If you think I'm s-s-staying here, you're crazy!"

Lyle gave a relieved chuckle. "You can ride with me, Betsy. Unless you'd rather ride with Morgan."

She scooted to the side of the bed, searching with her bare toes for her slippers. "Now, don't you two start fighting over me," she told them tartly, her spirits fast reviving. "It was bad enough when you were at odds over my daughter. I don't care which of you gets stuck with me. I just want to get home to Angus. He's probably worried sick by now."

Watson rode ahead of them. By the time Morgan and Drake dropped Betsy and Lyle off at the Salon for a tearful reunion, and caught up with Watson at the jail, Dave Arnett was safely ensconced behind bars.

"No trouble at all," the sheriff informed them wryly, fishing for his handcuff keys as Morgan removed Arlene's gag. "Dave's already started yammering fit to strangle a goose. Tellin' me all about how ole Widow Clancy here was the brains of their outlaw gang. How she planned which trains and banks to hit."

Despite the fact that Arnett was locked in the cell beyond her reach, Arlene made a lunge toward him, shrieking in rage as Morgan yanked her back. "I should have known you'd try to save your own neck, Dave Arnett!" she screeched. "You're just like the rest of them, and you'll meet the same end! Stupid bastards! The lot of you didn't have enough brains to fill a thimble. Without me telling you how to do it, you couldn't blow your own noses!''

The sheriff unlocked the abutting cell, and Morgan wrestled Arlene inside. He practically had to fight his way out again, dodging her flailing claws all the while.

Watson slammed the door shut with a clang and locked it. "Dave also claims Arlene instructed him to set fire to the saloon that night, as a means of getting everyone outdoors and creating enough confusion to abduct Mrs. Blair-Burns."

"Yeah, but Arlene's the one who nabbed the Burns woman," Arnett put in hastily. "I didn't touch her. You can't charge me with that part."

"No, you dumb son of a buck!" Arlene jeered with a crazed laugh. "But you wrote the ransom note, didn't you? It sure isn't in my handwriting. And as long as we're comparing crimes, you're the randy jackass who slit that whore's throat and stuck the Chinaman!"

"As if your hands are so clean?" Arnett scoffed. "At least I let Ginger die quick. Not like you was doin' to Gus, killing him inch by inch with that poppy poison."

"Given enough time, it would have all worked out, with no one the wiser. I could have been riding high, if that snippety daughter of his hadn't suddenly decided to visit. He'd have married me and willed me everything, and gone to his reward leaving me filthy rich. But those Boston bitches had to interfere," Arlene muttered.

Drawing herself into a ball on her cot, she clasped her arms around her knees and began to rock to and fro. A muscle twitched in her cheek. She rubbed at it frantically, then began tugging at her hair with fidgety fingers. "I spent three years priming that old coot for the grave. Cooking Sunday dinners, bolstering his inflated pride, listening to that god-awful accent of his." She gave a hoarse cackle. "I'd never have bothered if he didn't have a bank account bigger than Texas."

Peering out from the tangled strands of her hair, she smiled almost flirtatiously at Watson. "You didn't know about that, did you? No one knew but me. You know how I found out?" she added in a little-girl voice. "Gus talks in his sleep! And if you ask him questions right then, he answers them!"

Arlene went off in a fit of giggling that sent chills up Morgan's spine. "The woman's as balmy as a bedbug," he murmured.

"You're right," Drake agreed. "She's not just criminal, she's downright crazy!"

"Scares the begibbers out of me," Watson commented, staring at his female prisoner with nervous regard.

In a soft, soothing tone, Morgan said, "Arlene? Were you the one behind all those attempts to kill Heather?"

She chortled. "Had you running in circles, didn't I? Bet you never did figure it was me who put that face cream under her bed rug. I baked the nut bread, too, and snuck it into the saloon. The silly girl didn't even remember telling me she didn't dare eat yams."

"And the slivers of glass in her mug? And the snake?" he prompted gently. "Was that your doing, too?"

"It was so easy," she admitted, her eyes gleaming an eerie silver-gray. "I had the run of the place, and all of you took my presence for granted."

"What about the attack in the alley? Did you plan that, too, you clever minx?" Morgan inquired, feigning admiration for her cunning.

"Of course," she told him proudly. She frowned as she recalled why her plot hadn't succeeded. "Then you had to go running to her rescue and ruin everything. And that Chinaman, too, when my boys started the stampede. But we almost nailed three of you at once that day you went shopping with Heather and her mother. Gus would have mourned your deaths for a while, I suppose," she mused dreamily, "but I'd have been there to console him until he joined you." She cackled anew and resumed her rocking.

Watson took a deep breath and shook his head in amazement. "It was Arlene all along, makin' all that mischief for you. Even hearing it from her own mouth, I can hardly believe one puny woman could stir up so much trouble! I guess she wanted to kill all of you for messin' up her grand scheme. And when that failed, she still attempted to weasel money out of Gus by abducting Betsy and demanding that ransom. I reckon the only trouble she didn't instigate was that twister that hit Gus's ranch."

"Maybe you're not giving her enough credit, Sheriff," Morgan suggested wryly. "Could be she's on a first-name basis with the devil himself and managed the tornado, too."

Watson swallowed hard and offered in wary jest, "Then maybe we ought to burn her at the stake instead of hanging her."

By the next morning, the point was moot. After a second torrent of curses and a hysterical attempt to demolish her cell, Arlene calmed down again and went to sleep. When Watson tried to wake her for breakfast, she was dead to the world—quite literally. Upon examining the body, Doc Jenkins found an empty packet tucked inside her bodice. The dust left on the paper was opium, and the physician concluded that she'd swallowed enough of it to kill a herd of longhorns.

Dave Arnett was the only remaining member of their gang left alive to stand trial. It was a sure bet he'd be condemned to hang, despite his effort to avoid such a fate by telling Watson where the gang's stash of stolen loot was hidden. Several bags of money and jewels were recovered from a dry well on Willie Short's farm. Wells Fargo was overjoyed at the coup, and George Watson, Lyle Asher, Drake Evans, and Morgan Stone were being hailed as heroes of the first order.

"But you can't leave Dodge until after our wedding!" Betsy declared. "I want you to be my matron of honor, Heather. Morgan, surely you can wait a few more days before dragging Ching Yung and my daughter off to San Francisco. Lord knows when I'll see her again."

"Oh, ye'll see her, hinny, but not till after our weddin' trip."

While Betsy was frantically trying to organize their wedding, Gus was planning an extended tour of Europe, including a visit to Scotland. Moreover, he'd decided to sell the Salon to Jasmine, who had a good business head on her shoulders and wasn't as eager to trade her silk garters in for a wedding ring—unlike the other girls, who all had steady beaus now, thanks to the Courting Salon. As Gus put it, "I'm nae int'rested in runnin' a soda shop and wooin' parlor, and there's nae sense turnin' it back the way 'twas, when all o' Kansas is sure to be dry in a couple o' years anyway."

"What are you going to do after your honeymoon?" Heather inquired. "Are you going to start up another business of some sort here in Dodge, or move back to Boston?"

"Neither strikes my fancy right off," Gus admitted. He leaned over and gave Betsy a hug and a buss on the lips. "How does San Francisco sound to ye, hinny? We'd be close to these two and our grandchildren."

Betsy awarded him with a sunny smile. "Oh, Angus! That would be grand!"

"Aye." He nodded. "And mayhap I'll buy me a ship and go into business wi' Morgan's dad. Bring in goods from all over the world for his trading company."

"Trading company?" Heather repeated softly, her gaze swinging toward Morgan, who suddenly looked distinctly uncomfortable. "You said your father works on the docks."

Morgan offered a sheepish smile. "He does, darlin'. His shipping company is right on the waterfront."

Heather's temper exploded. "You lousy beast! Now I suppose you're going to tell me that he's as rich as Midas, after leading me to believe you were all as poor as church mice!"

Morgan gave a guilty shrug. "We are fairly well-off, I guess. I did tell you I'd always keep you in shoes."

She swatted at him. "You dirty rat! How could you? After you vowed to tell me the truth!"

"I would have, but the topic never came up again," he argued. "It was an oversight."

"Oversight, my foot! You lied to me by omission, and twisted the truth six ways from sundown! Are all Wells Fargo agents such proficient liars? Did they train you to be a devious, low-down sneak, or does that just come naturally to you?"

"Will you please stop bad-mouthing my occupation?" he grumbled. "Thunderation! There's no pleasing you, is there? You whined when you thought I sold shoes, and now you badger me because I have a more prestigious position."

"Be it ever so dangerous and dastardly," she quipped. "I suppose you relish deceiving people, since you do it so expertly. Do you also thrive on the danger?"

"It is exciting," he admitted.

"The travel must have its benefits, too. Do you seduce young women from coast to coast, or do I fall into a special category of fools?" she asked waspishly.

"Oh, you're special, all right," he intoned dryly.

"But I'll never mean as much to you as your precious career does, will I?" she accused. "How could I compete with all that titillating peril! And aren't you lucky to be able to justify your craving for glory by labeling it as duty to your job!"

He scowled at her. "If you'd shut up for two seconds, I could tell you that I'm considering resigning my position, if they can't assign me permanently to the San Francisco area. My reasoning, faulty as ever, is that I don't want to travel and be parted from my dear, sweet shrew of a wife! If I do quit Wells Fargo, I intend to go to work with my father. At the *docks*," he announced emphatically. "What have you got to say to that, sweetheart? Surely you can think of some worthwhile complaint."

"Don't you sweetheart me, Morgan Stone! And don't you dare try to pacify me, as if I were some cross child who's missed her nap. I'm so mad right now, I could gnaw your mustache to shreds!"

Her last comment caught him off guard, striking him as amusing. Humor defused his rising temper. While his lips feigned a grimace, his eyes danced like turquoise seas. "That sounds interesting . . . if painful."

"You deserve worse than that," she informed him. "You deserve . . ." Her words halted even as her own eyes slowly lit with an impish gleam.

"What?" he questioned hastily. "What are you plotting in that devious female mind of yours, Mrs. Stone?" She suddenly looked very pleased with herself, and that had him sweating.

"Never you mind, Morgan," she responded dulcetly, instantly all sweetness and light. "You'll find out in due course. Meanwhile, you can just stew in your own pot."

Privately she delighted in the thought that had just occurred to her. It was small revenge, but one she intended to have. Morgan had said he didn't want his son named after him, or his daughter after Heather, but she'd just conceived the most marvelous twist. If they had a boy, they could call him Heath, and if they had a girl, she'd be Morgana—and Morgan would still have a child bearing his name. Morgan might protest the idea at first, but Heather was sure she could talk him around by spring. Besides, the rotten rascal owed her that much after all his trickery.

"If you won't tell me what mischief you're planning, I'll simply have to resort to tried-and-true tactics, love," he warned, his tone deliberately seductive. "Measures that are guaranteed to pry even the most deep, dark secrets from your honeyed lips. Of course, the procedure I have in mind requires time, and privacy."

So saying, he swept her into his arms and headed for the staircase.

"Morgan Stone! You're going to have to break this Neanderthal habit of carting me off to the bedroom at every whipstitch."

He laughed, nuzzling his lips to her throat. "You love it, and you know it," he teased. "If I quit, you'd feel deprived."

She twisted around to nibble at his earlobe. "You're absolutely right," she admitted. "Don't ever stop, Morgan, until we're both too old to wobble up the steps. And don't ever stop loving me."

His mouth sought hers. "It's a promise, princess. A permanent, passionate promise."

Bestselling Author

CATHERINE HART

SPLENDOR
76878-X/$4.99 US/$5.99 CAN
"An absolute delight ...
Catherine Hart proves herself to be a true master"
Catherine Anderson, author of *Coming Up Roses*

TEMPTATION
76006-1/$4.99 US/$5.99 CAN
Tempted by passion, he gambled with his heart –
but a wily and beautiful cardsharp
held all the aces.

TEMPEST
76005-3/$4.95 US/$5.95 CAN

IRRESISTIBLE
76876-3/$5.50 US/$6.50 CAN

DAZZLED
77730-4/$5.50 US/$6.50 CAN

Buy these books at your local bookstore or use this coupon for ordering:

Mail to: Avon Books, Dept BP, Box 767, Rte 2, Dresden, TN 38225   D
Please send me the book(s) I have checked above.
❑ My check or money order—no cash or CODs please—for $_____is enclosed (please
add $1.50 to cover postage and handling for each book ordered—Canadian residents add 7%
GST).
❑ Charge my VISA/MC Acct#_____Exp Date_____
Minimum credit card order is two books or $7.50 (please add postage and handling
charge of $1.50 per book—Canadian residents add 7% GST). For faster service, call
1-800-762-0779. Residents of Tennessee, please call 1-800-633-1607. Prices and numbers are
subject to change without notice. Please allow six to eight weeks for delivery.

Name_____
Address_____
City_____State/Zip_____
Telephone No._____   CH 0595